Tyler Anne Snell lives in S   same-named husband, their   'lions' and a burning desire to meet Kurt Russell. Her superpowers include binge-watching TV and herding cats. When she isn't writing thrilling mysteries and romance, she's reading everything she can get her hands on. How she gets through each day starts and ends with a big cup of coffee. Visit her at tylerannesnell.com

Addison Fox is a lifelong romance reader, addicted to happily-ever-afters. After discovering she found as much joy writing about romance as she did reading it, she's never looked back. Addison lives in New York with an apartment full of books, a laptop that's rarely out of sight and a wily beagle who keeps her running. You can find her at her home on the web at addisonfox.com or on Facebook (addisonfoxauthor) and X (@addisonfox).

SEARCH FOR THE TRUTH

TYLER ANNE SNELL

RENEGADE REUNION

ADDISON FOX

MILLS & BOON

First Published in Great Britain 2025
by Mills & Boon, an imprint of HarperCollins*Publishers* Ltd
1 London Bridge Street, London, SE1 9GF

www.harpercollins.co.uk

HarperCollins*Publishers*
Macken House, 39/40 Mayor Street Upper,
Dublin 1, D01 C9W8, Ireland

Search for the Truth © 2025 Tyler Anne Snell
Renegade Reunion © 2025 Frances Karkosak

ISBN: 978-0-263-39705-5

0325

SEARCH FOR THE TRUTH

TYLER ANNE SNELL

This book is for Danielle Haas. If I could insert a ten-minute voice memo here, I would. Instead I'll just say this book exists simply because you're a wonderful friend. Thank you for always being there.

Prologue

The locals of Seven Roads, Georgia, were all saying the same thing. Missy Clearwater went and jumped off the old, haunted bridge near Becker Farm because she was mighty unhappy with her father, her ex and the fact that her best friend had taken all but two seconds to hook up with that same ex a week before.

It was a sad piece of news that traveled across the small, action-deprived town with breakneck speed. Starting with Abe Becker and his son, who had found her. Both of whom were still upset about it all, only for different reasons.

"Sheriff, I feel for the girl, I really do, but who's goin' to fix the damage she left behind?" Abe asked, thumbs hooked around his overall loops. He was nearing seventy, but the way he kept doing chores on his land would have made you double-check that math.

Liam Weaver, said sheriff, envied the man a little. He was in his thirties and was already fighting with a hip that locked up and ached if he skipped out on his physical therapy. Something he'd been lax about the last few weeks. The weather wasn't helping. It had been a surprisingly dreary and cold month. He tried to actively not favor his side and instead readjusted his belt, skimming his badge in the process. The metal was cold against his hand. Abe was a contrast with his reddening face.

"Are you talking about the wooden board that broke?" Liam had to ask to be sure. "The one that most likely gave way before she fell?"

Abe was a nodding mess.

"That bridge may be old, but it's still on my property," he said. "Not fixing it isn't an option for me."

Liam shared a quick look with Abe's son, Junior. He was closer to Liam's age and looked mighty ashamed.

"Dad, it was only one board," he tried. "We can fix it later."

Abe shooed the thought off with two in-sync and annoyed hand gestures.

"That's what I'm getting at." He motioned behind him where the great majority of his acreage sat. "Every penny counts in this place. Every single one has a purpose and a job. We take that money from somewhere it's needed and put it somewhere that it ain't, and we'll have problems. Problems I'm not paying for."

The last part was directed at Liam.

He tried to maintain an air of professionalism.

It was hard. His response was blunt.

"Well, Miss Clearwater can't pay for it, Abe, and I'll be honest. I'm not about to ask her parents for it while they're planning a funeral."

Junior's shame doubled in on itself, lining his face with a frown that sunk farther than a stone in water.

His daddy, at least, seemed to feel some of the ripples.

Abe let out a breath that was all frustration. He shook his head.

"I suppose I shouldn't go doing that right now," he relented. "Maybe it's something we can talk about down the line."

Junior saw his opportunity. He took his dad's shoulders and turned him away from the woods they were standing near.

"Until then we should leave the sheriff and deputies to do what it is they need to do." Junior nodded deep to Liam. "Y'all have our permission to come and go as you see fit until all of this gets settled. If you need anything, you know where to find us."

Abe looked like he wanted to gripe about that, but his son was faster. Liam only got one nod in before the two were back in their work truck and driving back the way they had come.

It left Liam with an ache in his hip but some contentedness in his chest.

He liked the silence that being alone brought.

That silence didn't last long.

Deputy Perry "Price" Collins got out of his cruiser rolling his eyes.

"Sorry to leave you hanging there, Sheriff," he said. "But I've spent almost all my life avoiding Old Man Becker ever since he caught me and my girlfriend hooking up in his barn in high school. That man not only tore into my hide for trespassing, he also *saw* my bare hide while he was doing it." Price shook his head. "That whole incident is why I learned to put my britches on faster than a lightning strike after that."

Liam liked the quiet, but of the constant noises in his work life, Price was one he disliked the least. For the past two years he had been more of a right-hand man than anyone else in the small-as-a-thimble McCoy County Sheriff's Department. He had also been the one who most respected privacy when it came to after-work hours. While they saw each other almost every day, they seldom spoke outside of the office.

"I've heard that story three times now, and I still don't know why you'd pick a barn to do that in. Especially on the Becker land. There had to be a better place."

Price snorted. "Believe me, that's the best we had at the time. My cousin Dwayne tried the whole parking-in-the-middle-of-nowhere thing and somehow had the entire law banging on his Ford's windows before the clock even struck nine." He shook his head again. "Give me Old Man Becker and him raising his voice at me over seeing someone with a badge holding a flashlight outside of my car door any day."

Liam wasn't sure which option was worse to him and decided it wasn't the time to get into it. Not with what they had to do next. He glanced up at the darkening sky and felt the wind try to bite into his jeans. It was only a matter of time before the rain came in and made things more difficult. A sentiment that Price seemed to agree with. He dropped his humor and secured his flashlight at his side.

"Ready when you are, boss."

The Becker Farm was the largest piece of acreage owned by a resident in the entirety of Seven Roads. The woods that took up the back end felt just as expansive. Once inside the tree line and it felt like another world.

A world that all the teens of Seven Roads at some point tried to sneak through to get to the bridge.

Stretching across one of the only major drop-offs on the property, the bridge stood over what used to be a deep creek. That creek had long since dried out. Which made the drop from the worn wood above so deadly.

Ten minutes later and Liam stopped just outside of the first plank with a sigh that pulled all of him down.

"Did you know Missy?" he asked when Price stopped next to him.

The younger man was quick to nod.

"I met her at a few birthday parties that my daughter, Winnie, went to when she was younger. Though Missy was there as friends of the older siblings since there was an age difference. I'm more familiar with her father."

That wasn't a surprise considering Jonathan Clearwater had run the tractor auction and supply business that had employed close to fifty people in town before he had sold it off, something that had happened way before Liam's time in town but that he'd heard about still. Seven Roads had less than one thousand residents. Things like fifty jobs leaving town was a big deal, even after the fact.

"It gives me a cold stomach thinking about it," Price added on. "Death is sad enough. Add in the fact that I have a picture with Missy and my little girl enjoying a birthday party at the arcade, and it hits different, you know?"

Liam didn't dispute that.

He did, however, get down to business.

"Let's go ahead and take the pictures Doc Ernest is asking for. You want the high ground or low?"

Price was quick.

"High." Liam's eyebrow went up at that. Price explained with a small smile. "Old Man Becker might have caught me full moon in his barn, but there isn't a kid who grew up in Seven Roads who hasn't navigated this bridge a hundred times at least. I know all the soft, squeaky parts. It'll be safer if I take the pictures up here. Trust me."

Liam snorted.

"You locals sure know how to party."

Price shrugged.

"Not all of us could be so cool as to grow up in a city. Us country folk had to make do."

Price pulled out his phone and was off. Liam took a beat before he took the path to the left. It led down a slope that hurt his hip but wasn't all that unmanageable otherwise. A few careful feet later and he was at the flat rock and dirt-covered ground beneath the bridge. It was an odd feeling being there again. He'd been the first one to arrive after the call was made, and while he'd seen horrible things during his deployments, seeing Missy had been different.

A young woman who had been pushed around so much that she'd found herself over the edge.

Cases like this never got easier.

Liam took out his phone and started snapping pictures of the area. Their medical examiner had asked for more pictures of the scene after the area had been cleared. He wasn't sure why, but he trusted that the good doctor had a reason.

So that's what Liam did for the next few minutes. He walked the area around and beneath the bridge, mindful of the details.

That's when he saw it.

Partially buried in the dirt, blending in next to some rocks. A slight shine to it, dirty silver.

On reflex Liam pulled out the pair of gloves he always had on him during work. He put them on and picked up the small object.

It was a USB drive. There were no markings on it, but there were two letters written in marker on one side.

"M.C.," he read out loud.

Missy Clearwater?

Liam turned the drive over again, then scanned the area once more.

His phone started to vibrate in his hand. Doc Ernest's name was on the screen.

"Hey, Sheriff, are you still at the scene?" she asked instead of a greeting.

There was a rush to her words. An urgency.

Liam's gut started grumbling.

"I am. We're finishing up with the pictures. What's up?"

There was movement on her side of the phone. When she spoke again, she was nearly whispering.

"I'm going to need you to take a lot more pictures. And do a dang good job of it."

Liam wanted to say he always gave the job his best, but something in her tone pulled a question out of him instead.

"What's up?"

There was hesitation.

But then there was certainty.

"Because I think Missy Clearwater might have already been dead before she hit the ground."

Chapter One

Blake Bennet had been to many crime scenes over the last ten years or so. It had come with the territory of being law enforcement, never mind the fact that she'd been a sheriff for many of those years. But her reign with a badge had ended and, she thought, with it any sense of being amid the chaotic aftermath of someone's life again.

Boy had she been wrong.

Currently her living room would have given the crime scene unit a run for their money.

"Blake! We're going to be late." A woman, brightly dressed but frowning severely, hurried into the room with bangles clanking and a baby on her hip squirming. In the last six months of sharing a home with her stepmother, Blake was still getting used to her jack-in-the-box sudden appearances around their house.

That went double for the toddler and baby who had managed to turn the room into a disaster movie within the blink of an eye.

"I can't find the keys," Blake yelled right back. "And unless you've learned how to fly in the last ten minutes, we need those to get going."

Lola had not in fact learned how to fly in the last ten minutes. She balanced Bruce on her hip and started throwing couch cushions and blankets around while Blake went back to her grid patterned search. Once she had been searching for a man buried alive and yet, somehow, the pressure she felt now was really grating. It didn't help that she already knew what would happen when they got to the school gym.

Everyone in Seven Roads would look at her.

The absent aunt come back home to take on the job title of inexperienced mother. Add in the fact that she was single, technically unemployed and living under the same roof with the stepmother she had barely known before coming back, and Blake was a walking, talking tabloid story for the town.

The gutsy Seven Roads locals would talk to her—the rest would talk in whispers.

It was, at best, annoying. At worst, it just plain hurt.

"Blake!" Lola exclaimed, pulling her attention with a start. She was pointing across the room to the one calm thing among the chaos. "Clem has them in her hand!"

Clementine Bennet was a quiet four. While her baby brother and her stepgrandma were expressive creatures, Clem was an observer first, a toddler second. Blake was reminded of the demeanor of the detectives she had worked with during her tenure in law enforcement. Watch people, take in the details and then communicate when necessary, if at all.

"Good girl, Clem," Blake said, relief washing over her. "Now let's get moving!"

That relief lasted for the time it took to get from the house to the Seven Roads High School's main gym. Since the town had limited space, any and every big event had been held in the same building since even before Blake had been a student there. Now in her thirties, it felt odd enough to park in the same lot she had when she was sixteen. It was a sentiment that she didn't have the luxury to let linger too long.

The second she had Clem out of her car seat, the child decided to become a world-class soccer player. Without a ball she made do with her shoes. One hit the floorboard, the other soared over Blake's shoulder like she had it headed straight for the game-winning goal.

"Forget the shoe," Lola said, hustling around. "Here, you take Bruce, I'll get Clem backstage, and you get us a seat. I already let Janie know we're heading in, so she's waiting at the door."

Blake was used to giving orders, but she had been finding that since moving back to her hometown, listening to Lola had become second nature. So she did as she was told. They switched kids and both sprinted off in different directions. Bruce squealed in delight at the rush. Blake just hoped there were seats available since they were downright late.

The gym lobby had a handmade banner that read Brightwell Daycare: What We Learned stretched over the three sets of double doors. Only two people were inside the lobby, but neither paid attention to Blake as she hurried to the doors. She peered through the glass and let out a breath.

The stage was empty.

The show hadn't started.

They still had time to grab some seats and maybe avoid people even noticing she was there.

She put her free hand on the door, ready to go inside, when that hope was dashed.

"Blake Bennet?"

One of the two other people in the lobby was now standing at her side. It had been years since Blake had been back to Seven Roads for any real length of time, and yet she recognized the woman instantly.

Corrie Daniels.

Blake would have preferred being trapped in an interrogation room with a feral tiger than talk with Corrie "Gossip Queen" Daniels.

But since that wasn't an option, Blake pulled her fake smile on tight.

"Hey there, Corrie. It's been a while."

"It has!" she exclaimed before letting out a trill of unnecessary laughter. She motioned to the front doors behind them. "I had to do a double take when I saw you. I mean, I heard you were back, but I guess seeing is believing, you know?"

Her gaze fell to Bruce.

Blake knew where this was going, and she wanted to nip it in the bud.

She made sure her smile stayed on and did her own little laugh.

"Actually, do you mind if we catch up later?" Blake asked. "Clem is in the program and we're running a bit late, so I still need to get some seats."

Corrie's entire expression fell into one of immense pity. Blake knew the look well by now. She had been getting it since her sister Beth's funeral. Never mind when word had gotten out that Blake would be raising her children. That pity seemed to split between the children losing their mother, Beth losing her life and Blake stumbling into a new reality she had never prepared for.

Blake had to hand it to Corrie though. While a lot of people tried to pretend that life had gone exactly the way they had planned it to, Corrie didn't even bother putting on airs. Why walk on eggshells when you only care about eating the omelet?

She reached out and patted Blake's shoulder.

"You come see me when you have the time," she cooed. "I know all of this must be so hard on you. I don't even know if I could do it. Never mind by myself. Poor thing."

Fake words. Fake concern. Fake pity.

Blake despised it.

Blake felt the strength behind her smile waver.

Anger was starting to claw its way up instead.

Thankfully, her personal jack-in-the-box popped up just in time.

"I suggest we save the chatter for later," Lola said, stopping at Blake's side. She nodded to Corrie. "You better go on in and find your seat. We'll be in right on after."

Corrie's mask of sympathy didn't slip, but she conceded with a nod. The hand already on Blake's shoulder squeezed once.

"Hang in there," she said. Then she did what Corrie did best. The perfect parting shot, the multitooled weapon of the South. "Bless your heart."

Blake's hand clenched into a fist at her side, but Corrie was already through the doors. She expected Lola to follow, but instead the older woman hung back.

It wasn't for support.

Lola turned Blake around to face her.

"I know you're probably getting near overwhelmed today, but I have to tell you something you're not going to like." Her expression softened. Blake couldn't help but brace herself.

Then Lola sighed out big.

"Bruce spit up."

Together they looked down at Blake's chest. Sure enough from her shoulder, down the yellow print on her dress, was baby Bruce spit up. She must have been more tired than she original thought. She hadn't even felt it.

"The one time I wear a dress," Blake breathed out.

Lola reached out for Bruce and laughed.

"The bathroom is around the corner. Hurry up and clean that so you're not smelling it the whole time. I'll get us seats."

So Lola took Bruce, and Blake was off and speed-walking to the same bathroom she had used countless times as a teen. She went to the task at hand with the same urgency, thinking about how she should have packed the towel parents used in this sort of situation.

She pictured it sitting on the dining room table.

Blake sighed again.

Her gaze shifted up to her reflection in the mirror.

Before six months ago she had always styled her hair into one long braid. Part habit, part utility. One single braid that always rested against her back. Contained. In order. Familiar.

Now her hair was down and short, a choice she had made to save time. To save energy.

But seeing herself now, seeing the bags under her eyes and the frown across her lips, the question that often bothered her came right on back.

If she couldn't take care of something simple like her hair, how could she take care of two little humans?

The ache in her chest grew cold.

It started to spread.

Blake shook her head.

"Now's not the time," she told herself. She straightened her dress and eyed the spot where the spit-up had been. She'd worn the wrong color of dress. The water stain was more than noticeable.

It made her grumble as she left the bathroom and hurried back to the lobby doors. Logically, she knew that no one would really care about it. That it wasn't a big deal. Yet, she hesitated before going inside.

Blake knew that it wasn't about the stain.

It was about the people.

And that made her feel shame.

She had dealt with all kinds of life-and-death situations, and here she was worried about gossip from people she had known all of her life.

On reflex her hand clenched again.

It was only by the grace of luck that she didn't use her fist when a man came up at her side and startled her.

"Excuse me."

The voice was a deep, deep baritone. A sound that almost felt like it was anchoring her to the spot. Which seemed to match perfectly with the man it had come from.

He was tall. A tall that would have been comical on most, yet the man was wearing his height, and everything else, well. He looked tailor-made by a group of women who had grown up watching romance movies, where the male lead was the rough-and-tumble handyman next door. Dark eyes, dark hair slightly unruly but in a neat way, facial hair clipped close, and all pleasing angles making up a face that was as handsome as it was alarming when it popped up out of nowhere. There was a scar, she thought, near his neck, but for the life of her, Blake's detail-oriented brain skittered a bit.

The best she could do was raise an eyebrow in question.

A question that the man answered before she could put it into words.

"I thought maybe this could help you out for the time being." He held out a denim shirt. Blake was so flustered she took it. The man nodded to the doors. "It might make you more comfortable in there."

Blake blinked a few times.

"You want me to wear this?"

The man shrugged.

"If you want to, you can. I've seen a few ladies come in wearing these things like jackets, so it might look trendy."

Blake was about to do the polite thing and refuse the offer, but feedback from the gym cut through the thought. Blake turned toward the window on the door. The daycare director was at the microphone onstage.

"If you don't want to wear it, it's no big deal," the man added. "You can just throw it on the chair over there."

He pointed to the corner of the lobby.

Blake eyed the shirt in her hands.

It was long-sleeved and blue. A button-up left open. It seemed clean enough and would certainly cover the water stain.

The man went through the doors without another word.

Blake opened her mouth to tell him no thanks, ask his name and ask why he was doing this, but the director's voice cut off all worries.

Blake put the shirt on like a jacket and hurried inside.

LIAM FOUND THE woman when a little girl onstage told the entire gym about the differences between moths and butterflies. While the girl was quiet and mostly still, a woman in the last row of seating was not. She shot up tall and wielding two cell phones, both of which were trained squarely on the kid. From Liam's angle, he could see her mouthing along with the short speech.

He could also she was wearing his shirt.

Liam was glad for it. Offering the piece of clothing to her had been an impulsive act. One that had been spurred on by her body language alone.

He hadn't meant to, but Liam watched as she tensed and panicked, as she balled her hands into fists, as she hesitated.

All while outside of a daycare program.

Liam had thought about his own mother when he was a kid. She'd had to do a lot solo since his father was deployed. Liam didn't know this woman's story—if she was single or if she was temporarily by herself—but the urge to help her had been one he couldn't ignore. He had only hoped it would be helpful.

He was glad to see that it must have been.

"Hey, I found her." Price sidled up to him, voice low. They were standing at the wall on the side of the open gym. The lights were mostly off, so the stage was the center of attention, but Liam could still see where Price pointed.

"She's in the flowery dress with the big hair," he added on.

Liam nodded and pushed his arm back down.

It was bad enough he'd had to come out to the daycare program to track down a potential lead, but then again, it wasn't like Cassandra West had given them many choices.

"Make sure you're casual about your run-in with her, or she's going to feel like we ambushed her," Price said, once again. "Cass might not be as popular as she once was, but tick her off, and it'll be like kicking a hornet's nest."

"I'm not here to ambush her," Liam defended. "I'm here to make an appointment, is all. It's not a big deal."

That was a lie. It was a big deal to Liam.

Cassandra was one of the last people to see Missy Clearwater alive.

It had been more than two months since Missy's body had been found. In the time since, her case had been ruled a suicide. It was a point of severe contention between Liam and the general public. Everyone had believed that Missy's life had taken such a turn that her ending had made sense. There was no hard evidence to say otherwise, and even her own flesh and blood had accepted this tragic outcome. Doc Ernest's original suspicion had also changed. Like Price, she had had an emotional reaction to the death of a woman she had watched grow up. So much so, she had mistaken a hope that Missy hadn't done it to herself for a gut instinct that someone had been behind it.

When, in reality, the fall had been what had done the girl in.

That should have been that, but Liam... He couldn't let it go.

He hadn't watched Missy Clearwater grow up, but his gut had doubled down on something not being quite right.

And that all started from the flash drive he had found beneath the bridge.

That's why, months later, he was still trying to piece together the day of Missy's death. Off the books. For his own peace of mind.

It's why he needed to talk to Cassandra West.

And if that meant starting that talk off casually, then he would.

Ten minutes later and that need was bristling under Liam's skin. He wasn't a man who fidgeted, but the urgency had him out of the gym and standing in the parking lot before the waves of people started to filter out.

However, he bumped into someone else first.

"Here."

Liam looked down at the woman who had tapped his shoulder. Red hair, green eyes and a pretty sun dress with a spit-up stain on it.

She smiled. She was holding his shirt.

"Thank you for this," she added. "It saved me from freezing under that AC for sure. I hope you weren't too cold."

Liam, not a man built for small talk, found an easy smile. He tapped his short sleeve.

"No worries here. I'm built warm."

Liam was about to ask where her kids were, genuinely curious, but the woman's gaze went behind him in the parking lot. With it, her smile disappeared.

Tension lined every inch of her so quickly that Liam's body mirrored that tension on reflex.

It was such a complete change that Liam was about to ask what was wrong, but the woman was faster than his concern.

She pressed his shirt into his chest.

"Thanks again," she said, words cold. "If you'll excuse me."

Liam turned around to watch the woman walk with purpose toward something else.

Someone else.

A man he didn't recognize was standing at the end of the parking lot, staring.

And it wasn't until the woman got closer to him that he turned tail and ran into the wooded area behind the school. And it wasn't until he was running that the woman gave chase, disappearing into the tree line in a flash.

And it wasn't until that moment that Liam forgot all about his potential lead.

He was off and running into the woods right after them, nothing but red hair in his mind.

Chapter Two

It had been years since Blake had been in the woods behind the high school. Set between the gym's parking lot and the old building that had housed a Kmart half a mile away, between the trees had become just another rite of passage for Seven Roads' teens.

They couldn't escape the boredom of small-town life; they could skip a few of their classes though.

Now Blake didn't see how she had navigated the area as carefree as she had back then. A few feet in and a tree root nearly took her down. She caught her balance halfway through the fall. Her dress wasn't as fortunate. She heard the tear but didn't stop to investigate.

Instead, she was all eyes on Ryan Reed.

"Stop running," she yelled out to him, rounding another tree he had tried to put between them.

Ryan had never been the fastest kid in school, but as an adult, he had seemed to inherit a talent for being slippery. He wove through the underbrush and oaks like the snake that he was.

Too bad for him that Blake had made a career out of having faster reflexes than most of the people she ended up chasing.

Instead of running behind him directly, Blake cut to the right and picked up speed. If her memory wasn't that far off, there was a slight hill that sloped up before sliding down into a small clearing. She could make up some space and cut him off.

So Blake followed her plan with total dedication. She didn't stop when she got tripped up again, she didn't stop when a low-hanging branch scratched at her face, and she didn't let up even an inch when her legs burned as she ran up and then down the small hill into the clearing.

She only stopped once she realized her plan had worked.

Ryan was holding his side and gasping. He broke through the tree line like he'd run a marathon. Blake closed the distance between them before Ryan realized she had cut him off.

His eyes widened.

Blake held out her hands in a stop motion.

"What are you—"

Before she could finish the question, Ryan did something Blake truly didn't expect.

He lunged at her.

Years of experience sang to her muscles. Instead of trying to avoid the hit, her legs and core braced themselves as her hands worked in sync while serving two different purposes.

Blake's left hand jabbed up in time to grab his wrist opposite her. Her right hand turned into a fist.

A fist that was angry.

It connected against the unsuspecting Ryan with enough power to throw him off his game. He stumbled to the side, only held up by her grip. Blake wasn't a petite woman, but Ryan still had some height on her. He lost his footing for a moment only to turn in the next and strike out with his free hand again.

It wasn't his fist that hit Blake but his elbow.

She cried out as pain exploded in her eyebrow.

Instead of trying to keep up with him, Blake decided to create some distance. She let go of his wrist and pivoted away.

"Stop this," she ground out.

Blake took a step back to try to meet his eye.

Ryan had both his fists up. Blake had only one ready. She knew what she was capable of and that she could do some damage. But that didn't mean she wanted to go against him again.

"What are you doing?" she tried. "Why did you run?"

Ryan's face was turning red. He shook his head with obvious aggression.

"Just tell me where it is," he spat. "I know you're—you're working on it."

Blake felt herself waver.

"What?" she asked, confused.

A guttural noise tore itself out of his throat. With the sound, Ryan moved again.

Blake was ready.

She let his punch go as far as it could before grabbing onto his arm with both of her hands. Then she turned into him, her back against his chest, and used his momentum and her balance to do something her previous trainer would have been proud to see.

Ryan didn't have time to stop the flip. Blake felt his full weight for a split second while she pushed up as he went over her.

If they had been on hardwood or tile, she was sure she would have heard a loud thud. Instead all she heard was Ryan's breath being knocked out of his chest. He wheezed. Then he was coughing on the ground, staring up at the sky.

Blake wasn't through.

She took two steps over to him and grabbed his arm for the third time since they had come into the woods. It wasn't easy to do in her dress, but she managed to flip him over. He kept coughing as she pinned his arm behind his back.

She wished she had her handcuffs.

Ryan started squirming. Blake thumped the back of his head. Then she winced as something stung her eye. It took a second to realize what it was.

She cussed low.

"You busted my eyebrow, Ryan. You better have a dang good reason for—"

Footsteps were coming fast from the tree line.

Blake tightened her grip on Ryan's arm.

Someone had followed them. Had Ryan not been alone?

Suddenly Blake regretted running blindly after the man. She should have been more observant to who was around them.

Worse came to worst she could run toward the old Kmart and to the main road for help. Or hide if needed.

Or she could fight some more.

Blake was still trying to figure out her plan of fight, flight, or find a tree to hide in, when the new potential opponent entered the clearing.

She recognized him.

"Shirt Guy," she said, the first thought coming out of her mouth.

Sure enough, it was the tall good-looking man from the gym's lobby. He even still had the shirt he'd let her borrow in his hand.

It was close to the badge on his hip.

He must have been eyeing her while Blake eyed it.

"You're the sheriff," she realized.

The man was breathing hard but not out of breath. He nodded, then motioned to Ryan.

"And this is…?"

Ryan started squirming again. Blake shifted her weight to stop him.

"A victim," he yelled.

Blake snorted. She looked down at the back of his head.

"Ryan, you've never been a victim a day in your life."

"You—you don't have any right to be doing this to me," he wailed back. "Now get off before I really get mad."

Blake had no intention of doing that at all, but the sheriff cleared his throat. He had gotten closer. Blake had to crane her head up to see into his eyes.

"I might not know what's happening, but I think I can take it from here." That deep baritone sure was nice.

Still, she hesitated and glanced down at his badge.

The pain in her eyebrow disappeared. The ache in her chest that had started six months ago flared to life.

Then she relented.

THE MAN SPENT their walk back to the parking lot trying his best to damn the woman walking behind them. It wasn't until Deputy Price met them at the tree line that he shut up. And that might have had more to do with Price's reaction.

In the middle of asking what was going on, he stopped himself and openly stared at the woman.

"Blake?"

Liam turned in time to see the woman smile briefly.

"Hey there, Price. It's been a minute. How are you?"

Price's eyes were wide, his excitement showing with ease.

"What do you mean, 'how are you?' What's going on? Who is—" Price stopped himself again. Now he was focusing on the man in cuffs. Whoever he was, Price seemed to recognize him. But only after seeing the woman.

His excitement dulled.

"What are you doing here?" he asked the man.

The chatterbox suddenly didn't like talking. He didn't answer.

Liam was annoyed at the lack of context he, the sheriff, had in this situation.

He also didn't like the wandering eyes of the people still in the parking lot. He motioned to Price's cruiser.

"I want to know what's going on, but let's go to the station," he said.

"Am I under arrest?" The man broke his silence.

Liam looked over his shoulder at Blake. Blood was coming down the side of her face. Her dress was torn at its side. There was a scratch or two along her left arm. She might have had the upper hand when he had shown up, but clearly the man had gotten a few licks in. He tried to keep his anger out of his response.

"I strongly suggest we all head that way to talk."

It wasn't technically an answer, but it did the trick.

The man hushed. Price took charge of him. Then he looked to Blake.

"Do you want to ride shotgun? Or—"

Liam cut him off.

"She can ride with me. You go on ahead." Liam turned around to face her straight on. She didn't look like she was going to argue. Instead, she pulled her cell phone out.

"Let me call my ride first."

Liam gave her some space to make her call and tried his best to keep himself close enough so he was blocking her from the onlookers still meandering through the parking lot. They were lucky that most of the cars were closer to the gym.

"Okay, I'm ready," she said after a minute or so. "I guess we're heading to the sheriff's truck."

She started to walk in its direction, but Liam caught her hand.

He felt her tension like a glass of ice water to the system.

He let go immediately.

Then he pulled the shirt he had slung over his shoulder off and handed it to her.

Again.

"I think it might be for the best if you just left this on for now."

He motioned to the tear in her dress but made sure to keep his eyes on her.

She didn't need any further explanation.

"I'm not sure if this is a lucky or unlucky shirt," she said, "but thank you again."

Her smile was strained, but she put the shirt on with no complaint.

Liam nodded. They started their walk to his truck. The few bystanders left made no attempt to pretend they weren't staring.

He noticed it wasn't at him though.

All eyes followed to Blake like moths to a red-haired flame.

Once again, Liam wondered who the heck she was.

Chapter Three

The McCoy County Sheriff's Department hadn't changed much in the fifteen years since she'd last been there. Neither had the locals who still staffed its halls.

Blake followed the sheriff through the lobby, taking pains to not make eye contact with the receptionist. Mary Kimball wasn't all that bad, but Blake wasn't great at chatting with the older woman. She wasn't a gossip, but she had been known to deeply pry into anyone's personal life if given the chance.

Blake didn't want to give her that chance, so she matched the sheriff's pace until her arm brushed against his.

He glanced over her at the movement but didn't speak. He had been just as quiet in the truck before, during, and after Blake had called Lola again. She had wanted to make sure her stepmom wasn't overwhelmed with getting Clem and Bruce back home solo.

"Shondra invited us for lunch," she'd repeated. "I just changed the location to the house. She loves these babies, and me, so don't you worry. You just take care of that man Ryan. Don't worry about rushing home."

Lola was a bright rainbow of optimism and love.

The way she said "that man" was laced with disgust and anger.

It was an uncomfortable but profound change.

Blake felt it too. She knew she was going to have to share it with Sheriff Weaver.

Maybe that's why she accepted the quiet ride to the department.

She was holding on to the last vestiges of peace before Ryan took it from her.

Blake sucked in a deep breath.

By the time she exhaled, they were in one of the department meeting rooms. Price Collins was already waiting for them.

He surprised Blake with an open arm hug.

"Sheriff Trouble!" he exclaimed, encircling her in a bear hug. He wasn't a particularly large man, but the embrace was all-encompassing. Blake couldn't even return it. So she let it happen and laughed a little.

"It's been a while since I've heard that one," she said.

Price stepped back, breaking the embrace, and was all smiles.

"You make a name like that for yourself, and you better believe I'm going to use it," he said. "I've been waiting to yell it at you since I heard it. I didn't realize you were back in town yet. I guess I'm behind on town talk."

He stepped to the side and rolled a chair away from the table for her. He did the same for his boss. They were in the middle of seating themselves as Price made a more dramatic introduction.

"Sheriff Weaver, let me reintroduce you to Sheriff Blake Bennet. Also known as Sheriff Trouble by some of her colleagues at her last two departments."

Sheriff Weaver's eyebrow rose high.

Blake tried to tamp down her grimace. She wasn't a fan of having to explain her current situation in detail. This situation, however, definitely needed the context.

"I didn't cause the trouble, I just kind of followed it," she tried.

Price laughed.

"And helped fix it." He swiveled so he was facing Sheriff Weaver directly. He pointed to Blake. "This here wonder woman has been elected sheriff of *two* different departments in Georgia and Alabama. That's to say nothing of her rocketing through every law enforcement establishment she's been a part of. Her last gig made national news. She was even hailed as an integral part of helping put an end to an entire town's corruption."

Blake couldn't help but stop him there.

"I didn't realize you were keeping tabs on me, Price. I'm almost flattered." She gave him a look that she hoped showed she wasn't in the mood for being flattered. He laughed again.

"Hey, when a Seven Roads local leaves the nest as a baby bird only to go fight with lions in their dens, you take notice." He met the sheriff's eye again. "Not saying you don't do us good here, Sheriff, but I just need you to know that who you're dealing with isn't some ordinary citizen. Blake Bennet has a knack for taming trouble."

Blake was about to scold her old friend, but his demeanor changed. He softened.

She knew what came next.

"I never got to say it, but I sure was sorry about what happened. How are you doin'? How are the kids?"

If it had been a gossip or Mrs. Kimball or any other local, Blake would have been curt. Instead, she gave Price a genuine answer. It was short but it was true.

"I'm still adjusting. We all are."

Price nodded.

"If anyone can handle it, I think it's you," he said. "If you ever need anything, you can let me and my kid know. She's at the babysitting age now too and wouldn't mind it a bit."

Blake took the offer with a quick smile.

Then she looked at the sheriff.

Two thoughts immediately popped into her head.

One, Sheriff Weaver was undeniably good-looking. Whether it was in a gym lobby, a parking lot, between the trees, or in a room full of fluorescents, the man was captivatingly handsome.

Two, despite his good looks and status as Seven Roads's main protector, he had no idea who she was.

Or, more accurately, what Price was talking about.

He didn't seem confused, but there was definitely a look of trying to connect the pieces he had just been given.

Blake felt the warmth of his shirt around her and decided to give him a hand.

"I moved back to Seven Roads a few months ago to take care of my niece and nephew," she said, trying to keep her voice as steady as possible. "My sister passed away six months ago, and now I'm their legal guardian. My niece was the one today who talked about moths and butterflies at the daycare assembly."

Blake gave another little smile. She hoped to undercut the potential pity coming her way. Thankfully, the sheriff didn't give it. At least he didn't give too much.

"I'm sorry for your loss." Then a slight pivot that she appreciated. "And I remember your niece. She spoke well."

Blake felt some pride at that. She merely accepted the compliment with a nod though. Then it was down to business.

"How does Ryan Reed figure into everything?" he asked. "You two clearly know him, but I've never run into him since I took up my badge."

Blake wasn't surprised. In fact, the only surprise she had was that Ryan had shown up in Seven Roads at all. She had been sure he wouldn't dare after their last encounter.

"Ryan was my sister Beth's brother-in-law," she explained.

"Former brother-in-law. Beth and his brother, Tim, divorced right after my nephew was born."

Blake cut her gaze to Price. She tried to find tactful words.

"Tim wasn't the best of guys," she continued. "He gave up his rights to the kids after letting anyone who would listen know that he didn't want to lose his life by being a father. After the divorce was finalized, he left town and moved somewhere up north. As far as I know, no one's heard from him since. He didn't even show up for Beth's funeral."

Old but violent rage welled up inside of Blake. She slipped her hand onto her lap and balled it into a fist. Her nails bit into the skin of her palm. Both men showed their displeasure. Price was shaking his head. The sheriff's frown was deep.

"Ryan, however, did," she kept on. "He pulled me aside and started asking about money. He kept wondering what I'd do now that I was back in town. If I'd get into the sheriff's department or if I'd sit around using up Beth's life insurance money to keep the kids and me going." Tiny points of pain radiated into her palm as Blake applied more pressure. "He didn't once ask about how the kids were doing otherwise."

"He was also really loud about the rest, from what I heard," Price added.

Blake nodded. She'd had no doubt that word would travel fast after Ryan had been so loud at the funeral. She had been relieved, however, to hear that the rumor mill hadn't churned out every detail. Maybe that had been more to Lola's credit than anything. Blake had long suspected that her stepmother had worked overtime to try to keep as much idle chatter about their family's tragedy under wraps as possible over the last six months or so. It was no one's business but their own that Blake was currently using her own life savings to take time off from working and make their transition as easy as possible. The insurance money was currently in a savings account that she wasn't touching unless absolutely necessary.

She hadn't told Ryan any of that.

And she definitely wouldn't.

"So this is the first time you've seen Ryan since the funeral?" the sheriff asked.

Blake nodded again.

"He doesn't, and hasn't, lived in Seven Roads for years, as far as I know," she said. "So seeing him at the school caught me off guard. I was going to go ask why he was there, but he started running. Past job experiences had me run after him on instinct."

"Did he say anything to you?" he asked.

"He asked where 'it' was and said he knows that I'm working on it. I have no idea what he's talking about." A cruel thought ran across her mind. "Unless he's referring to the insurance money Beth left behind."

Maybe it was her imagination, but Blake could have sworn she saw the sheriff's jaw twitch. Sheriff Weaver pushed his chair back with a little force too.

"Only one way to find out," he said. "I'll be right back."

Blake did the small-talk dance with Price while the sheriff interviewed Ryan. She caught up on his daughter's life, some mutual friends from school chatter, and then lightly on some of the bigger changes in town. That small talk had no choice but to lead back to the Grayton Steel Mill accident. It had been one of the most sensational things to happen in Seven Roads in the last few years.

"You know Mr. Grant's son started working a lot harder after the accident," Price made a point to say. "His name's Elijah. I met him once. He isn't as much of a social butterfly as his dad. He doesn't seem to need the attention. Still, I heard he stays at the mill enough that he's won over some of the workers. There was even some talk that they want him to take over the place instead of his daddy."

Blake didn't know how to feel about the steel mill anymore. Growing up, it had always just been a place that employed half the town. Even after the accident, it still was just the steel mill.

But then, one day, it became the last place that Beth had been seen alive.

She had finished her safety inspection and then gotten into the car accident on the way home.

It hadn't been the steel mill's fault, but now Blake felt an uncomfortable weight at its mention.

Still, she found the news interesting.

"I figured after Mr. Clearwater retired and shut down the tractor supply biz, his bestie Mr. Grant would eventually follow his lead," she admitted. "He's probably prepping his kid to take over for him. I doubt he'd just shut the mill down instead. The entire town would revolt."

Price agreed with that. Like her, he had grown up with the steel mill being the heart of the town's workforce. The idea of it shutting down was as bizarre as if Corrie Daniels decided to keep gossip to herself.

Not long after, the sheriff finally reappeared. He wasn't happy. Neither was Blake once she heard Ryan's excuse for his sudden reappearance.

Men lied, women too, but Ryan Reed was the worst of those who chose to twist the truth. He had been the same way before the divorce and shortly after. Lola had been livid recounting the way he had been loudly saying the entire thing was Beth's fault and none of it was his brother's fault. That's why Blake had a hard time believing anything the sheriff was saying. Then again, Weaver looked like he wasn't exactly buying it either.

"Ryan said he was in the area, saw the daycare program, and was curious," the sheriff continued to relay. "He claims he wasn't going to try to talk to you or the kids at all. He just wanted a peek at them to see how they were doing. He was trying to be inconspicuous, best I can guess."

Blake crossed her arms over her chest and snorted.

"When I saw him, he sure wasn't trying to seem inconspicuous. If he was Waldo, then every reader looking for him would have been disappointed at how easy it was to spot him."

Sheriff Weaver, leaning against the table, also had his arms crossed over his chest. Blake thought she saw his lips twitch. She continued with the other part of Ryan's sudden reappearance that had her questioning the man.

"Also, why the heck did he run?"

At this, the sheriff did a finger gun at her.

"I asked that actually," he said. He cleared his throat and surprised Blake with a mock impression of Ryan. It was a nasally sound that must have been hard for his naturally deep voice. "'I ran because she chased me like a bat outta hell.'"

Blake rolled her eyes.

"I took one step toward him, and he was the one out there running a relay." Blake leaned forward. "Not to mention, once I finally got him to stop, he attacked like a feral animal being caged. Why would you do that if you were only there with the best of intentions?"

The sheriff's gaze went to the Band-Aid over her eyebrow. It wasn't the best patch job she had done on herself, but it would do until she could take more care at the house.

"Has he never been physical before?" he asked.

Blake shook her head.

"Ryan, and Tim for that matter, have always been slimy guys but never abusive."

The sheriff tilted his head now a little.

"What about you?" he asked. "Have you gotten physical with him before?"

Blake snorted.

"I've wanted to smack both brothers upside the head since Tim married into the family." She sighed out long. "But I didn't want to upset my sister. Or my dad. So I only told my piece once about not liking them. I never brought it up again, especially after Clem was born."

Another, different kind of resentment pooled inside of Blake. She didn't often talk about her father, not even with her stepmother. He didn't live with them and, as far as Blake could guess, never would. Blake had only ever fallen short in her father's eyes. Nothing had changed that, even after Beth's passing.

Not even his optimistic and loving wife could sway Blake's father to change his poor opinion of her.

That was one reason Lola had moved in—she couldn't stand to see no one helping. So she had stepped in without a word.

Blake shifted in her seat, uncomfortable.

She shook her head.

"I've given Ryan no reason to run from me or attack me like that," she underlined. "And other than a hospital visit after Bruce was born, as far as I know, neither Ryan nor Tim have shown any interest in either him or Clementine."

The sheriff pushed off the table. His arms stayed crossed.

It sure was a powerful stance. Blake could imagine his campaign to be sheriff must have had some good-looking ad and marketing materials.

Price was silent but was obviously not a fan of the story either.

"It's up to you if you want to press charges, but just know he's already talked about reaching out to a lawyer," the sheriff said. "Plus, you did chase him into the woods. Even if you were only following him to talk."

Blake already knew she looked like the instigator in the situation. Still, it made her snarl.

The sheriff didn't directly address the less-than-professional noise. Then again, it wasn't like she was at work here. She was just a citizen now.

"I'll leave then," she said, standing. "I assume talking to him beforehand would be discouraged."

"Strongly so," Weaver agreed. "Unless you want to keep dealing with him and his lawyer too."

Blake didn't want that. Plus, she needed to get home. Lola was already a saint for sacrificing her retirement to help Blake and the kids. She didn't need to add a new stressor to their already chaotic lives.

"I think this morning was enough of a detour for us."

The sheriff nodded.

"Good choice."

A moment of silence bubbled up between them. Sheriff Weaver wasn't the least talkative man she had met, but with his size and demeanor, that quiet had its own presence. One that made her feel a bit squirmy.

"Can I go now, or do I need to do anything else?" she asked, trying to move away from yet another uncomfortable feeling.

He nodded to Price.

"Price can drop you off at your house whenever you're ready. We'll let Mr. Reed go after you've already left." He took something from his pocket and handed it over.

It was his business card.

Liam Weaver, Sheriff

"You can call the department or me directly if there's any more trouble with him. It would be faster to call the department though."

Blake nodded. She didn't have her purse or a pocket to put it in, so she held it against the side of her dress. She suddenly felt a wave of vulnerability in wearing it. Or, really, wearing it without some kind of badge out in front.

Her eyes flitted to the sheriff's star. She averted her gaze right after.

"Hopefully I won't have to use it," she said. "But thanks."

The sheriff didn't hesitate.

"Hopefully not." He walked to the door and opened it wide. A deputy was walking by. The sheriff caught his attention. "Make sure Mr. Reed doesn't leave until Miss Bennet here is gone. I don't want him starting anything in the parking lot."

Blake spied the deputy's name tag: Mel Gavin.

He looked familiar, but the name wasn't landing.

That was okay though. She had no intention of making friends at the moment. Even reconnecting with Price wasn't going to go past their shared ride.

It couldn't.

Blake had enough to deal with. Enough to juggle. Enough to worry about.

She smiled up at the sheriff, thanked him again, and started to walk on by.

His eyes followed her every step of the way.

Maybe if things had been different, Blake would have said something more. Done something more.

Instead, she let the smile be the end of it.

It wasn't until she was sitting the car with Price later that she realized she was still wearing the sheriff's shirt.

Chapter Four

The sunset was nice. Liam watched it from his apartment's balcony with a beer in one hand and his phone in the other.

A call he was waiting for hadn't come. He figured it wouldn't.

Still, he had waited.

It wasn't until the sun had completely gone that he put the phone down on the balcony's table.

A few minutes later, a rock hit the chair arm next to it. Liam set down his beer as another small rock came over the balcony railing at him.

"You know, throwing rocks at the sheriff isn't the smartest move," he called out.

Laughter came back.

"Is your door unlocked?" the voice from the ground asked.

"No."

A groan sounded.

Liam stood.

"You have thirty seconds," he called out again.

The sound of footsteps running to the outdoor stairwell echoed behind him as Liam made his way back into the apartment. He didn't slow his steps even a little. Yet when he unlocked the front door, a second later it was opening. Theo Chasten was out of breath but grinning.

"I'm—I'm getting faster," he panted. "I even skipped like six steps coming—coming up here."

Liam backtracked to the kitchen. He pointed to the refrigerator as he set his aim to the balcony again.

"There's leftovers in the fridge, superstar."

He didn't have to say any more than that. Which was a relief. Liam had come to Seven Roads after a divorce had left him tapped out on being any kind of social. He'd wanted quiet; he'd wanted peace.

Then he'd run into a teenaged boy sitting in the stairwell of their apartment complex while a storm raged on a few feet outside. Theo had been quiet then, but a strong quiet. It wasn't fear or worry that kept his mouth shut tight. It was his choice. His armor. Getting him to admit he was locked out of his apartment and unable to get a hold of his mother had been a chore. If it hadn't been for the tornado sirens going off, Liam doubted he could have convinced the teen to seek shelter in his apartment until his mom came home.

But those sirens went off and Theo had begrudgingly taken Liam up on the offer.

It was the first time Theo had been given help without asking for it but not the last. Now, almost two years later, Liam had become a mentor of sorts to the boy. He helped him with school, made sure he ate well, and answered any life questions that came his way. Liam had even taught the boy how to drive. Though, no one had been happy during that ordeal.

Liam had been deployed in combat zones before. Teaching an anxious teen to drive had tested his nerves almost as much.

In the end, it all led to Theo finally not fighting the offer of food anymore. It saved them both more time and Liam more sanity.

"Also grab you a water, fast guy," he added. "Because I can almost bet you haven't had a drop all day. Just that energy drink crap or sodas."

Theo laughed from the kitchen.

"You sure do know me really well, Sheriff." He cleared his throat. When he spoke again, his accent had more syrup in it. "Much obliged."

The night air was cool but not cold enough that the balcony door could stay open without messing with the air conditioner. Without saying it, though, Theo slid the glass door closed when he came out. It was little things like that that made Liam realize how much his relationship with the sixteen-year-old had changed since they had met.

First there had been yelling.

Then there had been annoyance.

Now Theo threw rocks, Liam left him food, and the former thought about the AC.

"Didn't you have a study group tonight? Don't tell me you bailed to come hang out with me. You'll never get that girl's attention if you aren't actually there to get it."

Theo dropped down into his usual spot on the chair next to Liam. He was already in the process of eating the leftovers.

"Her name is Sammy, thank you very much," he said around some food in his mouth. "And she's the reason I bailed. She had to babysit her little sister so her parents could go somewhere."

"Is the rest of the study group still meeting up?"

Liam saw the boy's head nod forward in the near darkness.

"Yeah but I'm not about to go sit in some coffee shop with a bunch of people I don't even talk to only to pretend that I'm not good at calculus."

Liam held in a chuckle at that.

Theo Chasten was a smart aleck, but there was a heavy emphasis on the smart part. Liam had been quick to pick up on the fact that Theo's mom wasn't exactly one to dote on her son. She worked hard, it was true, but she often overlooked him and his needs. He'd already been dropped into foster care once as a younger kid. He didn't talk about that time much though. Once his mom worked her plan to get him back, she'd done enough to keep him out. Still, that had weighed heavy on his little shoulders, and he had acted out more than not when he was younger. It had earned him a less-than-favorable reputation in town.

Most of Seven Roads had written him off already, thinking he didn't know a thing. Liam, his teachers, and thankfully Theo himself knew otherwise. Though that didn't mean he wanted others to know it. He hid his capabilities behind a facade of teenage angst and annoyance, especially from his peers.

"Plus," Theo continued, "I heard you chased some woman through the woods today, so I thought I'd rather waste my time here talking to you."

The image of Blake Bennet perfectly popped up in Liam's mind. Standing there in a ripped yellow dress wearing his shirt, which swallowed her, her eyebrows scrunched, the Band-Aid she had applied moving as she was thoughtful. Sending her off with Deputy Price had bothered him more than it should have.

"I didn't chase a woman through the woods. I chased after a man *she* was chasing," he corrected. Liam took a pull from his beer. "But that whole thing hasn't been resolved, so I'm not talking about it here."

The shadow of Theo's head bobbed again.

"I figured you weren't out there terrorizing civilians today," he said. "Especially not when I heard it was that sheriff lady. What do you call a former sheriff, by the way? Is it like the president, where you still call them Sheriff even though they've left the office? Or is it more like *Star Trek* and once you've left the captain's chair you're just whatever position you're in?"

Liam quickly sidestepped the additional ramble and instead got to the part that surprised him.

"You know Blake Bennet?"

His question came out a little strong. Luckily, Theo didn't pick up on it.

"I know *of* her, but I've only seen her once or twice in person," he answered. "Some of the workers at the steel mill have talked about her. Apparently, she was on TV a few times. It sounded like she upset a lot of people where she used to live."

Liam started to fiddle with the label on his bottle.

"People at the factory were talking about her?" This wasn't the first time that Theo, working part-time in the cafeteria, had gotten him an inside scoop.

"You've heard about her too. Or at least her sister. You know that guy, Hector Martinez, the guy Missy Clearwater was really good friends with before her own life got depressing, who got really badly burned when one of the furnaces started melting down a while back? That sheriff lady's sister was the safety person who came out to do a safety report on it. Later she got into a car accident on the county road. You know, the gnarly one that had every ambulance in the county there."

The label on the bottle started to slide off. Liam paused.

Then it finally clicked.

"Beth Bennet." He swore under his breath. "I knew the name sounded familiar."

Liam remembered the accident that had killed Blake's sister. He hadn't been in town for it, but the briefing had been enough when he'd come back. Doc Ernest had been visibly upset. The only solace she had given was that the woman had been killed instantly in the rollover. Her funeral had been a private event. Liam had meant to send his condolences but hadn't been able to find the right time.

Then, he felt ashamed to think, he had forgotten. His mind

had gone to cases and work, and now here he was putting together old pieces to a current puzzle.

"Apparently she's been in town for a while now, but no one's really seen her," Theo went on. "The talk from the cafeteria wasn't exactly nice about her either. They talked about her trying really hard to stay out of sight, but it also sounded like they didn't try to go see her at all either."

There was distaste in the teen's words. For good reason, he'd never been a fan of public opinion.

Liam went back to slowly peeling off the label of his bottle. He tried to keep his tone casual.

"Is there anything else you heard about her? The sheriff, I mean." Liam regretted how *not* casual-sounding the question came out.

He had overreached. Judging by the quick head turn, Theo had realized it too.

"Whoa, whoa, whoa!" he exclaimed. "Did I hear that right? Is our dear sheriff finally, *finally* giving in to the drama that is Seven Roads and its people? Are you really sitting here trying to gossip with me?"

Liam rolled his eyes and made sure the breath he let out was unmistakably annoyed.

"All right," he said. "I think this conversation has run its course."

He started to get up, but Theo grabbed at the leg of his jeans. He was laughing.

"Calm down there, Sheriff," he said. "No need to get all defensive. Everyone in town knows you don't put up with the rumor mill. I was just thrown a little, is all."

Liam stayed where he was.

He knew he had successfully moved the boy out of his teasing and right to where he wanted him—answering his original question without additional commentary.

"The only other thing I know about the Bennet family is that they used to be one of the longtime families of Seven Roads, but then everyone started leaving. The lady who passed was the last one who was here before her sister showed up again. Seems like there was family drama before that." He shut the leftover container with a click. His next words sounded thoughtful. "If the sheriff has been back for a while, then she really must have tried hard to keep to herself. I mean, it's hard not to notice someone in this place after all."

He wasn't wrong. Seven Roads was thimble-sized small. Even if you wanted to stay off the radar, a local would put you right back on it the second you stepped foot into any store or venue. Maybe that was some of the hesitance he'd seen in Blake before the daycare program. It was the general public that had her wavering outside of the gym doors.

If that was true, then it also made Liam even more irritated with Ryan Reed.

It sounded like Blake had earned her right to silence, and he'd gone and forced her into the public eye.

Theo quieted after that. Liam too. Eventually the teen pulled out his homework. He went to bed as soon as it was finished.

His mother had never once been against Liam stepping in to help take care of Theo. The guest bedroom was more his room than the teen's own bedroom in the apartment on the first floor. Still, there were moments when Liam wished the boy wouldn't come by. That he would, instead, find comfort and happiness in his own home.

But life didn't always work out as easy as that.

Theo knew that. Liam knew that.

Blake Bennet knew that too.

Liam's hip ached a little. He kneaded it with his fist and then checked his phone one last time for the night.

There was no reason for her to call or text.

Still, he checked.

There was nothing and he decided that was that.

Today had been an offshoot of his investigation. A side quest that had concluded, and now he had to get back to the main one.

Missy Clearwater.

The young woman whose last two weeks of existence had been sad enough for everyone to believe that her taking her own life made more sense than someone else being responsible. Though Doc Ernest was sure to give credit to the ones that had, in most people's opinion, been the motivation behind her action.

"Blunt trauma killed her," Doc Ernest had announced once she had reconsidered her autopsy conclusions. "But if you ask me, it's the ones closest to her that got her falling off that bridge. She has a big fight with her dad that everyone hears about, then her boyfriend leaves her, only to get with her best friend a week later?" Doc Ernest had shaken her head, sorrow lining her features. "That's a rough go of it, especially on someone so young and sweet as Missy."

But Liam couldn't ignore the suspicion that the flash drive had created. It had spider-webbed through every story he heard, through the autopsy report, through the town chatter, and through the evidence they did have.

That's why he wasn't going to stop until he could put those suspicions to rest. Or find out what had really happened.

Which is why he needed to talk to Cassandra about Missy's last interaction.

It could either help him move on or give him something to go on to find another piece to the puzzle.

Blake Bennet might have been intriguing, but her time with him was obviously done. She had her own life to live while he had Missy's death to put to rest.

Yet, when the next morning rolled around, Liam found the

woman leaning against his truck in the parking lot of the gas station. It was all he could do to hide his surprise.

"I've thought about it," Blake said in greeting with all the confidence in the world, "and I'm pretty sure I can help you. And I think you should let me."

Chapter Five

"You think you can help me."

The sheriff's baritone sure was something, even repeating her own words right back to her. Blake pushed off the truck and nodded, resolute. She held up the second reason she had come to find the man before explaining.

"There's also this," she said. "Your shirt washed, dried, and ironed with care. You wouldn't even know it's been through the wringer."

The button-up had gone directly into the washer when Blake had gotten home from the sheriff's department. She had never been the best at remembering the laundry in a timely manner, but when it came to this particular denim shirt, she had been unusually attentive. It had, after all, helped cover her as much as its owner had. It only seemed right to be just as courteous.

The sheriff eyed the shirt with a raised brow. She thought he was going to refuse the gesture for a second, but then he grabbed it and held it against his side with the one arm and kept his coffee in his other. The man was a Ralph Lauren ad come to life as far as Blake was concerned.

"You didn't have to do all that," he said, tipping his chin a little to get a better angle on her gaze. "But thanks."

Blake waved the comment off.

"I might have been a little chaotic recently, but I'm not without manners. Plus, if I hadn't done it, Lola wouldn't have let me hear the end of it. Lola being my mom. Aka the lady who will have my hide if I don't have all my social p's and q's together."

Sheriff Weaver snorted.

Blake paused in what she had intended to say next.

The sheriff looked right near caught.

His humored expression smoothed.

She wasn't letting him go.

"What was that for?" she asked.

He didn't hesitate.

"What was what for?"

Blake crossed her arms over her chest. She gave him a mock snort, then pointed to herself.

"You snorted at me just now. I want to know why." She tilted her head to the side and feigned politeness. "Don't tell me you've got something against people washing your clothes at home. What was I supposed to do? Dry-clean it?" Blake glanced down at the shirt that was pinned against him. "No offense, but it's not *that* nice of a shirt."

This time there was no snort, but she could have sworn a smile was trying to tug up at the edges of his lips. It failed.

"You said you washed my shirt because of good manners. Then you said you only did it because of your mother. You only were nice because of the consequence of not being so. I just think it's funny how you contradicted yourself so fast."

Blake opened her mouth.

Then she shut it.

Her face was growing hot. Her words would come out boiling next if she didn't calm down.

So she decided to acknowledge instead of defend herself.

"Hey, not all of us can be so domestic," she said. "Just be-cause I had a consequence that forced my hand doesn't mean

I also didn't have good intentions. It's like baking a cake for someone's birthday. Normally most people don't bake cakes at random for you, but if they miss giving you one on your birthday that's kind of a bummer. I did it because those are the unwritten rules, but I also genuinely wanted to be helpful after everything that happened. So follow the same rules and say thank you and let's move on."

The sheriff wasn't smiling. He wasn't frowning either.

Blake took that as acceptance. His nod helped prove it further.

"I suppose you're right about that. Thank you."

Blake felt like she had given the man some humble pie.

No sooner had she felt some satisfaction did she have to eat a slice herself.

The sheriff had the audacity to start walking around her toward his truck door.

"That's it?" she asked, doing a little hop, skip, and shuffle to follow. "I didn't tell you what I could help you with yet."

She stopped between him and the driver's-side door, sliding in before he could even reach the handle. His eyebrow rose again at the move. Blake watched it with a surge of annoyance. His tone when he spoke next didn't help.

"I didn't ask for anything from you. So don't worry yourself over me."

His eyes dropped to the door handle next to her.

She took a deep breath and moved out of the way. She could fight him, get huffier and turn into a Southern woman who just so happened to be a former sheriff, but instead, Blake decided to play it as cool as she could. She had dealt with strong-willed people all her life. Just because this one was a sheriff didn't mean a thing.

She watched him open his door, deposit the shirt on the passenger's seat, and place his coffee in the cup holder, all like he didn't have an audience.

When he settled into his seat and went to close the door, Blake cleared her throat and threw bait in the water.

"I can give you Cassandra West."

Blake was ready to add context, but something changed. The man's entire body tensed. His brows went up. His eyes found and then swallowed hers. She didn't need to give him anything more.

He was already hooked.

"What do you mean, you can 'give me Cassandra West'?" he asked.

Blake took a small step forward and lowered her voice.

"When Price was driving me home yesterday, he mentioned you had been having a hard time getting her to talk to you. Since she seems to be skirting you, I'm assuming it's not for a case. At least not one where your badge would work, or else you would have already had her talking." Blake patted her chest. "I can get you a casual conversation with her."

"*You're* friends with Cassandra West?"

Blake didn't like his tone. Hers came out a little huffier, regardless of trying to remain completely civil.

"We go way back. She'll talk if I'm there. Of that, I'm sure."

"If you're there," he deadpanned.

"If I'm there," she repeated.

Blake took another small step forward. She made a show of turning her wrist over to look at her watch.

"And, as it so happens, my presence can be helpful right about now." Blake gave the man a big old grin. "What do you say, Sheriff? Do you want my help or not?"

A part of Blake expected the man to grumble or try to dissuade the notion that he needed help. Instead, he surprised her.

He nodded.

"Your car or mine?"

Blake mentally hiccupped. Her face started to heat.

Both states made her mentally scold herself.

"Follow me in yours, or else the whole town will be talking about us riding together," she said, regaining her composure. "Meeting up is fine, showing up together will get everyone's mouths flapping."

He nodded again.

"After you," he said, motioning out to the parking lot.

And that was that.

Blake had hooked the sheriff and would be repaying her debt to him. All while the kids were in daycare and Lola was out being social.

It felt good.

It felt—

"Miss Bennet?"

Blake's body turned back on reflex.

"Yeah?"

The sheriff wasn't smiling, but she heard something different in his tone when he spoke.

"Call me Liam."

THERE WERE TWO cars parked outside of the Twenty-Two Coffee Shop. Liam let Blake take the last open parking spot, and he slid his truck into the drug store's lot across the street. By the time he was crossing over Main on foot, Blake was standing on the sidewalk and staring up at the café's sign. Her hair was loose. It looked nice against the light-colored blouse she was wearing. Her expression, however, was flitting between a scowl and a smirk.

When she saw him, she nodded up to the sign.

"We might have all gotten older, but some things really haven't changed a bit."

Liam waited for an explanation. Blake didn't give one.

"Make sure you order something frilly-sounding," she followed up instead. "You don't want to offend Corrie."

"Why? She doesn't own this place."

Blake snorted.

"No, but Cassandra does, and if you make Corrie happy, Cassandra will follow. Same with the opposite end of the experience. Make one twin angry, you get the other one angry too." That scowl-smirk combo smoothed into an easy-to-define feeling. She gave him a raised brow. "Don't tell me you've been in Seven Roads for two years, and this is the first you're hearing of the twins. The Daniels family is a part of town lore 101."

Blake didn't give him space to respond.

He was finding she was a point-A-to-point-B kind of woman. She didn't stray from her target. At least, not long enough for him to get a few more words in.

Liam wasn't sure if he disliked that quality though. The South had a habit of churning out people who spent more time talking about nothing than not. At least with Blake, she seemed to edit out the time-wasting part.

The little bell over the front door dinged as she led the way inside of the shop. Liam had been in the café several times but had never really lingered. It was a small space with only a handful of tables and chairs and a bar that took up more than half of the tight area. Having a quiet cup of coffee to himself had never been an option in the shop. Their to-go service had been his best plan.

Now he settled into a chair next to one of the larger plate glass windows that looked out at the sidewalk that wrapped around the edge of the corner lot. The old pocked road that led from Main to one of the older established neighborhoods was in desperate need of repair. According to Mayor Tufton, that was an almost impossible task given their current town funds.

Mayor Tufton and his little sports car never drove down Main unless it was campaign time.

The mayor had a habit of keeping his head down outside of town repair too. The moment he had heard that Liam was still looking into Missy's death had been the moment he had decided to have a lot of opinions on why they *shouldn't* have a lot of opinions on the matter.

It was true that Liam had no solid evidence to suggest that anything had happened to Missy other than her jumping off the bridge, but it still made Liam angry now at how the mayor's reasoning for stopping had been about "the optics." The mayor didn't want bad press.

Liam curled his fist against the knee of his jeans.

Blake didn't notice. Instead, her attention seemed to have gone behind them and out of the room.

She didn't sigh, but when she spoke, her words were heavy.

"If Corrie's here, she'll come out first, and she'll talk our ears off, but I'm hoping that since all I saw was Cassandra's car, we're safe for now. If not, we'll just have to endure."

Liam tilted his head to the side in question.

"You haven't lived in Seven Roads in years, how are you so sure they'll even mind you're here?"

He didn't mean it to sound as patronizing as it did, but Liam also couldn't deny he was genuinely curious. Even Theo had talked about this Bennet woman with reverence. He didn't understand why Blake was so interesting to the whole town. Was it because she had been a sheriff outside? One who had made the news?

Was it because her sister had been killed?

Sure, that warranted talk, Liam understood that, but where was this confidence stemming from? Why did Blake Bennet know she would be treated so differently?

Was it because she was beautiful?

The thought crossed Liam's mind as the woman smiled.

Her hair was lit up by the sun pouring through the window. Its red seemed to liven into something warmer than before she had sat down.

Her words were still on the cold side.

"Because a long time ago, a teenager promised she would never come back in a very public way." A door opened behind the bar. Liam kept his eyes on Blake as she finished. "That teenager was wrong. Now I'm back and the townspeople want me to eat crow for it."

Her eyes attached to the woman who took a pointed path toward them.

Liam recognized her as none other than Corrie Daniels.

"Well, if it isn't Blake Bennet here in front of me again!"

Corrie stopped beside their table with a thin smile. Liam had interacted with her enough to not be a novelty, but his relationship with her was, at best, a passing acquaintance.

Then again, he could have been her flesh and blood, and she probably wouldn't have cared. Like Blake had predicted, the woman's focus attached to Blake and didn't let go. She had her hands clasped in front of her, and that smile went from thin to overbearing in a flash.

A shark in the waters who smelled blood.

"What can I say, running into you yesterday helped open my eyes to the fact that I needed to get out and be more social," Blake returned. Her words were as genuine as Corrie's smile. She motioned to the bar. "I mean, I didn't even realize that you and Cassandra took over the old coffee place and turned it into your dream shop. You've been wanting to open Twenty-Two since we were, what, sixteen? I can't believe it's taken me this long to finally visit."

Corrie couldn't have smiled any wider. Yet Liam felt like she was stretching herself. She laughed lightly.

"I can't believe you even remember something like that," Corrie said. "It was so long ago. I figured you had probably forgotten all about us since you left. To be honest, there were a few times between then and now that I'd forgotten all about that girl who fought her daddy in the park. Now I'm hearing that you had to come back and fight with someone else too."

Liam didn't understand the first reference, but he knew Corrie meant Ryan in the second. He also knew that Blake had been absolutely right. Corrie was trying to hit a nerve.

And, he might not be familiar with entire account of Blake Bennet's backstory, but he could see that a nerve had definitely been struck.

Blake's expression pulled tight. Her shoulders lined with undeniable tension.

That wasn't going to do.

Liam cleared his throat and put his cellphone on the table with a thud.

Corrie didn't seem too keen on redirecting her attention, but she did so with that customer service polite on.

"Sorry to interrupt you two playing catch-up," Liam started, "but I've been told that the faster I try your newest coffee, the faster I'll be happy. And, well, I'm sure not going to turn down happy today. Could I trouble you for the newest coffee item on the menu?"

Liam watched as her eyes widened a little. Probably because it was the most he had ever said to her. Or, maybe, Corrie was finally realizing who exactly had come in with Blake. She glanced between them but nodded.

"As it would happen, our new frozen mocha has been all the rage recently," she responded. "I would be more than happy to get you one, Sheriff."

"I'd like just a black coffee, if you don't mind," Blake added. "No whip."

Corrie did seem to mind, but she nodded all the same.

"Sure thing. I'll be back in a jiffy."

Liam waited until he was sure she was out of earshot. He fixed Blake with a narrow-eyed look.

"I thought you said to order something fancy-sounding or we'd offend them," he pointed out.

This time, Blake did sigh.

"I wanted you to order something fancy so *you* wouldn't offend them." Her gaze fell to her hand. She was rubbing her thumb along her index finger. It was like her focus shifted with it to something else entirely. Still, she finished explaining. "Me simply being back in Seven Roads has already offended them enough. There's nothing I can do to fix that. Now, if you'll excuse me, I need to use the restroom."

It happened then, as he watched her walk away.

Liam realized that his singular mission to solve the circumstances behind Missy's death had picked up another mission along the way.

Finding out who exactly Blake Bennet was.

Chapter Six

"I lied to the sheriff for you."

Blake was sitting on the edge of the back office's desk and trying to find a candy from the candy dish that she wanted to eat. Cassandra West was watching the attempt from her office chair, no doubt frowning.

"That's a bad habit to start," Cassandra replied. "I'd think someone like you, who held the same title in the past, would avoid such mistakes."

Blake grinned. She found a golden-wrapped toffee and went to work peeling back the paper.

"I lied saying I was going to the bathroom for your benefit, not mine," she said. "So save your judgment for the end of his program, thank you very much."

Cassandra let out a breath that wobbled. She was stressed. That didn't stop her from trying to cover up that fact.

"I didn't ask you for anything. Especially lying."

Blake waved the comment off with her hand and popped the candy in her mouth. It tasted like visiting her grandmother's. She rolled her neck around and met Cassandra's eye.

"No, but I figured I'd buy you some time to tell me why you're avoiding the sheriff out there," she said. "I heard he's been trying to talk to you, and you've been doing anything but."

Cassandra was the same age as Blake, which made her twin, Corrie, the same age as well. Yet Cassandra had always seemed older. Maternal, a worrier. She was also practical and leaned more conservative, especially in comparison to her sister. If Blake had to guess, she was the one who kept the coffee shop running, the workers paid, and she dealt with the day-to-day stresses of owning a business.

Cassandra was a straight shooter.

Which was why Blake didn't understand her hesitance with Liam.

"I'm not avoiding the sheriff," Cassandra defended. "I'm just not seeking him, or any sheriffs, out. It's not like I'm under investigation. I don't have to chat with him."

Blake sucked on her hard candy for a few beats. Cassandra's gaze didn't waver.

She apparently had grown up into a straight, stubborn shooter.

"Listen, I'm only here because the sheriff helped me out," Blake started. "And he seems to be really in need of talking to you. You don't have to say anything to him, but at least tell me what's going on, and let's see if I can't get him off your back." Cassandra didn't look too sure. Blake flashed her a smile. "You know me, Cassie. The good, the bad, the ugly. Whatever your personal feelings are for me, you have to know I'm not here to cause trouble. I've had enough of that for a lifetime. Now tell me why Sheriff Weaver thinks you're the answer to whatever question he has."

Blake's smile dissolved.

Cassandra looked like she had aged ten years within the last minute. She shook her head but spoke all the same. Blake put her hand back in the candy dish and twirled the candies around while the other woman explained.

"Missy Clearwater," she said, defeat in each syllable. "The reason for her death is what he's after. Did you manage to hear about it? Or has your seclusion only let in food delivery and Walmart runs?"

Blake sidestepped the barb and recalled that the news had indeed reached her through Lola's social circle. The news had been sad, but she'd been dealing with a lot at the time. She hadn't thought too much about it past a wave of sympathy. She might have known most of the Seven Roads locals, but she'd never met the young Missy.

"I heard about her passing. Her daddy is Jonathan Clearwater, the owner of the tractor supply before he retired and sold, right?"

"Yeah, that's him." A grimace passed over Cassandra's face. "He was a big part of her problems. After he shut the tractor supply down and laid everyone off, a lot of people were angry. It's not like we have a big job pool here, you know? Especially the older folks who'd been there for a minute. But it's not exactly like they could have told him off or said anything but nice words in his direction. So they turned to the safer option of pushing that frustration onto the easier target. People were passive-aggressive and sometimes outright rude to Missy. Nothing too bad in the beginning, but after a while, it became a thing that had people whispering whenever she was around. She must've gone to her dad about it, but it backfired. They had a big fight near the diner. Yelling so loud that Mrs. Thomas almost made them leave."

Cassandra cast her a look. If she had been Corrie, she would have no doubt commented on the similarities of the last part with Blake's own past, but thankfully, she stayed on topic. She leaned back slightly, shaking her head a little more.

"Then her boyfriend went and left her—Corrie thinks because he couldn't take the unflattering spotlight—and *then* to make matters worse, he had the gall to start dating her best friend. Like it was out of a sitcom or something. They're still together, by the way. I sold them coffee last week."

Blake didn't have any other words than "Yeesh."

Cassandra seconded the sentiment.

"If that wasn't enough of a sad story, Missy died a week after that news broke. She was found beneath the bridge out at Becker Farm."

Blake stopped twirling her hand through the candy dish. That part she hadn't heard through Lola's rumor mill.

"Did she fall or jump?"

Hesitation. It lined every beat of time between Blake's question and Cassandra's answer. When it broke, her words had become notably colder.

"She was found at the bottom, in the dirt. That's all I know."

Blake averted her eyes to the dish.

"What did the newspaper say?"

There was no hesitation this time.

"That Missy jumped."

"And what does the sheriff out there think?"

No hesitation again.

"From what I've heard, that she didn't."

"He thinks she fell?" Blake asked the question, but she suspected that wasn't the answer.

"You'd have to ask him that."

Cassandra sighed out long and loud. Her patience with Blake seemed to be running out. So Blake went in for one last go.

"Why is he barking around your tree then?" she asked. "Were you and Missy close?"

Cassie shook her head.

"No. But I supposedly was the last person to see her alive." She pointed toward the door. Beyond that was the hallway that led to the main coffee shop room. "She came to get a coffee a few hours before she was found beneath the bridge."

"You two talk?"

"Unlike the rest of the town, I thought it would have been

impolite to ignore her. Or heckle her. We talked about the weather, about laptop brands, and then about how expensive whipped cream had gotten. She left when she was done with her coffee. She tipped well, smiled nice, and then was just gone. That's the long and short of it."

"Laptop brands?" That wasn't exactly normal chatter, especially with Cassandra, who had never been a fan of technology in school.

"She had one with her and seemed capable enough with it. I asked if she liked it well enough since my youngest, Hunter, spilled milk all over mine and I needed to get another. She was nice about that too."

Talking about laptops, the weather, and whipped cream hours before potentially jumping off a bridge. Drinking coffee too. It didn't sound like a woman who was planning not to see the end of the day.

Then again, not everyone was so cut and dry with their actions.

Cassandra pushed back in her chair but didn't stand. It seemed she had finally reached the end of her patience.

"You can tell your sheriff that that's all I know and that's all we did. Past that, I'm not going to talk about Missy again. He's the one who signed off on the end of her case in the first place. He needs to let it go and move on, like the rest of town. That goes for you too, Blake. Don't go poking your nose around me or mine."

Her words were harsh.

Blake respected them.

She selected another candy from the dish and nodded.

"I can take him with me now, but I'll never make it out of the shop if Corrie is still waiting for me," she pointed out.

Cassandra picked up her cell phone and typed a message out for a bit.

Then she pointed back to the door.

"I called her off. You can leave now and she won't bother you."

Blake chuckled.

"If only I could have that power over my sister."

The thought slipped out before Blake even realized she'd had it. All humor vanished. She tried to overcompensate and gave her old friend a smile and pivoted back to an earlier thought.

"So, why didn't you just talk to the sheriff about all this?" Blake asked. "It doesn't seem like any information that was worth dodging the law for."

Cassandra seemed to consider her answer for a moment. Her lips twisted a little before she spoke, like she was regretting it before she said a word.

"Word got around that the sheriff was asking questions about Missy even after everything was finished up. It really upset her dad, but it struck even more sour with those old goons who still worship him from their time at the supply. You know, the ones who started working there in their teens and managed to retire before he sold it off?" She shook her head. "It might have been nothing that I told you, but if it got around that I said that nothing to the sheriff, I might get some looks I don't want."

"Ah." So there it was. "So now it's on me."

Cassandra didn't try to deny it.

"If it gets around town that you're talking about Missy to the sheriff, then that's on you. Even if they find out I'm the one who told you, it's still on you."

Blake snorted. She wasn't mad at the intention. In fact, she understood it.

"Whoever says that Corrie is the scarier twin hasn't met the real you."

But Blake smiled true.

"It was good to see you, Cassie," she added. "I'm glad you're doing well. Truly."

Cassandra didn't return the smile, but she did nod.

It wasn't until Blake was one foot out of the door that she called out to her.

"Hey, Blake, I'm sorry about Beth."

Blake paused.

"Me too."

Blake refocused her attention as she made her way back to the main dining room. On the way, she passed Corrie. The woman was scowling but also silent. She met Blake's eye with a barely contained sneer and was gone right after.

Then there was Liam.

Blake stopped next to their table. She handed him the candy in her hand.

"I'm not in the mood for coffee anymore, so how about we do dinner tonight instead?"

LIAM WAS STARING into his closet. Theo was inside and sporting a brown blazer that had only seen the world twice since being purchased at a strip mall in Florida. The teen flapped his arms, then did another twirl.

"This isn't the worst thing you own," he said. "It actually looks pretty decent, good with your jeans too." Theo made a show of looking him up and down. "Unless you want to change into something else."

Liam almost rolled his eyes. He avoided the urge. Theo had been in his apartment for less than a half hour and, in that time, had already made several jabs about his appearance.

"This isn't some kind of date," Liam said, once again. "I'm just going out to dinner. I don't need to dress up any more than this."

Theo didn't hold back his urge to roll his eyes.

"You're finally doing something social after business hours. With a woman." He shrugged. "I feel like that's as close to a date as you're going to get. Why not make more of an effort?"

"Says the guy who refuses to say hi to his crush of, what did you say, five years?"

That seemed to hit home. Theo took off the blazer. Liam pointed to the hanger.

"Hey, I'm just trying to help a divorced man get his groove back." He hung the blazer back up. "That's not a crime. That's *charity.*"

"That's sticking your nose where it doesn't belong," Liam corrected. He backtracked through his bedroom to the kitchen. His badge was on the counter, his cell phone next to it.

Fifteen more minutes until he would be leaving.

Fifteen more minutes until he would be meeting Blake at the restaurant.

"Plus, this isn't remotely a date. This isn't even a social call. It's about work."

Liam said it with a little too much vigor. Maybe he was trying to underline the reason he had agreed to Blake's invitation for himself too.

"After work hours though?" Theo prodded. "Do you know how rare that is for you? Sheriff No Work Talk After Clocking Out. You can't expect me not to question this. Unless there's something *else* going on."

"There's nothing else going on. Blake just has a busy schedule I'm trying to accommodate. It's not like turning down Deputy Gavin for some beers when he wants to complain about the medical examiner hurting his pride."

Theo crossed his arms over his chest. He still looked skeptical.

"You met her for coffee this morning, you're going to dinner with her tonight. What's next?" he asked. "Staying at her house until morning?"

The boy cracked a grin.

Liam made sure to be stern.

"Don't even joke about that," he warned. "One word like that gets out, and all our ears are going to be filled with gossip that will most definitely put me in a mood. A mood that locks that front door, and that fridge, from a no-good, talkative teen."

Theo rolled his eyes again but then caught whatever snarky remark he was about to say. Instead, he put his hands up in mock surrender.

"I won't make a peep about your nighttime *work* meeting with the beautiful, and rumored to be single, Miss Bennet at the fanciest restaurant in town. My lips are officially sealed."

So, she *was* single.

Liam hadn't asked and hadn't planned on it either.

But now, he knew.

"Good," Liam said to the boy's promised silence. "I'll grab you a plate to eat tomorrow if you don't say another word about it, starting now."

Theo mocked a loud gasp. Then he bowed.

"I won't tell a soul you even left the complex. Much appreciated."

This time Liam did roll his eyes.

"Your mom said she won't be home until tomorrow night, so you can crash here. But you better not stay up too late. I know school is boring for a smarty like you, but that doesn't mean you're allowed to sleep through it. Got it?"

Theo saluted him.

"There's food in the fridge. Lock the door behind me."

Theo was fast. As soon as the door was closed behind him, Liam heard the dead bolt slide into place. Knowing Theo, this wouldn't be the end of date-talk between the two of him. It should have grated on Liam, but he was finding that Blake Bennet continually popping up on his radar didn't exactly bother him. However, it was starting to bother him when other people forced her to surface.

While Blake had excused herself to the bathroom at the coffee shop—which Liam now knew was her sneaking away to talk to Cassandra herself—Corrie Daniels had tried her best to grill him about the woman. She had been fishing without even throwing her own line in.

Liam hadn't fallen for it.

After her second mention of Ryan's name and his sudden reappearance in town, Liam had done something he very rarely did.

He had made small talk.

The weather came first, then the coffee shop and how business was doing.

Liam had stayed in those conversations with his feet dug in and resolution clear.

Maybe that's why Corrie had been so quick to leave once she had gotten a text on her phone.

Or, maybe, whoever was texting had way more power than he did over the woman.

Either way, she had gone and Blake had come back…different.

It was why he had agreed to her dinner invitation so quickly.

He wanted to know what Cassandra had said, sure, but he wanted to know why it had changed Blake.

So he got into his truck and pointed it in the direction of the restaurant she had picked. The streetlamps outside of the apartment complex gave way to the dark of night while the stretch between residential and commercial held nothing but road, dirt, and trees.

The song on the radio belted out some catchy beat with a guy crooning about love.

He was still singing when Liam found his way back to the light, and the song was still going when Liam saw the woman of the hour standing outside of the restaurant, waiting for him.

Her hair was braided. Her blouse was red. Her jeans looked nice.

Her smile, when she saw him, was warm.

Blake Bennet might have been Sheriff Trouble in the past, but right then and there, she was simply one thing to Liam.

Breathtaking.

Even when she was hustling to his window and motioning for him to roll it down.

She didn't waste any time in her request.

"I only had your office number or else I would have called, but is there any way we could change locations?" She dove in. "Bruce kind of destroyed the kitchen earlier and threw off our family schedules. Lola is back at the house with him now, and I have Clem with me."

Liam finally saw the rolled-down window of the car behind her. The little girl from the daycare program was staring intently at them. She seemed calmer than her aunt, that was for sure.

"She's a good kid, but there's not a thing she'll eat off the menu here. The diner, however, has some of her favorite chicken nuggets."

Blake's eyebrow rose. She didn't give him space to respond as she added, "Or we can reschedule? Or maybe I can just talk to you on the phone instead?"

Liam would later wonder if his answer would have been the same had someone else been asking. In the moment, however, his response was quick.

"I happen to be a chicken nugget fan myself. You lead the way and I'll follow."

Chapter Seven

The change of location had been a simple request, but Blake had found herself oddly nervous about it. No doubt Lola's parting speech hadn't helped.

"The fact that he already agreed to eat with you is a good sign that he won't mind Clem being there or y'all going to the diner," she had said over her mop and bucket. "I'm still surprised he said yes in the first place. Since he moved to town, that man hasn't been very social. Some think that's why he got his divorce, and some think he's closed off *because* of his divorce. Either way, he doesn't seem like the kind of man to get snobby about a kid or a change in plans."

Lola had shrugged.

"And if he makes a fuss, then fuss right on back," she'd added. "If that doesn't work, give me a call and Bruce and I will show up and fuss too. That'll teach him to get into a snit over nothing."

Blake had waved off the offer of the fussing backup, though she'd been touched. Not just anyone would go to bat against a sheriff for her.

Lola's words, as supportive as they were, however, had Blake antsier than she had anticipated when driving up to the restaurant.

She wanted to talk to Liam.

She wanted him to *want* to talk to her.

Maybe it was because he had helped her with Ryan. Maybe it was because they both understood what it meant to be a sheriff. Maybe it was because, other than Lola, he was the first adult in town not to ask the hard questions.

Talking to Liam had so far been an easy thing to do.

So when he was quick to assure her that their change of plans wouldn't make him leave, Blake couldn't help but feel some relief.

In fact, there was some excitement too.

"We're going to eat with an actual adult, Clem," she called over her shoulder once she was back in her car. "Someone who *doesn't* live in our house. That means we need to be on our best behavior. No yelling from me, no throwing food for you. We don't want to scare the sheriff off."

Clem was in a jumper covered in cartoon ducks. Her hair was braided and, in the right light, looked identical to Blake's. It was a point of pride for Blake that she was the only one Clem would let play with her hair. And play it had become since Blake learned quickly that doing her own hair in braids was one thing. Doing a toddler's hair in braids was another.

"You ready to go?" Blake asked the girl, reversing into position in front of Liam's truck. Surely he knew how to get to the diner, yet he was waiting for them. It was sweet.

Clem apparently agreed.

"He's gonna eat chicken nuggs too," she squealed in delight. Blake saw her wave in the truck's direction. She couldn't see if Liam waved back. "Chicken nuggs with ranch," Clem added once they were going forward again. "Ranch, ranch, ranch."

Blake laughed at that.

"You and your ranch. You know I told your grandma that it might not be a bad idea to throw you a ranch-themed party for your next birthday."

Clem broke out into giggles.

"With chicken nuggs?" she asked between them.

Blake nodded.

"With chicken nuggs."

Clem started to talk about food some more, and Blake navigated the stretch between the restaurant's parking lot right out to the town's biggest collective grievance—the new intersection. One that Blake had only experienced a handful of times since coming back.

"It's like whoever added in that intersection was paid to make it as much as a pain in the tuchus as possible," Lola had once complained about the spot. "I went the wrong way twice there, and I don't even feel bad about it. None of it makes sense!"

Blake had done enough driving in enough less-than-ideal areas that the intersection didn't bother her as much. That didn't mean she let her guard down though. She was hyperaware of the cars around them as she rolled to a stop. It's why she noticed that the vehicle behind her was not, in fact, the sheriff's truck.

"I guess Liam is one of those Sunday drivers," Blake mused aloud. "He probably let me lead because he likes taking his time behind the wheel."

The idea of someone as intimidating-looking as Liam being a passive driver really got into Blake's system. One more laugh and Clem caught on, and when the light changed to green both were giggling nonsense.

Blake's heart softened and squeezed all at once.

Beth should have been able to hear it too.

That ache bloomed.

Blake had never regretted her decision to leave Seven Roads years ago. She hadn't regretted her choices after that either. Each step she had taken after crossing the town limits line was done with confidence and pride. Even the mis-steps. They had been hers and she had embraced them all.

She had created an unmovable foundation for her future.

It was only after coming back that she realized there had always been a crack that ran through it.

Beth.

The golden child. The baby of the family. The little sister who had made all the right choices in the eyes of their father while Blake had done everything wrong.

That's how she had seen Beth in her mind, even if she had convinced herself that she hadn't.

Beth, though, had never once said a word against her. She had supported each choice Blake had made, forced her to en-dure phone calls and video chats at least once a month, and had always kept her updated on her life. She had also always asked for updates from Blake's.

Their mother had left them. Their father had let Blake go. Beth?

She had held on as best she could until she had been forced to leave too.

It wasn't until Blake was sitting in an attorney's office, holding a small note written in her sister's silly little hand-writing that Blake had finally found the crack in her life. The one that would now forever be filled with regret.

If you're reading this, then I guess something not-so-great happened to me, the note had begun. *So let's skip the sad part and get to the nice. I love you, Blakey. Let my kids love you too. Take care of each other. And make sure to eat some-thing yummy. Love, your sister, Beth.*

Regret. Grief. Immense sadness. Total love.

Just under fifty words in total and Blake felt everything all at once.

She was living in Beth's home, raising her children a week later.

Now, she knew Clem had a passion for ranch dressing that rivaled most epic love stories. That Bruce kicked his feet a little when he was content. That Clem didn't talk at all while watching TV but would sing the intro songs loudly and with delight as soon as the screen went dark. That Bruce happy-danced when his sister started her singing and became even louder when Lola joined in.

Blake had learned a lot of little things since she'd come home.

The biggest thing?

She missed her sister something fierce.

"Hey, Clem?" Blake said, clearing her throat to stave off tears she knew would come if she kept on with her current thoughts. Instead, she went to a happier memory. "Let me tell you about something your mama used to eat that ran me up the wall when we were kids."

They were moving along the access road that eventually would take them to the side of the diner. The lighting along the road consisted of exactly one outdated streetlamp. It left an orange glow in the dark across Clem's curious expression as Blake glanced at her in the rearview mirror.

The headlights coming up fast behind them cut through that glow with startling quickness.

Blake pressed the gas pedal down hard.

It was the only reason the approaching vehicle didn't rear-end them.

Adrenaline flooded her system, but Blake reserved her gut reaction to curse the driver. It was surely an accident. The driver probably wasn't paying attention. The alarms in her head going off had nothing to do with some kind of on-going danger.

Why would there be any here in Seven Roads, after all?

No sooner than she had the thought than it vanished.

The headlights became bigger as the car behind them sped up again.

Blake didn't leave room for interpretation now.

The car was trying to hit them.

And there was no time to figure out why.

"Hold on, Clem."

A DRIVER WENT when they weren't supposed to at the headache of an intersection. Once they realized their mistake, they panicked and stopped in the middle of the street. Blake and the car that had been able to slip in between her and Liam had managed to get ahead of the confusion. Liam, however, rolled down his window and slowed next to it.

He recognized the older woman behind the wheel and motioned for her to roll her window down too.

She did so, eyes wide.

Liam cut off any lengthy explanation or apology.

"It's okay, Mrs. Connie," he called out. "The light changes here don't make much sense. Just try to be more careful. You can go on now."

She had been trying to turn into the same lane as he was in, so Liam waved her ahead, glad that they were the only cars around.

Mrs. Connie wasn't so sure, so he called out to her again and told her to go ahead with more assurances.

She did so after a few more moments that seemed to crawl by. Not everyone became nervous around Liam, but Mrs. Connie always acted as though she'd been on the fence about law enforcement. Her overcautiousness showed as Liam's speed was reduced by twenty following her down the two-lane road.

He sighed and accepted the delay. Blake's taillights were nowhere in sight. He idly wondered how people had treated her during her times as a sheriff. She had left a small town that hadn't known her originally and yet she'd managed to be elected during her time living there.

It was the same as his story, but Liam would bet money that Blake had blazed her way into her position. He, on the other hand, had been elected for McCoy County's sheriff in a calm, quiet event. There had been no pushback, no fuss that he wasn't a true local. There had simply been a need for the position to be filled after the former sheriff had retired. Liam just so happened to be there with the right résumé.

He had been suspicious though at first. Why hadn't someone else tried to run against him?

Price had been open about the answer.

"We're boring here in McCoy County," he'd said. "Not a bad thing, but there's not many people who want to be in charge of all of that boring."

Boring equated to still. Still meant quiet.

Liam started to knead his hip with his fist.

Quiet is what he'd been wanting.

The current silence in the cab of his truck didn't last long. It was only humorous timing that a few moments after recalling his memory with Price did his name pop up on the phone screen.

It was just past seven. Both men were off work.

Liam answered with an eyebrow raise that no one could see.

"Hello?"

Price's words came out through the truck's speakers strong but rushed.

"Where are you right now?"

Liam's back zipped straight to attention.

"Just left the cluster intersection. Running along the access road that goes to County 22. Why?"

Mrs. Connie was still going too slow. It now made Liam feel anxious.

What Price asked next didn't help matters.

"Can you see Blake?"

Both hands went to the steering wheel.

"No. Why?"

Price was moving. Rustling came through the line.

"She just called me saying someone is trying to drive her off the road," he hurried out. "She can't get your business card while she's defensive driving, so I'm sending her contact now. She said she needs your help."

Liam flipped on his hazards. His phone made an additional beep.

The text came in fast.

Liam was faster.

He was already passing Mrs. Connie when he clicked the number link.

"Hang up with me and get out here," Liam ordered.

Price didn't respond. The call ended.

Liam hit the call button on the new number.

It rang once before Blake answered.

The road noise coming through the call was startling loud.

"Liam?" she asked before he could say a word.

His name had never made him sit at such attention before. "I'm here."

That's all Blake seemed to need. She launched into the situation with notable calm.

"Some four-door car—I can't tell the make—has been trying to run us off the road. They already managed to bump me at the turn. I— Hold on, Clem." She cut herself off and filled in the space with some cussing.

Liam's grip tightened on the wheel and his foot pushed the gas pedal down hard.

The access road's end was in the distance. She would have had to turn left toward town or right, taking her along County

22. He needed to know where she went but only managed a quick question.

"Which way?"

Thankfully, she understood.

"County 22."

Clem was making noise, but he couldn't tell if she was just talking or crying. Blake's voice was strained as she continued.

Liam readied to make the right turn.

"I'm not going to go on the offense because Clem's in the car. I can't chance us wrecking. I'm guessing you're not too far behind me. Can you—"

"I'll end this," he promised. "Getting on County 22 now."

His tires squealed a little, his heart was pounding a lot.

Blake cussed again. Clem started clearly crying.

"We're going too fast." Blake was talking fast too. "If I go any faster and they hit us again, we'll crash. I—I don't think you're going to get to us in time. We've been flying since I got on here."

Liam was filling with anger.

He should have never let any car get between them.

"How much of the road do you have left?" he asked. His speedometer was topping out. If County 22 hadn't been a straight shot, he wouldn't have been able to do it as quickly. That was probably why Blake was confident that her and her tail were already so far ahead of him.

"The curve near Becker Farm's back end is coming up. If he hits us, we'll flip." Blake's voice drastically changed. "We can't do that, Liam."

He'd only known her for two days, and yet Liam understood that the panic he heard was rare for the woman.

It pulled at every part of him.

Especially since he couldn't help her yet.

And even more so since the advice he was about to give her was less than ideal.

"Don't take the curve then," he said. "Hit the field to the left of it. It's flat, just mowed last week. Reduce speed enough that the entry won't rock you too hard. It'll force him to slow down too. If they even decide to follow."

If she didn't agree with the plan, there wasn't time to come up with another.

She agreed.

"Okay. Clem? Clem. I need you to hold on to your seat. Okay?"

Liam was running the math. He was a minute behind them, give or take. He could get there in thirty seconds if he didn't reduce his own speed. Clem's crying quieted.

"I don't have a weapon with me, Liam." Blake's voice had changed again. It was back to being hard. "You have until the field runs out to save us."

Liam felt straight fire in his veins.

"Yes, ma'am."

Chapter Eight

Blake pressed the brakes enough to drop their speed to keep them from wrecking as soon as the tires hit the grass shoulder. Every part of her was clenched, her knuckles white on the steering wheel. Her back so straight it wasn't even touching the seat.

She didn't have time to look back at Clem, but the silence in the car was astonishing. She had listened to Blake.

Blake hoped her promise to the girl that they would be okay would hold true.

The only break in focus from the field lasted long enough to see if the car followed them off the road.

Once she confirmed it did, Blake became single-minded.

They weren't going to crash.

That meant handling the field first.

The old Becker Farm had the most acreage in Seven Roads. The back end was part of that land but was notorious for never being used for anything practical. Mostly because Abe Becker didn't like being so close to a well-traveled road. Still, Abe was a proud man and kept every bit of his land maintained, especially the parts that were visible to the public.

Blake could have kissed the man for his decision.

The field was flat enough and freshly mowed, as Liam had

said. Blake's car hit the grass without any dips or rises taking out her tires or crunching her bumper. That didn't mean the car was handling the change in terrain all that well.

The speedometer was at forty miles per hour when they went in, and she had to drop even farther the deeper they went.

Everything rattled.

Clem's quiet lasted a few yards in and then she was crying again.

The car chasing them followed but had to drop their speed just as fast. It made Blake's stomach drop. She'd been hoping that whatever the driver had wanted from them wouldn't continue with the added trouble.

She was wrong.

"Did you make it?" Liam's voice could barely be heard over the sound of the field beating against the car that dared run through it.

"Yeah," Blake yelled out. "They did too." She looked down at the speedometer again. "I'm slowing but we're going to hit the tree line sooner rather than later. Where are—"

The call dropped. Blake heard the familiar beep sound play through the car's speaker. The spotty service that Seven Roads's more rural areas usually sported had finally claimed their call.

It couldn't have happened at a worse time.

"We're—we're okay," Blake yelled back to Clem, trying to be as soothing as possible. The truth was they sounded like they were in a tin can during a tornado. The darkness around them made it even more terrifying. As an adult it wound Blake's nerves tight.

But now wasn't the time to worry about their feelings.

The tree line that ended the field was near the edge of the bouncing headlight beams.

There was no way she could keep driving once she got there.

She was going to have to turn and hope the car didn't—

The headlights behind them shifted. Blake watched in the rearview as the car behind them seemingly lost control. It took a hard right.

She didn't waste the breakaway.

Blake turned left with every intention of driving along the tree line before going back to the main road. But a horrifying sound followed by an awful shuddering changed that plan quick.

"Hold on, Clem!"

The front right tire didn't just blow. It exploded.

Blake felt it through the floorboard.

It was the nail in the coffin of her plan to flee.

She let off the gas pedal and held on to the steering wheel for dear life.

The next moment felt like it stretched hours when really it must have been only a few seconds. The car wobbled violently until coming to a stop a few feet from massive oak trees.

Blake whipped her head around to look out of the back windshield.

The pursuing car must have also been disabled. It was stopped a few yards diagonal to them. Without waiting to see what the driver did next, Blake made a split-second decision.

She tore her seat belt off and threw open her door. She repeated the sequence in reverse as she hurried to get Clem out of her car seat. The girl didn't fight her, but her sobbing pushed against Blake's chest when she had her out and against her.

"Wrap your legs around me," she told the girl firmly. "We're going to run now."

No sooner than she said it did Clem follow the directive. Her little arms wound around Blake's neck just as her legs fastened around Blake's waist. The added weight would make her slow, but Blake could at least gain enough distance to maybe turn the tables and ambush whoever followed.

If they followed. Maybe wrecking was enough to deter the driver?

A new terrifying sound broke through the night.

A car door opened.

Then another.

Blake didn't mean to—she couldn't afford the time—but she turned around.

Sure enough, two people had exited the car that had been chasing them.

Two men.

And one was holding something in his hand.

Clem's sobs racked Blake's body.

There was nothing between them and the men if they decided to run and attack them—if they decided to shoot.

Blake's mind tried to come up with solutions. What-ifs in which she kept Clem out of harm's way, but everything seemed to stall.

For the first time in her life, Blake felt immeasurable fear.

Her grip on Clem tightened.

It was why she didn't register the new set of headlights right away.

By the time she understood what she was seeing, the truck shuttered to a violent stop right between the cars. It effectively cut off Blake's view from the men.

It didn't keep her from seeing the new driver.

Or hearing him.

"Hands up or I'm shooting!"

Liam's voice was the loudest thing she had ever heard. It echoed through the field and bounced back from the trees behind her.

His passenger-side window must have been open. His arm was raised and, she assumed, a gun in his hand aimed at the men. He didn't break his focus even as he got out. Instead, he kept his arm straight and trained on the men over the hood of the truck, adjusting as he went around it.

"Do it now!" he roared.

It was enough to get Blake moving again. She ran around her car to put another barricade between Clem and the men just in case they decided to resist.

A siren started blaring in the distance.

Another long second stretched by.

Whether it was because of backup coming or Liam's command, the men must have decided that resisting wasn't a good idea.

Blake could hear Liam going through the normal directions for apprehending suspects. His tone notably less aggressive as he did so.

Relief poured through Blake at the change.

She rubbed at Clem's back and spoke softly into the girl's hair as she hugged her tight.

"We're okay now," she said. "The sheriff is here."

THE MCCOY COUNTY SHERIFF'S DEPARTMENT showed up in fine force. Price came in first, followed by Deputy Mel Gavin, who had been nearby with his cruiser when Price had rallied the troops, and then in third had been Darius Williams, the ace—and only—detective in Seven Roads. However, he was the first person to identify the two men Liam had on the ground after their arrival.

Now, nearly two hours later and currently standing opposite Liam in a hallway at the sheriff's department, Detective Williams went into more depth about who they were.

"Chase and Ray McClennan are the youngest two of the McClennan families still living in town. They're cousins. Cousins who, up until now, haven't taken a step out of line in regards to the law. No criminal history. No nasty rumors.

Just two good, average young twentysomethings who've been
around town since they were born."

Liam cussed as big as an elephant. He would have curbed
the urge if Blake and Clem were in the room with him, but
both were sitting in his office a few doors down, Price with
them, until Liam finished up. Until he was in the same space
again, he let his anger flare.

"They chased down a woman and her child at night in the
middle of nowhere. While one of them was holding." Liam
shook his head. "They could be heaven-picked saints before
this, and it wouldn't change how much I want to wring their
necks. They didn't give you any idea why they went after
Blake?"

Darius shook his head now.

"Ray just repeated what he'd already told you when you
were handcuffing him in the field," he said. "'We got the
wrong car. We thought it was our friend's and wanted to
mess around.'"

Liam snorted at the direct quote. The older one, who he'd
find out later was Ray, had been the one to spout that nonsense.

"Do you believe that?" he asked Darius.

The detective didn't nod but also didn't shake his head.

"Considering I couldn't get them to tell me what friend
they thought it was, I'm thinking they aren't being truth-
ful about it. I can't say for sure yet since I didn't get much
else from them before they were hollering for a lawyer." He
flipped his wrist over to see the face of his watch. "It's too
late to talk to them tonight. I'll have to wait until the morning. You want to be in there with me?"

Liam wanted nothing more than to get the truth from the
cousins. He gave the detective a reserved "Yes" but could
still feel himself boiling.

From the time their phone call had cut out to seeing both

cars stopped in the field, Liam had felt utterly helpless. When he'd gotten close enough to see that the men were outside of the car staring at Blake? He'd felt worry replace it.

When he'd seen the gun that Ray had been holding? Anger had come into play.

When he'd heard that baby girl crying for all she was worth after they had secured Ray and Chase in handcuffs? Liam had seen absolute red.

He wanted the cousins to explain themselves.

If they were lying, he wanted to know why.

And he wanted to know the absolute truth so he could make sure it would never happen again.

"I'll be back first thing in the morning," Liam added before they parted ways. "Don't start without me."

Darius said he wouldn't and left.

Next was Liam's office. He took a beat before entering, checking his anger at the door. At least, any traces of it. He was glad for the chance. As soon as he walked through the door, all eyes were on him.

All eyes that were awake.

Clem was fast asleep against Blake, both sitting on the love seat against the far wall. Price was cleaning up food wrappers from their fast-food supper. Not that the adults had eaten all that much. Clem, however, had stopped crying at the sight of chicken nuggets. Liam wasn't experienced with little kids, but he thought that was less of an age thing and more of a comfort thing.

She'd just been through a lot and had been scared and confused.

Just like the woman currently giving him a wide-eyed stare.

Liam lowered his voice and motioned to the door.

"If you're ready, I'll take you two home now."

Blake looked like she wanted to ask every question she

had right then and there, but Clem shifted against her. That look turned to acceptance.

"I just finished my statement, so we're good to go."

She started to stand. It was an effort with the sleeping girl in her arms. The same sight had met him when he had finally been able to check on them after Ray and Chase were dealt with. Clem was glued to her aunt and her aunt wasn't complaining.

That didn't mean she didn't need help.

Liam stood in front of them and leaned over, arms outstretched.

"Let me carry her to the truck," he said.

Blake was quick to decline.

"It's okay. I can—"

Liam fixed her with a level stare and interrupted with an excuse.

"I need your hands free so you can set up the car seat," he said. "So help me out and let me carry her."

Blake was exhausted. He could see it in every part of her face. He could also hear it in her relenting.

"Okay. If you don't mind."

He didn't, and soon the three of them were walking slowly out to the parking lot. Lightning forked in the distance and the breeze had taken on some moisture. Still, the world was quiet around them.

They didn't disturb that silence.

Blake set up the baby seat in the back seat of his truck while Liam moved slightly side to side. Clem kept sleeping, warm against his chest. She didn't wake when he transferred her into the seat and stayed just as asleep as he started driving.

It was only after Blake had finished giving directions to her home that Liam repeated what Darius had told him about the McClennan cousins. Blake was as unimpressed with their answer as he was.

"We could have been seriously hurt, or worse, and that's all they're saying?" She actually snarled. "Do they not realize how serious this is? My sister died the same way, for goodness sake. And this time her child was in the car."

The parallel wasn't lost on him.

"We're talking to them again tomorrow, first thing," he said. "Don't worry. Whether they thought you were someone else or not, they're definitely about to learn a hard lesson."

Blake nodded. A few moments later she sighed.

"I should have just told you about my conversation with Cassandra at the café this morning instead of dragging it out," she said. "But I guess I got that feeling again and wanted to make it last as long as I could."

Liam didn't take his eyes off the road but inclined his head a little at that.

"That feeling?"

Out of his periphery, he could see her tap the upper part of her chest.

"Working a case, chasing justice, that kind of feeling," she answered. "I've been out of the game for half a year, and sometimes it feels like a whole life slipped away in between. Still, dragging out your investigation into a girl who died just to play pseudo sheriff again was cruel of me. I'm sorry."

Liam hadn't expected that. Much like the panic in her voice earlier, the sheer defeat that he heard in her words caught him off guard. The walls that Blake Bennet must have had around her dropped away for the second time that night.

He didn't like that she had to do it alone.

"I'm the one who should be apologizing," he said. "I'm sure Cassandra told you about what happened with Missy and how the case is closed—and that I closed it—but now can't let it go. The truth is, I've been going off only one thing that doesn't add up and a gut feeling. I shouldn't have pulled you into that. We both know how dangerous it can be to become obsessed over a case."

But that didn't mean he was going to let Missy's death go. Not until he was sure no one else had been involved. He wasn't going to admit that to the woman sitting next to him though. Blake had been through enough.

Her hair shifted in his periphery as she nodded.

Once again, he could see how tired she was. Her next words even came out in an air of quiet.

"They talked about whipped cream, laptop brands, and the weather. That was the long and short of it. Cassandra said Missy left after that." Blake laughed quietly. It had no humor in it. "This whole night could have been avoided if I'd said that earlier. No muss, no 'plowing through a field and terrifying my poor niece' fuss."

Liam should have consoled her once again. Reassured her that none of what had happened was her fault.

Yet he had gotten hung up on something.

"They talked about laptop brands?" he asked.

"Mm-hmm. Missy had hers at the counter and Cassandra was asking how she liked it since she needed to buy a new one and is notoriously bad at all technology. Missy was nice enough to answer."

Liam didn't respond.

The sound of Blake shifting in her seat had him guess that she had turned toward him.

"Why? Is there something there?"

Liam shook his head.

"There was nothing there."

Blake sighed out long.

"There was nothing there," she repeated, like the topic was done.

But for Liam it had just started.

"No," he said. "I mean we never found a laptop with Missy or with her belongings. There was nothing there."

This time he did glance at his passenger. Light from the approaching intersection showed him an expression that was all thoughtful.

"Then what happened to it between the café and the bridge?"

Liam didn't know, but he sure was going to try to find out.

Chapter Nine

Rain started to fall two steps after they were inside of the house. Once again Liam took charge of carrying Clem. If Blake hadn't called ahead to let Lola know they were coming, she was sure the older woman would have been shocked quiet at the sudden appearance of the big man holding their small kiddo.

Instead, she greeted them all at the door with a tight hug for Blake, a soft back rub for the sleeping Clem, and a little pat on Liam's arm. It wasn't until Clem had been settled in her room and all three adults were standing around the living room that Lola and Liam were officially introduced.

"I would have liked meeting you under better circumstances, but I have to say, Sheriff, I'm sure glad you were around." Lola reached out for Blake's hand. "When Blake called me earlier to tell me about what happened... I, well, I'm just really glad everything worked out the way it did."

Liam gave her a small smile. He waved his hand a little as if swatting away the nice.

"I didn't do much," he said. "Blake here is the one that did all the work. I just showed up at the end."

They all knew that wasn't true—Liam had put a stop to the madness—but it was late, and they weren't there to rehash what had happened. Lola wasn't letting him go that fast though. While Blake and Clem had eaten takeout at the sheriff's department, Liam hadn't had one bite. Once Lola realized he had an empty stomach, her Southern manners refused to let him leave.

"I'm making you an egg-and-bacon scramble," she announced. "Unless you really want to fight me on it, why don't the two of you go take the weight off your poor feet?" Lola caught Blake's eye. "The chairs are ready."

The sheriff raised his eyebrow at that.

"The chairs?"

Blake led the way back outside to the front porch. She motioned to the random assortment of outdoor chairs lined up next to the railing. There were two adult-sized and one miniature chair, covered in rainbows. Around those were a few wayward dinosaur figurines, an empty can of Play-Doh, two bottles of bubbles, and a smattering of shoes lined haphazardly along the wall.

"We're a family who really likes to watch the rain," Blake explained. She eyed the slight chaos that was around the chairs. "And apparently a family who forgets to clean the front porch. Sorry for the mess."

Liam settled into one of the chairs. He laughed.

Blake followed suit and settled in the chair next to him. The rain was still falling outside, but it was a soft shower. Soothing. Cool. Relaxing. At least as much as it could be considering the last few hours.

"It's not mess," he said. "It's breadcrumbs."

"Breadcrumbs?" Blake parroted.

She watched as the corner of Liam's lip turned up ever so slightly.

"A buddy of mine used to say the thing he missed the most about home while we were deployed were the breadcrumbs. You know, the little things people leave around their homes that prove a family lives there." He laughed. "He used to talk about the hair ties his daughter and wife would leave lying around everywhere. The cats would find them, eat them, and then cough them up, making a mess. He'd say he'd get up in the middle of the night for some water, and if he could make it to the fridge without stepping on one or the other, it was a win. Things like that. A chipped bowl no one ever throws away, discarded socks in random places, toys and books and the pen you can never find when you need it, but it's always in the way when you don't. His family called that breadcrumbs. You follow them, you'll find a family."

It was the most Liam had ever said to her in one go.

Which made the idea of breadcrumbs even more endearing to her.

"Breadcrumbs," she repeated. "I like that. It's a more charming way to call something messy, that's for sure. Though I'm not sure Lola would take breadcrumbs as a good excuse to skip cleaning day. That might be pushing my luck." Blake smiled at the thought. Liam caught it.

"You two seem really close. Lola, I mean. She lives here with you full time?"

Blake nodded.

"That's how we got close, to be honest," she admitted. "She's technically my stepmom. My dad married her after I'd already left town, so I'd only met her a few times before coming back to Seven Roads." Blake hesitated. She didn't want to unload any more sad family stories, so instead of detailing what had led Lola to move in with her, she decided to be brief. "She already had a good relationship with the kids and came to live with us to help out."

"Did your dad come too?"

It was a reasonable question. He didn't know that there had been a falling-out between her father and Blake when she was younger. He didn't know about the falling-out that had happened again after Beth's death.

So Blake didn't answer that in detail either.

"No. He lives in Alabama."

Whether he wanted to know more or simply took the hint, Liam accepted her answer as enough. Blake capitalized on that and switched back to an earlier subject.

"You texted Darius asking about Missy's laptop right after we got here, right? Did he respond yet?"

Missy having a laptop the day she died had indeed been news to Liam. After admitting he had never seen it, he'd sent a few messages to Darius after parking in her driveway. He'd buttoned up about it right after, focusing on getting Clem in the house. Blake had momentarily forgotten about the news the moment she had seen Lola's worried gaze.

And when they were tucking Clem in?

All Blake had been thinking about was how hard the girl had cried against her.

Now she had the space to backtrack, though the excitement from the morning at working a case had dulled. Blake wouldn't admit it, but she was exhausted. Physically and emotionally. Once Liam was done eating, she was going to check on Bruce and then probably lie down next to Clem on her bed for comfort.

Hers more than Clem's, if she was being honest.

Liam pulled his cell phone out but didn't check it. He nodded.

"He just confirmed that none of us saw a laptop," he said. "I told him we'd talk about it after we talk to the McClennan cousins tomorrow. We'll see if it was an oversight on our part."

"What do you think the alternative could be?"

The question popped out before she could stop it. Liam's expression went impassive.

"Sorry," she said. "Old habit."

Blake returned her gaze to the rain past the railing.

She was surprised when Liam didn't skip a beat in answering her.

"I don't think Missy jumped off that bridge voluntarily. I think something might have happened to get her there. That laptop might be the missing thing that either proves my hunch or finally puts it to rest."

Resolution, calm and clear, came through every word.

It was still strong as he snorted.

"It's been like pulling teeth to try to piece together Missy's last day. I've never run into so much resistance from an entire town."

Blake knew that feeling.

"That's an old Seven Roads habit right there," she said. "If one person thinks you're in the wrong, it won't be long before the whole town thinks it too. Especially if that one happens to be someone like Mr. Clearwater."

Liam turned to her. She gave him an apologetic look.

"Cassandra said you had his fans all up in arms by asking questions after the case closed."

He grumbled.

"I'll never understand how a retired businessman has so many folks sticking up for him. You'd think he was a celebrity or something."

"He might as well be one," Blake said. "Jobs are a big deal here. Some of those guys had been working at the tractor supply straight from high school up until retirement." She became angry again. "You know, Ray and Chase McClennan's fathers were like that. They started working at the tractor supply alongside Mr. Clearwater when they were all in their twenties. They managed to retire before he shut down the business. He kept them and their families fed and clothed for their entire lives basically. That's where the loyalty comes from."

That was also why Missy had taken the general public's

criticism for her father's decision to sell the business. No one would go up against the elder Clearwater since they would potentially have to deal with those older folks who had been through thick and thin with her daddy.

It hadn't been fair to Missy.

"I wonder how they'll act when they find out what their kids did."

Blake shrugged.

"Not every parent will go to bat for their kids. They might come down harder on them than even you could. I don't know much about their dynamic, but I bet, regardless, they'll all be loud about it."

The door behind them opened right in time to stop their conversation. Lola presented Liam with her scramble bowl with a flourish. That flourish extended in part to Blake when she handed her a bag of little cookies.

"You earned it," she said, all smiles.

Blake let out a breath and returned the affection.

A year ago, she had barely known Lola. Now she couldn't imagine her not being around.

Blake's gaze fell onto the man next to her.

A week ago, he hadn't even been on her radar. Now? Would Blake be okay not seeing him again?

Blake decided not to think about any of that yet.

Instead, she listened to the rain with the sheriff at her side.

Chapter Ten

A week passed and nothing about it was satisfying.

Ray and Chase McClennan remained committed to their story. They had believed Blake was their friend Henry, driving a new car and messing with them. They had followed her into the field because they thought it was funny. Chase hadn't known about the gun Ray had in his hand, and Ray had been insistent that he had simply had it to give Henry a funny scare. If Ray hadn't had a permit for the gun, he would still be in jail. But both of them were now out and about.

It had absolutely riled Liam up.

That wasn't even figuring in the lack of laptop either. Liam had gone through every part of the original investigation again to try to find the computer that Missy had had at the coffee shop, but he had come up short. He was on the fence about reaching out to her father again to see if maybe he had any idea where it might have gone and was still thinking about it when Price knocked on his office door and let himself in.

"Winnie heard some talk at school about the McClennan boys," Price said, bypassing a traditional start to a new conversation. He sat down opposite him in a chair that squeaked at the weight.

"We're still talking about those two?" Liam asked, instantly grumpy. "Also, isn't your daughter in high school? What talk about the McClennan cousins are going around there?"

Price adopted a high-pitched, flitty voice.

"'Oh, Sheriff, haven't you *seen* Chase McClennan?'" He dropped into a more dramatic voice. "He's young enough that the high school girls think they might have a chance with him if they say just the right thing. He's also just old enough that flirting with him at the restaurant he works at has become the 'it' dare in the past few months. According to Winnie, Amber Bell even live-streamed her asking for his number. He declined. She was mortified."

Price said everything with a straight face. And with an absolute sincerity. Liam could always tell the difference when Price was talking about anything that had to do with Winnie, including the talk that she was simply relaying to him.

Price Collins loved his daughter immensely.

Liam didn't have children, but he couldn't deny that his deputy's dedication to his daughter made him appreciate the man more.

"So even the high school has its own rumor mill about the rest of us," Liam mused.

Price nodded to that.

"Based on what I've heard since Winnie started, it's way more vicious than this fluff we have out here." He sat straighter and leaned forward a little. "And they get some of theirs from eavesdropping on their parents, which makes the new theory floating around the school more interesting than it already is."

Liam couldn't help it. He leaned in a little too. "Theory?"

Price's retelling of the news he had heard from his daughter was delivered in his own voice this time.

"No one at that school thinks that the guys were going

after a friend but instead trying to mess with—drumroll please—you."

"Me?"

Price nodded.

"Apparently a lot of the parents have been talking and, when they found out Blake was helping you with looking into Missy's death, they all decided that Ray and Chase went after her to scare her off or maybe send you a message." Price held up his hands in defense before Liam could start in. "This is just what Winnie said she heard from a group of seniors. The word is that Blake went back to her old ways of being an outcast sheriff and teamed up with you, *another* outcast sheriff, to dig into the Missy thing."

Liam balled his fist.

"Why would they even care? Ray and Chase, I mean." He was trying very hard not to go on a tangent. "Were they friends with Missy?"

Price's expression tightened a bit. He was annoyed at his own words.

"I asked Winnie, and she said the only friend Chase ever really hangs around is Cooper Han. He's a senior, I've met him once or twice. Good kid, as far as I can tell, a whiz with computers too. Not exactly on brand for someone who might want to send the sheriff a threatening message. Ray was acquainted with Missy, but they never ran in the same social circles. But their fathers…"

Liam nearly growled. He remembered Blake's words from the week before when they were sitting out on the porch.

"They're fans of Jonathan Clearwater, Missy's dad," he finished.

Price nodded.

"Bingo," he said. "Winnie said she's heard the theory that Ray and Chase were following their dads' orders, or they were trying to win some points with them. Both men have been pretty vocal about you being a problem since word got around that you were still investigating on the sly."

Liam took the pen he had in his hand and slammed it down on the desktop.

"This is absolutely ridiculous," he said.

"It's also just a bundle of rumors from teenagers who were eavesdropping on adults, probably just shooting the breeze to pass the time. Either way, it doesn't look good on the boys' intelligence." He held up two fingers. "If their story about thinking they were messing with a friend is true, that was an absolutely ridiculous plan. If the story about them trying to mess with you and Blake because of the Missy investigation? Well, that's a special kind of stupid if you ask me."

Liam had to agree with that.

"I think Blake is the kind of woman who digs her heels in when someone tries to make her stop doing something she wants to do," Liam added after a moment. He shook his head. "That would have been a really bad plan on their part for sure."

Price nodded his agreement. Then he was all sighs.

"I know Seven Roads is a small town, but when you start seeing how everyone is connected, it sure feels smaller." He stood and stretched. "Either way, I thought you should hear what's going around. I'm not sure it holds any water, but I wanted you to know just in case. I'm heading out for now, though, unless you need me for something else."

"I appreciate it, but, no, I'm good here."

A smile stretched wide across Price's face.

"Good. I'm doing a movie night with Winnie, and those have become rare since she hit teenagehood. You have any plans on this fine Friday, Sheriff?"

Liam motioned to the paperwork piled in his inbox tray.

"You're looking at it."

Price whistled, already moving to the door.

"Give me a deputy's badge over a sheriff's any day."

He left with a laugh. Liam went back to his paperwork. However, his attention strayed once again.

Had the McClennan cousins really tried to use Blake to shake them away from looking into Missy? Did their fathers' loyalty to Missy's father really run so deep that the children would risk such harsh consequences?

And why go after Blake and not him directly?

Unless Ray had simply pulled up behind the wrong car and had meant to target him instead.

This wasn't helping his hunch that something had happened to Missy that led to her death. If she really had taken her own life, then why was there this much resistance to his investigation?

And what about the flash drive?

Liam looked down at the locked drawer of his desk.

As far as he knew, only two people knew about the flash drive he had found under the bridge. Price and his friend who had analyzed the information he had found on the drive.

It was the main reason his gut wouldn't let her death go.

Liam had almost told Blake about the flash drive that night out on the porch. Instead, he'd stopped himself. Then he'd told her he could handle it alone.

And a week had gone by with no word from her.

Not that he could say a thing about that. He hadn't reached out either.

Liam glanced at his cell phone on the desk. He could send her a text to see how she was? To see how Clem was doing? How Bruce and Lola were too?

As if he willed it, his cell phone lit up right before it started to vibrate.

It wasn't Blake's number. It was Theo's, and he said just about the only thing that would make Liam leave his work behind without hesitation.

"Hey there, boss." Theo was whispering. "I just thought you should know there's a woman and a baby in your apartment right now. The lady's looking for you, and if I'm being honest, I don't think she's doing too hot."

BLAKE'S HEAD FELT like a vise was squeezing it. She blamed sinus pressure. She squinted through the pain at a picture frame on the TV stand. She was standing in Liam's apartment and staring at a photo in a nice wooden frame.

It was easy to find Liam at first glance. Among the group of men in the picture, he was the tallest. A tree among weeds. If Blake had felt better, she would have laughed at her own analogy at that. Instead, she traced the weeds with her eyes. Six men in total, all in varying stages of laughter. They were in military uniforms, but it looked to her like basic training rather than active deployment. Each man, Liam included, was covered in mud. Liam had some on his cheek. It made the gigantic smile on his face all the more charming.

Blake couldn't help but wonder when the last time he smiled like that was.

Maybe he was always that happy-go-lucky, but it was just reserved for certain people.

Maybe there was a special woman who did it for him too.

A thought that only popped into Blake's head after she had knocked on the sheriff's apartment door. It wasn't like they had talked about their personal lives that much. Apart from scanning his ring finger, she hadn't inquired about a wife, girlfriend or anyone else in that relationship realm.

You're only here to tell him something, not interrogate him, she had reminded herself while waiting for the door to unlock. Though bringing a baby probably wasn't a move she should have taken. Clem was at home doing crafts with Lola and Blake had to admit the situation last week had given her all kinds of feelings about the kids. She'd been sleeping with

Clem, and anytime Bruce was near, she felt the urge to pull him up into her arms.

When she realized she wanted to loop Liam into her new little plan, she scooped Bruce up without a second thought. He'd even giggled when a teenager had opened the door with wide eyes.

After Theo had introduced himself, he'd been quick to cut off the questions popping up one after the other from her.

"I'm not his kid, by the way," he had exclaimed. "I live in the apartment complex. Liam lets me hang out here when my mom's working."

Bruce had trilled in delight at a new face, while Blake had spied a full meal on a plate at the table behind the teen. She also noted his shoes by the door and what appeared to be another set of the same size shoes next to them. There was a book bag too, slung on the couch arm. A cell phone was on top of it. He excused himself to make a call to Liam.

Theo had seemingly marked Liam's apartment as a safe space. It had warmed Blake's heart.

Now her heart did a little flutter as the dead bolt on the front door slid open. Bruce swiveled hard enough that Blake's balance tipped. Her head swam as she took a step to keep herself right. The ache around her head pulsed.

Sinuses.

That's all it was.

The door was open, and Liam was frowning. Blake pulled on a smile she hoped would defuse it. Theo spoke before either of them could.

"Wow, boss, you made some good time," he said. "You must have broken some of those speeding laws you were supposed to be keeping good."

Liam's gaze slid to the boy's.

"And you must be done with all of your schoolwork?"

Liam motioned to a door that must have been the second bedroom. "Why don't you go check?"

Theo raised his hands in defense but laughed. He gave a deep nod to Blake and scooped up his book bag.

"And on that note, I'll give y'all some space."

Blake felt bad for her intrusion and making the boy leave the living space, but at the same time, she didn't want him to listen to what she had to say.

"It was nice meeting you," she returned. Her smile was nothing compared to Bruce's. He did a little dance when Theo waved.

Then it was just the three of them in the living room.

Blake took a deep breath as dark eyes settled on hers.

There was no point in beating around the bush.

"I did something that you're not going to like."

Chapter Eleven

Blake was holding Bruce so that the boy was facing Liam. He started to babble, waving a toy in his hand, but neither adult was in a playful mood.

Liam didn't understand why Blake had shown up to his house with Bruce at night after a week of silence. There was also no diaper bag with her. Like she'd had to come there in a hurry.

Her statement definitely wasn't making him feel at ease.

What had gone wrong?

"What am I not going to like?" Liam asked.

Green eyes were locked on him and him only, but the sigh that escaped Blake's lips seemed to be for the entire world. She held up her free hand in a *Stop* gesture.

"Before you go scolding me, let me get everything out first, and then you have carte blanche on telling me I'm wrong. Okay?"

Liam felt his eyes narrow. He nodded still.

"Okay."

There was no more sighing after that. Blake dove in and didn't stop once.

"I know you said you'd handle it by yourself, but I've spent the last week looking for Missy's laptop, and I think I have a bead on it. After I started thinking about it and how this town really doesn't seem to be on your side about looking into Missy's death, I decided that I could at least just poke around a little to see if I could get something you couldn't. Specifically about the laptop. Since I don't know what all you've done in the primary investigation, I went to the coffee shop and heard that your talk with Missy's ex was less than helpful."

Kyle Langdon, Missy Clearwater's ex-boyfriend.

"Less than helpful" was an understatement. Liam had interviewed Missy's ex and had been thoroughly ticked at his behavior. Kyle had shown signs of being truly upset at her death but seemed to have no remorse for the possibility that his cheating scandal with Missy's best friend had contributed to her supposed leap off the haunted bridge. The man had instead acted as if he had done nothing wrong at all.

"We broke up for the greater good," was what he had said when Liam asked about the breakup. "Some things you just can't see eye to eye on, and there's nothing you can do about it."

It had been an off-putting response.

If Kyle hadn't had an airtight alibi of working at the steel mill during the window of time surrounding Missy's death, with security footage to confirm it, Liam would have bet money that he had been out on the bridge with Missy. The same went for Missy's former best friend, Miranda. She had said only a few words to Liam, and of those words, none of them had been regret or guilt.

They were sorry Missy had died, but they didn't believe their actions had had anything to do with it.

"Kyle doesn't know me," Blake continued. "So when I *casually* bumped into him and mentioned I had just moved to town, he got really chatty and weirdly accepting. That led to him inviting me out tomorrow. He was shooting for dinner, I switched it to afternoon coffee."

Liam broke his deal and broke his silence.

"You're not going."

Liam heard the hammer drop in his own words.

Blake paused at it. Green eyes searched his expression. It gave him enough time to edit himself.

"I don't like that man," he said, trying not to physically bristle at the idea. "There's something about him that rubs me the wrong way. Also inviting someone he just met out to dinner? That's another mark against him in my opinion."

Blake's eyebrow rose up.

"Didn't I ask you out and you agreed to dinner right after we met?"

Liam didn't have to think even once on that one.

"We're different," he defended. "This Kyle guy isn't me or you. I don't want you to go out with him."

He meant every word of what he said, Liam realized. He didn't like the idea of Blake sitting across from the man, dressed nice and smiling. It grated on him.

Blake blew out a huff. Bruce caught her finger as she tried to motion to him.

"That's why I'm here," she said. "I want to be bait. I figure we can do the same thing we did with Cassandra at the coffee shop. I'll sit down with him, ask a few questions, and then you can swoop in."

"Swoop in," he repeated. "I doubt he'll tell me anything else, even if you're there."

She shook her head.

"No, I mean swoop in to take *me* away. Not try to talk to him again."

It was such a simple request and she said it with such ease.

"I'll take you away," he repeated again.

Blake was unfazed.

"Yeah, but do it in a way that doesn't make him think we trapped him," she added. "Maybe don't wear the badge. Just, you know, come over and say we have plans later, and I'll just go with you. Like we have a date or something."

Liam's eyebrow went high of its own volition.

For the first time since they had met, Liam thought he saw the woman's cheeks start to tint red.

She cleared her throat.

"Or, you know, I can come up with something on my own. It's no biggie, I can—"

Liam cut her off.

"I'll be there. Don't worry."

She cut eye contact with him and cleared her throat again. If he hadn't been looking at her so intently, he wouldn't have noticed her flinch. For a second, he thought it was because of their conversation. Then he really took a good look at her.

She was tired. More pale than usual. Even standing still there was an uncomfortable slant to her.

"Something's wrong with you. What is it?" Liam nodded toward her. "You're hurting somewhere. Where? Don't lie. I can tell."

Blake motioned to her head. Bruce's finger, still wrapped around hers, went with it.

"My head," she said. "We were actually at the store for some sinus meds and ran into Price on his way home. Then I became impulsive and decided to show up here. Price, quite easily I might add, gave up your address with no questions asked. You might want to have a chat with him about that."

Liam had no doubt that the man had a soft spot for Blake, and if it had been just anybody, the information wouldn't have come out.

"Which, by the way, I'm going to go ahead and grab and take home now," Blake added. "Since I have officially intruded and we've officially come up with a plan, it's time to go home and see if I can't attempt some kind of supper."

The smile looked as tired as she sounded. It was almost

the same expression she'd been wearing while sitting in the sheriff's office after Ray and Chase had gone after her.

The McClennan cousins and the same questions came to mind again.

Had they been going after him and gotten her instead? Or had they gone after her trying to shake him?

Coincidence?

Accident?

A poorly laid out plan?

A feeling of protectiveness pushed through him so fast that he didn't have time to think about his words until they were already out there between them.

"I can cook."

HOURS LATER AND all Blake could think was that life sure was a blur.

Next to her in bed was none other than the sheriff of Seven Roads. If she had been a shier woman, she wouldn't have pointed out the oddness. Instead, she snorted and said exactly what was on her mind.

"Had you asked me who would be the first man to share my bed since coming back to Seven Roads, I don't think its sheriff would even be in the top ten of my guesses."

Blake was wearing an oversized baseball T-shirt that read Kelby Creek Fighters and a pair of extremely unattractive flannel sleep shorts. Her wet hair was sloppy in its short braid, and she knew from a hesitant glance in the mirror before getting into bed that her face was pale and flushed all at once.

Her sinus issue had revealed itself to be more of a cold. Before that realization, though, Liam had insisted on following them home to cook. She had started running a fever before Liam had even started making dinner. It had given her enough time to switch to the right medicine and to also let Lola know how *normal* this was. Liam was there as an investigative partner. An acquaintance that had been in the trenches with her during their field escapade.

A friend?

Blake wasn't sure why she couldn't bring herself to label the man as that.

After all, would she let someone less than that into her home? Into her bed?

She glanced over at the man in question. He was sitting next to her with a children's pink plastic desk between them. On its top was an empty bowl of chicken noodle soup.

If he was offended by her joke, he didn't show it. Instead, he actually lobbed one back.

"Funny, I thought this was exactly how I was going to spend my first bedroom experience with the opposite sex after my divorce."

Blake let her mouth hang open for a second. He laughed after seeing her expression.

"What? You didn't expect the quiet guy to make a divorce joke?"

Blake couldn't help herself.

"No," she admitted. "I'm still getting used to hearing you say more than one or two words at a time, and now you're getting personal? Maybe the cold meds are making me hallucinate."

Liam rolled his eyes, but there was a good-naturedness to it. He pointed to the covers that had shifted off her when reaching for the TV remote. Wordlessly, Blake pulled it back up and over her lap. Surprisingly, or maybe not, Liam had been quick to take on a mothering roll once he realized she was sick. He'd been fussing after her worse than Lola.

"Stay warm and I'll talk your head off."

Blake wasn't a woman who liked taking any kind of orders but, as Lola had stated during their earlier, very quiet conversation. "If this good-looking man is here to worry about you and cook for you, don't spit in the face of *that* blessing."

So Blake listened to him. When he told her to shower, eat, stay warm, and now when he was on her again about the blanket she kept throwing off.

"Fine," she said. "But give me some backstory on you. And make it something good that would make the rumor mill go wild if they heard it instead of me. Tell me about your life before Seven Roads."

Liam settled back on the headboard, crossed his arms over his chest and stretched his long legs out. There was something slightly endearing about seeing that he wore socks with patterns on them. The pair he had on had little golf flags across them.

"You're not the first person to get a little grouchy with me when I'm telling you what to do when you're sick," he started, humor in his voice. "My unit used to call me the Mother Hen."

"Mother Hen?"

Blake felt the movement of his nod.

"I had a tendency to take care of everyone when they were sick. Even when they didn't want it. I 'made a fuss,' but instead of being a pretty woman, I was treating grown men like little kids." He chuckled. "They were equally grateful and annoyed. Hence the Mother Hen nickname."

Blake heard the pretty comment but latched onto the overall point he'd made.

"Oh, so this little production isn't rare, huh?" She motioned to the empty bowl between them on the desk. "And here I thought the sheriff was giving me special treatment."

Liam played ball with the joke with startling speed.

"The food is the standard package, but the served-in-bed portion is definitely on the secret menu. Morning service has to be ordered separately."

The heat that ran up Blake's neck was fast. It pooled in her cheeks. She was glad, at least, that she could blame the flush on her fever.

"You might not talk a lot, but you sure know what to say when you do," she returned. "That sweet-talking must get all the ladies."

At this, Liam didn't laugh. Blake peeked over at him, worried she had offended him somehow. He was staring right at her. There was a tilt to his head. Almost like a curiosity.

"I don't think I've sweet-talked anyone since the beginning of my marriage. And even then, it wasn't like this."

Blake felt like a parrot the more she spoke with Liam.

"Like this?"

The world went slow for a bit. Liam kept her gaze, then it started searching. She knew he went from her eyes to her lips then to her brow. After that, she lost track. He was tracing her, maybe looking for something? But what?

He opened his mouth—to answer her, right?—but the next sound that came out was from the bedroom door.

"Excuse me."

Blake nearly jumped. Lola was standing in the doorway, all apologetic with her smile. The little girl behind her leg was peeking out, all shy.

"I hate to interrupt, but Clem wants you," the older woman said. She looked at Liam. "Our Blake here started a dangerous trend. When this one doesn't want to sleep, the two of them watch TV in bed for a bit. We call it wind-down time."

Blake was immediately defensive.

"Hey, not all of us can sleep like logs, like you and Bruce," she said. "I personally think it's smart of me and Clem to partner up on a different path sometimes. Isn't that right, Clem?"

She might be a quiet four, but Clem was always vocal about their occasional late-night TV time.

"Yeah!" she exclaimed. Her hair bounced along with her little hop of excitement. After that she was nothing but speed. Liam barely had enough time to move the desk from the middle of the bed as Clem rocketed herself up and into space in the middle of them.

Lola's smile fell. Concern, fast and deep, lined her frown. "I can come back and get her in a little bit," she offered.

Blake shook her head.

"You can head to bed. I've got her."

Lola was silent a moment. Clem didn't hesitate, becoming a drill and burrowing under the blanket.

"Are you sure?" Lola added.

"I'm sure. I already feel way better thanks to the meds and food." Blake thumbed over at the sheriff. "Worst case, Mother Hen here can give me a hand if I need it."

Liam was fast.

"Don't worry," he said. "I'll make sure they're good."

Lola didn't fight the offer. During the last week, she had continued to talk about his heroics in the field and, now that he had cooked for them and had clearly been accepted by Clem? Blake had a feeling she'd be singing Liam's praises for a good while. Lola told him thank you and wished them a good-night before leaving.

Blake waited a few seconds before whispering to the man at her side.

"You don't have to stick around," Blake tried. "We're just going to watch some TV."

"I don't mind sticking around a little longer." He notably paused. "Unless you want some space."

Blake didn't.

Not from him.

An acquaintance my tushy, she couldn't help but think.

But instead she said, "You can stay."

Liam took the remote off the nightstand next to him. He

said only one word next, but it was enough to make the heat in her cheeks grow warmer again.

"Good."

Chapter Twelve

His hip was hurting, but it wasn't because of his old injury.

Liam opened his eyes.

The bed was different. Too big, too soft. He smelled lavender. He felt warm. Light moved across the room.

It was the TV, still on but muted. A cartoon dancing across the screen.

Liam hadn't been sleeping all that much during the last week. He'd be the first to admit that. However, he hadn't realized how tired he'd actually been. He couldn't deny it now though. One second he'd been talking to Blake about their show, and the next?

Liam realized why his hip felt different.

Clem was pressed against his side, wrapped tightly in her blanket and fast asleep. Just as he had been moments before.

He had fallen asleep slightly sitting up.

At Blake's house.

In her bed.

And she wasn't there next to him anymore.

The spot on the other side of Clem was empty. Adrenaline surged as worry took over all his senses.

That surge turned into an all-out flood when he realized he'd not simply woken up on his own. Movement at the side of the bed came at him quick.

Liam reached one arm out above Clem and the other at the person in motion. His hand wrapped around the person's forearm.

It didn't stop that person from moving though. Instead, they brought their face merely inches from his.

"Keep quiet."

The only light in the room was coming from the TV, but it was more than enough to see the green eyes of Blake Bennet. It was easier to see the worry in them. In her. She was still in the shorts and T-shirt she'd worn to bed. Her hair was down and wild. Her skin was warm and slightly slick with sweat.

She lowered herself even closer to him. She angled her chin so her lips were almost against his ear.

"There're two men outside," she whispered. "One has a gun. I can't tell about the other."

That did it.

Liam let go of Blake and eased himself off the bed as she backed up.

"What are they doing?" He kept his voice low and palmed his cell phone off the nightstand. He internally cursed every decision he had made up until now that meant he didn't have his service weapon on him. It was shut away tight in his truck's lockbox. He hadn't intended to stay long at Blake's, certainly not fall asleep there.

Thankfully, Blake had an answer to that problem. She took that wrist and pulled him along to the closet. It was a small walk-in but big enough to hold a safe. She flipped on the light and went right to it.

"I got up for a glass of water and noticed them at the side yard. They were standing in the tree line," she hurried to say. "I can't tell who they are, but it feels like they're waiting. There's no car outside either, so I don't know where they came from. Take this and go look for yourself."

There was only one gun inside. It was a pistol. She handed

it to him. Liam grabbed the ammo that had been kept separately. He assembled the weapon.

"You can see them if you look outside the kitchen window."

Liam wasn't slow when speed was needed. He made it to the kitchen by the grace of memory and a few motion sensor nightlights plugged into outlets turning on along the way. The light over the stove was at his side. He could see the men clearly from the window.

Just as Blake described, there were two of them standing at the edge of the yard, the tree line just behind them. They were dressed casually, shirts and jeans, and tennis shoes. One had a dark hat on, the other a gun in the hand hanging at his side. They were too far away for Liam to make out their faces, but even if he had, there was no person in the world who had a reason to be at Blake's home in the late hours of the night, armed with a gun at that.

Liam did some quick mental math. Instead of calling the sheriff's department, he called someone closer.

It was just after two in the morning, but Price answered on the third ring.

Liam didn't waste a second. He forwent any kind of greeting and dove right in.

"I'm at Blake's house and there are two men standing outside. One is armed, I can't tell about the other. We put my truck in the garage earlier so the neighbors wouldn't see. Lola's car is in there too. Blake's is in the driveway. Me, Blake, Lola, and the kids are in here. We have only one gun between us."

After the first statement, the sound of movement had come through from the other side of the call.

"Did you call dispatch yet?" Price asked. Based on the noise Liam assumed he was dressing.

"No. You're closer and I'm thinking we might need help sooner rather than—"

The two men outside turned in tandem toward the trees. Liam watched as a third person stepped out into the open. There was a gun at his hip.

"A third guy just showed up. He has a gun." One of the original two men pointed toward the house. Liam's gut was all-out growling. "Can you call the department on another phone? I want to stay on the line with you."

Price wasn't playing around. His usual casual tone had been hardened into absolute focus.

"I'll use Winnie's. I'm putting you in my pocket on speaker."

The sound of movement let Liam know the man was doing just that. He too followed suit. Liam slid his cell phone into his breast pocket. He didn't want to break the line of sight he had on the three men, but their situation had just changed drastically.

Who were they?

Why were they here?

Their body language wasn't aggressive. It was like they were waiting for something. Or someone.

Blake was on the same wavelength.

"What are they waiting for?" she whispered.

No sooner had the question came out, than an answer followed.

It wasn't at all what they wanted.

A sound echoed from the back of the house. Metal clinking. Cracking? Had they been asleep, it might not have woken them, but now it was like a gunshot in the night.

Blake's hand slid around his forearm.

"That's the back door," she breathed out. "Someone's trying to come in."

Those words would be the last before the chaos of the next

several minutes, but before his legs got ahead of him, Liam glanced back through the kitchen window. The men were no longer standing around chatting. All three were looking at the house now.

Liam realized it then.

They weren't waiting to cause trouble. They were waiting for someone else to start it.

PRESSURE MADE DIAMONDS.

Blake didn't talk about or even think about her mother all that often, but her telling Blake this while growing up had firmly stuck into place. If anything was hard or tiring or brought on waves of stress, it was a necessary part of life. In fact, it was almost a good luck of sorts. Without pressure, there would be no diamonds after all.

That had been a soothing saying for Blake as a kid because it had made the most sense. It wasn't a promise of a stress-free life or a guarantee that life would always go the way you wanted it to. It was practical. It was an if-and-when situation. Not a what-if situation.

When life became hard, endure.

Not *if* life became hard.

That's how you became a diamond.

That saying, however, lost some of its shine when their mother left the family behind. Apparently, Blake's mom could be a diamond. Just not with them.

Years and years had passed since the Bennet matriarch had gone her own way, and yet Blake had found that out of everything she learned—good and bad—from her mother, this sentiment was the loudest. The second the back door started breaking, Blake heard her mother's words as if she were standing next to her.

"Pressure makes diamonds, Blakey. All you have to do is endure the squirmy parts first."

There were four people in the house who absolutely couldn't get hurt.

Bruce, Clem, Lola and Liam.

But one of those took the lead quick. It made Blake's heart skip a little beat.

"Get the kids," Liam said, words and movements hurrying. "We don't know how many are coming in. Hide until backup gets here."

He was already moving, gun raised and ready. For a split second Blake was torn. She wasn't used to taking the back seat in situations like this. She was the one who ran in, gun raised and ready to take on the trouble. Then again, she wasn't in her old life. She was in charge of protecting two little ones. From the known and unknown.

And she had no idea how many armed men were coming. *Endure the squirmy parts first*, she thought.

Then all thoughts went on autopilot.

Liam outstepped her, pinpoint focus on the back of the house and the continued sound of someone trying to get the door open. He was a wall of strength and grit. Blake wouldn't have known that ten minutes prior, he was fast asleep with a four-year-old had she not seen it herself.

He didn't even have shoes on at the moment.

Yet somehow that made him more intimidating. A man in his home, ready to defend it.

Blake's gaze left him as she went to the bedroom with the most vulnerable Bennet first.

The hallway had four rooms branching off from it before it forked to the right for the guest bathroom and laundry room. The back door was past the last room. Liam disappeared around the corner, the hallway sensor light flashing on low as he went. It was the only source of light as Blake went into the kids' room.

When things became more settled Blake, planned on giving Clem and Bruce their own room but for now, she shut the door behind her, sidestepped Clem's stuffed animals, the bottom of her twin-sized bed, and a cluster of Barbies on the floor until she was at Bruce's crib. His zoo-print onesie had always made Blake's heart feel warm, but seeing it now, the low light from the rocket-shaped lamp in the corner making most of the room visible, and Blake's stomach went to ice.

Why were the men here?

"Endure the squirmy parts." Blake's mother's words sounded in her head again.

Blake went to work.

She started to reach for Bruce but bumped the baby monitor mounted to the crib. It gave her an idea. She kept her voice low, hoped the sound machine would keep her muffled enough to keep the boy asleep, and leaned close to the speaker.

"Lola. Lola." Blake reached into the crib. Bruce didn't startle at her touch. She got straight to the point. "Lola. Men with guns are here. Liam's at the back door. Be quiet and go to my room."

It was dramatic but urgent. Lola was a light sleeper, so hopefully that would get her going.

Bruce, thankfully, wasn't as easy to wake. Blake had him against her with minimal noise coming from him. She knew that wouldn't last long the more she moved.

Blake walked past the Barbie pile and opened the door as slowly as she could. Movement opposite her almost pulled out a yell in reflex. The same must have been true for Lola. Her eyes were wide as she finished opening her bedroom door all the way.

Bless the woman's speed.

She was still clutching the receiving end of the baby monitor, but she understood her assignment.

Blake nodded toward the primary bedroom to her right.

A heavy thud sounded from her left.

There was no time to investigate.

Lola was quick and quiet as they went to the bedroom at the opposite end of the hallway. As soon as they cleared the doorway, she had the door shut and locked.

"The bathroom," Blake whispered. Another locked door between them and the intruder would make her feel better. Plus the room only had one window, and it didn't open.

Sounds from the hallway became louder. If there had been an element of surprise on Liam's behalf, it was undoubtedly gone. Neither woman commented on the escalation. They were focused. Lola took Bruce, and Blake scooped up Clem. As soon as all four were in the bathroom, Blake started moving. She took the blanket she had grabbed from the bed and threw it in the garden tub. Clem went in next. She started to stir. Lola put a hand on her stomach and started patting, Bruce was still asleep against her shoulder. The motion-sensor light next to the vanity cast shadows over Lola's face. She was terrified.

Blake hated it.

That didn't mean she wasn't going to give out the facts.

"There were three men outside near the trees," she whispered. "Liam called in backup, but then someone started coming in the back door. At least two of the three outside were armed."

Lola had, as far as Blake knew, never been in a violent situation like this. She didn't own a gun, she had never been in a fight, and the most chaos she had endured had to do with the children she was currently guarding.

But now, she was a diamond.

Her voice was even as she asked a practical question.

"Do we have guns?"

Blake shook her head.

"Liam has the only one in the house."

Fate was interesting.

No sooner than she answered, the house was rocked by a sound that Blake had hoped never to hear.

A gunshot.

After that, no one stayed quiet.

Chapter Thirteen

Ray McClennan hadn't expected Liam to be waiting for him inside the house. That much was evident when Liam had slid behind him, gun raised and pressed it to the small of his back.

"Don't move." Liam's voice had been deathly quiet, but he knew Ray heard him loud and clear.

It's just that the man didn't care to listen.

He spun around while throwing himself off-balance on purpose. It was a wild move that might have had him dodging a bullet had Liam intended on shooting the man on the spot. There were two reasons why he didn't want to use a gun if he could help it.

One, he didn't know exactly where the Bennet family was inside the house, and no matter how great his aim was or how close he was with his target, there was always the possibility that something could go wrong. He didn't want to chance an accident with Blake, Lola, or the kids close by.

Two, and this was just as strong as a point as the first, Liam didn't want the men outside to know that their presence was needed. He wanted them to keep standing next to the trees while they thought Ray had everything handled.

A shot going off in the night surely would do the opposite.

So Liam kept his finger away from the trigger and instead dealt with Ray with the length of his arm and elbow.

He used this and his sheer weight as a battering ram. Instead of going forward, however, he smashed into the man's side and threw him into the laundry room's wall.

Something cracked, but Liam wasn't in the position to inspect. He just knew that Ray hadn't been put out of commission. The man swung his elbow out with undeniable panicked strength. Liam was too close and took the hit to the side of his face.

Pain burst along his cheek.

He didn't have time for it either.

Using his gun as a fist, he brought its butt against Ray's shoulder. It was such an odd spot, but the sudden force did wonders. Ray grunted and tried his best to grab the new pain while also trying to dance away from it.

Space bloomed between them, and in that space, Liam was able to see that Ray wasn't one of the men without a weapon.

He had a gun.

The shot was quick but sloppy. It could have been a kill shot, easy, but Ray was still operating like he had been caught off guard. Instead of a direct chest or head shot, pressure pushed into Liam's right arm. Liam lost his grip on the gun.

So he kicked it away from both of them on reflex as Ray lunged forward with his left.

Liam's hand wrapped around Ray's wrist, and he pulled back with all his might. This time he knew the cracking he heard was the man's bone.

Ray howled in pain. More importantly, he dropped his gun to the wood floor.

Liam kept going. He brought Ray's broken wrist and arm with him as he got behind the man put him in a hold. His plan was to use his knee and the hold to put Ray on the floor.

He never could have accounted for what happened next.

A man wearing a rain slicker and a head so bald it shone with the limited light appeared in the back doorway. He was built like the letter T, and although he wasn't the same height as Liam, he wasn't far off either.

He also had a gun that he didn't hesitate to use.

Liam had no room to move once the gunshot split through the air.

Neither did Ray.

Still pinned against Liam's chest, Ray took the full force of the shot to the chest, and it pushed both men over, Liam hitting the floor hard. The air left his lungs. He struggled to stand and breathe all at once, coughing and trying to pull Ray out of the way at the same time.

He was left unprotected. Vulnerable. An easy target.

He should have remembered Sheriff Trouble was still in the house.

Liam watched in bewildered awe as Blake coolly walked around him and planted herself near his feet. Her arm was raised. Liam realized a beat too late that Blake had a gun.

And she wasn't waiting for an invitation to use it.

Blake opened fire with a steady hand and even steadier focus.

Liam collected his breath and awe to not waste the attack. He looped his arm around Ray's waist, then pushed and pulled him around the corner and into the longer main hallway that split the house.

The second he was clear, he yelled back as much to Blake.

She let out the third shot and then was a flurry of motion rounding the corner.

"He ran," she hurried to say. "No hit."

"Are you okay?"

Blake nodded. If Liam had more time, he would have really taken the situation in, looked at the woman and her calm, but now everyone outside knew they were needed. Though, he was hoping the shots had scared them away. Liam was hauling Ray into the first room to their left when Blake slipped the phone out of his pocket.

The light flashed on at the movement. He could see he was still on the call with Price.

"Price, Ray's been shot, maybe dead, and Liam looks like he took a bullet to the arm too," she hurried. "There's a man in a dark red rain jacket, bald, with a gun. I think I scared him off, but he might come back. The other two are unaccounted for."

Liam straightened to stand.

He'd been shot in the arm?

"The kids and Lola are locked in my bathroom," she added. "I'm putting you back in Liam's pocket and hushing until y'all get here."

Blake did exactly as she said. She put the phone in Liam's pocket and set her gun back to ready.

"Can you still fight?" she asked him. Her eyes flashed to his right arm.

That pressure he felt earlier was starting to fill with pain. He guessed Ray's shot hadn't just been a graze.

That wasn't going to stop Liam.

He nodded.

"Take the gun and stand guard in the bedroom. I can handle things out here."

Blake didn't like that.

Her voice was steel.

"I'm not leaving you."

It was such a direct and resolute statement that Liam was momentarily caught off guard. He wanted to combat it in the next, but the sound of footsteps sounded near the back door.

Were they really that brazen to come in despite knowing the people inside were armed?

Then again, hadn't the bald man shot Ray without hesitation?

Was he coming back with help? Were they about to be caught by three men instead of one?

Blake had her hand wrapped around the gun. She positioned her body to have the best shot at whoever came into view.

It wasn't a good angle.

It would leave her exposed if she wanted a good shot.

Liam had an idea.

He took his phone out and as low as he possibly could, he whispered out a command.

"Price, make noise."

The second the words left his mouth, Liam tossed his phone across the hallway and into the bedroom opposite them. There was a faint light in the room, and because of it, he saw the phone hit something that looked like a pillow on the ground.

The soft thud was still enough to alert whoever had come inside.

Then Price started making noise.

Liam placed his hand on Blake's shoulder. He moved her soundlessly back a few steps. Then his hand dropped to her waist. He adjusted her stance until she was squarely looking into the other room. She didn't fight him.

The footsteps were in the hallway next to both doors.

Price continued making noise on the other end of the phone. There must have been a sound machine going in that room. It made Price sound even more natural, as if there were people trying to talk in hushed, hurried voices.

Liam hoped it would be enough to draw whoever was in the hallway that way first.

He slid his hand back up to Blake's shoulder and kept it there.

She didn't as so much as breathe.

That's how they were standing when the first man came

into view. He wore a baseball cap and jeans. There was no gun in his hand but a slight tremor in the way he slowly moved. Liam squeezed Blake's shoulder lightly. She continued to be still.

Which was a feat in itself considering the baseball-capped man made a stunning move.

Instead of walking into the room opposite them, he started to walk backward into theirs.

Liam put pressure on Blake's shoulder with his index and middle fingers. Two quick prods. The man slowly backing up into their space was also using his hands to wordlessly signal. He motioned forward to the room where Price was still doing whatever it was to draw any and all attention.

It seemed the man was going to let his friend do the work of fighting while he backed himself away into a safer space.

Which meant that maybe he really wasn't armed.

And meant that his friend probably was.

Liam released his hold on Blake and took a step forward. Blake didn't move a muscle. He wished he could tell her his plan, but there was no time.

They were outnumbered, and he was hurt.

If they didn't execute the next part of his new plan flawlessly, they could lose their lives. Or, worse, the family hiding in the house could.

But they were also out of any other good options.

So Liam did something he hadn't done since he was in the Marines.

He decided to trust another soul explicitly, no room for hesitation or second thought.

Just pure, unbridled trust.

Then, and only then, did Liam make his move.

THE MAN SEEMED to have no idea he wasn't alone. He had even less of an inkling that the wall of strength that was Liam was waiting behind him. Had he walked back even one more step, he would have collided with him. Instead, he stopped within the relative darkness, staring straight ahead.

He was waiting for his friend and his gun to make the first move.

Too bad for them that Blake and Liam had their own plan.

One that happened in a flash.

A new figure entered the space in front of the man. All Blake could see over his shoulder was that it wasn't the man in the rain jacket. The way he held himself, though, she was almost certain he had a gun in hand.

Liam must have seen it too.

Without a word, he sprung into action and Blake was ready for it.

Liam wrapped his arm and hand around the man in the hat's mouth and torso and pulled them both down and out of the way. The other man about to move into the nursery heard the commotion.

But it was too late.

Now Blake had a perfect line of sight.

There was no room for errors.

She shot her mark with a perfect score.

The man yowled in pain and crumpled.

Then it was a dance between Blake and Liam.

He left the man in the baseball hat on the floor and took two quick steps to the man she'd just sent to the hardwood. Blake didn't watch what he did next but instead switched her attention to the man next to her.

"Don't move," she ground out, gun aimed down at him. "Understand?"

It probably helped matters that Ray's unmoving body was next to him.

She saw his head move in what she assumed was agreement.

Liam took his own unknown man and pulled him into the nursery all the way, keeping himself out of the open hallway.

Blake saw the gun in his hand. The man he had by the back of the shirt was still yowling and thrashing around. It didn't shake Liam one bit.

He met her eye. Shadows danced across his face, but Blake could still see the absolute strength in him.

Now if the bald man appeared, they could outnumber him.

Blake strained to listen for more footsteps. It wasn't easy. The man she had shot in the leg was still wailing. The man on the ground next to her and Ray, however, was obedient in his silence.

Liam looked like he was about to deal with his captive, but another sound broke through the night around them.

Sirens.

And not just one.

Blake didn't dare loosen her defense.

She did, however, let out a small exhale.

Backup had finally arrived.

Chapter Fourteen

Blake slapped her hand down on the table with force. She curled her fingers and dragged her nails against the top until she was making a fist.

"That's Mater Calhoun," she said through gritted teeth. The cell phone next to her showed the image of the smiling man in work clothes. The same man whom she had shot in the leg in her home earlier.

Liam settled into the chair next to her.

"Unfortunate name," he observed. He was mindful of the sling on his arm.

Like several hours before, Price was with them again. This time, though, he was in person, sitting opposite them. It was now morning, but the McCoy County Sheriff's Department paid no mind to the change. The meeting room they were in had one window, and its blinds were drawn tight.

Price shook his head in what seemed to be equal parts anger and disbelief.

That feeling was amplified in Blake.

He could see her fist tightening still. Liam reached out and gently tapped that fist twice.

Blake's gaze flew to him. She silently released her own hold.

"I know of the family but not Mater specifically," Liam

admitted, hand back on his phone. "Other than the obvious reasons why we should be upset, why are you two *this* upset?"

Price was in a full snit, but he acquiesced to Blake for her answer. It almost felt like a hierarchy move, like Blake had seniority, and it was his job to let her take the lead. A part of Liam couldn't blame him for the instinct. Despite being on cold medicine, forced to violence in her own home, and then dealing with the aftermath of getting her scared family together and settled in the sheriff department's break room, she still was a pillar.

Liam didn't know if it made him proud or worried. Or both.

She needed to rest; she couldn't yet.

And apparently, some of that had to do with this Mater Calhoun person.

"Mater Calhoun—" Blake's voice was undeniably angry, even the pause she forced herself to take after his name felt weighted. Whatever she had originally been about to say, she looked like she changed her mind about it. Instead, she was steady with her next words. "He's the reason I left Seven Roads all those years ago."

Liam couldn't help but lean a little toward her.

He quirked an eyebrow.

She was quick to wave her hand at the first thought that sprang up at the statement.

"He was only a friend at the time, and, well, even that's generous," she continued. "He lived on the same block my dad did and liked to come over to the house to hang out a lot. Whether it was with me or Beth, he was an easy guy to get along with. Even my dad liked him, which is saying something." She let out a breath. It was hot with anger still. "Then one day Mater came to the house all upset—like really upset—saying that he needed my dad's help. He'd gone and messed up at his summer job at the steel mill and gotten into a fight with a new hire there, and now everyone wanted a piece of him, including the sheriff's department."

She snorted. There was no humor in it.

"My dad, someone who'd only had daughters but wanted sons, told Mater to stay hidden at our place until he could get things sorted. He told me I was in charge of making sure he was okay. I didn't mind it at first, but then, well, then I found out what he did."

Price cut in with a sharper edge than Liam had expected of him.

"The trouble he'd gotten into was because he beat that guy so badly that he ended up losing an eye," he said. "And the man didn't even start the fight. He only swung back in defense, and even then, he looked like he was pawing at pillows."

"The security footage of the fight was spread around pretty decent before Dad could even make it to his lawyer's office," Blake tagged back in. "I tried talking to Mater about it, but he just got more and more tight-lipped. But you could tell he was in the wrong and he knew it. Then he'd come to the only place in town where someone would fight for him."

Blake looked like she was about to say one thing again but, instead, switched to something else.

"Then Sheriff Dean showed up on our doorstep," she said. "He knew my dad saw Mater as a surrogate son and came at me with the same feeling. He gave me a speech about doing the right thing, about people who did the wrong thing, and he really dug deep into the idea that one bad choice doesn't necessarily mean a life filled with them. But it didn't matter what he said, because I already made up my mind. I let him in the house and let him take Mater, only stalling long enough to put on my shoes."

Blake's expression grew more solemn. She readjusted in her chair before continuing.

"Dad showed up right as Mater was being driven off by a deputy. He was so spitting mad, face all red and running up like he was about to fight the entire sheriff's department." Blake paused again. This time, Liam knew there was a lot that she wanted to say but didn't. "Sheriff Dean didn't budge at anything my dad said, and after that, my dad never forgave me. We got into a yelling match out near the park on the way home from the department and… Well, it was good for everyone that I left town. Mater, even with a lawyer, ended up in prison later. His sentence was ten years, last I heard."

Blake looked to Price.

He nodded confirmation.

"He got out early for good behavior but stayed out of Seven Roads until a few years ago," he said. "He's been living in the duplex out on Grantham Street. He married a woman he met after he got out. Forget her name, but would you believe where she works? Steel mill. Same place that caused him all the grief. That's probably why he's been doing so many odd jobs through the years, trying to make enough to get her to leave the place."

"And tonight he was with Ray," Liam finally said.

"And tonight he was with Ray," Blake repeated.

Price shook his head.

"I'm guessing that Ray really could be targeting you, Sheriff," he said. "First they go after your dinner companion in the field and now this? Ray might've hired Mater to help, and Mater's been hard up on cash, so he said yes to it. That's best I can guess as to why Mater would get involved. As far as I know, Mater doesn't have a connection to Missy, her father, or her case. I wish we could just ask Ray though. At least get him to tell us who Rain Slicker Guy and Baseball Cap Guy are."

Liam had been able to leave the hospital within an hour of the ambulance dropping their party off. The bullet wound in his arm had been only a little more severe than a graze. He'd needed stitches, sure, but he could manage just fine now. Ray, on the other hand, was in much worse shape and fighting to stay alive. The bald man had done a serious number on him.

Which was one more reason why Liam felt the urgency to find him, the savage one who had managed to run off earlier. The other man with the baseball cap who hadn't even attempted to understand his surroundings, had buttoned up his mouth with speed. No one had recognized him, but Detective Williams would make quick work of him, Liam was sure.

Mater wasn't one to help with this problem either. He was in the hospital post-surgery for his gunshot to the leg. Despite his yelling, he wouldn't say much of anything with or without a lawyer.

"I still don't understand why they're coming after you," Price said after a moment, turning his gaze to Liam. "I mean I kind of understood misplaced anger coming in from his dad because you're looking into Missy's death, but grabbing three other guys and busting into a family home just to—what? Scare you? Hurt you? I don't get it." Price dragged his hand down his face. "Darius is talking to Chase McClennan in a few hours, so maybe we can get some kind of answer there if Darius can't grab anything from Baseball Cap Guy."

Chase McClennan's alibi had been solid. He definitely wasn't at Blake's home that night. Still, that didn't mean he didn't know the men who had been.

Liam looked sidelong at Blake.

He was angry for many reasons, but the grief that Blake had been put through topped the list. Seeing her worry over the kids and Lola had made him exponentially more so, considering he was the reason they had been traumatized in the first place.

He should have kept his distance from the woman.

That's why he had kept so quiet during the last week.

That's why he had asked to put the truck in the garage while he was at her home—to sidestep gossip, sure, but to also keep his associations with her as limited as possible in the public's eye.

He should have actually kept his distance instead, not offer himself up the second she came around.

Now she was going through trouble again because of him.

Liam could feel the anger in his chest boil again. It hadn't left since the night before.

If he hadn't been around, they would be enjoying their morning together in peace, not sitting in the department scared.

"But they didn't know you were there."

Liam's eyes widened as Blake spoke. For a split second he wondered if he had spoken his last thought aloud.

"What?" he asked.

Blake was staring at the fist she had made earlier. She brought her gaze slowly up to Liam's before repeating herself.

"They didn't know you were there."

The men stopped. Liam tilted his head a little, thoughtful.

"We didn't plan on you coming to my house last night," she explained. "Your truck was locked up in the garage and out of sight, and then we all fell asleep. You stayed late on accident. If *we* didn't even know you were going to be there, then how would they?"

"They could have followed you?" Price said.

"But why did they seem so surprised when Liam started fighting?" she ventured. "Surely they would have expected him to do so. Instead, Ray and Mater waited before coming in. They—"

"They didn't plan on me," Liam interrupted. "Ray seemed genuinely surprised when I appeared. I thought maybe because it was late and they expected us to be asleep, but the sight of me made him hesitate."

Blake nodded, unclenched her fist and used her index finger to tap out another point on the tabletop.

"They followed me last week. Maybe they really had no idea you were driving behind me. You weren't ever in their plan."

Price was shaking his head.

"So—what?—you're saying that they came just to break in? To what? To rob you when they knew you and the kids would be home? There's got to be easier places to get a nicer score, no offense."

She shook her head.

"Even if I had a house full of valuables, why would you bring *that* much manpower? Why bring *four* men, armed, to a home when everyone's supposed to be sleeping?" She met Liam's eye again. "And why, even if that's your plan to break in and steal, do you send only one out when you know resistance is probably going to happen?"

Liam was sure of it now.

"They had no idea I was there," he agreed. "They expected only you to be a threat."

Blake tapped her finger against the table again.

"Which brings us to another question we might have an answer to," she said. "Why not wait until we weren't home? We have a set routine taking the kids to daycare and doing errands when none of us would be home. When there wouldn't even be a chance of resistance. But instead, it's like they came prepared for battle…a battle they didn't think you would be there for."

Price's eyebrow rose.

"What are you thinking?" Price said.

But Liam had already followed her thought process.

He wasn't a fan of where it led.

"They came for you."

APART FROM SOME THEORIES, they didn't have a strand of evidence to make sense of the men or their actions. Sitting there talking about it wasn't helping either. Try as she might to appear the epitome of composure, Blake was finally starting to openly struggle.

Not only had she missed sleep and gone through a traumatic experience in which she'd had to shoot someone, there was the simple and annoying fact that she had a cold tugging at her. Her head hurt, her nose was starting to stuff up again, and although she didn't feel as if a fever was hanging around, there were a few body aches that were nagging her.

When Liam said it was time for her to go, however, she was split between agreement and a stubborn need to stay. She pushed; he didn't budge. He told her no once more to her suggesting she go in to talk to Mater or the man who'd worn the baseball cap with absolute resolution.

"Running yourself ragged isn't going to help anyone," he said, standing tall in front of her in his office. "Not you, your family, or solving whatever is going on here. So let's go."

Even though the sheriff had been a lot more social with her in the last twenty-four hours or so, Blake found that it was her turn to hesitate at the sight of him. It wasn't the first time she had wondered how she and her family would have fared if he hadn't been there to help. She eyed his bandaged bicep and the sling keeping his arm steady.

Her mind wandered to perhaps the real reason she wasn't ready to leave.

If she hadn't already been preoccupied, she would have avoided his next movement.

Liam stroked a warm thumb down between her eyebrows, smoothing out the crinkle there.

"Go ahead and tell me what you're thinking," he said. "That way I can join the conversation."

The touch might have unsettled her before, but now she sighed as it withdrew.

"Let's say that I really am a target. Is it because of you? Because of me? Because of Missy's case? Or what if it's belated revenge from me turning on Mater back when we were young with an added bonus of Ray helping?"

"There's no way we can know yet," Liam pointed out.

"Exactly. Which means, how can we know if Rain Slicker Guy isn't out there waiting to try again? Whether it's against me or you." She put her hand to her chest. "I'm good with me being in a bull's-eye, but what about the kids? Lola? Won't me being with them put them in danger again?"

Liam did something so unexpected, all Blake could do was stare.

He laughed.

"What did you think I was about to do?" he asked when done. "Send you off alone?"

Blake didn't respond. That's exactly what she thought.

He shook his head. His voice thrummed low and strong as he explained.

"Until we have this whole thing figured out and settled, I'm not leaving your side. Sorry to say, you're stuck with me now, Sheriff Trouble. And that's that."

Chapter Fifteen

Once that decision was made, Blake and Liam didn't speak much.

It was understandable, they both were moving parts that needed to be moved. Liam saw to the department, assigned jobs and made phone calls while doing both. Blake wasn't connected to his movements but was always near. She had the kids, her and Lola packed in a flash. In the next, she had them unpacked at the only house in Seven Roads that could be considered a secret.

At least, according to Price.

"A lot of people don't know this, but I once tried my hand at flipping houses a few years before you showed up," he explained once Liam and him had inspected every inch before ushering the Bennet clan inside. "And by 'tried my hand,' I mean I've been renovating my aunt's house for a long time... with a slow hand and thin patience."

He pointed to the field behind the two-story home and then brought it around to the two houses on either side, though with a lot of space between all three.

"This backs up to the Becker Farm's western pasture and no one's home in any of these. They've been that way for ages though. One's an inheritance to a city dweller who hasn't set foot in town in years, and the other has another lazy renovator who hasn't done much over the years."

"And no one knows you own this place and you're letting us all stay here." Liam wanted to make sure.

Price nodded.

"Despite popular belief, there *are* some places in town that even gossip gets bored of. No one comes out here anymore. There's no point in it." He clapped Liam on the back and smiled. "That said, I'm not a man who just leaves an empty house sitting alone. This baby has a security system and cameras around the outside and the inside of the front and back door. If anyone comes by unannounced, you'll know it quicker than a second sneeze."

Price didn't add onto the fact that, unlike last night, this time Liam was also prepared. His service weapon, along with a bag he'd packed quickly, had definitely come along with them.

"Thanks for this," Liam said once they had done another recap of what needed to be done next. "I know as sheriff I probably should be hanging around the department during a time like this but..."

He didn't finish his sentence. He didn't have to for Price to understand. Or for him to respond about the woman on his mind.

"Sheriff Trouble and her family have been through a lot already. If you can help ease some of their burden, I would think less of you if you didn't try." Price smiled. That smile changed a little in the next moment. "Plus, from what I know of her, Blake doesn't often let people into her life so easy, never mind letting them help her. Other than Lola, I can't think of a single person she'd let get as close as you've gotten to her and the kids. It'd be a waste if you didn't use that to help her out."

Liam couldn't deny that hearing those words meant a little

more than they maybe should have. It felt like only yester-day that he had handed Blake his shirt, and yet at the same time, he realized he was as comfortable around her as if she had been in his life for a long while.

Though, his lack of information on her was a quick re-minder that that wasn't the case.

A question that had been in the back of Liam's mind came out of his mouth.

"By the way, did anything else happen with Mater Cal-houn? Back then, I mean. When he was arrested."

Price's eyebrow went up in question. Liam clarified his meaning.

"Anything else, that is," he said. "When Mater was brought up, you and she just seemed to have a lot of anger directed toward him. A lot more than I thought there would be for the situation. I was wondering if there was part of the story I was missing."

They were standing in front of Price's cruiser, a good dis-tance from the house and the family inside. Still, he lowered his voice a little when he answered.

"It's not so much about what Mater did as what happened after he was arrested." He nodded toward the house. "Blake really undersold the fight she had with her dad. He was so mad at her for letting the sheriff in to take Mater that he kicked her out of the car downtown on the way home from the department. He yelled at her pretty badly on the sidewalk with an audience and everything."

"What was he fighting with *her* for?" Liam couldn't help but feel defensive.

Price sighed.

"Loyalty. And how she didn't know what that word meant. There was more to it—I wasn't there personally—but a few bystanders at the time stepped in to try to calm him down."

"What did Blake do?"

Price shrugged.

"She took as much as she could stand. Then she yelled right on back about Mater being in the wrong, and, well, she kept going. They started yelling about her mom leaving them, and then suddenly she said she was going to do the same. She kind of dragged the town through it too, calling it small and noisy and a place she never ever wanted to come back to." He shrugged. "We've all said some mean stuff in a fight before but that's where a lot of Seven Roads's locals get their anti-Blake feelings from. No matter if she meant it or not, the rumors and gossip were really bad after that. For her, her dad, and Mater. A month later she was gone. Honestly, I thought she'd never come home again." The deputy let out a breath. There was some defeat in it. "Though, I guess she didn't come back for really happy reasons in the end since her sister passed. Now...now all of this is happening."

They let that sit for a moment.

Then they said their goodbyes.

Liam watched the deputy drive away with some residual anger still in his chest.

At Mater, at Blake's father, at the men who had invaded the Bennet home.

When Liam had told the woman that he wasn't leaving her side, he had meant it. Now, he somehow meant it even more.

Price's house was furnished but only with the basics. Had it been just the two of them, it probably would have felt cold and empty, but when Liam finally went back inside, he was met with a slew of toys, mats and little knickknacks that came with the territory of children.

Breadcrumbs, he thought while scooping up a little alien stuffed creature by the door. He hadn't had much time to interact with Bruce and Clem but had noticed the girl clinging to the stuffed creature earlier that day.

Liam was going to bring the toy to her when he spotted someone on the couch in the living room.

Blake looked ready to drop, but when she saw Liam, she gave him a little nod.

"Did Price leave?" she asked.

"Mm-hmm," he confirmed. Liam spotted the baby monitor on the coffee table next to her. He could see Bruce and Clem on the display, both asleep on the main bed.

"Lola's on the couch next to them. She's using nap time to catch up on sleep herself." Liam was about to suggest Blake do the same, but a change overtook her expression so quickly that it momentarily made him pause. She took advantage of the space. "I want to use this time to ask you a question. One I haven't actually asked yet."

Liam felt his eyebrow rise.

"What is it?" he asked.

Blake, obviously tired and in need of sleep herself, had a voice that was suddenly as hard as steel.

Those eyes kept his entire attention as she spoke.

"Whether or not I'm being targeted, or you're being targeted, I'm going to focus on the one thing we've had in common the last week or so."

"Missy Clearwater's death?"

She nodded.

"But now I want you to tell me—why do you really think Missy Clearwater was murdered?"

Liam had to be tired, but he didn't look it. Instead, he somehow managed to exude an energy that sent a surge of steadiness up Blake's spine. He was calm. He was focused.

He was very good-looking.

It had a cold-water-to-the-face kind of effect on her.

The drag of her cold meds and the aching exhaustion that

had been pressing down on her since that morning temporarily disappeared.

"I guess keeping you in the dark isn't going to keep you safe, like I once thought," he said, a slight teasing in his words. It was another small break from the normally quiet man. She leaned into it with a snort.

"Keeping me in the dark just leaves me in the dark, and I'd like at least a flashlight beam in here," she said in return.

Liam nodded to that. He let out a breath and sank onto the couch cushion next to her. Blake angled her body to be able to meet his eye the best she could, given how the man was just as tall sitting as he was standing.

"First off, are you familiar with Doc Ernest?"

"The medical examiner for the county? Yeah, I know her. More from when we were younger though. She's a good egg."

He nodded again.

"That was my impression of her too, despite not having many reasons to interact with her through the years," he said. "So when she called and told me that she thought Missy was already dead before she hit the ground, I had no reason to not believe her."

"Missy was already dead?"

If that was true, that was news to Blake. And apparently not common knowledge that many others had heard. After first meeting Liam, Blake had scoured the internet for news of Missy's death. No sources had mentioned her taking a post-death tumble.

"It became a several-day conversation between us. One that the doc ended up walking back after having another look at the examination. She said she thought she'd become too emotionally invested since she knew Missy and had been wrong with her original report. I would have left it at that, but I'd already found this. That's when the hunch I haven't been able to get free of came in."

The man was wearing some nice snug-fitting jeans but managed to pull a small black case out of his pocket. He opened it to show a flash drive. It looked like it had seen better days. There were initials written in marker on its side.

"M.C.," Blake read aloud. "Missy Clearwater?"

"I assume so," he said. "Considering I found this under the bridge when I was taking pictures there the day after her death."

Blake didn't reach for the flash drive but leaned in a little as if seeing it closer would give her more answers. The movement put her thigh up against his in the process. If he minded the closeness, he didn't say anything.

"That's a weird thing to have on you normally, never mind before your death," she said. "What's on it?"

At this, Liam's expression grew thoughtful.

"One Notepad document," he answered. "It's a code."

"Code? Like as in computer commands that looks like the green font in the Matrix movies?"

He nodded.

"Exactly that. But according to an old computer hacker friend of mine from college, it's only a partial piece of a much longer series of coding. A copied and pasted snippet from something else."

Blake smoothed over the fact that Liam had casually mentioned having an old computer hacker friend for later discussion and posed another question.

"Why was Missy carrying a flash drive with a partial computer code on it? Are you sure it's hers? Though I guess if it wasn't, it would be one heck of a coincidence. Ugh. I wish we could find her laptop. If she had that code, then the rest is probably there."

Liam was watching her. It was the only reason she didn't

go on a stream-of-conscious rant with her thought process. Instead, she bottom-lined the answer to her own original question.

"So, it's all suspicious," she said. "A medical examiner who wavered on her belief that Missy was already dead when she fell and a flash drive with the unknown code on it near her body. That's how you got your gut feeling that something is seriously off."

Liam dipped his chin down a little.

"And now the missing laptop and the McClennan cousins last week and Ray, plus the three men who came to my house last night, a place that they either did or did not know you were inside of."

Was this whole thing about Missy's case? About the code?

That made more sense than everyone coming at her for no reason.

Blake didn't know the answers, but she knew she wanted to help get them.

"I missed my meet-up with Missy's ex-boyfriend Kyle at the coffee shop, so let's reschedule for tomorrow, if we can, and that way, maybe we can figure out at least where Missy's laptop is or why she might have had this flash drive and code."

Liam was still watching her. Which made sense. They were talking after all.

Yet, Blake stopped herself.

Because, well, it didn't exactly feel like they were on the same page anymore. Instead, it felt like Liam had gone to a different metaphorical book altogether.

Then, as if to prove that point, he did something that froze Blake to spot.

His gaze dropped to her lips.

Adrenaline shot through Blake. Her heartbeat started to gallop with its encouragement.

Slowly, like syrup sliding, he reversed his gaze and trailed back up to her eyes.

Heat, not warmth, but heat ignited within her.

It was surprising; it wasn't surprising.

Liam Weaver was perhaps the only person who Blake had met in the last few years that she had felt this comfortable with. The only man who she had let into her home so easily. The only man who hadn't made her occupation, her personality and her unusual life choices and circumstances feel less than.

He had helped her. She had helped him. He had a problem. She wanted to help. He wanted to help keep her safe. She wanted to help keep him safe too.

He was so very handsome.

And they were so very close right now.

Blake knew she probably could have helped it, but in that moment, she decided her actions were out of her control.

Liam leaned down, closing the distance between them, and Blake was ready to accept anything he gave. Her eyes almost fluttered closed.

But then a noise made them stay wide open.

"I'm hungry."

Blake whirled around to see Clem standing at the foot of the stairs, eyes sleepy but tummy apparently growling.

Normally, that would have given Blake a laugh. Clem was quiet only until she was hungry, then she would chat the entire alphabet until she had food in hand.

However, when Blake saw her, she couldn't stop the first thought that came into her head.

She looks just like Beth.

All at once, Blake remembered why she was in Seven Roads. Just as she remembered why she left.

And why she hadn't come back. Till now.

Guilt and anger and immense sadness gripped her chest tight.

She got off the couch, not looking back at Liam.

It was for the better.

Blake wasn't back in town for her life after all.

Chapter Sixteen

That night, Blake slept. Though not soundly.

She was sharing a bed with Lola, and Lola was moving to every toss and turn. It wasn't until the morning sun started to creep through the slit in the curtains that the older woman finally whispered into the quiet.

"What's hurtin' on you? Your nose, mind, or heart?"

Blake went still, though she opened her eyes wide. There was no use in pretending she had been anything but restless.

"I think I'm finally over the hump with this cold crud I got from the kids," she hedged at first. "Liam gave me the nod of approval after supper, if you don't believe me."

"So, not the nose. Then is it the mind or heart that's got you all jumbling the sheets?"

Blake sighed.

She could lie, but with everything Lola had done for her, there wasn't a good enough reason in the world to tell the woman anything but the truth.

Too bad the truth for her wasn't as easy to answer herself.

"I'm not sure," she admitted. "I keep thinking about how close y'all were to danger. Clem for the second time. I keep thinking about Liam's arm bleeding. I keep thinking about Mater and Ray. Then I'm thinking about Beth. Then I'm thinking about how she trusted her kids to me, and I'm already having to shuttle them off to a safe house with no clear plan on how to make sure they stay safe."

Blake let out another long breath. Even though she was lying down, it felt like she was dragged farther down into the mattress.

"I think the loudest thing in my head is Beth," she added. "She's probably looking down at me, wondering why it's me who's here and not the other way around."

Blake knew she had a lot on her plate that she could have been mentally chewing on, but that thought seemed to have been bothering her the most.

There she had been thinking about kissing the sheriff when she should have been thinking about how to get the kids back to their normal, safe lives.

Beth wouldn't have her kids in danger and thinking about anything else.

She was ashamed even now at the move.

A shame Blake thought Lola would understand.

However, the older woman did something she hadn't expected.

"I'm sorry."

Those two words were enough to get Blake's head to turn on her pillow. Lola was staring up at the ceiling.

"You're sorry?" Blake repeated. "Why? What for?"

There wasn't a thing Lola Bennet ever had to be sorry for, at least not to Blake's knowledge. Still, she sure did sound it in those two words.

She kept staring at the ceiling as she spoke.

"Beth dying was a dang shame, there's no two ways about that," Lola started. "Her leaving behind those two angels in the other room, well that makes her passing hurt even more. Knowing that they won't get to know their mama and knowing she won't get to raise them... It sure does hurt. But, Blake, she's gone and her going doesn't take away from something I don't guess anyone has talked about yet."

Lola reached out. Her hand wrapped around Blake's over the covers.

"You lost your life too. The moment you learned she passed was the moment your life jumped track. Everything you worked for, your career, your dreams, the life you were building, and the life you had planned...it ended when you knew Beth was gone."

Lola squeezed her hand.

"And, honey, you didn't bat an eye at it. You packed up that life, those dreams, your everything, and you came back to a place you didn't want to, and you stood tall. You didn't have time to prepare, and more importantly, you didn't have time to grieve. And I'm not talking about grieving Beth. I'm talking about grieving you. The life *you* lost."

She sighed.

"I bet you talked to countless people during your time in law enforcement about moving on after tragedy. After the death of loved ones. I bet you spoke about peace and time healing wounds. But I'm starting to think that, maybe, you haven't actually seen that your loss needs some peace too."

Lola squeezed her hand again. Blake didn't dare move.

"Beth is gone," she said. "From now until we go, that won't change. But you? You're here, kiddo. Every choice you make is yours now. Beth can't do a thing, and if you ask me, Beth wouldn't if she could. She'd know as well as I do that while we can tell those children about her and do our best to make sure they never forget her, *you* are going to be the mama who takes them through most of their lives."

She let go of Blake's hand. The sudden lack of warmth startled her. She turned to see Lola had turned to look at her.

"Beth might not agree with every little thing you decide to do in your life, but don't you forget for a second that she picked you to take care of the most important things in hers. So don't be too hard on yourself. You've done everything just right, even the wrong things. Stop putting your life on hold because you think you have to live Beth's. It isn't fair to you, her or the kids if you stop being Blake." She reached out and put a hand on Blake's cheek. The baby monitor for the kids asleep in the guest bedroom next door cast a glow across Lola's face. Blake saw her smile. "And I'm sorry that no one has said any of this to you yet. To be fair, I would have said it sooner, but, well, I've also never had to raise little ones and—my goodness—they sure make the time fly by."

She rubbed her thumb across Blake's cheek. It pushed the tears running down it away.

Blake hadn't even realized she had started crying.

After a moment, when Lola pulled her hand back, she laughed a little.

"Did I ever tell you what my favorite thing about my father was?" Blake asked. She ignored the slight rasp to her voice.

Lola shook her head.

"No. What?"

Blake smiled.

"The fact that he made you my mom."

Lola paused, caught off guard no doubt by Blake showing such emotion. That shock didn't last long.

"That's funny, because you want to know my favorite thing that man ever did was?" she asked.

"What?"

Lola's smile grew.

"He made you girls."

After that, there wasn't much to say. Blake cried a little more; Lola consoled her with pats and hand squeezes. The sun rose higher outside and the room grew brighter. Eventually, the weight pressing against Blake's chest started to lift.

Then, sometime after that, her thoughts found their way to Liam.

Blake thought it was important that she started to feel even better after that.

PRICE WAS GOING above and beyond his job as a deputy. In fact, he seemed to be going above and beyond that of a friend too. Liam only said the former in a comment at the dining table after lunch.

"I can't order you to stay here," he told the man again. "So if it's not something you have time for…"

Price, who was dressed down in street clothes and had his daughter, Winnie, in the kitchen behind them with Lola, waved the concern away.

"Listen, I wouldn't offer to do this if I wasn't confident in my abilities, the safety of this house and the fact that I think you have a better chance at getting the information we need to potentially put this entire fiasco to bed than me." Price looked down at Liam's lap.

Or, really, Clem.

Since that morning the little girl had been stuck to his side, in his arms and on his lap. It seemed returning her alien stuffed creature had curried unflappable good favor for him. Liam wasn't complaining. He was quick to notice that she was quick to notice things herself. They had made fast work of the two puzzles that Lola had brought along in their toy bag. Even a tablet game about cupcakes had been a breeze for the two of them.

Now she was holding her alien and watching Price speak like she was memorizing every inch of the man and his words.

He smiled at her, but Clem didn't return the gesture. Instead, she leaned her weight back against Liam's chest and just kept staring.

"Tough crowd," Price muttered. There was humor in it though.

Liam snorted, but it was Lola who came in with a comment.

"Don't act like Blake hasn't given you the same look before," she said. "The Bennet women need to scrutinize before they fraternize."

She stopped next to Liam and held out her hand to the girl.

"Though, I will say, Sheriff, you've sure earned the acceptance of the very same women in record time." Price couldn't see the wink that Lola threw him. He cleared his throat as her attention went to Clem. "Now, it's time for Sheriff Weaver and Sheriff Trouble to go get some answers, so why don't us girls and Bruce go watch a movie with Miss Winnie? I heard she brought us *Frozen*, which I'm pretty sure is your—"

Clem was already throwing herself off Liam at the mention of *Frozen*. All three adults laughed as the four-year-old started to sing one of the movie's songs as she ran into the living room.

"That's my cue," Lola said. She started to leave the room but paused as Blake walked in. Liam watched as she lightly tapped the back of Blake's hand before telling her to be safe. "That's to you too, Sheriff. I know Blake here is trouble, but let's keep it to a minimum if we can."

He nodded to her.

"Will do."

"And that's my cue to tell y'all the same," Price said. He stood between them and told them to be safe and to keep him in the loop. He also reiterated his vigilance in keeping the family safe on his end.

Then it was just the two of them.

Liam made sure to keep his gaze firmly locked with hers.

Not on the outfit that looked so good on her, not on the way her small smile made the room feel brighter, and not on the way her lips shone with whatever makeup she had put on for their outing.

Liam had already messed up the day before. One second he had been listening to her excitedly rattle off ways to help him solve their current complicated questions, and the next he'd wanted something so simple all other thoughts had left his mind.

He wanted to kiss her.

That was it.

Liam wanted to kiss Blake in the middle of their chaos. Not out of worry or pity or attraction only.

He had wanted to be closer to her, simple as could be.

It had been such a strong yet singular desire that he had thought about it for a long while later that night when alone on the couch.

No matter what he was feeling, no matter why, he wasn't about to make Blake uncomfortable. Something he had clearly already done by the move. So he had made a resolution to keep things professional as could be.

As normal as could be.

Definitely no thinking about how beautiful she was.

Definitely no staring at her lips.

So he cleared his throat again and returned her small smile.

"Ready to go?" he asked.

Blake nodded.

"Are you ready to keep your cool around a man we both have already agreed we dislike?"

Liam grumbled as he grabbed his keys. He waited until they were inside his truck and pulling out to answer with words.

"You get this no-good guy talking and I'll keep him going," he said. "But I'm here to let you know that if you had asked me last week if I was going to tag along on a coffee date with Kyle Langdon, I never would have had meeting Missy's ex for a coffee date on my Bingo card."

Blake let out a chuckle.

"If it means we might figure out where that laptop of hers is, you'll just have to learn to endure there, Sheriff."

Liam grumbled again.

"I just don't get a man like that," he said after they made their way back to the main road. He didn't say it, but Liam had been focused on making sure no one was around or following them. He had no doubt Blake was doing the same.

"What do you mean? A man who cheats, or a man who immediately gets with his girlfriend's best friend after they break up?"

"Both," Liam said. "But what I meant was how he's taken Missy's death. No matter how it happened or why it happened, he doesn't seem…like I think he should. I mean, they broke up, and a week later this happened to her. I've been divorced from my ex for years, and I think I'd still be upset if she died."

The thought was true, but Liam felt the need to correct it just a little.

"I mean not because I still have feelings for her like that but just because she's a human I used to spend all my time with." He shook his head. "Unless he's really just a despicable piece of scum, I would have thought he would be more… affected. Even with his new girlfriend."

"Maybe he's hiding it," Blake offered.

Liam shrugged.

"He did, and is doing, a good job of it then. Might have to tell him to try his hand at acting."

She let that thread of thought sit. A small silence stretched between them.

Blake broke it a few blocks before they made it the Twenty-Two Coffee Shop.

"How long were you with your ex?"

The question came out a little strong. Liam glanced sideways at the woman.

Blake was already looking at him. She rolled her eyes.

"I'm only asking because that's the first time you've brought up some gossip that I've already heard. I figured I'd give you a chance to let me hear *your* side of the story since we're already talking about it."

"Ah, the divorce rumors." Liam laughed. "Theo's told me a few he's heard since I came to town. My favorite one was where I didn't talk to her for a month straight, and that's what pushed us to divorce. Is that what you think happened?"

He was genuinely curious.

Blake was quick with her response.

"You talk to me just fine, so I don't think it's that."

A simple answer.

And it was true.

While he was a quiet guy, he was finding that talking was less of an effort and more natural around Blake.

He didn't say that though.

He took a turn to get them to the community parking lot for Main Street. Then he told her a truth he hadn't said out loud in a long time.

"We got married young—high school sweethearts—and still were growing up together when I went into the Marines. Then I started deploying, and the time we actually spent together became less and less." No matter what mood he was in, no matter who he was talking about, when mention of his time in the military came up, the dull pain in his hip pulsed. Liam fought the urge to readjust in his seat. "I was in an accident on my last deployment and had to come home. That time helped us realize that life for both of us had changed while I was away. We weren't the same kids we were in high school. Though we did try to say together. It just turned into the two of us being unhappy all the time. We divorced after eight years. It was the best option for us."

He smiled as he parked the truck.

He meant it.

"We still keep in touch and wish each other happy birthday and catch up occasionally," he added. "She's remarried to a good guy and they have a little boy and another on the way. It isn't what we thought would happen for us when we first married, but we've already agreed we wouldn't change a thing. We're where we are meant to be now."

It was true, all of it. He wouldn't take away his marriage or the divorce. Both led him to Seven Roads and the driver's seat right next to Blake. He couldn't be mad at that now, could he?

He cut the engine, thinking the topic was well and done, and turned to go over their plan one more time for meeting Missy's ex.

It was wholly a shock to, instead, find Blake already in motion.

She closed the space between them in one fluid movement.

Her lips were warm.

Chapter Seventeen

News of their attack had made it around Seven Roads but, apparently, had a few key facts omitted in the retelling. The first was who exactly it was who broke into the house. Sure, word had gotten caught in the rumor mill nets that Ray and Mater had gone to the hospital, but as for the third and fourth unknown men who had attacked, no one spoke of them.

Blake wondered belatedly if that had been due to Liam's constant low-voice talking he had been doing to everyone who had stepped onto the scene that morning. Or maybe it was fear. There hadn't been an outpouring of violence like this in a long while in town. Maybe they didn't want to incur the unknown men's wrath by idly chatting about them.

Either way, it was perhaps the second piece of information that was absent that really surprised Blake.

No one seemed to know that Liam had been with her.

That was apparent in how Corrie greeted them as they walked into the coffee shop. She side-eyed Blake while motioning to a separate table for Liam.

Her face was wholly shocked when he shook his head and declined.

"I'm with her," he said simply.

Corrie's eyes went wide. Blake's nearly did too.

Heat started to whirl in her belly. Damn that baritone.

Though, could she really only blame the octave of his voice for making her have to fight a blush?

Blake didn't need to have a good memory to recall the fact that no more than two minutes ago, she had kissed the sheriff in the front seat of his truck like they were teens parking. She hadn't lingered as long though. As quickly as she had moved to him, as quickly as she had felt the soft strength of him, smelled some kind of spice on him, heard his breath momentarily pause, Blake had ended the kiss.

Then, as if she had reverted right past that confident teen making out in a parked car mindset, she had settled on an awkward resolution.

Pretend it didn't happen while not addressing it at all.

She'd broken the kiss and then coughed.

Then said, "Let's go."

And, to his credit, Liam had.

Now he stood firm at her side until Corrie redirected her open hands to one of the tables against the window. Instead of following her suggestion, however, Blake felt his hand on the small of her back.

"We'll sit over there instead, thanks."

Blake let herself be guided to a table in the corner of the room with a good sightline to all entrances and exits. She would be lying if she said she didn't enjoy Corrie's dumbfounded expression as they walked around her.

There wasn't time to talk, or not talk, about their kiss as Blake settled into a chair. Liam left her to go to the main counter to order, and no sooner had he done that, a man with golden floppy hair and a too-wide smile came into the coffee shop.

Kyle Langdon, Missy Clearwater's ex-boyfriend.

Like she couldn't deny seeing Corrie baffled by Liam wanting to be next to her, there was no denying that Kyle heard the news about the attack.

He was barely holding it together as he took the seat opposite Blake. He didn't even notice Liam or Corrie at the counter.

Which was good. That way he wouldn't leave before she could start prying.

"Are you okay?" Kyle said. He had those big doe eyes and they suited him nicely. He was handsome and, she'd bet, charming. The stereotypical image of a good old Southern fraternity brother who went to the beach for spring break and wore the same shirt for every football game his team played.

Blake smiled into his concern.

"Bad news travels fast, I see. But I'm good. I just needed a change of scenery, is all."

She motioned to the room around them. Kyle's eyes were glued to hers.

"I bet! I couldn't believe it when I heard, and then you texted me to reschedule? I really couldn't believe something like that happened here in town."

Blake had already suspected that Kyle would hear the news and, with it, would figure out who she was with all the additional town talk through the years. Kyle, however, went in a different direction.

"If I knew you were Beth's sister, I would have been way chattier when we first met."

Blake, who had been at the ready to pepper in questions that would lead to Missy and her life right before her death, stalled. She'd been 100 percent focused on a Missy conversation. Talk of her sister hadn't even been on her radar.

"Beth? You knew my sister?"

The Bennet family had never been a simple one. Their go-to family move was to leave after all. Their mother, Blake, Beth's husband, and then their dad after Beth's death. Even Beth had found a way to go, though she hadn't intended to.

There had been a lot of time between Blake's exit and Beth's, and logically, Blake had known that.

But, sitting across the table from the smiling man, Blake finally understood that space. She had no idea if Kyle Langdon knew her sister. She had no idea if they had been friends. If they had passed each other on the streets every day or went to the same church. If they only knew of each other or if they had gone to a party or two as friends.

And it wasn't just Kyle.

The last time Blake had spoken to Beth about her life and not just updating her about her own, they had been texting. Beth was trying to remember a song but hadn't known enough of the words to search it. So she'd sent a voice message to Blake humming it poorly. Yet Blake had gotten it and answered correctly. Beth had been excited and said thanks.

Remember to eat something yummy was the last text she got back from Beth after.

Then, a month later, Beth was gone.

Blake might have known the song, but she was faced with an awful coldness of realization now.

She had already lost her sister before she had even died.

Kyle, however, didn't have a clue in the world about the emotional turmoil Blake had just found herself in. He nodded to her question with enthusiasm.

"Of course I knew Beth," he said. "I was there when she tore Mr. Grant a new one."

"Tore Mr. Grant a new one?" she repeated.

Kyle nodded deep.

"We couldn't believe it, you know, the factory workers in that section," he said. "I've been at the steel mill since high school and never seen someone even raise their voice at Mr. Grant, and there she was with a red face and so loud."

Blake was stunned.

"What was she yelling about?"

Kyle still hadn't caught on that he had, once again, thrown her for an emotional loop.

He shrugged.

"I couldn't hear the specifics, but I think he turned down one of her suggestions for something to do with the furnaces. But to be fair, he gets a lot of suggestions from safety advisors so—"

"When did this fight happen?" Blake interrupted. Her voice had raised but she couldn't help it. Kyle's eyebrows went higher with it. He looked like he was finally realizing that he had said something that bothered her.

"Uh, she never really came to the steel mill unless she was working, so I guess that was around..." He let his words trail off. His eyes widened. "Oh, man. I'm sorry. I didn't think—"

The chair scraped against the tile as Blake pushed it back and stood. She crossed the room in one fluid movement, only pausing at the counter for one question.

"Is Cassandra in the back?"

Corrie had a coffee cup stopped midair between her and Liam.

She nodded.

"She's on a call—"

Blake kept moving, eyes on the hallway that led to the office.

She heard Liam ask after her, but there was no stopping her.

Blake flung open the manager's office door and closed it right back behind her once inside. Cassandra was indeed on the phone, but Blake took it from her and slammed it down on the cradle to hang up.

Cassandra seemed rightly angry, but Blake spoke over any and all questions and concerns.

"Why didn't you tell me that Beth fought with Mr. Grant before she died?"

Cassandra took the words and spat back a question with just as much heat.

"What the heck do you mean?"

Blake pointed in the direction of the main room behind her.

"Kyle Langdon said he saw Beth yelling at Mr. Grant at the steel mill and Beth only went there twice in the last year. Once to do the inspection on the furnaces and the day she died. How come I didn't hear about the fight? You had to have known!"

She was so angry. So heated. Her hands shook, her heartbeat sped.

Had the fight been the reason Beth had been speeding? Had it distracted her and led to the accident that killed her?

Why hadn't a town that thrived on gossip not spread that tidbit around?

And why was it making her so angry?

And why was *that* making Cassandra so angry right on back?

The other woman stood so fast her chair fell over behind her.

"Do you think just because I run a coffee shop that I get every piece of news that this town has to give?" she countered. "Do you think that everyone in this town runs to *me* like I'm a bartender and tells me everything?"

"Yes!"

Cassandra stood firm.

"No!" she exclaimed. "They don't. I had no idea that Beth fought with Mr. Grant, and even if I had, it's not like I know to tell you every single little detail. Who do you think you are and who do you think *I* am? I mean, is that what you and your sheriff think of me? Do you really think I need to tell you every little piece of information I hear? Every little detail? And even if I did, am I supposed to remember everything I see and hear?"

Blake had apparently hit a nerve. Cassandra was fuming. She walked around the desk, anger in every movement.

"The last time you two barged in here, I was nice," she continued. "I was polite. I told you about Missy, about her mood, her personality, her laptop with the little panda sticker, what I thought about her death, and did all of that without anyone forcing my hand. Now you come in here, hanging up my phone to vent to me about—"

"Panda sticker?" Blake interrupted.

Cassandra looked ready to fight even harder at the rudeness but stopped. She must have noticed the shift in Blake's tone.

"Yeah. Missy's laptop had a little panda sticker on it," she said a moment later. "I only noticed it because it was covering the logo."

Blake's mind stalled for the second time since walking into the coffee shop. She didn't explain to the second person either what had caused it.

She turned on her heel and went back out into the hallway. Cassandra's footsteps hurried behind her.

"You're just going to yell at me and leave?" she asked. "Why? What's wrong?"

Blake didn't answer her. She didn't answer Corrie's questioning look from behind the counter either. There were only two people she acknowledged.

"Sorry, I'm going to have to cancel this time," she told Kyle, his face nothing but confused. She didn't wait around to explain more.

Instead, the second person she acknowledged came to her side without a word.

Liam followed her to the truck and had it started, no explanation needed. Even when Blake asked for him to drive them to her house, he did so without follow-up.

There was police tape still across the back door, but it

had been repaired, so it was still locked when they searched the house to make sure no one was inside. Then Blake went with purpose to the guest bedroom that used to be her sister's study.

She went to the desk, took a key from the top drawer and unlocked the side bottom one with it. She set her eyes on a panda sticker covering a logo.

Before she did anything, she finally gave Liam an explanation.

"After going through all the paperwork and legal things it took to adopt the kids, to take over the house and to sort out her life insurance and get my head around all the new bills, accounts and leftover debt, I let the easier stuff rest." Blake waved a hand through the air. "This room became where I put things I wanted to look at more closely when life settled down. A few months ago, I had a burst of inspiration and decided to come in and finally start combing through Beth's things and boxing up what I wanted to save and donating what I thought she would be okay with."

She reached into the bottom drawer and put the object she was aiming for on the desktop.

Her finger traced the panda sticker on the laptop's cover.

"Cassandra said that Missy's laptop had this same sticker covering the logo. I'd almost feel like waving it off as a coincidence, but *this* particular sticker is a one of a kind. I know because Beth sent me a picture of it after she made it. For *her* laptop."

"Her laptop," Liam repeated.

Blake nodded.

"A few months ago I came in here and the laptop wasn't where I remembered putting it," she said. "I thought maybe I had just been distracted last time, but now I think it definitely had been moved. That would have been around the time Missy died. She—or someone else—could have put it back before her death."

Blake clapped, finally having two pieces of their very confusing puzzle attach.

"We've been having a hard time finding Missy's laptop because it wasn't hers to begin with."

Liam's voice was low, and it rumbled deep. If she hadn't already come to the same conclusion, she would have gotten chills at the new turn of events.

"The laptop we've been looking for was Beth's."

Blake nodded again.

"And whatever is on it was important enough that Missy must have been sneaking around here the day she died, and who else knows when."

Liam came around to her side. He looked down at the electronic as if it might answer.

"But why? What's the connection between Missy and Beth?"

Blake hadn't had the mental space yet to really think about that. Had there been any crossover between Missy and Beth? Just like Kyle, Blake felt the discrepancy between what she should have known and what she did know about her sister.

"I didn't even know Missy," Blake thought out loud. "Other than what was in the papers or Lola told me. Which was about her death and the accident—"

"The accident at the steel mill," Liam interrupted, "where, according to Theo, Missy's friend Hector Martinez was almost killed by the furnaces overheating."

Adrenaline surged through Blake's entire being.

"Which is the accident that Beth investigated. Kyle just told me that Beth had a loud fight with Mr. Grant at the steel mill about some safety suggestions regarding the furnaces. Her car accident happened after she left that day. Everyone assumed she had gone to the steel mill that day to finish some paperwork. I never heard that she talked to—let alone yelled at—Mr. Grant."

Blake's mind was spinning.

She whipped her head up to stare into his eyes.

"What if that's what Missy was doing with the laptop? What if Missy was looking into Hector's accident? What if that's what actually caused her death? And, if any of that's true, what does that mean about Beth? Did she find something she shouldn't have during her investigation at the steel mill? And if she did, does that mean that her death wasn't an accident either?"

Had someone killed Beth to keep her quiet?

Had the same someone killed Missy?

Blake didn't know when it happened, but Liam's hand was over hers. The pressure felt grounding in a way.

His words even more so.

"Don't worry. No matter what, I'm going to take care of this."

Chapter Eighteen

The laptop didn't appear to have anything of note on it. At least none that were accessible to them. Half of the files were locked and encrypted and fell under the name of Beth's former job. Though none of them were labeled as Grayton Steel Mill.

"From what the press release after Hector Martinez's accident said, it was caused by human error," Blake had said, not for the first time since they had gone through Beth's laptop. They had also paid more attention to the details of Beth's former office, looking through materials Blake had yet to organize.

Liam had never really known Beth Bennet, but he got the feeling that she had been against bringing her work home with her. They had only found a few papers that seemed to be work-related. The rest were mailer odds and ends and things pertaining to the kids.

"A claim that Hector didn't dispute," Liam pointed out. "Not even his mother who took him with her back up north tried to make anyone believe otherwise."

Blake was still staring at the laptop.

They had been at it for over an hour since arriving at the house. In that time Blake had seemed to settle a little. Or had at least started masking all the emotions she must have been going through better than she had.

Liam didn't want her to have to hide anything from him, but he also understood that sometimes you needed time to process new information, and usually, that was easier with a clear head. Even if you had to temporarily force it clear to get there.

"But for Beth to publicly scold Mr. Grant?" Blake shook her head. "There must have been something that upset her about what she found during her investigation into the furnaces. She wasn't the type to just fly off the handle, especially not at a man like Mr. Grant. He holds more weight in this town than the mayor or the—" She stopped short.

Liam snorted.

"Or the sheriff," he finished. "Believe me, I may not be a true local, but I know the social standings of everyone. If Missy's dad has a loyal following for his old tractor supply business, the man who employs half of the town is close to God."

She nodded.

"Small towns give you a run for your money, that's for sure."

They had already gotten caught in the same questions before, just as they had with questions about Missy.

Why had Missy had Beth Bennet's laptop the day of her death? Had she broken into the Bennet home to get it? But then, if she had, why return it?

And did all roads lead back to the steel mill?

Liam ran a hand down his face, then stood. He extended his hand back down to where Blake was sitting. He had her on her feet in a blink.

"We need answers, so let's ask the right people questions," he said. "Looks like we're going to the steel mill."

THE PLAN SEEMED SIMPLE, but it took two hours on the phone to get an appointment set up to speak to Mr. Grant himself the next day. And even though Liam wanted to be the one taking the job on, it was Blake who ended up making the plans.

"Mr. Grant will see me faster than he will you," she had explained before calling. "He knows my father and I can play the sympathy card too. I'll just say I found something about my sister's investigation there and had some questions. He'll have to see me one way or the other."

And that's exactly what had happened.

Mr. Grant's assistant had confirmed the appointment for the next afternoon at his office. Like meeting with Kyle, Liam hadn't liked the idea of her going alone.

To which she had responded with a slight teasing to her tone.

"You're coming too, so don't worry about that. We just need to figure out how to get you in there without making anyone clam up."

That had been on his mind too but shifted to the back burner as day turned to night. They returned to Price's house and Liam relieved him. They spoke at the car after dinner was finished and before he left.

"Darius is still working on getting that guy with the baseball cap that y'all caught at the house to talk," he updated him. "He has a lawyer though and isn't budging. Then there's the whole Mater situation. Ray too."

Ray McClennan had flatlined twice and was still in the ICU. Mater was still in the hospital but wasn't saying a word either. Liam didn't like their only lead being the steel mill, but as the shadows of night grew darker, he couldn't think of another way to get an answer. At the very least, they could cross off some of their new questions.

Liam was still going over those questions as he took a new change of clothes into the guest bathroom downstairs when soft footsteps sounded in the hallway. He peeked his head out to see Blake shuffling across the hardwoods toward him.

Since meeting the woman, he had been aware of her—from the lobby of the high school to the coffee shop to the department to her home to his apartment—but now it was like every sense Liam had went on a higher alert.

Her hair was wet from the shower she had taken after supper. It made the normal red into a dark heat, waving to the tops of her shirt and making the fabric darker too for it. Her shirt was oversized and swallowed her body all the way to her thighs. He could just make out the bottom of some shorts but only barely so. Then those legs were free and clear until the pair of socks that were helping her slide so quietly along the floor.

She had no make-up on. No lip anything.

Those lips.

They still hadn't talked about the kiss from earlier that day.

He wasn't going to bring it up now.

Blake had the baby monitor in her hand.

She shook it in the air a little when she met his eye.

"Unlike the three of them up there, I can't sleep," she said, voice low. "I was coming down to see if you wanted to chat."

Blake eyed the clothes in his hand.

"Oh, you're going *into* the shower. Not out." Her face fell. "I can wait. Or, well, I guess you might want to get some sleep, so maybe I'll just talk to you tomorrow."

Maybe it was because of that kiss that they weren't talking about, or maybe it was because, in that moment, something happened that had never happened before.

Blake Bennet looked lost.

Holding a baby monitor in her pajamas, hair wet, and wanting to talk, Blake looked tired and lonely and restless. It was a combination that Liam knew well. She wanted someone next to her.

And Liam wanted to be that person for her.

So he reached out and took her hand, pulled her gently with him into the bathroom and then shut the door behind them.

BLAKE WAS HOLDING on to the baby monitor like it was a lifesaver and she had just been thrown into the sea without a hope of treading water.

Liam locked the bathroom door and put his folded clothes on top of the closed toilet seat. Then, like it was the most natural thing in the world, he reached past the shower curtain along the opposite wall and turned on the water.

When he turned back around to face her, Blake knew her face was the color of a stop sign.

He smirked. He pointed to the counter next to the sink.

"As long as you don't peek, you can sit there and we can chat while I shower," he said. "I wouldn't mind the company, if I'm being honest. It'll be nice to get out of my head for a little bit."

Blake opened her mouth. Then closed it. Then opened it again.

She didn't hate the idea, but was it appropriate?

You already kissed him earlier, what's talking to him in the bathroom? It's not like you'll be in the shower with him.

Her internal battle ended quickly.

She pretended to think about it a little longer, though, before making a big show of relenting.

"I guess we've already been through a firefight together," she said. "What's talking in the bathroom compared to that?"

Liam waited to undress after Blake settled on top of the counter. She closed her eyes just in time to see his shirt flutter to the ground. Her face went all flames at the sound of the rest of his clothes hitting the floor. She kept her eyes tight until the shower curtain moved twice. Even then she didn't open them all the way until he called out to her.

"You're safe."

Blake let out a little breath she had been holding and positioned the baby monitor so she could see it without holding on to it. She double-checked that her side was on Mute, and the other side was on Loud. They had brought the travel basinet for Bruce, so Lola and Clem were on the bed beside it, all three fast asleep. Blake envied their ability to sleep that easily. She had tossed and turned until she had needed to escape.

Though, did it count as escape if she had gotten out of bed with Liam in mind?

Running toward someone was its own plan after all.

"I was worried me walking around had woken you up," Liam said from the other side of the shower curtain. Blake glanced at it. She couldn't even see his silhouette. It would be a bold-faced lie if she pretended that didn't annoy her a little. "The only person I usually have to worry about waking up is Theo, and that boy can sleep through a bomb blast, I'm pretty sure. He's still upset that I wouldn't let him come stay with us, by the way. He said he's more than ready to fight if he needs to. I told him that's not needed."

Blake had originally wanted to talk more about their investigation but found her curiosity of the man overriding that never-ending circle of questions.

"You two must be close. He said you're like a babysitter to him?"

The sound of water shifted. Liam must have moved out of its spray a little.

"Yes and no," he said. "The first time I met him was in the middle of a really nasty storm. His mom was out of town, and he lost his key and was huddled in the stairwell, scared out of his mind. I let him come to my place to wait out the storm. Almost two years later, and now he's at my place, eating my food, come rain or shine." Before Blake could ask about his parents, Liam added the answer on. "His dad passed away when he was a baby, and his mom remarried a guy who travels for work a lot and doesn't really like kids. His mom asked me to look after him one time, and after I said I would, she kind of stopped coming home regularly. It's kind of an unspoken thing that he can come and go as he likes. Just like it's an unspoken thing that he has to show me his grades, do chores, and stay out of trouble, or else." Liam laughed. "The first time I grounded him from TV because of his math grades was the last time he brought home bad math grades."

Blake smiled.

"Who knew the cold sheriff of Seven Roads had such a caring side?"

Liam snorted loud enough to be heard above the shower.

"Nice gossip travels slow, I suppose. It's much more fun to speculate about my divorce and lack of friends."

She nodded to that, though he couldn't see it.

"Lola said it's like hearing tires screech in the distance and waiting for the crash. Only to be kind of disappointed when it doesn't happen. Humans like a little chaos."

The sound of the water shifting let Blake know Liam was doing something different. She kicked her feet a little in the air and tried to keep her mind out of his space. A feat made easier by his next question.

"Speaking of Lola, you said she was your stepmom, right?"

Blake knew where this was going. It was touching in itself that Liam had held off bringing it up as long as he had.

"Yeah, she married my dad about ten years ago. They dated for a year or so before that. I didn't really know her all that well until I came back to Seven Roads." There was a silence. Blake addressed it with a chuckle. "Let me guess, you're trying to find a nice way to ask why she lives with us but my dad doesn't."

The sound of water shifted again.

"You got me," he admitted. He was quick to add on, "But you don't have to answer if you don't want to. It's not my business."

"As someone who is talking to you while you shower, I think we're past you not being a part of my business." It was meant to come off as a joke, but Blake faltered after saying it.

Would it really bother her for Liam to know this truth? One she hadn't told anyone ever before? One she hadn't *wanted* to tell anyone ever?

It wouldn't, she realized.

"When I was younger, my mom left," she started. "But even before that, I can't ever remember her and my dad getting along all that well. I think that's why he seemed to prefer Beth over me. I was, or am, my mom's twin. A carbon copy of her lookswise and, apparently, in the ways that we're stubborn." Blake sat up straighter. The wall was uncomfortable behind her but she made do.

"Dad and I butted heads a lot after that, but I thought that was pretty normal for single dads and their teenage daughters. But then the Mater thing happened, it was like it broke whatever was keeping the peace between us." Blake didn't say so, but she could never forget the way her father looked at her when he accused her of not knowing what loyalty meant. Still, at thirty-five, it made her heart upset a little. "I didn't stick around long after that. I wasn't even sure what I wanted to do in life when I left but eventually realized that the entire ordeal with Mater actually inspired me too. Out of everything that had happened, Sheriff Dean left an impression. Before I knew it, that was my goal. Fighting for justice with a badge on my chest."

She continued. "Dad, though, saw it as me rubbing salt in our old wound. I only saw him on holidays when I came home, and we both knew that was just to see Beth. As the years went by that became okay for me. I saw Beth, and after

Dad married Lola, she'd reach out for him. That was enough for me. But then Beth passed away."

Blake looked down at her hands.

She felt wholly uncomfortable at the next part. Like getting pricked by several cactus needles but not knowing which one to take out first.

"When I first came back to deal with the funeral, Dad told me that life wasn't fair in taking her away. That she was the sweet one. The kind one. But me? I was the one in law enforcement, risking my life every day, dealing with violence. I was the one who didn't have a husband or kids. But Beth? It wasn't fair that the wrong daughter had died." Blake rubbed at her finger, eyes unfocused at the memory. "It wasn't fun to hear, but I agreed. I'd pick Beth to live too. Plus, this man had just lost his favorite kid. He could yell at me all he wanted, and I couldn't be mad, right? And then when he said it again after the funeral, I still believed that grief was powerful, and I only had to endure it for a while until he could get out of the shock of it all. I even held on to that belief when he said it again after I moved into Beth's house to take care of the kids."

Blake stopped rubbing her hand.

Her vision blurred a little.

She was embarrassed at the tears that threatened to come, but for some reason, she felt like she had to finish the story for him. So she did.

"But then one day, Lola showed up. She had two suitcases, and my dad was nowhere to be seen. I knew it then, without her saying a word, what that meant. Dad wasn't just talking because he was hurt. He meant what he said. He wished it was me who had died, not Beth, and no matter how he looked at it, he couldn't get past it." Blake watched as a tear hit her leg. She was seeing Lola though. Standing at the end of the driveway, looking a world of sorry for her. "Lola never said it. Not out loud. She's kind like that. Instead, she asked if she could stay with us to help for a while, and when I tried to turn her away, she just walked past me and went inside. She hasn't left my side since, and my dad hasn't shown up either."

Blake laughed.

"For a family who's good at leaving each other, it sure hits different when outsiders just decide to stay. That's why—"

She hadn't heard the water stop or the shower curtain move to the side.

She hadn't seen him get out or wrap the towel around his waist.

She hadn't seen or heard him move to the spot right in front of her.

Blake, however, felt Liam's hand cup the side of her face and gently move her gaze up to his.

And for the kiss he pressed against her lips right after? Everything else in the world disappeared in an instant.

Then there was just Liam Weaver.

Chapter Nineteen

Liam pulled her to the edge of the counter, closer to him. It forced her legs to make a choice—block him or accommodate him. Blake chose the latter.

She wrapped her legs around him and his towel so there was no space left between them. Not that there was any to begin with up top.

Liam's kiss had lost its surprise. Now it had given way to something else.

Something heated.

Blake opened her mouth to let him in and Liam gladly accepted the invite. His tongue swiped inside as one of his hands tangled up into the back of her hair. He lightly pulled so her head tilted back. It made it easier to consume her that way, she decided. Because even with her up on the counter and him standing, his impressive height was still very much there.

Much like what she had felt that morning when she had been the one to kiss him.

She wanted him.

She didn't know why exactly, but she did.

She *wanted* him.

And she wanted him to want her.

Which she now knew, considering she could feel him through his towel, the desire was mutual.

With one arm fastening her against him and the other hand holding her head, Blake decided to do some positioning of her own. She let her hands blindly explore the wet body of the man against her, trailing his chest and back until she decided that it wasn't fair that he was the only one so exposed.

Blake pushed against him hard enough to let him know she wanted to stop.

Maybe it was too hard.

Liam not only stopped; he took two steps away from her.

His lips were red and swollen, his face was flushed, his expression was turning to apologetic.

"I—I'm sorry," he said uneasily. "I just think you're the most incredible woman I've ever met, and it was driving me crazy not to—"

He cut himself off, stopping amid his frazzled statement.

Probably because Blake had just thrown her shirt off from over her head and tossed it on the floor.

For a moment, Liam reminded her of a teenage boy. His eyes dropped dramatically, landing on her bra. That gaze didn't flinch as she undid said bra and let it hit the floor too.

"Turn the shower back on," she ordered, breathless but proudly still in control. "Then prove to me how incredible you think I am."

That shy, inexperienced teenager facade absolutely died on spot.

Liam was nothing but all man as he whirled around, turned the water on, and then came back to her. His lips crashed into hers while his hands did work.

One steadied her, the other slid beneath her shorts and underwear and expertly pulled both down in another fluid movement. No sooner were they on the floor than his towel joined them.

Then it was just Blake and Liam pressed against each other with nothing in between.

Still, Blake wanted to explore.

Liam was now the accommodating one.

With one arm, he helped guide her into the shower, not once breaking their stride. The back wall of it was cool to the touch, the water above them was warm.

When Liam finally made his way inside of her, Blake felt nothing but blessed heat.

By the time they left the shower, the water had long turned cold.

HIS HIP HURT.

Liam didn't mind. The pressure against his leg in the dark more than made up for any discomfort. Blake's even breathing let him know that she was still asleep. She seemed to be comfortable too. Her leg and arm were thrown across his and his chest. Her head was on her pillow, but her hair was fanned across his shoulder.

He smelled his own shampoo on it.

He couldn't help but smile at that.

The sun hadn't yet risen, and the only small source of light was coming from the baby monitor on the nightstand next to him. He wondered if someone on that end had been what had woken him, but a quick look showed that all three people, young and old, were still asleep in the room next door.

He started to wonder if he'd simply just woken when a noise pulled his attention farther across the nightstand.

It was his phone.

Someone was calling him.

Liam picked the phone up off the table so the vibrating wouldn't wake Blake. With as much care as he could, he detangled from the sleeping woman and hurried downstairs. By the time he was confident he hadn't woken anyone, the call went to voicemail. Instead of checking it, he called the number right back.

Price answered on the first ring.

"Sorry if I woke you, Sheriff," he said in greeting. "But I think we might need you."

Liam glanced at the time on his phone. It was just after four.

"What happened?"

The sound of movement shifted between them before he responded.

"A few minutes ago, there was a shooting at the hospital. Ray McClennan is dead."

Liam was wide awake now.

"What?"

"There were no other causalities or injuries. The guy walked into the ICU and shot Ray quick. Then he rabbited before the security guards on duty could do a thing. Now the whole hospital is a mess."

Liam was walking back up the stairs but kept his voice low.

"Any idea who the shooter was?"

"Deputy Little is on scene and said that so far, she can't find anything that identifies him. Getting a statement from the staff is kind of chaotic too. Before he bolted, the gunman made a mess of the ICU. I can head there now or do you want me to—"

"Come here and watch the house," Liam finished for him. "If Ray was targeted, I want to see by who, but I'm not leaving this place unprotected."

If he was abusing his power to use one of his deputies as protection for Blake, he didn't care. Price must not have either. He agreed and said he would be there soon.

The call ended just as Liam was thinking about where he had left his work clothes. He found them when the lamp next to the bed flicked on. There was a pillow imprint on the side of Blake's face. However, her eyes were sharp.

There was no reason or need to withhold the truth from her, so Liam bowled right in with it.

"There was a shooting at the hospital. Ray McClennan is dead. I need to go help with the aftermath and manhunt. Price is on his way here until I can come back. I'll have my phone on me, but if you can't get a hold of me for whatever reason, Price will help find me."

Blake was quick.

She was out of bed in a flash. To his surprise it was to hand him his shirt.

"I'll make you a quick cup of coffee. Price too." She was absolute speed-pulling on her own jeans and hurrying out of the room.

It wasn't until he was fully dressed and downstairs that he took a moment to think about the night before.

After they had shared more than a few moments in the shower, they had settled into the bed in a contented quiet. They hadn't yet talked about the two of them. About what their time together then meant for the future. If the stress of everything had made them impulsive. If, when they finished with the investigation and the need for close proximity ended, they would still want to be close to each other.

They didn't talk at all.

They just slept, holding on to each other.

Now didn't seem like the right time to talk about it either. So they didn't.

Blake handed him a coffee and told him to be safe.

Price showed up soon after, and together they told Liam not to worry.

Yet, as he drove away from the little house, now all lit up, he couldn't help but feel a new weight pressing down hard against his chest.

He didn't want to leave them.

And, only later in hindsight would he realize that he shouldn't have.

THERE WAS A lot of movement at the hospital. That didn't slow once the sun came up, and it didn't slow by the time shift change happened. Liam became the man in charge at the scene and directed his deputies in a search for the gunman. Then he helped Darius Williams speak to Ray's mother.

Doc Ernest helped her when she broke down in tears.

Ray's father was absent.

The security footage didn't help anyone. The man wore a mask, had been fast, and had known exactly where he was going.

"He targeted Ray," Liam had said to Darius while both standing outside of the security room.

The detective had nodded.

"Now I think we might know why our dear Glenn isn't saying a word," Detective Williams said.

Glenn Lowell had been the man in the baseball cap who had broken into Blake's home. Although he had finally given up his name, he had refused to explain anything else. Considering he was from a small town in Alabama and seemingly had no connection to anyone involved, his presence was still a mystery. One that now he might be more inclined to keep unsolved.

"It could be the fourth guy, the bald man in the rain jacket, tying up loose ends," Darius had added. "Ray didn't have any law attached to his bed because of the state he was in. Mater had Deputy Little outside of his room. So maybe he went for the easier target."

Still, it didn't sit quite right for Liam.

"Killing him seems like an extreme consequence, but for

what?" Liam had asked. "The chance that they might talk about their plan for why they broke into the Bennet house?"

Darius had shrugged.

He still didn't know the whole story or about the laptop connecting Missy and Beth together. Liam was about to let him in when Liam was called to the hospital front desk.

He went there, for a moment thinking it might be Blake, when instead he was met with a stone-faced and determined teenaged boy.

The boy didn't waste any time.

"I need to talk to you," he said. "In private."

Liam quirked an eyebrow.

"And who are you?"

The teen lifted his chin a little. Liam noticed his eyes were a little swollen.

"My name's Cooper. Cooper Han."

Liam did the mental math fast. He was the best friend of Chase McClennan.

"I need to talk to you," Cooper said again. "Now, please."

Liam said okay and directed them to the closest, most private area they could find. They sat on either side of a small table next to a cluster of vending machines. Liam could tell the boy was serious, but he could also tell he was nervous.

Still, the nerves didn't win.

He got straight to the point.

"I hid Chase McClennan away, and I'm not telling anyone where he is until you arrest the man who killed Ray and the man who told him to do it."

Liam was gobsmacked.

"Come again?"

Cooper didn't back down.

"While Chase made a mistake listening to Ray during the car chase, nothing that has happened has been his fault," he said. "He just fell into his cousin's problems and didn't know how to get out. So I decided to take him out of all of this until all you professionals get it fixed. You can't see or talk to him until I know it's safe."

A part of Liam admired the conviction and obvious care. The other part, the sheriff taking the demands of a teen without any background information, wanted more to go on.

"The car chase? When you say he fell into Ray's problems, what do you mean? Does Chase know who killed Ray? And you said there's someone else behind that gunman? Does Chase know who?"

Despite his nerves, Cooper seemed to have come prepared for the questions.

"Ray was the one with all of the answers, Chase doesn't know anything."

Liam tilted his head to the side a little in disbelief.

"Then why would he be in danger if he doesn't know anything? Because, to me, it seems like Chase and Ray shared some anger, and that anger somehow got to me and maybe even one of my friends. Now that anger has led to a murder and I'm still trying to put all the pieces together to make sure nothing else bad happens. How can I do that? How can I protect anyone if I don't even know who I'm protecting them from?"

This question stumped the boy. His brow knitted together, he bit at his bottom lip. Then, that resolution that had demanded the sheriff to do his job all at once disappeared.

Cooper balled his fists and squeezed his eyes shut. His words came out quick but clear.

"Chase isn't the one who knows anything. It's me. I'm the one who told him about the code, and Ray's the one who overheard me do it. I'm the one who started this. I'm the one who—"

Liam froze.

His question didn't.

"The code?" he interrupted. "What code?"

Cooper opened his eyes. He looked pained again, but his answer was as clear as day.

"The code that I gave to Missy before she died."

Chapter Twenty

Price was upset. He made that clear. Blake made it even clearer that she wasn't going to lose her chance to get some answers.

"Listen, this isn't my first rodeo," she told him, swinging into the open car door. "I'm Sheriff Trouble remember? I should be able to handle talking to Mr. Grant senior."

Price wasn't so sure.

Just as he hadn't been sure the first time she had told him she had received the call from Mr. Grant's assistant that the meeting needed to be moved up or canceled until further notice.

"At least let me touch base with the sheriff first," he said, not for the first time. "I gave him my word that I'd keep the house safe, and now part of that house is leaving by herself. Let me just call Darius and see if he can't find him."

Blake rolled her eyes.

"Listen, Price, I appreciate the concern. So much so that I'm going to skip over the fact that it feels like you need his permission to let *me* do what I want and instead ask you very sweetly to continue keeping my family safe." She motioned to the car. "This is the only thing I can do for my family right now—try to get some answers—so let me go before I'm late and the almighty Mr. Grant decides he doesn't want to talk anymore."

Price looked like he wanted to keep arguing.

He also looked like he understood it was pointless.

Sheriff Trouble, who he had initially admired, had her mind made up. And, what's more, Lola had already backed her up once Blake had told her the entire truth about everything they had learned over the last week or so. With two fierce women going against him, he had little room to do anything other than protest.

"Keep your phone on," he finally said, relenting. "If anything feels off or weird, call immediately. And I'll track the sheriff down while you do it. So don't be surprised if he shows up grumpy that you left without him."

"Understood."

AND THAT WAS how Blake found herself alone at the steel mill.

Grayton Steel Mill was on the largest plot of commercial land that Seven Roads had to offer. It was a collection of warehouses, offices, storage rooms and production lines that expanded such a distance that some workers used buggies to drive around from place to place. The main office was the largest office buildings, mainly due to the cafeteria housed inside and the second floor corporate offices.

It was on that second floor that Mr. Grant was waiting for her.

Blake parked, made sure her phone's ringer was on loud, and struck out across the parking lot. As she walked, she hoped Liam was okay. She knew all too well how stressful the job could be, never mind when it came to a case that had personally touched you. That was another reason Blake wanted to get this over with.

She wanted answers for herself, Beth and Missy.

She also wanted them for Liam.

He had been targeted, he had been hurt, and Blake didn't want that to happen again.

Not to her man.

Her face heated a little at the last thought. It had sprung up so suddenly she didn't know how to dissect it.

Thankfully, she was distracted away from it.

Someone was calling her name. Or, rather, an old name.

"Sheriff Bennet!"

Blake turned to see a surprising face running up to meet her.

"Theo?"

Theo was wearing coveralls and a name tag. He was smiling ear to ear.

"What are you doing here?" he asked. He made a show of looking behind her. "Is Liam with you? I heard about the shooting at the hospital, but he didn't answer when I called."

"He's still there working, I think. I'm here to talk to Mr. Grant. We have an appointment. Why are *you* here?"

Theo tapped his name tag.

"I have a part-time job in the cafeteria. I usually work the weekend shifts. You caught me on my lunch break. I was just about to head out." His smile brightened even more. "Here, I'll take you up to his office. I've been there a few times before, delivering meals."

Blake accepted the help simply because, of all of the places she had been in Seven Roads, Mr. Grant's office had never been one of them.

"I didn't even know Mr. Grant was in today," he said as they walked. "He must have parked in the private lot behind the building. Him and his son are the only ones who really use that though. It floods something wicked when it rains."

"So, his son, Elijah, does actually work a lot, huh?" she asked. "I heard he's won over workers because he pulls his weight."

They had entered the lobby, so Theo lowered his voice. Though his snort was easy to hear.

"He works, yeah, but Elijah Grant walks around this place like he's some kind of god when his dad isn't around. You should feel the vibe of the workers in the cafeteria when he's nearby versus when he's not. A total mood shift."

He led them up some stairs to a second smaller lobby. There was no one behind the desk, but Theo went to check it anyway.

"Are you sure you're supposed to meet Mr. Grant today?" he asked. "I know sometimes he'll work during the weekend shifts, but it doesn't look like Rhonda's here. She's his personal assistant. Do you have the time right?"

Blake was about to check her phone again when the door down the hall to their right opened.

The man was tall, wore a crisp business suit and didn't skip a beat at the sight of them.

"Mr. Grant," Theo said in greeting.

Mr. Grant?

He was all smiles as he walked over to them.

"Oh, sorry, I thought you had an appointment with Grant Senior," Theo said. He didn't bother to lower his voice. The man approaching laughed.

"I realized after the fact that my assistant might have confused you with that." He looked to Blake and extended his hand. "You must be Blake Bennet. I'm Elijah Grant Junior. I'm the one who made the appointment with you since my father is out of town on business."

Red flag.

It sprung up quickly.

Blake shook his hand with grace.

"Oh, that's no problem. Maybe you can help me too. If you don't mind, that is. I'm sure you're a busy man."

Elijah Grant.

Blake didn't know much about him other than he was Mr. Grant's only child. Even though his father's company employed half the town, he had never been one to fraternize in the social aspects of Seven Roads. Elijah was a few years older than Blake, but she knew he hadn't attended any of Seven Roads's schools either. She wasn't even sure she had been in the same room with him in any of her thirty-five years of living.

Yet, she was good at reading people.

She had a strong feeling that Elijah wasn't as nice as his smile.

But neither was Blake.

She turned to nod to Theo. The boy was looking between them with not-so-sure eyes. Blake tapped his hand in what she hoped was a casual way.

"Thanks for walking me here," she said. "Make sure you give your dad a call and tell him you were kind enough to show me around. He'd be proud of your manners."

Blake was, of course, talking about Liam. While she was fine to go talk to Elijah in private, the change was enough to make her feel the need to update Liam. She was still ready to handle herself, and even if she hadn't been, leaving now might spook the man. How and why, she wasn't sure, but Blake did know that he had heard her request and accepted it instead of his father.

And that made her mighty curious.

Thankfully, Theo played his part cool.

"I'll let him know," he said. "I was just about to call him anyways since it's my break. Y'all have a nice chat. I'll be going now."

She imagined if he had a hat, he would have tipped it to them.

He cast her a quick look, and she returned the gesture with her own little nod.

Elijah seemed wholly unaware of their secret exchange. He swept his hands in the direction of his office with a smile still hanging on his lips.

"This way."

He wasn't the CEO of the company and it showed. Elijah's office was only big enough to fit a desk, a love seat, and a coffee table. His view wasn't the greatest either. It faced the mill instead of the front view of trees and a nicer landscape of the town. There was also the metal roof of the first floor that was right outside the window. Storm debris and rust patches sat along its creases. There was also a damp smell that met Blake's nose as she was guided into the lone chair opposite his desk.

All in all, it didn't seem to fit the man wearing a suit on a Sunday.

"Sorry again for the misunderstanding," Elijah began. "Rhonda, my father's assistant, will contact me if there's business after hours or on the weekends so as to give my dad some space. When the request came in for you to talk to him, it came to me first. I felt like I was just as capable of answering, and, well, she said there sounded like there was some urgency there too."

Blake decided to play it sweet for a while. She upped her southern twang and made sure to smile nice.

"Well, I sure do appreciate you taking the time to see me, especially on the weekend and on such short notice. You must be plenty busy as it is."

That seemed to stroke his ego just right.

His shoulders relaxed as he sat forward and domed his fingers together.

"I'm just happy to be of help. I heard you wanted to talk about your sister, Beth Bennet?"

Blake was curious as to how much Elijah actually knew

of what happened. She watched his expression closely as she spoke.

"Yes. I recently heard that Beth had a fight with your father about the safety investigation she performed here on the Hector Martinez incident. I know it's none of my business, especially if it was about work, but it happened to be the day she passed, and, well, I've been trying to get a better idea about my sister's life leading up to her last days. So I thought I'd ask your father what that fight might have been about, especially since it's so unusual for Beth to get heated."

Elijah was as cool as a cucumber. No surprise.

"Ah, yes, I remember the fight. Though it was more of a misunderstanding. She thought my father had disregarded her suggestion for a several-step authentication system for the furnaces' computer system. *In reality* it was me who went in a different direction." He swapped out his smile for a look of concern. "My father was trying to explain I had already implemented a new security system that would take care of any future human-caused errors."

If he had stopped right there, if he had ended his side at that moment, then Blake might have wavered in her initial thought of the man. She might have questioned if Missy's ex, Kyle, had seen the end of the fight instead of just the yelling. Then, realizing she had never asked, felt a bit guilty and frustrated that she hadn't thought to at the coffee shop the day before. She would have felt a sliver of negligence, all her fault.

But Elijah kept talking.

"I was ready to personally reach out to her to explain the situation, but, well, I never got the chance."

It was a simple statement and understandable. He couldn't have talked to Beth about the change because Beth had had her accident right after.

It made sense.

However, Blake had made a career of reading people. Of following her gut.

He'd met her on the weekend instead of his father. It didn't feel like an obligation.

It felt like Elijah Grant wanted to talk to her for his own reasons.

So she kept going to see which one of them would get what they wanted first.

"I guess you can explain it to me, then?" she asked sweetly. "I mean, I don't know a lot about computers, or anything really about them, but it sounds like you do. I'm sure my sister would have loved to hear it."

Elijah's smile lifted.

It wasn't like Liam's at all. Liam's made her feel warm. This man's made her feel like she had just accidentally touched something wet while using public transportation.

He waved his hand through the air, all nonchalance.

"I won't get into the specifics, but the new system that's in place is all automated, minus a few initial commands."

"Automated? The furnaces can run on their own?"

"Once set up and given specific times to run, yes," he said. "We still need people to man them, but now we don't have to worry about people like Mr. Martinez getting hurt during their maintenance."

"But he wasn't hurt during their maintenance." The words came out as Sheriff Bennet instead of coy Blake before she could stop them. She tried to save face in the next breath. "I mean, I heard that Hector's accident was him trying to manually shut them down after one started overheating. He was worried the whole warehouse might go if one had a meltdown and that the entire mill would be affected. That's the word around town at least."

That part was partially true. The rumor mill had split between Hector being negligent and Hector trying to be a hero.

The negligence story had gained more traction after the steel mill sent out the press release about his accident being human error. That's why Beth had been sent in after all.

Elijah took the barb without emoting anything other than coolness.

"Mr. Martinez made a judgment call that was sadly not a call he should have made at all. We had many safety protocols in place to facilitate a solution that would have been safe and effective. Instead, Mr. Martinez put his own life in danger and paid dearly." Once again, if Elijah had stopped there, a seed of doubt might have sprouted within Blake. Yet the man couldn't help himself. This time, though, the addition cost him.

"In fact, the person in charge of the safety protocol put in place is here today. I thought maybe you might be interested in talking to him."

Blake felt the familiar rush of adrenaline flood her system. The red flag that had sprouted was now in a forest of them.

To think, after everything she had been through in the last week, she had walked willingly into the final boss's lair.

Because in that moment, Blake was sure she was talking to none other than the man behind Missy's death and behind her sister's accident. And who very much wanted to add Blake's death to the list.

But why wait?

Why not kill her on sight at her house? Why not go in guns blazing to take her out? Why make an appointment to sit down and talk to her? Why ask questions? What could he want? What could—

Missy's flash drive and Beth's laptop.

But nothing of note had seemed to be on Beth's laptop.

So that left the code on the flash drive.

Blake wasn't sure where it fit exactly, but she bet her life that it was this man's downfall.

"Oh, that would be nice," she said to his offer. Though it was less of an offer and more of a warning. He had already texted something on his phone. "But, first, I have one last question, if you don't mind."

Elijah met her eye with a new smugness.

"Sure. What do you have for me?"

She decided it would be impolite to keep pretending to be someone she wasn't.

So Blake dropped her smile and did something she had become quite good at during her career in law enforcement. She applied pressure where she thought she might break the man's no-doubt carefully applied facade.

"How angry were you after you realized Missy hid her flash drive with the code before you killed her?"

It was like wiping red marker off a white board.

That fake politeness was no match for the burn of his rage.

Blake's shot in the dark had landed. And it had hit a bulls-eye to boot.

But he wasn't the only one shooting.

The door to the office flung open. Blake threw herself back, toppling over with her chair but managing to stay upright as she tried to scramble away from the new intruder.

However, the person who ran inside and immediately slammed the door closed behind him wasn't a no-name lackey.

It was Theo, and he was breathing heavy.

"Gunman outside!" he yelled. He whirled around and pointed to Elijah. "Gun in here!"

Blake was so startled by Theo's entrance she hadn't noticed that Elijah was reaching for something. Her body went on autopilot. She threw herself across the desk ready to disarm the man.

Everything after that seemed to go in double speed.
A gunshot.
Glass breaking.
Then chaos.

Chapter Twenty-One

Liam was pissed. At everyone.

He was angry at Cooper Han because the boy had waited so long to tell anyone about the code. It was only when someone he loved was threatened that he even dared come out to say a word. Though, Liam knew it counted that the teen had tried to correct his hesitance and had done so in the face of potential danger. So he couldn't hold on to that anger too long.

Which worked out, because next he became angry at Price.

Once he had finished his conversation with Cooper, he had noticed his calls weren't coming through or going out. That happened occasionally near the hospital and across a few other spots in town. Panic had risen through him in an instant, then anger came in swiftly on its heels once he finally spoke with Price, who explained what was going on with Blake.

Mr. Grant had changed his appointment time with Blake, and she had simply gone along with the flow.

Solo.

So then the anger at Price for letting her go had gone and attached to the stubborn woman who hadn't waited for him.

She hadn't even called him, only left a text saying where she was going. Nothing else.

At that point Liam had already been in the truck and heading over to the steel mill as fast as the wind.

Then he had gotten a call from Theo.

Normally, he would have sent the call to voicemail if he thought he was heading into danger and needed to focus, but the timing of the call was too coincidental.

Liam had answered on the second ring.

He didn't have time to say hello. Theo was rattling off information fast.

"Sheriff Bennet is at the steel mill talking to Elijah Grant, Mr. Grant's son, in his office. I think she was supposed to meet Mr. Grant instead, but something changed. Then she told *me* to call *my* dad and let him know that I had walked her in. Which I think she meant to call you and tell you."

Liam's anger had switched one more time.

Right onto Elijah Grant. The same man Cooper had just said had installed the code that everyone kept dying for.

"Find a way to let her know that Elijah is dangerous and then you both get out of there," Liam said, not bothering with the backstory. "I'm a minute or so away from the mill."

Bless him, Theo didn't ask any questions. He said okay and then started moving fast on his side of the phone.

All at once, that noise stopped.

His whisper was the loudest Liam had ever heard.

"The man who you said attacked y'all at the Bennet house but got away. Was he tall and bald?"

Adrenaline skyrocketed from the tips of Liam's toes all the way up to the ends of his hair.

"Yes."

"Then I think he's walking down the hallway and—and he has a gun!" The sound on Theo's end of the call wasn't still after that. He was all out yelling. "Second floor to the right. End of the hallway and—"

A loud *clatter* vibrated through the phone and across the

silence of the cab of the truck. Liam looked at his phone to see the call was still going. He heard what sounded like running in the background.

Theo had dropped his phone.

Liam cussed and pressed the gas pedal to the floorboard.

The call ended right after that.

Liam cussed again.

He called back, but no one answered. By the time he made it to the parking lot and was out of his truck and running, he had already called in every able-bodied person from the McCoy County Sheriff's Department.

But he wasn't about to wait around for them.

Liam checked his gun as he ran through the parking lot and burst through the lobby doors of the main office. He took the stairs two at a time and put all of his attention on the hallway that led to the offices at the right end.

A cell phone was discarded on the tile halfway between him and the open door at the end of the hallway.

It was Theo's.

Liam stepped over it and kept his gun aimed straight ahead and ready.

Yet no one appeared.

Liam swung into the office and found it empty. He would have backtracked had he not noticed the windows.

One was broken. The other was opened wide.

Surely no one had gone out them…

He hurried to check. His stomach lurched at what he saw outside.

The metal overhang from the first story stretched across the full width of the building. It wasn't until midway across that the slope led to a flat roof that was connected to a storage building. There the roof was flat and easier to manage.

There he could just make out four figures, all moving fast.

Even at the distance, Liam could see Blake clearly.

As much as she didn't want to admit it, Blake was at a serious disadvantage.

Their rooftop escape might have worked had Elijah's helper not broken into the office the second that she had been able to disarm Elijah. Instead, the best she and Theo could do in the moment was flee through the window that had been shot out by accident.

She had let the boy lead the way, and again had the bald man not been right on their heels, they might have been able to scramble down the side of the current building they were on and make a run for it.

Instead, they had been cornered on a rooftop with two men both holding guns.

Blake extended her arms out as wide as she could and put herself firmly in front of Theo.

She was out of breath but managed to keep her voice steady.

"He doesn't know anything. Let him go and we can talk."

Elijah, who seemed to be struggling the most, laughed through his spurts of trying to regain his breath.

"You're—you're in no position to—to negotiate," he said. "We—we will talk though."

He lowered his gun after looking at the bald man at his side. The fourth man from the ambush at her home. He was unmoving as he kept his gun aimed at her.

"Tell me where—where it is," Elijah said, holding his side until breathing seemed to come easier. "Tell me where the flash drive is."

Blake shook her head.

"I do that and we're dead," she said. "Let him go, though, and I'll tell you whatever you want."

It was a bluff.

But it didn't matter. She knew neither man was going to let Theo or her go.

Now the best she could do was stall for time and hope that the boy had gotten her hint to call Liam.

If he had, then Blake didn't doubt for a second that the sheriff wasn't on his way to save them.

Elijah laughed, very much a man with no intention of letting them live.

"Do you know, the last person who tried to negotiate with me found herself at the bottom of a dried-up creek. I suggest what you focus on now is how easy to make this next part for the both of you. Because, believe me, I can make you suffer if I need to."

Blake narrowed her gaze.

"So you really did kill Missy Clearwater," she said.

The man rolled his eyes. It was an unbecoming sight.

"All I did was hit her a little. It's not my fault she took a tumble right after that. If she had simply listened to me and handed over that damned little flash drive, we would have been fine. But, no. All you women like playing hero. I think it's only poetic that you'll be the one to end the cycle, considering it was your sister who started it."

Blake lowered her arms. Theo was right at her back.

"Beth's car accident wasn't an accident," she stated.

"Beth's car accident wasn't an accident," Elijah confirmed. He snorted. "Though it was her fault, not ours. My friend here just wanted to talk about her findings. It isn't his fault that she got scared and started driving like a lunatic."

Blake's hands fisted.

If she hadn't been trying to shield the teen behind her, she would have lunged at the man. Instead, she tried to get answers.

"Which means that she *did* find something she wasn't supposed to."

Elijah was back to smug.

"Do you know how many safety inspectors we've had

come out to the mill over the years? Do you know how many have turned a blind eye or taken money to overlook an infraction? But no. Not Beth Bennet. She was a woman who wanted to stick her nose where she shouldn't.''

He laughed.

He actually laughed.

"Who knew that she was so fast? Squirreling away the one thing that could mess up everything?"

"Her laptop."

Elijah nodded.

"Since we couldn't find it anywhere after so many months, though, we thought that was that." He breathed out his annoyance. "Then Missy Clearwater, the beloved daughter of my father's best friend, used her name to start asking questions. Who did she even think she was? Acting like she had been the one hurt when it was just that good-for-nothing friend of hers Hector?" He shook his head. "Then suddenly *she* had the code and then, *then*, she had the audacity to try to bring my father into this whole thing? Trying to mess up my inheritance? I don't think so."

Elijah blew out another short huff of air.

"She should have known better. After the way this town treated her when her father decided to shut down their business? Can you imagine the flak I would have caught had they found out I was the one trying to burn this place down for a payout?"

Blake's mouth opened on its own accord.

Elijah saw the shock and seemed to revel in it.

"And there it is," he said, the smile from earlier returning. "You can't fake that kind of surprise, Eric. Did you know that?" He patted the bald man's shoulder. His smugness was returning as well. He looked to Blake again. "I don't think Miss Bennet here knows as much as she's pretending to. Let's see. Miss Bennet, can you tell me what exactly the code is for? Or did you come here for a fishing expedition only?"

Blake hated that she didn't have a good answer.

She also hated that the feeling of dread in her had tripled.

Elijah had found out that she was more expendable than he had originally thought. Which meant they didn't have long.

Blake wished she could hear sirens in the distance.

She wished she had her gun.

She wished she hadn't come to the mill by herself.

She wished she had waited for Liam.

She wished that she could turn back time to them all sitting at the dinner table, Clem on his lap, Bruce in her arms, and Lola fussing over the food between them.

She wished she could hug the kids again. Kiss Liam. Laugh with Lola.

She wished she could tell her dad she was sorry that life for them had gotten so offtrack.

She wished she could hear her sister tell her to make sure she ate something yummy.

Instead, she was about to become another tragedy and trauma in Seven Roads history.

Or so she thought.

Movement caught the corner of Blake's eye just as it alerted the man with the gun trained on her, Eric. He whirled around and shot without waiting.

Blake didn't waste that time worrying about his target. She closed the distance between her and Elijah before he could lift his gun. Pain exploded along her fist as it connected with his jaw.

Another shot went off, then another, on the roof behind them.

Elijah's gun hadn't gone off yet, but it also hadn't fallen.

Blake struggled against him, throwing hits and kicks as hard as she could.

The man knew how to play dirty though. He slammed his head into Blake's so hard that all she could do was try not to pass out as she fell backward against the ground. Theo was already there, trying to pull her away.

He yelled something, but despite everything, Blake was getting tunnel vision.

That vision had Elijah at its center. He had his gun coming up to aim at her.

With everything she had left in her, Blake willed karma to see him pay for all the bad he had done.

A split second later, another boom sounded.

Elijah crumpled to the ground.

As darkness took her, Blake could only think of one word. *Good.*

Chapter Twenty-Two

The world was a lot nicer when Blake opened her eyes next. She had to admit that was probably mostly due to the man staring down at her.

Liam's gaze didn't waver.

"You know, I've been to war and been less stressed than I was today," he told her. "Being a loner, not talking to people? That's easy stuff. Falling for Sheriff Trouble? Hardest thing I've done yet."

Blake had questions, but her focus was watered down. She wanted to ask about that falling-for thing but was getting distracted by what was above his head.

"Where am I?"

Her throat hurt at the question. She flinched.

Liam's face softened. His fingers traced the side of her jaw before his hand enveloped her own at her side.

"You landed yourself in the hospital. We're in a private room. You just cleared a round of doctors."

Blake's brow scrunched of its own accord.

"Concussion?" she asked.

He nodded.

"And one heck of a bruise and bump for it." His face darkened. "Who knew Elijah Grant had such a damned hard head."

The name brought a bad taste into her mouth.

It wasn't the only thing.

"Did I get sick?" she asked. Blake felt like she was extremely hungover. He confirmed her suspicion.

"You came to in the ambulance and got sick a whole bunch. Poor Theo nearly lost it at the sight but didn't want me to tell you that." He smiled, lopsided. "He says he's not like most teenagers, but he really wants to keep that reputation of his tight."

Blake was relieved to see Liam joking about the boy.

"He's okay, then?"

He nodded. Then became serious again.

"I actually don't think I could have pulled off getting you to the ambulance without him. You're easy to carry under normal circumstances but off a building's roof—well, it was a bit trickier. Plus, he kept fussing after the stitches on my arm. They didn't pop, though, and he kept his cool."

Blake was trying to think back.

All she remembered was Elijah's head hitting hers.

That and his admissions. The old ache in her heart started to hurt. She decided to push it to the side for now.

"What happened?"

Liam held her hand tight as he recounted the rooftop fight. While she had taken on Elijah, he had made his way out onto the roof from the office and shot the man named Eric the moment he was close enough to get a good opening. Before he could knock the man out with a bone-crunching hit, Elijah had already attacked Blake.

"That's when you shot Elijah," she guessed.

She was wrong.

"Someone followed me and came out onto the rooftop too. He's the one who shot Elijah."

Blake didn't understand his expression. She raised her eyebrow in question.

"Who was it?"

She wasn't sure she heard him clearly, so she asked him to repeat himself.

The second time, it was clear enough.

"Ryan Reed, your sister's former brother-in-law. He's the one who shot Elijah."

"Ryan? As in Tim's brother? Clem and Bruce's uncle?" Blake didn't understand, so she had to make sure she clarified.

Liam nodded.

"Apparently he didn't leave town. A good thing too that he showed up. His shot was right on target." Liam squeezed her hand. "It was a kill shot too. Elijah Grant is dead."

For so many reasons, and probably more that she couldn't think of, this made Blake cry. Her tears were hot and big and made her head hurt even more.

Liam didn't say a word. Instead he kept her hand safe and secure within his until, a few minutes later, she stopped.

"We can talk about everything after you get some rest," he told her, wiping his thumb over her cheek. "Until then, I just want to ask you one question and one question only."

Blake was so drained. All she could do was nod.

Liam smiled.

"I'm sure there is a more suave way to do this, but the cold sheriff of Seven Roads sure doesn't know how to do anything but ask outright." He cleared his throat. "Blake Bennet, when you're feeling better, how about we go out on a date? Dinner, movies, playing in the park with the kids—I don't care what it is. As long as it's with you, I'll be happy."

Exhaustion momentarily paused.

Blake returned his smile.

"As long as we eat something yummy, I'm in."

A DAY PASSED before they finally got the rest of their answers. However, Blake ended up getting them from an unlikely source.

Ryan Reed was in handcuffs but sitting in the sunlight on a bench outside the hospital. He had already told his story to Detective Williams and Liam back at the department. Now it was her turn, thanks to Liam pulling some strings to make the conversation happen.

"Missy called me a month or so after Beth's death looking for my brother," he said, starting the story of why he had killed Elijah Grant. "You know Tim. Once he left Beth and the kids, he left any thought about this life behind. I tried to tell her it was useless to call him, and then, in the middle of all of that, she said it could be a matter of life and death, and she brought up Beth's accident. The way she said it… I couldn't shake it. Then she asked me to meet her since I was still family and maybe could talk to you."

He looked sheepish at that.

"She didn't hear that we had fallen out. About how much of an ass I made out of myself at the funeral. How out of line I was with you talking about the insurance money. I just couldn't believe how we'd all gotten there. I know I wasn't a rock star uncle, but Tim just up and leaving like that as a dad? And then Beth was just gone. No matter what, though, I shouldn't have done what I did. I'm sorry about it all, really I am. Guess I should have said that sooner."

He kept on without waiting to see if Blake accepted his apology or not.

"When we met, Missy told me everything, starting from the beginning. She wasn't suspicious about the steel mill or Elijah until after she heard about Beth's accident. That's why she went down the rabbit hole. Beth's death and, well, that friend of hers. That Hector fella." He shook his head. "She was sure as the sun shines that Hector wouldn't have made such a mistake with those furnaces. So she went to her daddy about it, who, in turn, asked Mr. Grant about it. I guess her questions got to Elijah in the end. And he wasn't appreciative of it. He met her at the mill, but she said he was acting weird. He kept asking for proof and if she'd been close to Beth."

Ryan sighed. It had dragged him down.

"Missy said that she snuck into the furnace room after that, saying she was visiting her boyfriend that worked out there. She didn't know what to look for but suspected it might have something to do with the computer. So she copied every-thing she could onto one of those flash drive things. Some-one caught her doing it too."

That someone was Cooper Han. As part of his tech pro-gram, he had found Missy there during one of their tours fumbling around with the computer. If it hadn't been for his aversion to judging people without giving them a chance, he might have turned her in. Instead, he offered to help her.

"That boy is a far throw from the likes of me, I'll tell you that," Ryan said. "He was able to find some kind of code in all of that garble that shouldn't have been there. He can prob-ably explain it better than I can, but they realized—as far as I can tell—it basically could make the furnaces overheat by themselves, eventually causing a catastrophic meltdown. He guessed it had been put in manually by someone to make ev-erything melt down. But there was no way to figure out who."

"That's what happened with Hector," Blake realized. "He thought it was an error that caused the meltdown and tried to help. But it was on purpose."

Ryan nodded.

"Missy told Cooper to be quiet about it, worried it was dangerous information to have, and that's when she called me looking for Tim. She was trying to figure out if Beth had found the code during her investigation or if she had any info on her work laptop about it. I didn't have any idea but told her that if Beth had a laptop that it should be at the house with you." Ryan laughed. "So she actually went and stole it from you. I guess you were busy with the kids and didn't notice, but, sure as sure, she had it with her, trying to figure out if the code was there."

Blake couldn't believe it. Then again, maybe she could. Missy Clearwater had more than proven she was a clever girl.

"Then she told me she was putting it back, worried that if anyone found it on her, they might think you had a part in this. And she didn't want you or the kids in danger."

A look she couldn't decipher went across Ryan's face. He continued.

"I met with Missy the day she died. She said her father had gotten drunk the night before and wondered if his friend, Mr. Grant, was going to cash out of the steel mill while he could or give the massive debt to his son. She prodded her daddy until she got a better picture of the situation."

The situation, which they would later confirm through an investigation, was that the senior Mr. Grant had used a lot of his fortune to help pull his son Elijah out of severe debt before he'd come back to Seven Roads. It was only after Mr. Clearwater, his good friend, had sold his business to retire that he had started to think about letting his son inherit the mill, only to leave him strapped with the financial fallout.

Something that Elijah had found out about.

And tried to plan for.

"Elijah wanted the mill to burn down so he could collect the insurance payout. Simple as that," Ryan finished.

"So, did Beth even know about the code?"

Ryan shrugged.

"Missy never found out, and you know me, I'm not exactly book smart. The most I've done was try to figure out who all was connected to Elijah. I didn't want a one of them to escape."

Blake hurt for her sister. They would never know for certain if Beth had figured out what was going on, but Blake liked to think she had. That's why she had been so angry the

218

day she had died. That's why she had been so scared when the man named Eric, a favorite employee of Elijah's, had come after her while driving that day.

Eric never said a word on the matter, but a security camera outside the hospital had caught him fleeing the scene after he killed Ray McClennan. Chase had become Ray's voice in the end, admitting that Elijah had paid Ray to try to stop Liam at all costs from digging into Missy's death. At the time, Ray had lied to Chase about what was happening, saying that the sheriff was a bad man who had done bad things. It was only after Cooper Han had heard what had happened that he had told his best friend Chase about the code.

He hadn't realized that Ray had been listening.

Or that Ray would raise the flag of alarm to Elijah, who had had no idea there was a code floating around out there somewhere. That's where the panic had come in and that's where he'd gotten sloppy.

He'd wanted Beth's laptop, sure she had a copy of the code. In his mind, the only way to get what he wanted was to use the kids to threaten Blake to find it. His panic had only ratcheted higher when Blake and the sheriff were seen around town together. He'd been sure they were looking for the code too.

So, in came Ray McClennan. A young man who had his own set of daddy issues. He'd been more than willing to do whatever for the youngest Grant.

Too bad for him that Elijah had always planned to frame Ray for whatever misdeeds took place. They'd find that out later, when Glenn Lowell, the man in the baseball cap, finally opened up. The ambush at Blake's home had been Elijah's plan. The car chase had been Ray's bad makeshift first attempt after seeing the sheriff and Blake outside of the restaurant that Chase worked at by chance.

"All these seemingly smart guys sure made a lot of bad

decisions, all because they were worrying about two women who were chasing the truth," Ryan said after a moment. "I went to tell you at the school gym that day, but I lost my nerve. I wish I hadn't. I wish I'd helped Missy even more."

Blake looked at Ryan with new eyes.

He looked right on back and was as serious as she had ever seen him.

"I know my brother wasn't a good husband or dad, and I'm really sorry for him. I'm also real sorry I didn't step up like you did. But I tried to make things right. As right as I could. From us. From Tim and me. Because Beth was a good, good woman. So was Missy. They both deserved a long, happy life. That's why I killed Elijah without an ounce of doubt in me, and that's why I'm not sorry for it."

He shook his head.

"Though, I suppose I am sorry for the trouble it might bring you and the kids in town. I'm sure Mr. Grant isn't going to be happy with our family after I killed his son."

Mr. Grant, and the steel mill, would be in a fierce legal battle for the next year, until eventually an outside company would purchase it. The jobs would stay for the Seven Roads employees, but the name and management would change.

But, at the time, Blake wasn't worried about any of that.

"There are some things you could apologize to me for, Ryan Reed," she said. "But that's not one of them."

He nodded and stood. The story was over, and it was time for him to leave. He paused though and seemed to become a little sheepish.

"Maybe if it suits you and them, you could send me some pictures and updates about y'all," he said. "I know I won't ever be uncle of the year to the kids, but maybe I can be kind of like a distant uncle who sends them birthday cards and asks after their grades on occasion. Only if it's okay with you though."

Despite herself, Blake agreed. She also surprised herself by hugging the man. His parting words hit deep in her heart.

"Take care of our family, Blake."

She smiled, her eyes starting to water.

"I will."

Ryan seemed satisfied with her answer.

Then he grinned.

"And keep that sheriff around too," he added. "He seems like he'd be one of those really good husbands and dads."

Blake didn't say it then, but she absolutely agreed.

RYAN ENDED UP getting sentenced to several years in prison with the chance of parole. In his first letter home to Blake, he said he accepted the sentence but couldn't deny he was also glad he didn't get more than what he had. Blake wrote back with more or less the same sentiment. She included a picture of them at Clem's preschool graduation and re-capped the whole affair, right down to when Bruce squealed for his sister so loud that it started a wave of giggles from the crowd.

The next letter would talk about Bruce starting to run. His first long sprint was the same week that Clem started kindergarten.

Both kids used his new ability to play chase with Liam, but the boy really seemed to enjoy their game the most. He would squeal and laugh, running around the yard full tilt. It was only when Liam had to slow down because of his hip that Bruce would slow down a little too, as if trying to help Liam out. If he wasn't paying attention too closely, however, Clem would run past Liam and catch her brother for him. This became a little game all their own while Lola and Blake usually chatted from the front porch in their chairs, watching.

It was on those chairs one day that Lola finally told them that she had decided to divorce Blake's father.

"We all know that life changes quick," she had said. "In a perfect world, maybe your father and I could have been happy. But life happened, and I think it's better for the both of us that we go on our own paths now. I'm okay and I think he will be too."

Blake had been supportive of whatever Lola wanted but made sure to let Lola know that she could change all she wanted, but her home never would. Lola had laughed.

"Oh, I'm not going anywhere," she had said. "I wouldn't miss this chaos for anything."

Liam had helped her move the rest of her things into the house one day later. Blake's father hadn't been there, something Blake had been worried about. Lola had pulled Liam aside before leaving.

"Don't worry," she'd said. "One day he'll come around and realize how sorry he's been. Until then, all we can do is love Blake hard and love her true. The rest will work itself out."

Liam had liked the advice and thought it was more than easy enough to take. Together he and Lola buckled down on giving Blake love and support until she was finally comfortable enough to talk about her own future. Since she had helped solve quite the scandal and mystery without the help of a badge, they suggested Blake officially end her time off from work and join the McCoy County Sheriff's Department.

Something that garnered a lot of support, mostly from an unlikely source. Gossip Queen Corrie Daniels was pro-Blake becoming the law again.

"Can you imagine the optics of you working alongside your sheriff boyfriend? I mean, just think about it. You solve a case as a civilian, start dating him, and then y'all are working together on another case and saving each other from bad guys in the nick of time, like in the movies!"

Blake had laughed and so had Corrie's sister, Cassandra. Lola had admitted it would be fun to see Blake even run for sheriff. Price did too. He lightly punched Liam in the shoulder as he laughed while they were all sitting around a table at the coffee shop.

"What if she really did become sheriff? Could you really be okay with that job switch?" he asked.

Liam had laughed.

"Hey, you're not the only one who is a fan of Sheriff Trouble."

By the time Clem's birthday came around, Blake had decided she would in fact start up her law enforcement career again. What position she wanted to apply for, however, was still up in the air. Liam could see even just the talk of it made her happier.

He also bought a ring. Theo helped him pick it out and was mighty proud of it. Despite Liam moving into Blake's house, no one had minded Theo making the guest bedroom his home away from home. He spent several nights a week with them, much to the little ones' delight.

Now he, Lola, and the kids were all inside the house fast asleep. Liam, sitting back in his lawn chair on the front porch, had his hand wrapped around Blake's as both rested on her lap. She was sitting next to him in her own chair, staring out at the rain that had been falling for a few hours.

There were toys scattered around them, a pair of Theo's shoes by the door, and a glass that had held sweet tea Lola had been drinking but forgot to take in when done in one of the cupholders.

Liam took them all in.

Blake noticed his new attention. She raised her eyebrows. "What is it?" she asked.

Liam smiled. The answer was simple.

"Breadcrumbs."

* * * * *

RENEGADE
REUNION

ADDISON FOX

For Beth and Eric.

A life in service protecting others is an incredible sacrifice, both for the one who protects and the one who waits each day for their return. Your love, support and belief in each other is an inspiration.

Chapter One

"And just as it always does, water seeks the lowest level. Just like you, you hungover idiot."

Trace Withrow knelt down beside the rushing stream, fresh with spring rain and winter snowmelt, and washed his face. The water was freezing, which meant it did wonders for the hangover he was still sporting. Even if it froze his fingers in the process.

Damn, but his friends knew how to throw a party. And welcoming home one of their own had certainly been worth every minute of his monumentally painful ride this morning. It couldn't, however, erase one unalienable fact.

"I'm getting too old for this crap."

Trace sat up, wiping the ice-cold water from his face. His horse, Magnum, was seemingly oblivious to his pain as he bent his head, drinking from the same stream. Although Magnum was a faithful companion and Trace trusted him implicitly, the horse had little in the way of equine compassion.

A trait Trace admired in spades.

Magnum lifted his head, his dark brown gaze hard and unyielding. Although the Arabian had never gone all Mr. Ed on him, that look spoke more than a thousand words.

Get your sorry butt in gear and let's finish up our work.

"So noted."

Trace got to his feet, the vast, sprawling Wyoming mountains spreading out in all directions. It was a far cry from
DC—what wasn't, outside the Beltway?—and that had only
added to its appeal.

Liar's Gulch, Wyoming. A vast, Western wilderness that
had surprisingly become home. And, despite its name, had
far more good people than the liars, backstabbers and power
players he'd called colleagues back in Washington.

Liar's Gulch had also become his haven. His respite from
a life that he still sharply remembered, even if the edges had
gone blessedly dull as he healed out in the big, wide-open
West, running a horse-training-and-rescue operation on the
four hundred acres that he now called home.

The air around them was quiet as Trace gave one last stretch
before moving back to Magnum. He'd nearly placed a foot in
the stirrups, ready to mount, when something stopped him.

A stillness, maybe?

It made little sense, but he'd trained too long and too hard
to ignore the hairs that stood up on the back of his neck.
And he'd managed to stay alive because he—never once—
doubted them.

Patting Magnum's neck in a casual gesture, Trace considered the gun at his waistband and the other clutch piece
at his ankle. He could have both in hand and firing in less
than two seconds.

Which was two seconds too long if whatever had him in
its crosshairs decided to move.

And that left him with only one choice.

Swinging around as he drew his gun, Trace faced off
against his enemy.

And laid eyes on the only woman he'd ever loved.

NICOLA MILES HELD her position, the safety off her gun and
her stance fixed as she stared down Trace Withrow. Realis-

tically, she didn't want to shoot him. His body was way too fine to put a bullet into if she could help it.

But sometimes fate had other ideas.

"Nic." The edges of his lips twitched, but other than that slight movement, the rest of him was eerily still.

"Jackass." She meant it in greeting and had to hold back the wince when she registered the extra-sharp note in her voice. She knew her upper hand was tenuous at best, and giving even the slightest sense that she was at a disadvantage simply would not do.

To his credit, he didn't seem to register the greeting, but neither did he relax his own stance or lower the piece in his hands that matched her own.

Old habits died hard.

"This is a surprise."

"I don't doubt that."

And she didn't. When they'd left each other two years ago, there had been a finality to the parting that hadn't characterized their other battles. Fights that had always ended in the sweetest sort of détente.

But not that one.

That one had been nuclear in its destruction. The sort where even the cockroaches died and mass-produced cheese actually melted.

The one that ended it all.

"To what do I owe the pleasure?" Those compelling gray eyes of his were as inscrutable as ever. So was his tone. Flat. Uncompromising.

Just like the man.

Traits she admired in a colleague and an opponent that were wildly out of place in a lover and a life partner.

Unless you added *uncompromising in his thoroughness* when he loved her.

Nicola shook off the heated images that brought. She

would not think of the hot, thick air that had filled their humid hotel room in a run-down section of Buenos Aires. Nor would she think about the impossible cold they'd fought off in the wilds of Siberia, with a small fire, two thick coats and only each other to stay warm.

She knew this man.

Knew his body and his mind, his values and his blind spots.

And he knew her. Knew her in ways no one else ever had or, she now keenly understood, ever would.

"You going to make me ask again?" One lone eyebrow rose above those eyes she knew so well. So well, in fact, that she still dreamed about them.

Regularly.

"I need your help."

"By holding me at gunpoint?"

Nicola allowed her gaze to flash ever so briefly to the cold metal at the end of her hands. "It's an effective enticement."

"So is sex, but I don't see you offering that."

Damn him, he knew just what to say to get under her skin. "I'd rather put a bullet in your ass than touch it."

He took a few steps closer, his voice like silk, even as his own gun stayed firmly in place. "You didn't always feel that way. Even at your maddest, you never felt that way."

"Things change."

"Actually, most things don't change." Without warning, Trace dropped his gun. "Not one single bit."

She'd never been afraid of handling a gun. A fact that wasn't only handy but absolutely necessary in her line of work. But she'd never been comfortable holding one steady on someone who posed no threat.

And while she might understand how threatening, tough and all around badass Trace Withrow could be when riled, this moment wasn't it.

Her own gun fell to her side before she took another precious moment to put on the safety. A moment that gave him the advantage—if he wanted it—to grab his clutch piece.

A moment—if he took it—that would give her some perverse pleasure in battling him hand to hand.

Yet in the end, it was a moment that passed without any further movement, threatening or otherwise.

"Why are you here, Nic?"

"I told you. I need your help."

"How'd you find me?"

The question was flat, devoid of emotion, which was almost enough to push her own ire back to the surface. She didn't want to need him, damn it. Didn't want his help.

Even if she had no say in the matter.

Add on the fact that she was still smarting from those sexy, overwhelming flashbacks, and she would have done anything else on earth but stand before him, vulnerable and alone. She could still picture his naked body, a towel around his lean, whipcord hips, his inky-black hair still dark from a shower, just like it was now at the edges. She'd watched him dip his head in that rushing stream, shivering to herself when she imagined him bracing against the cold of the water.

Thoughts of the water had led right into images of him fresh out of a shower, which had then blended with memories of the cold, and then her mind was right back in Siberia and…

Oh, it had been a long twenty-four months.

"Well? I deserve to know."

His question still hanging between them, she considered her approach. It would be so easy to poke at his pride, dismissing the question and, with a laugh, suggest just how quickly she'd found his location.

Only it would be a lie.

When Trace Withrow had walked out of the CIA, he'd meant it. No matter how well she knew how to use the tools at her disposal, the man had been nearly impossible to find. In the end, it had been the fact that she knew him—and remembered a throwaway conversation on assignment in Geneva. He'd talked of a small corner of Wyoming where he loved to fish while on his personal holidays away from DC.

His dark, husky voice had been filled with awe as he spoke of nature's bounty. She'd only ever heard that tone when they made love. When his lips were pressed against the shell of her ear, his large body finding a rhythm over hers. In those precious hours together, his voice had held both the promise of pleasure and the wonder at what flared and flamed between them.

She'd taken it for granted at the time. Had believed the pleasure was something born of the moment. A product of their intense jobs and schedules, the work they did grueling and satisfying all at the same time.

They'd been attracted to one another from the start, and she'd entered into the affair well aware neither of them were relationship material. She'd always known that about herself, cementing the truth of it once she entered the rarefied air of the Central Intelligence Agency.

The CIA had offered all she ever wanted. Since the day she'd gotten the agency as her group study project in high school civics, she'd recognized it as the perfect place for her. A place where she could do work that mattered. Where she would matter.

It was an idea that had enticed, even as it was in short supply in her young life. After being bumped from place to place as a child, she'd nearly run away out of the foster system.

Until the Bakers.

They showed up around the same time as that civics class.

Nic wasn't a big believer in fate, but figured someone, somewhere was looking out for her when, at fourteen, she'd finally found a permanent home with a sweet older couple.

They'd given her a soft place to land, with minimal judgment and even fewer rules, but a roof, three squares and a gentle insistence she get an education.

Through that education, she'd found her true calling.

Once that civics project had finished, she'd researched the hell out of the CIA on her own. Where most of her fellow students were hunting up the latest makeup tutorial or endless photo-filled articles on their favorite boy band, Nic scoured the internet for details on the CIA. She'd trained body and mind, working up to five miles a day for her daily run and acing all her classes to get into a good college in DC.

It never once dawned on her to deviate from her path. Nor had she ever questioned that she was made for dangerous assignments with the highest of stakes. Those stakes never bothered her because they provided the very best outcomes should they succeed.

Until Trace.

He'd been as driven as she, yet he knew how to play. How to walk away when the situation got so intense it singed you from every angle. And how to give perspective to the work so that even when it was all-consuming, it wasn't everything.

"I'm not asking again, Nic. How'd you find me?"

The smooth, casual attitude had vanished, leaving behind the reality of who and what he was. Trace Withrow might wear any number of facades, but he was an inherently dangerous man, with or without a loaded gun in his hand.

"You talked about this place. That endless week we spent in Geneva staking out those insurgents. It was a mindless, empty conversation about four coffees into our day."

His eyes narrowed. "The one about vacation spots. You were particularly keen on Maui, as I recall."

"Have you ever met anyone, ever, who doesn't love Maui?"

He ignored her stall tactic. "And that's how you found me here?"

Damn it, she couldn't tell him the truth. How that conversation had haunted her long after they'd caught the insurgents. That there was something wistful in his voice when he spoke of the mountains and the land and the endlessly clear streams. Something that had drawn her in and made her think that there was a place in the world where she wasn't a reject foster kid. Where nature was bright enough and pure enough to wash away any number of sins.

And where, if she was with him, she might actually be worthy of him.

HE REMEMBERED THAT CONVERSATION. That stakeout. That time in his life. He remembered it all with a clarity that was so vivid it hurt to breathe through the memories.

What he couldn't reconcile was that she had remembered.

Trace had never doubted Nicola Miles in any way. Her intelligence. Her courage. Or her willingness to do what was needed to achieve their goals.

But it was humbling—even as stubborn hope sparked in his chest and through the raging headache that pounded his temples—to realize he might have underestimated his impact on her.

Had she not shared the memory from that stakeout, he'd have continued on in his beliefs. The ones that had haunted him for two years now. The ones that said he was the hopeless fool.

He'd been the one to fall in love. To break the unspoken agreement between them that they'd use the sheer combustion that fueled their encounters as a pleasurable way to blow off steam while on assignment. Nothing more.

Only now, he had to wonder.

Had she felt something?

Or was she just that damn good? Remembering a throwaway comment in a throwaway conversation on an endless stakeout.

Disgusted with himself for opening the "deeper meaning" door even a crack, Trace moved a few steps forward. Nic's vivid blue—almost crystal—gaze never left his, nor did she move back a step.

This was a woman who knew how to stand her ground.

A fact that delighted him and infuriated him in equal measure.

He gave himself another few beats to look his fill—that vivid blue, the sweep of blond that arced behind her ear, the firm line of her jaw that was so sharp it should have been a warning—before offering the denial she had to have anticipated. "We don't have the same boss anymore. And since there's only about three planks still holding up the bridge I tried to burn, no one back at Uncle Sam's ranch is going to give you a parade for coming to find me."

"No one knows I'm here."

"If you actually believe that, then let me sell you those three remaining planks, sweetheart."

"No, Trace. No one knows."

He'd had a long time to come to grips with what he knew about her, but one thing he'd never doubted was her honesty. She had an unwavering faith in her colleagues and the organization she'd devoted her life to for over a decade. It had been a point of contention between them—one they'd never come close to reconciling—and it had only added to their implosion at the end.

"Since when does Nicola Miles work outside the auspices of the mighty CIA?"

Her gaze darted down toward the rocky scrub grass beneath their feet before determinedly shooting back up to rest on his face. "I'm not working outside anything."

"You are if you're telling me the truth. The CIA takes care of its own. It doesn't need help from ex-agents who left on bad terms."

"This has nothing to do with the CIA. This has to do with me."

"You are the CIA, Nic. You have been since the day you walked in the door. Nothing could dislodge that boulder of trust and self-righteousness off your shoulder."

For a long time, he'd accepted it. Oh, he'd poked at her plenty about it, but he'd trusted that she was smart enough and well trained enough to hold her own, no matter the situation. And if she had a deep-seated belief that the organization she worked for was focused on fundamentally doing good, what did it hurt?

It was better than his piss-poor attitude. The one that had burned those bridge planks, one by one, in his fifteen years with the agency. Because while she liked to believe her fellow agents were fundamentally good, made even better by the structure and intelligence and security around them, Trace opted for the opposing view.

Anyone who chose the life—who understood the shadowy underbelly of how the world worked—wasn't immune from those shadows themselves.

She still stood close enough to touch. Close enough he could feel the heat emanating off her body in the cold morning air. Close enough he could see the throb of her pulse against the delicate skin of her throat.

But it was the whisper, thick and nearly strangled in that morning air, that caught him up as cleanly as the fish he loved to drag from the river. "I think you might be right, Trace. Have always been right."

"About what?"

"There are traitors in our midst. Whether by choice or by consequence, I don't know. But I do know I can't fight them alone." She hesitated, before adding, "I can't fight an enemy I can't see."

"And you think I can?"

"I think you always have. I just never wanted to believe you."

"What changed your mind?"

"It's a kid this time. She's fifteen and brilliant and—" She broke off, but there was something in the hesitation that told Trace all he needed to know.

Somehow, some way, her case had turned personal.

And that was the biggest danger an agent could face. He'd learned that lesson the hard way, and now it appeared she had, too.

"Why this kid?"

"She's a computer genius, and she was my asset. I was protecting her, and she vanished three days ago."

"Runaway?"

"It was made to look like it. I don't believe it."

"Why not? Genius kids have a lot of attitude. And at fifteen, you think you can do anything. Who wants to be cooped up in a crappy safe house, protected by strangers?"

"It's not like that, Trace. It's—"

The gunshot burst through the air, birds taking flight in the melee.

Trace didn't think. Didn't question the instinct.

He threw himself at Nic, wrapping her in his arms and cushioning her with his body as they hit the ground.

Chapter Two

"Smooth moves, Romeo. I'm sure it's every woman's dream to lie buried in a patch of scrub grass."

His brother's amused voice floated over him as Trace rolled off Nicola with an alacrity he didn't know he possessed based on the way his head still throbbed.

"What the hell are you doing, Garner? And for the record, she wouldn't be lying in a pile of scrub grass if you weren't shooting at us."

"I wasn't shooting at you. I came to help."

Trace heard the subtle distinction in his brother's voice and ignored it. "Right."

He got to his feet and extended a hand to Nic. He saw her eye his fingers and guessed she was near to shaking him off before thinking better of their audience. It was only as her hand closed around his that Trace recognized his mistake.

Despite the cool air, her hand was smooth and soft and warm. Even better than how she felt was the way her fingers nestled beneath his, a perfect fit.

A remembered fit.

"You going to introduce me?"

Although Trace loved his brother beyond reason, at the moment he'd have been happy if the ground opened up and swallowed Garner whole. Not only was his little brother in the way, but he'd drunk as much the night before and appeared to be no worse for wear.

Perhaps because *little* was a poor description of the six-foot-three-inch former navy SEAL who could still bench three hundred and had shoulders roughly the size of a small truck.

Pissed at the situation and the odd hand fate had just dropped in his lap, Trace tilted his head toward Nic before firmly turning his back. "Nic Miles. My brother, Garner Withrow."

Garner moved up beside Nic as Trace headed off for Magnum, who even now stood about ten feet away. Despite the lack of a tether, the animal had remained in place. Out of boredom or some equine curiosity, Trace had no idea. But he counted himself fortunate he didn't have to add horse wrangling to the morning's adventure.

Especially with his brother's random gunshot.

Magnum had earned himself some extra sugar cubes for the equanimity and serious demonstration of his training.

What the horse couldn't manage, unfortunately, was figuring out how to pick up the pieces. Because while she still hadn't told him much in the way of usable information, Nic was scared. He'd seen her a lot of ways in a lot of situations, but this was a first. Add on a clear streak of maternal—or at least familial—concern, and something had her spooked.

And he was the one she'd hunted down for help.

Her comments suggested someone on the inside, but why now? Or maybe a better question was what had her spooked enough to suddenly take his advice to perpetually watch her back?

Again, all he could come up with was *why.*

Or perhaps a modified: *Why him?*

The day he walked out of CIA headquarters was also the

last day he'd seen her. And he'd spent the past twenty-four months well aware he'd never see either again.

Yet she'd come for him. And remembered vacation story or not, she had to have done some digging to find him. He technically hadn't gone off the grid, but he knew how to bury himself deep, and old habits of self-preservation died hard. Even the horse training business he was building was shrouded deliberately in a corporate shell.

His new life was his choice, but he'd made a lot of choices in the old one that could haunt him if he wasn't careful. When he'd made the decision to start fresh in Liar's Gulch, it was to truly do just that.

Besides, he liked Liar's Gulch specifically because it was hard to find. And he'd further buried his personal information to avoid any visitors from his past. Since Garner had felt the same way after his last SEAL mission gone horribly wrong, their new situation suited them well.

Both of the Withrow brothers were well trained, with years of professional skills still honed sharp. Out here, they could build their equine business as they saw fit. Along with that work—if they decided to act—they could also choose the occasional job that utilized those still-sharp skills for the genuine betterment of others. *Mercenary* was a term with challenging overtones, but it was essentially what they'd become. Only instead of taking jobs for the pay, they each took jobs that provided a way to pay back a former sin.

Trace found missing people and dispatched relatives who regularly overstepped the bounds of what family should endure to far-off places. Garner had taken a particular interest in cold cases, his tenacity and sheer stubbornness serving him well.

And the best part of it all was that each job came with a discreet referral from someone they trusted. Trace's time in the CIA and Garner's in the SEALs ensured they had a strong network of connections. Connections who'd proven themselves over time as determined to work on the right side of the law. As of this week, they'd become a trio when they added Garner's buddy from high school, Jake Stilton, into their midst. A former detective for the Las Vegas PD, Jake seemed happy enough with the decision to trade the Strip for this small corner of nowhere.

As happy as any of them could be anyway.

Jake's arrival had also coincided with the evening's questionable fun at the town bar.

Trace patted Magnum's neck before turning back to where his brother still stood by Nic. He'd overheard their polite conversation, which was an odd joke all its own since *polite* wasn't an adjective he'd use for either his brother or the woman who still haunted his dreams.

A fact his brother was aware of.

Garner might not know Nic by name, but he knew there'd been someone in the past. He'd stayed quiet about it, but Trace knew Garner knew. Another night like last evening, shortly after Garner had settled in Liar's Gulch, had brought on a degree of soul-searching and confessing Trace normally avoided like the plague.

Only that night the whiskey had loosened his tongue. Happy to see his brother again and happier that Garner had survived his last mission—a fate three of his fellow SEAL brothers didn't have—Trace had talked of the woman who nearly did him in.

A decade and a half as an elite operative hadn't been the thing to break him.

A woman had.

So yeah, he'd spilled his guts and given up the real reason he left DC. Why he'd given up the CIA. And why he was determined to live his life with minimal attachment, brotherly bonds the rare exception.

Only now she was here.

And his carefully constructed world had just gone down like a house of cards.

"SO YOU'RE THE BROTHER," Nic murmured as she traipsed back along the rushing stream that led toward Trace's property. She'd checked the area out thoroughly, having already seen the entrance to the large property from the front when she drove by the day before. This morning had been the second part of the exploration, working her way through the hundreds of acres that backed the wide expanse and culminated in this small tributary of the Snake River.

She hadn't lied to Trace—she was desperate, and she was increasingly running out of time—but even with the ticking clock in her mind counting down over Olivia's head, Nic had known she had to be prepared to meet Trace head-on.

She was on his turf, and that required preparation and an understanding of what she was walking into.

But the brother, too?

"And you're the ex," Garner whispered back, his voice equally low.

He knew about her?

Whatever she might have anticipated, Trace sharing the details of his sex life wasn't on the list. The man was a vault, almost in the literal sense of the word. It was a challenge to get anything out of him, and she'd always counted herself lucky somehow whenever she gleaned a small nugget about him or his past.

He could carry a conversation, that was for sure. He was charming and oddly sweet, and it still galled her that it had taken her as long as it had to realize how smoothly he could talk about any number of subjects and still avoid saying anything of substance about himself.

The reference to his wilderness haven had been one of

those rarities. And the talk of a brother late one night after a difficult mission had been another. The rest of what she actually knew about him beyond the physical could be ticked off on the remaining fingers of one hand.

"You going to tell him why you're really here?" Garner's voice remained low, but still loud enough she suspected Trace could pick up on it.

"I already did."

"And?"

"And what? Ball's in your brother's court now."

The muttered "the hell it is" that came winging back through the crisp morning air was the only sign he'd heard her.

But he had.

Garner fell silent, drifting away to make his own path back to the house. She was grateful for the reprieve and took in the surroundings as they walked, careful to look at the landscape and not at Trace's impressive shoulders and delectable backside. She was basically just reversing her early morning course, but she looked out over the landscape with fresh eyes.

Determined eyes.

Because there was no way they could remain on Trace for any longer than necessary. Besides. She'd conquered the first hurdle. Trace hadn't actually shot her, nor she him.

Which was a relief.

Since the discovery Olivia had been taken three days ago, Nic had gone through any number of scenarios in her mind. The first day she'd spent tracking and tracing the child's whereabouts for the previous week. Although technically under federal protection, Olivia was being watched versus held in place. A reality Nic regretted now but which the child's mother had insisted upon.

No one in the Brigante family actually believed Olivia was in danger. And while the CIA had done their best to convince

Eloisa Brigante, the child's mother, that her daughter was at risk from her brother's shadowy organization, the guidance was disregarded as laughable.

"My brother runs an import-export business." Eloisa held up a hand replete with gold rings, her perfect, pink-tipped nails waving in the air. "I realize that you government people often think that's code for any number of crimes, but it's not. Richie's been part of the family business thirty years, first working in it and now running it for almost two decades. He's a good man. The best. I would never put my daughter in harm's way."

"But, Ms. Brigante," Nic tried again. "We've intercepted several suspicious containers across three different ports. All shipments not noted in any manifest. Your daughter's computer abilities are cause for concern."

"Because she knows how to code?"

"Yes. That combined with her rather precocious attempts at interacting with government websites."

Interacting was a subtle euphemism and *precocious* actually translated to successful intrusion into three different government databases, which was the only reason Nic had managed to secure an audience with the child's mother. She had more than enough ammunition to make life difficult for the kid, and the mother knew it.

But once her team had done some digging of their own, they realized that a kid who helped the government's overworked computer geeks find and quickly patch holes was worth her weight in gold.

She was also an in with Brigante Container Corporation, which was how Nic was brought in on the project.

Eloisa's perfectly plucked eyebrows slashed down. "That was a misunderstanding, nothing more. And the coding is for a project at the private school she goes to. All that…" another wave of the hand "…STEM stuff. She's a bright girl. That's all."

With the brick wall standing firm and high, Nic tried another tack. "Allow us to watch out for her then. Our officers are discreet and will blend in."

Eloisa stared her up and down. "You'd blend in with a bunch of kids?"

"We're trained for it."

Eloisa shook her head. "My kid'd make you in thirty paces. So would the rest of them. They're sharp, and they pay attention."

Nic heard the protest, but she also saw the discernible edges of fear in the woman's dark eyes. Eloisa might want to believe her brother was running an aboveboard business, but that small skitter of fear suggested she did have questions.

Nic considered how to play it, her mind whirling through each approach before discarding several. Whatever else she was, Eloisa Brigante was clearly used to hiding that fear behind confident bravado. She wasn't going to be swayed by a sympathetic ear. Nor was she going to be bullied into a decision over her child.

In the end, Nic went with the simplest answer. "Then it's up to me to make sure I blend in, and the kids don't make me or anyone on my team. It's a good thing I still fit into my high school uniform."

An approach that had worked until it didn't, Nic thought with no small measure of disgust as they crossed out of the woods ringing Trace's property and onto the grounds of what was clearly his living area. A rambling two-story farmhouse was visible about three hundred yards off, with land still stretching beyond it. A dirt road cut through the land, and in the far-off distance she could see a small quaint-looking log cabin.

Where Garner lived?

It would make sense. They might be brothers, but it would be difficult to combine lives under one roof at their ages. Nic made a mental note to ask before coming back to her senses and firmly striking it. She didn't care where or how Trace Withrow lived or who he lived with. She needed his help, and that was all.

Then she'd be gone.

And he'd go back to living whatever life it was he'd chosen up here in the Wyoming wilderness.

A large sturdy-looking stable sat off to the north of the main house, and Trace led his horse determinedly in that direction. Garner was already heading for the main house without a backward glance, his interest in what was going on either quelled or he was using that lack of concern as a ruse to get more dirt later.

Which left her to choose the lesser of two evils. Follow a stranger into the main house or follow a man she knew far too well into the stable?

As images of Olivia's cheeky little wave as she headed into school this past Friday filled the forefront of her thoughts— the last time Nic had seen her—she opted for the devil she knew.

And the one she'd come to for help.

TRACE HAD FELT her gaze hard and heavy on his back the entire walk back to the stables. He'd have preferred to ride Magnum, but even he wasn't such an ass that he'd leave Nic behind.

And stuck with his brother, no less.

"You really must need my help." He shot the comment back at her, damning himself by turning around.

She stood in the open doorway of the stable, early morning light haloing her in the frame. Something clenched hard and low in his gut.

Desire? Probably.

But even that was too simple for the swamp of feelings that hadn't let go of him since he turned around to find her staring at him down the barrel of her gun.

Unwilling to spend any longer with the ghosts of his past, he shifted his full attention back to his horse. He made quick work of Magnum's saddle and riding tack before providing the sugar cubes he'd already promised in his mind. The horse's lips feathered over his palm, the sugar gone in an instant before Magnum nuzzled his shoulder for more. The move was as affectionate as the horse got, but Trace took it for the genuine compliment that it was. Magnum's respect might be grudging in his own equine way, but it was absolute. Trace dug a few more cubes out of his pocket, more than grateful for the camaraderie.

As the sugar disappeared, Trace was satisfied he'd settled his immediate debt. He closed the horse's stall door and offered the promise of a return for a midday snack and some time with the currycomb.

He couldn't delay any longer.

Turning toward Nic, Trace was relieved she no longer stood in the doorway, the sunlight a halo over her blond hair. The woman wasn't an angel, and he'd do well to remember that, most recent imagery aside. She had moved fully into the stable, standing beside an empty stall door.

When he bought the property, he'd selected it specifically for the acreage and the ability to build out a proper stable facility. The existing structure had been small, and other than using it as a temporary space for his and Garner's mounts, he'd set about immediately working on the new state-of-the-art facility that he imagined for his program.

His focus was twofold: building a strong program that could both train horses from a young age as well as rehabilitate those that might not move into working ranches but could make wonderful horses for individuals. Since he'd finished out the stables the previous winter, the structure now housed Magnum, a pretty bay quarter horse Garner loved named Lucille, as well as six more that were swiftly moving through the program.

"This is quite a stable." Nic had moved closer, her attention focused on the large brown-and-white Appaloosa peeking over his stall in curiosity at the new visitor.

"It's the heart of my business. I'm determined to build the finest horse-training program in Wyoming."

It was oddly satisfying to see the surprise flash in her blue gaze. Nic had always known how to hold her emotions close, so that slip was as interesting as it was intriguing. "I thought—"

"I came up here to loaf around and play at ranching."

"No, of course not. I guess I just didn't realize you had such a thing for horses."

If asked even a few years earlier, Trace wouldn't have said he had a *thing for horses*, either, but the decision to leave the CIA and all he'd ever known had forced him to reconsider what he did want out of his life.

The animals were simple—real—and they provided a level of solace he'd never imagined. Along with the selective assignments he and Garner chose to take on, Trace had used the past two years to regain control of his life. It was hardwon, but it felt real and right and true, even as recently as his hungover ride out this morning.

Which made it such a shock that this woman had managed to upend the equilibrium he'd finely honed these past twenty-four months. A truth that hit him like a ton of bricks as Nicola Miles still stood fully in his line of sight.

"I am sorry about the gun," Nic added when he still hadn't responded, that crystalline gaze never leaving his. "I was pretty sure you'd help me, but I needed to hedge my bets."

"Sure. Right."

"And a kid's involved."

That was the second time she'd brought up the kid, and Trace wasn't sure what to make of it. While they'd spent precious little time together discussing future hopes and dreams, when they did discuss anything beyond their world at the CIA, it wasn't to talk about children. Did she want them?

And what was it about this one child in particular that had her so insistent?

Trace might have his own personal lingering issues with the CIA and how the agency operated, but he'd always taken his work seriously. He believed in what he was doing and took pride in the fact that their work ensured the safety of millions of people. But he'd learned early in his training that you didn't get attached to an asset. That way lay madness.

Not to mention a personal attachment could get you and the asset killed.

Nic knew that as well as he did. So what was going on here?

He didn't want this. Had actively left DC to avoid facing any of it ever again.

Yet as he stood there, staring at her, he knew the truth.

He was in. He had been since the moment he caught sight of her with that damn gun pointed at his chest.

It had never been anything else with her.

Whether he wanted it or not, Trace didn't need the details to know the truth. He was all in.

Chapter Three

Although she'd have preferred the more earthy air of the stables and the space to move around, in the end, Nic suggested they head into the house. Coffee and a computer were in order for what she needed to do, and both were in short supply out with the horses.

Soon, coffee, hot and black, was in a mug in front of her. Trace had a matched mug of his own as he took a seat opposite her in the kitchen. "What's the CIA doing playing bodyguard to a kid? On US soil, no less."

Right to the point.

Which was what Nic needed, not to mention the reason she was here. But would it kill him to ask a few pleasantries first? How was she doing? Was that bistro they loved in Georgetown still open? Who's running the department now?

With that uncanny knack he'd always had, Trace eyed her over the rim of his mug. "And does Mick's still serve that mussels-in-garlic appetizer I loved?"

"I don't know. I haven't been ba—" Nic hated the prim tone. Hated even more that he'd read her so easily. "I haven't been there in a while."

He shrugged, but she saw the first semblance of a smile at the corner of his lips. "I'll have to look up the menu online."

The smile vanished, falling away quickly enough. "Now. Walk me through it."

"The CIA's been following the Brigante family's activities for a few years now."

"Brigante?" Trace's eyebrows rose. "Shipping?"

His question was proof that she'd come to the right place. He might believe himself long past his time in the CIA, but it was clear he was still on the pulse of, well, everything.

"The owner hit the radar the first time a shipment came up short versus its manifest, and we've been keeping tabs ever since."

"What does the kid have to do with it?"

"Niece to said shipping owner. Genius IQ. And a special sort of skill with the computer."

Trace sat back at that and stared down into his coffee. "You think the kid's helping?"

"I think the kid's being forced to help. And because of those superior skills, she's been kidnapped by the uncle. Her mother wouldn't let us put her under protection, and other than a lot of suspicion we don't have anything to make the situation a more formal arrangement."

"So why are you pushing this without proof?"

"Because I know. I recognize the kid's skill and vulnerability. She's at risk, Trace. And now that she's gone missing, it's on me that I didn't push the issue and follow the instincts that have been clamoring about this from the first."

"What do you have on the uncle?"

She enumerated the list of details they'd secured over the past few months: the continued gaps in the manifests each time a Brigante freighter came into port; the suspicious loss at sea of a ship bound for the Middle East; and a strange run-in with pirates in the South China Sea that had the air of a faked tragedy stamped all over it.

Trace listened to it all, taking it in and saying little. Yet as Nic watched him, she saw what she always had: the way thoughts and ideas moved through his mind. Saw the way a plan built and evolved and came together as he listened to her.

It was only when she was done that he finally spoke.

"And you say the mother's firm that her brother's clean and the kid isn't in danger."

"Yes."

"Any reason to think the mom's involved? Or worse, the kid?"

Nic set her mug down. The thought was the logical next step—it was what they'd trained for—and the speed with which he'd arrived at the conclusion was one thing. The fact that it matched her thoughts as she'd worked this case, even more so.

She'd dug hard into the mother, especially after Eloisa seemed so reluctant to have her child placed under protection. And from the start, Nic had looked every which way she could think of against Olivia. It went against every instinct to think a kid was capable at that level, but she'd learned long ago not to assume. Or to underestimate the power and skill of a child. Especially at fifteen.

Although she was now twice that age, Nic still remembered that time. Remembered how clearly she saw the world and her role in it. And could recall, with absolute ease, how determined she was to make the life she wanted.

For her, that was the CIA.

It wouldn't be a huge leap to assume Olivia could be recruited into the family business. Especially if the computer work gave her a chance to flex muscles she was already proud of. In control of.

"Any chance the kid just went under for a few days? Played hooky on Friday and laid low for the weekend? Does she have a boyfriend? Girlfriend? Secret passion project?" Trace listed off the possibilities, and Nic recognized the validity in walking through all of them again with fresh eyes.

Even though she'd discarded each and every one already.

"Nope. None of those things."

He got up to refill his mug, crossing back over to her to give her a top-up as well. "Looks like you've got a missing asset then."

"And?"

"And it looks like I'm going to help you find her."

TRACE WAS STILL cursing himself an hour later as Nic flipped through various files on her computer. Although he'd known damn well that he was going to say yes about eight nanoseconds after she asked him for help, he'd envisioned himself playing it a bit cooler. Probing for more details. Pressing her on what work they'd done to date to protect the kid.

Hell, even just sitting there with his resting jerk face to make her sweat for a few minutes.

But damn it all, there was a kid involved. A smart kid who had to be scared out of her mind if she was being held by someone she would have trusted. It was the vulnerability that tugged at him. That lack of power that defined childhood. It had certainly defined him and Garner and, from what he'd pieced together in their time with each other, Nic as well.

Nic tapped a few keystrokes, screen after screen lighting up with information as she walked him through the case file. The tech she'd logged in to was impressive. He'd been gone two years, but in that time the security had advanced several generations. Her log-in from a SAT phone had followed with an extensive VPN protocol that would make a tech geek weep.

But once she got through… Hoo boy, it was the mother lode.

"Is there any file you can't access there?"

"No."

They were sitting side by side at the kitchen table, and just the way she tilted her head to look at him nearly had his breath catching in his throat.

How could he have forgotten how beautiful she was?

Her beauty had always been something that could stop him in his tracks, and he was suddenly grateful for the firm chair beneath him. She wasn't classically beautiful. Her features were too sharp for what would technically pass as physical perfection. Yet there was something about the way all those angles fit together, set off by a soft sweep of hair that framed her chin, that had done him in from the first.

From the moment he met her, he'd longed to touch all those hard angles and explore what he just knew would be soft skin beneath his fingers. Those sharp edges had always suggested a man should back off, yet all he'd wanted to do was move in close.

And he hadn't been alone in his attraction. They'd worked together for nearly a year before they'd given in. Before those three glorious months when she was his. Through the ups and downs of their job. Through the nights that never stayed dark quite long enough to satisfy his need for her. And through the moments—far too few of them in the end—when he'd felt himself giving in to something that was bigger than he was.

A need so fierce and deep that it had scared him beyond measure.

Guns and criminals and the world's safety hanging in the balance…he'd trained for that.

But love with an equal? Nothing could be harder. And, in the end, impossible.

"Flip back to the page on the uncle."

She did as he asked, the dossier on Richie Brigante filling the screen. Trace was grateful for the distraction and turned his attention to the always-thorough briefing document.

The guy was in his late forties and had been involved with Brigante Container Corporation since high school. Despite it being a family business, young Richie had needed to earn his keep along with the rest of the staff that worked there.

Trace scanned further, noting the guy had done it all. He'd filed paperwork in the home office, done a six-month rotation in the shipping yard and then followed it up with three rotations at sea. Far-flung places, too, with real challenges to cargo ships, not some rich-kid pleasure cruise down to the Caribbean. The man was trained in the family business from the ground up.

"What about the mother?"

Before Nic could do it, Trace was following the thought with action. His hand brushed over hers as he reached for the keyboard, and he felt the warmth of her fingers where they brushed his.

It was a stupid accident, but he felt the touch echo more keenly through his body than any physical encounter he'd had in the past two years.

And he didn't miss how she snatched her hand back as if singed.

He ignored it, already feeling stupid for the well of emotion he wasn't able to hold back and hadn't yet figured out a way to ignore. The coffee had kicked in and, along with three aspirin, was holding the headache at bay, but the rush of seeing her again was still too close to the surface.

He needed to get control.

And there was no better way to do that than to bury himself in work.

He was free at the moment, his last job having wrapped a week ago and nothing new on the horizon. What was likely going to be another week of fishing, working with the horses and doing some cleanup around the ranch wasn't meant to be.

They had a kid to find.

Trace toggled up and down the page with the arrow keys, reading the dossier on Eloisa Brigante. She'd married the kid's father briefly around the time she got pregnant but had kept her maiden name.

"Didn't want to give up the prestige of the family moniker," Trace muttered. Even as he thought it, he recognized that the kid had the name, too. "That's interesting."

"What?"

"The mother did marry the father but kept her own name. Big money and lots of influence, that makes sense. But she gave the kid the same last name."

"Rich people do strange things."

"Sure." They did do strange things, and Trace had been around long enough to know there was no accounting for any number of human quirks, but it still struck him as a bit…off. "Didn't the father have a say in it?"

"We looked at him early on. Nothing much popped. He visits Olivia for birthdays and holidays, and that's about it."

"So not involved in supersmart kiddo's life."

"Maybe it works for them."

He caught the edge of something in her voice, and curiosity tugged at him. "Maybe it does. Or maybe it doesn't."

"You think the father's involved?" Nic asked.

He shifted his attention off the screen, careful to keep his expression neutral. "I think I'm asking."

She sighed but eased off a bit. "All I mean is that I've already looked under that rock. Just like I looked at extended family, friends, any other rich kids' families she goes to school with. Sometimes kids just get a crappy family deal."

He almost believed her. The nonchalant way she went through the list. The idea that she'd turned over every stone. But it was there at the end, when she mentioned that oh-so-true reality of childhood for some, that he saw it.

Crystal fire.

It lit the depths of her blue eyes, flashing like a lightning storm, and added even more proof that something about this job had become personal for her.

"Okay, fine. Maybe it's not the father. But maybe it turns right back to Olivia. What if the kid resents the crappy family deal? And what if the crappy family deal makes her even more willing to help the uncle?"

"That's an awful big leap, Trace."

"Is it? Childhood experiences, especially trauma, can drive a hell of a lot of bad decisions." They'd certainly driven his life.

But this wasn't about him. A fact that was increasingly clear as he watched the emotions play across her normally stoic face.

Nicola Miles was a highly trained agent of the government. She knew how to assess any situation and adapt. And she never let her own emotions come through.

So why now?

And why this case?

That lone question continued to hammer at him. Yes, she saw something in the kid. Even if it was something kindred, the fact remained Nic knew how to keep her professional priorities intact. Always. Hadn't he learned that the hard way?

She was the consummate professional, and she never let her emotions interfere with…

"Well, hell." He spit out the words along with a few more choice curses as the truth sank in. She'd even told him herself, yet he'd blithely ignored whatever problems she was battling inside the organization. "Who's involved in this?"

"No one. I mean, I can't prove—"

"Nic." He let her name hang there, unwilling to give another inch. Damn it, not even another millimeter.

"I—" She stopped, the most indecisive he'd ever seen her.

And that was when the last puzzle piece fell into place.

Nic, the ever-steady champion of the CIA, had well and truly had her blinders torn off.

"Who betrayed you on this?"

"I don't know."

"Don't know? Or won't tell me?"

Once more, something flickered in the depth of those eyes that were so good at shutting everyone out. Recognition? Or even just her own suspicions? "I don't know, Trace. But I know it's someone inside. They made sure the agents on duty on Friday were called off the scent for a matter of minutes. And in that time Olivia vanished."

Images of his life before flooded his mind. Trace had always known—or maybe more to the point, accepted—that the CIA operated under its own rules. Along with every other aspect of intelligence, there was no other way to manage the shadowy world that existed around information gathering, spy tactics and covert operations.

Anyone who believed otherwise was fooling themselves. Hard.

Nic had always claimed she understood that, yet believed in the underlying purpose of what she was doing. She believed in the men and women she worked with to achieve a common set of goals. And she believed that in the end the organization would always do what was right.

Not *easy*, she'd argued with him the few times their differing beliefs blew up into a full-out fight. But *right*.

"So you don't think she's with the uncle at all? You think the CIA's got someone kidnapping kids?"

"I'm assuming she is with the uncle. But that one of our agents let him have her."

Sure, money was a powerful lure. And Brigante was wealthy, but enough for an agent to ruin their career over? Enough to put a kid in jeopardy?

Something didn't add up, and he was about to press her

when the screen flickered, grabbing his attention. What he'd assumed was the screen fading to black as it went into energy-saving mode did the opposite.

"Nic? What is this?"

The gaze that had been tight on him flipped to the screen. "What's what?"

The dossier files onscreen faded to the background as a large terminal window popped up. It was the sort of window that came up before instructions to reboot kicked in. "What's it doing?"

The new window filled with code, the image at odds with the slick interface it replaced. This was rudimentary at best, and hardly a time for her computer to crap out on them.

"Should you restart—" The question died on his lips as words became visible in the command line.

Nic. It's me Olivia. I'm in trouble.

A cursor blinked at the end of the word *trouble*, like a flashing sign.

Are you there? You were just there. I saw you typing a few minutes ago.

"What does she mean she saw us typing?" Trace reached for the computer, but Nic beat him to it, tilting the machine toward her. A hard sigh whistled through her lips as she set her hands on the keyboard. Where are you?

The cursor barely had time to blink as Olivia's response came winging back. I don't know.

Who are you with?

I don't

The screen went blank, the code terminal winking out as if it had never been.

"What the hell was that?"

Nic tapped at keys, but no matter what she tried she couldn't seem to get the kid back.

"Can I try?"

She pushed the laptop toward him. "I think we need to act fast."

He wouldn't classify himself as highly proficient, but he'd had basic coding as part of his training. But after three attempts, he had to admit that he had no idea how to get the terminal back up onscreen. "The kid hacked a CIA VPN."

"I know."

Nic's words seemed to hang in the air between them before Trace pressed again, "A highly specialized, deeply veiled government database. And the kid hacked it."

"I know."

"Those are more than 'some skills,' Nic. That's a walking felony with a side of treason tossed in."

"I know!" She scrubbed a hand over her face before shoving her hair out of her eyes. "All right, Trace. I get it."

"What the hell are you involved with?"

"I'm not sure anymore."

Chapter Four

Why had she come here?

The question had drifted in and out of her mind throughout the long flights with three plane changes to Cheyenne. It grew more intense as she made the drive across the state to the barely-a-dot-on-the-map Liar's Gulch.

But it was nearly deafening earlier as she'd watched Trace walk around the stables, currying his horse, putting up tack and asking the pointed questions he was so good at.

It accompanied the other question that hadn't drifted far from her thoughts.

Who was this man?

She'd believed she knew him, but in the time since they'd been apart, Nic realized it was quite possible she hadn't known him at all. If she had, would she really have walked away?

Because that truth—the fact that *she'd* walked—had haunted her every moment of every minute they'd been apart these past two years.

Whatever she'd believed about their differences of opinion, she never doubted his competence or his inner drive. Neither had she ever doubted the core values and tenets he chose to live by.

He wasn't by the book, but he wasn't a villain, either. In

fact, she'd increasingly come to admit he was one of the good guys. Maybe the very best.

Here in this completely foreign environment, he was calm, cool and competent. Just as he'd been in war-torn countries or in high-level tactical meetings in Washington, DC. And now he'd gone and done it again, those enigmatic gray eyes totally focused on her and the question of what had happened to Olivia Brigante.

"You owe me an answer."

She did owe him an answer, Nic admitted to herself. She owed him far more, if she were honest, but it was a place to start.

"I know. Truly, I do. But I can't say I know myself."

He sighed, but she saw a new level of acceptance in his gaze. It gave her the slightest shot of hope. And, maybe, a little voice whispered, proof she'd come to the right place.

He glanced at her dark laptop once more before nodding. "All right. Let's shift things a bit. You've got a missing kid and suspicious CIA behavior at the time the kid went missing. What else is off?"

"Off how?"

"This didn't just happen. You're a company man through and through."

She shot him a dark eye at that one. "Last time I checked, my equipment was fully female."

"Don't I know it." That gray of his eyes heated ever so slightly, and she wasn't dead enough inside not to register it. Was even more honest with herself to admit she'd have loved to see it flash a few seconds longer before he pressed on, "You know what I mean. 'Company man' isn't gender-specific but a type of agent. And you've been one since the day you walked in."

"As opposed to your shoot-first-ask-later renegade approach to it all?"

This time that grin flashed hard and long, and damn it if her breath didn't catch in her throat. "It worked for a long time. Until it didn't."

Since that smile was still firmly in place, Nic avoided going too far down the fanciful path her memories seemed determined to follow.

And then he made it a wee bit easier when he went straight back into interrogation mode, that smile falling only to be replaced with grim determination. "What else has been nagging your mind on this? Odd coincidences. Off moments. Strange flickers of awareness you can't shake. Something has to have your senses on high alert, or you wouldn't be so convinced this was an inside job."

"That's the problem. I can't point to anything specific. Nothing that I can clearly say is off. Yet it is. It all is."

"So someone's covering their tracks very well."

Was that it?

Before she could say anything, he pushed on, "You're on Rannell's team now, right?"

"How'd you know? You were gone before I moved over."

Trace shrugged, but the move was anything but casual. Did the man even do casual? She'd never seen it.

Instead, that laid-back veneer had always reminded her of a lion on the Serengeti, yawning one minute in the afternoon sun and then moving at warp speed toward a gazelle the next.

Nic had never considered herself a shy, retiring violet, but she'd also never been able to shake the mix of silent thrill and subtle admission that she was happy Trace Withrow was her ally, not her enemy.

"He's had his eye on you for a while. Figured he'd get his way sooner or later."

"Dirk Rannell is a highly respected member of the agency." One who'd first been a highly respected analyst who worked his way up the ladder into management. She'd always found him somewhat unconventional—the man's analytical talents were robust, but as a consequence he lived in his head. Still, he didn't suffer fools. Nor did he live so deeply in his head that he missed what was happening around him.

Despite all that, she liked working for him, thought him to be a fair man and often found the two of them simpatico on the analytical aspects of their work.

"Besides, it was a mutual move onto his team when you left, and Bane retired. Why do you ask?"

"Rannell's also a company man. Which leads me to believe he'd be hard-pressed to see some of his team members for who they were if you've got a snake in your midst."

"That's not very broad-minded of you."

"Yet I'm the one you came to for help."

The easy congeniality that had hovered between them even a few minutes before had faded, replaced by a simmering anger Nic recognized. Wasn't this how it always went down between them?

A big part of her knew she needed to keep her cool. She was on wickedly thin ice, after all. Especially with starting their reunion by pulling a gun on him.

But damn it all, why was he insistent on going straight back to jerk territory at the earliest sign of a difference of opinion?

"Before you start poking at me, would you give me a damn minute to follow you? You make assumptions about who I am, who I'm working for, why I'm here. You readily accuse others of having biases, but you refuse to see your own."

"You're right. And because of it, I got out."

Before she could respond to that, he was out of his chair, marching across the kitchen to a sleek coffee maker that looked like it could calculate the algorithms to put a man on the moon while it brewed a fresh cup.

Nic sat there a full thirty seconds, stunned.

Was he actually admitting he'd contributed to his exit from the CIA? Because whatever she'd thought about his departure two years ago, nothing would have made her think that decision was a mutual one.

"What's this about?" Nic asked, careful to keep her tone neutral.

"It's not about anything."

"Oh no. You don't get to do that. You don't get to drop bombs and then clam up like it's none of my business."

Whatever had immobilized her initially had her moving out of her chair, crossing to where he stood at the counter, his back still to her.

It dawned on her a heartbeat too late that she'd gotten too close. Heat radiated off that broad back in waves and she could practically feel the hard lines of his body beneath her fingertips, even if it had been twenty-four endlessly long months since she'd last touched him.

"It's not your business, Nic." The words were low. Feral. And tinged with a level of pain she'd never have imagined. Gone was that congenial man who grinned at her with a gleam in his eye that affirmed he'd seen her naked. In its place was a wounded animal. One who'd never fully healed.

So she reached out and placed her hand on that back, heat searing through her palm and radiating up her arm.

Only it was the wounded animal who turned on her, pain filling his gray eyes while a sense of isolation and loneliness she'd never seen before seemed to pulse in lockstep with that heat.

It was that moment when she admitted she'd overstepped.

Especially when his arms wrapped around her, pulling her close. Determination carved harsh lines in his face, and she had the briefest thought he looked like a fallen angel.

And then his head bent toward her, his lips so close they brushed hers when he finally spoke.

"What do you want, Nicola? Because I'm losing my patience waiting for you to answer my questions."

HE WAS BEYOND THIS.

He *should* be beyond this.

He *needed* to be beyond this.

Yet less than an hour in her company, and all he could think of was getting his hands on this woman and touching all the places he knew ignited a blaze between them. And still, he held himself back, his lips hovering over hers.

"I want to find a lost child."

"Nope." He shook his head slightly, their breaths mingling. "That's too easy an answer. Try again."

"It's the only answer I've got."

He stepped back then, his body sending up flares to keep holding her while his will exerted a last fleeting attempt at saving himself. "Not buying it."

"You don't think this is about a child?"

He had to give her credit that she could manifest that stern voice even when her breath was still ragged and her pupils were wide in those crystalline blue eyes. "I think you've convinced yourself it's only about a child, and we both know that's a lie."

"Her safety is essential."

"Without question. And I've already told you, I'll help you. What I want to know is why the first time you decided to run from your ivory federal tower you headed straight for me?"

"Looks like I'm not the only one running. In a span of ninety seconds, you've tried to change the subject, kiss me and twist the conversation back at me. What are *you* running from, Trace?"

He'd spent the past two years determinedly convincing himself he hadn't run from anything. That his time in the

CIA was simply over, a tenure that ended when enough was enough.

Even if *enough* was finding out your boss and team leader had funneled secrets overseas to one of the worst terrorist groups in the world.

And even when *worse than enough* was when you took the intel to upper management who affirmed in no uncertain terms, yet without *actually* confirming a damn thing, that they'd sanctioned it.

All the memories mixed in with those truths swirled around the ones of him and Nic at the same time. Their liaison had started as a way to blow off steam out on missions and had turned too quickly into something more.

In the end, he'd accepted it meant more to him than it did to her, but he'd still have bet his last breath she'd felt the *more*, too.

"It was another time and place, more than two thousand miles from here," he said. "It's over and past."

"Yeah, right. If it's so over, why do you live up here so far away from civilization? And if your time in DC is so over, why can't you just respond to my questions?"

"Because I don't owe you answers anymore."

Without knowing why, Trace pushed off the counter and headed out of the kitchen without a backward glance.

It put him at a disadvantage, leaving when the conversation went dark and twisty, his parting shot bordering on petulant, but he couldn't stand there any longer. Couldn't stand there with his still-pounding head and the endless swaths of memories that wouldn't abate.

Most of all, he couldn't stand there with the gentle heat of her body and the scent that was distinctly Nicola Miles washing over him.

She'd still be there whether or not he escaped to tend the horses for a while. The kid would still be missing, too. And, damn it to hell, two years of secrets he wasn't able to face yet would still carve a chasm between them.

Each of those facts blazed through his mind as he stomped back into the stables five minutes later. He changed into work boots and set about mucking stalls, spending some quiet time with each of their equine charges and doing his level best to calm himself right out of his miserable memories.

It nearly worked until Garner breezed in an hour later. "There's an incredibly attractive woman working on a computer in our kitchen."

"Her prerogative."

Dark brows over deep brown eyes so like their mother's shot up into his brother's forehead. "You sure about that?"

"Don't you have somewhere to be?"

"Nope."

"I thought you were going to show Jake around a bit."

"He's still sleeping off his warm welcome into town last night."

Sleeping? Trace was about to think less of their new tenant when he glanced down at his watch only to realize it still wasn't even ten in the morning.

A fact Garner quickly punctuated with another reminder of last night's fun. "We didn't walk in until after two, and the guy spent nearly all day yesterday driving up from Vegas."

"Yeah. Right. Got it."

"Looks like you're stuck with me."

Trace narrowly avoided grunting at his brother before turning on his heel and heading down to Libby's stall. Their sweet girl—a black-and-white quarter horse they'd purchased the prior summer—leaned in to nuzzle his neck as he patted hers in turn. "How are you doing in this cold weather, baby girl?"

He moved into her stall, checking her water as he kept up a steady stream of nonsense about the expected snowstorm predicted for later that week and how they'd take good care of her through it all.

Despite his pointed attempt to ignore his brother, the man obviously missed the memo. "Those storm predictions sound like they're no joke."

Trace glanced up to find Garner's large form hulking in the doorway of Libby's stall. "It's snowed before, it'll snow again. We'll work through it."

"I suppose *we* will. But you and Nicola might need to travel in it."

Trace leaned on the broom he was using to clean Libby's stall and stared at his brother. "Why are you poking at this?"

"Consider this volunteering myself for service."

"Service for what?"

"Helping you get your head out of your ass. A state you'd better figure out pretty damn quick if you mean to actually help her."

The expletive hovered there, just at the edge of Trace's tongue. It nearly slipped out—he and Garner didn't exactly tiptoe around each other—but something held him back. And before he could think better of it, something even more uncomfortable fell from his lips. "You think I can't handle this?"

"I don't question your ability to handle things, Trace. I never have. What I question is your ability to come back from this."

Although they'd spent nearly their entire adult lives apart until Garner's move to Wyoming almost two years before, there was no one Trace respected more. Even in the moments when he'd happily punch his brother in the face.

"I know how to take care of myself."

"Something I never question. But your only focus in this will be taking care of her, and that's the real danger."

Trace heard something just beneath that answer—an honesty even more raw than Garner's words. "You don't like Nic."

"It's not that simple."

"You sure?"

Garner sighed and stepped backward through the stall door. "You keep leaping to answers that aren't mine. Why don't you finish up what you're doing, and we'll talk later?"

There were endless dimensions to their relationship—both steeped in being siblings *and* government operatives—but nowhere before had either of them ever used those things as an excuse not to hash out a problem.

The anger was already washing over Trace in a tsunami at the idea Garner would walk away when stark reality slammed into it with the force of an earthquake.

Neither of them *ever* walked away.

Yet Garner was now.

Avoiding the urge to toss the heavy broom across Libby's stall, Trace lightly settled it against the far wall. Refusing to allow a single bit of that anger to reflect at her, he gave the horse a small pat and a few murmured words before gently closing and locking the stall door.

And then he went on the attack.

"I'm finished!" Trace hollered at his brother's retreating back.

"Later!"

"Sonofabitch," he muttered, chasing off after Garner. His head still throbbed with the hangover, and his emotions still roiled at Nic's return, and despite it all, Trace forced himself to remain in control.

Barely.

"What the hell is this all about?" He reached Garner just before he could cross the threshold of the barn.

His brother turned, but where Trace expected a matched wall of anger, all he saw was quiet resignation. And how was it *that* sparked more of his anger than actually locking horns like two angry bulls?

"You tell me."

"Oh, cut the cryptic BS, G. What is with you?"

The easygoing smile that normally filled Garner's face was nowhere in sight. Instead, all Trace saw was a grim sort of resolve. "What's the end game here?"

"I help Nic, and we save a child in grave danger."

"I don't doubt you'll do that. I mean after you save the kid. The real end game. When the mission is over, and you're finally forced to deal with having Nic back in your life."

"Why would I deal with anything? She's walking right back out the way she came in."

Garner's gaze never left his, even as his dark eyebrows slashed over narrowed eyes. "And you're gonna be okay with that?"

"Of course."

"Then you're telling yourself lies."

"I'm not—" Trace stopped and shook his head. He would not let his brother do this to him. He needed to keep himself mentally sharp and prepared, because no matter how much faith he had in himself and Nic that they'd bring the child home safely, it wasn't going to be a cakewalk. Wasn't that why Nic had come to him in the first place? "I can do whatever needs to be done."

"And you will do it. Being in love with the woman has nothing to do with that."

"I'm not in love with her."

"Then I'm forced to repeat myself." Garner's gaze only grew darker. "The end game matters a hell of a lot, and you're lying to yourself if you think otherwise."

Trace only stared at his brother, unwilling to ask the unspoken *why*. Even when Garner's unrelenting honesty continued unabated.

"Because you are in love with her, and I don't think you have it in you to watch her walk away twice."

NIC STARED AT her laptop screen, frustrated when each and every programming trick she possessed—though limited— failed to produce another connection with Olivia.

She could call in a favor and ask one of her tech geeks to help her, but she had no way of knowing where loyalties were held right now. She wasn't taking help off the table, but she'd been in Wyoming less than twelve hours. She'd like to give it a bit more time before tapping back into home base for help when the problems in Langley were the exact reason she'd left.

A raspy cough pulled her out of her musings when she looked up to find a tall, lean man with a few days' scruff, no shirt and jeans come strolling into the kitchen, a German shepherd by his side.

"Hello?"

He looked startled as steel blue eyes, shot through with red, met hers. The dog, on the other hand, seemed unaffected as he stared at her with big brown eyes, his stance perfectly still beside the man. "Hey." Before she could say anything, he added, "I'm sorry. I didn't know... I mean, I didn't realize—" He broke off, confusion adding to the mix of an obvious hangover. "Did you come home with me?"

"No."

"With Trace or Garner?"

"No."

"That's a relief."

He turned toward the counter and the coffeepot without a backward glance, and Nic was amused despite the odd greeting and obvious lack of memory from the night before. She normally wouldn't be quite so forgiving of such an oblivious reaction to sex with a stranger, but there was something about the guy that tugged at her.

A strange loneliness blanketed him—which was an exceptionally odd reaction to a total stranger—but the sense rolling off him was overwhelmingly clear.

Or at least it was to her.

"Is that how you greet all your one-night stands?"

The man never turned around, his words gravelly as he remained facing the coffeepot. "I've never been a big fan of them, so I couldn't quite say."

After a hearty gulp of what had to be scalding coffee, the man busied himself filling a bowl beside the fridge with fresh water and a second bowl with kibble he pulled from under the sink.

With the dog happily scarfing down his food—after the command that he could, of course—a few minutes later, the man finally took a seat opposite her at the table, extending a hand. "Jake Stilton." He nodded a head toward the dog. "That's Hogan."

"I'm Nic."

"How'd you wander in here?"

"I used to work with Trace."

Jake's gaze narrowed, and for the first time she had the subtle sense the dazed-and-confused routine might all be a bit of an act. "Man's a horse trainer now."

"I know."

"Do you?" Jake stared at her over the top of his mug that still puffed steam, and she couldn't deny the continued concern that he was burning a path down his esophagus.

She also couldn't deny the obvious questions of why she was here and what sort of problems she'd brought to Trace's doorstep.

Before she could summon up a response, Trace and Garner came into the kitchen. When she'd first settled herself at the large rectangular table, she'd thought the room rather expansive, but the space suddenly felt small with three large men and a dangerous-looking dog that had just finished its breakfast.

"Jake." Trace's voice held a raw edge she recognized. She'd heard it rarely in the time they worked together, but those ragged edges suggested he was keeping his patience on a very short leash.

"Morning." Jake nodded.

"I see you've met Nicola."

"Just sat down. We were getting acquainted." The wry tilt that edged Jake's mouth almost had her smiling in return, but Nic wasn't ready to poke the bear that was Trace Withrow in this moment.

Even if he had gotten all up in her space, then left her for an hour in the kitchen alone to reflect on…*easier* times between them.

"Yes, we were. Jake was unduly concerned I might have been a one-night stand who was overstaying her welcome." She added a syrupy sweet smile for good measure, only to get a wicked smile in return from the half-naked man across the table.

"A man can't be too sure when a pretty woman looking fresh as a daisy is sitting in his still-unfamiliar kitchen."

"Nic and Trace used to work together." Garner reiterated the path she'd already started down, before jerking a thumb over his shoulder. "Why don't we leave them to it since it looks like they're going to be working together again?"

Jake's steely gaze flashed with interest, but he stood and headed for the coffeepot. "Anyone need a refill?"

Trace's "no" came as fast as her own.

Which left Jake to offer up one more of those knowing smiles before he headed out, whistling for the dog. "Come on, Hogan. Let's go explore our new home."

Garner followed, giving the dog a wide berth, but Nic didn't miss the last glance he gave his brother before leaving the room.

Trace remained standing but did settle himself against the counter. "I see you met Jake."

"Another musketeer?"

"Maybe yes, maybe no. He's Garner's friend from way back. He's giving Liar's Gulch a try."

"I'd say best of luck to him, but he's not going to get very far unless he exorcises those ghosts in his eyes."

"That's an awfully quick take."

"One I'm well trained to make."

The mulish expression never left Trace's face, his mouth a grim line beneath the day's growth of beard. He did, however, back off a tiny bit as he pushed off the counter and crossed to the table. "Did Olivia reach back out?"

"No, and I haven't found a way to reverse whatever it was that she did to get into my system."

"Kid's smart."

"The kid is off the charts in every way. That's what worries me."

Whatever tension had gripped them from the start faded as Trace leaned into the case. "Isn't that a good thing?"

"Yes and no."

"If she's with family, that has to give her some protection. It's not an ideal situation, and we'll get her out, but do you really think her uncle's going to hurt her?"

Nic had weighed this problem since the moment she learned Olivia had been taken. It had consumed her all the way to Wyoming. The wild card in all this was Olivia. She was in danger *because* of how smart she was. "A child with such formidable abilities? That's what worries me the most."

"Her ability to use those smarts has gotten her this far," Trace said.

"And it's her lack of understanding of how to wield them that's put her in grave danger."

Chapter Five

Trace carefully folded the stack of laundry on his bed and cycled through all he'd learned that morning. His former colleagues had really fouled up the mission if they let a kid under their protection go missing. Ops weren't foolproof, but mistakes like this didn't rest easy on a team.

It certainly didn't rest easy on Nic. But more than that, there was a huge risk of embarrassment and head rolls for the higher-ups for a screwup like this.

His own experience there at the end had Trace considering if the loss of the child was deliberate. It couldn't be ruled out, but it did make him wonder if it was also a sign of more dysfunction in the organization than anyone wanted to admit.

When the world's a dumpster fire, you fight the biggest ones first.

Those prophetic words—offered by his first mentor once he'd joined the agency—drifted through his mind as he stowed his clothes in his dresser.

He wasn't immune to the global challenges faced by everyone in law enforcement, no matter the level or jurisdiction. The work was hard. For a long time, he'd believed it was supposed to be hard. That was how he knew he was making a difference.

It was only when he understood the lines between good

and bad were blurrier than he ever could have imagined that
he'd given in and jumped ship.

What I question is your ability to come back from this...

*The end game matters a hell of a lot, and you're lying to
yourself if you think otherwise...*

*Because you are in love with her, and I don't think you
have it in you to watch her walk away twice...*

Trace shook off Garner's words, unwilling to think of them
as anything but his brother's overactive protection gene kicking into high gear. He knew his own damn mind, and he'd
done just fine protecting himself for nearly four decades.
He didn't need platitudes or questions, no matter how well-
meaning.

Which would have been fine, Trace considered as he
dropped down on the bed, bending forward to put his head
in his hands, if Garner wasn't right.

He *was* in love with Nic.

Hopelessly.

Desperately.

Two truths that flew in the face of every act of self-preservation he'd attempted.

Images he'd ruthlessly refused purchase in his mind's eye
these past few years filled him on a rush.

The two of them laughing together over a bottle of wine
at a sidewalk café in Paris the night they recovered nuclear
codes put at risk by a double agent.

The hot, thick air that surrounded them on a mission in
Colombia in the middle of August. The languid heat had only
added to his need for her as they'd come together over and
over in their small hotel room.

And that last time together, in his bedroom in DC. Their
lovemaking had carried an urgency he'd never experienced
in his life.

It had held anger, too, Trace admitted to himself as he

stood up from the bed. Anger that carried him out of the city and more than two thousand miles across the country to live practically off the grid. Oh, he wasn't quite ready to make himself invisible, but he'd done a damn good job of locking down the essentials.

"And she found you anyway," he muttered to himself. A reality that wasn't going to change by hiding in his room.

A few minutes later, Trace walked back into the kitchen, only to find her closed laptop on the table. He supposed that act sent a bit of a message. The woman he knew wouldn't be parted from her work tech for any reason. The fact she'd left it there on the table had to mean that while she might be in Wyoming grudgingly, she did trust them.

It did leave him curious, though...

Where had she gone?

He hadn't seen a car when they walked back to the house from their initial meeting in the woods, and she had to be staying somewhere.

Snagging his winter jacket from the old coatrack near the back door, he headed outside. The driveway looked the same as earlier, Jake's truck still where he'd parked it yesterday when he arrived. Garner's SUV was visible through the open garage doors, and Trace's own was parked right beside it.

Where had she gone?

Even as he wondered, those heated thoughts from earlier in his room came winging back. For as intimate as those shared moments had been, he'd had no claim on her. Did he actually think he had one now? She didn't owe him her comings and goings. Nor did she need to check in.

But damn it, where was she?

The thought was punctuated by the sound of pinging gravel against steel, and a large black SUV came bumping down the long unpaved driveway.

The car looked like something they'd ridden in throughout their careers. *Large and in charge* was always how he'd thought of those enormous vehicles with their dark tinted windows and undeniable presence as they ate up the road.

But seeing her through the windshield now? Why did it tug at something he had no business feeling?

Because what should have given him the sense that she was in charge and prepared for anything, several tons of cool machinery under her perfectly formed ass, left him feeling differently now.

All he saw now was a woman alone.

Perched up there in the driver's seat, that cage of black steel around her, he saw vulnerability and a deep sense of loneliness as he looked at her. Maybe because he knew the truth. Reinforced metal and a large agency of professionals couldn't help her now. Nor would they save her if the mission went sideways.

It was all on the two of them to make this right.

Maybe it was because he recognized that look, staring back at him through the windshield. Had worn it himself for two long years.

There were moments it felt like a solid victory when it was you against the world. And there were others when you realized the bigger truth.

When the weight of it sat upon you.

NIC PRIDED HERSELF on thinking before leaping.

She'd learned early in foster care that a few extra seconds to consider a situation before acting would pay dividends on the outcome.

Determine who was friend and who was foe.

Pick a fight and leap in, or stay the hell out.

Stay or run.

It was a philosophy that had kept her safe, out of trouble

and, eventually, in a home with decent enough people who chose to truly care for her.

As an adult she was well aware that part of actually *being* a child was having impulses and acting on them like a kid would. Children weren't mini adults and expecting them to be lay the road to mindless frustration.

But it was her own deliberateness that had led to her career. A damn successful one.

Which made the image of Trace Withrow standing at the end of the driveway, looking at her through the big front window of the SUV, both unnerving and welcoming at the same time.

Trace was an impulse.

One of the few she'd ever given into and by far the biggest. He was also the biggest risk of her life. She still didn't understand if that was a good thing or a bad thing, but, well, she was here, wasn't she?

And they had work to do.

Hopping out of the vehicle, she slammed the door and walked deliberately toward him. "I left this parked about a half a mile up in the woods."

"A convenient getaway vehicle if you needed to kidnap me out there on the trail?"

"Maybe." She shrugged but couldn't quite rise to the bait.

Especially because it was true. She'd come prepared for her conversation with him, and part of that had been the gun she'd carried on her person and the rope and ties she'd carried in the pack on her back. To be honest, she'd had no idea what she'd find catching him unawares, and she hadn't been willing to take chances.

It was only now, a few hours later, that she realized just how much she'd miscalculated. Because where she was expecting resistance, she'd gotten a heck of a lot of acceptance.

"It also gives us the needed comfort to go off searching for Olivia."

"In that?" Trace's gaze drifted toward the SUV before returning to her face.

Unyielding. The lone word drifted through her mind as that gray gaze held hers.

He'd always been solid and seemingly impenetrable, no matter how much she wanted to trip him up. But he simply *was.* This unmovable force that fascinated her as much as it confused her and kept her off-kilter. He'd done it professionally. And he'd managed it in their personal moments, too.

Oh, they'd always been on a level playing field sexually. She'd never have slept with him otherwise.

But all the rest of it?

As soon as their moments of intimacy were gone, Trace went right back to that place she couldn't touch. Or understand. Or break through. All those places where he refused to let her in or see the man beneath the undeniably capable veneer.

The unending frustration of that came out in a snappish tone at his question. "Why not in this?"

"Because it screams government agents."

"It's a rental."

"It plays to type. As does the low-rent, nondescript motel you're likely staying in. So no, we're not going in that."

The superior tone chafed, but Nic refused to give in. This was part of their patter, and she was damned if she wanted to fall so easily back into old habits.

Old, deliciously warm habits…

Instead, she did a quick scan of the area, from the battered truck in the driveway to the open garage doors across the way. "I haven't checked in to a hotel yet. Besides, what do you think will be better?"

"We've got a work truck parked out on the other side of the stables. It'll be our best bet."

Her hands went up to her hips without her even thinking about it. "Sitting up high in a truck without tinted windows that likely can't hit fifty in under thirty seconds?"

"You wound me." Trace slapped a hand on his chest in mock horror before shaking his head. "As if I'd ever have such a piece of crap on my property."

"Let me see it."

Trace waved her on, and they circumnavigated the same building they'd walked into earlier. His body was large beside hers, his steps moderated to account for her slightly shorter strides.

He'd always done that. That subtle suggestion that he was aware of her and considerate of her even when he had no reason to be.

She was highly capable. Well trained.

And damn it, that subtle accommodation still managed to make her heart rumble happily in her chest.

As advertised, an old work truck was parked in the back, looking like it had seen more than a few Wyoming winters and far, far better days.

"Clearly we have a wildly different definition of the term 'piece of crap.'"

Without saying a word, Trace went straight to the driver side door and, after opening it, hit a button to pop the hood. Nodding toward her, he smiled. "Take a look."

Her training had covered any number of topics, and one of those included vehicle maintenance of all different types. Even without a single bit of it, she'd have recognized the very large, polished-to-a-gleam engine shining beneath that hood.

"Is she street legal?"

"Barely." He smiled, his grin nearly feral. "Garner and I both believe in owning top-notch equipment. Regardless of what it might look like on the outside."

"I stand corrected."

He shrugged. "I might have led the witness a bit with the work truck reference."

That frustrating hour at the kitchen table when she'd done her best to backtrack Olivia's hacks into her system had been painful and fruitless. And suddenly felt overwhelming.

"It won't do us a bit of good if we can't find her."

"She found you once. That's got to count for something."

"Unless someone caught her reaching out to me."

Trace's gaze narrowed at that as he came around to drop the hood back into place. "From all you've told me, she's smart. She's evaded detection this long."

"She's still a kid."

"I'm not suggesting otherwise. But she's also proven herself resourceful and downright sneaky."

It was an honest assessment. Realistically, she knew that. And still… "You talk like she's brought this on herself."

"Don't mistake my meaning. Those skills are keeping her alive."

"Because she's a bratty kid?"

"Because she's resourceful and clearly has the ability to look out for herself, despite being surrounded by adults who should stand for her no matter what."

Nic had no idea why she was pushing this. Worse, why she was so unable to get out of her head when it came to this case. The one that kept telling her she'd be too late to save an innocent child.

But it was his solemn promise that went a long way toward allaying that unending swirl that refused to settle.

Lips set in a grim line, Trace said, "Which is why we will."

OLIVIA BRIGANTE TUCKED her computer under a pillow and switched over to the one her uncle had demanded she use when he picked her up the other day. He liked to think he indulged her with fun things to keep her occupied, and she played along so he wouldn't figure out what she was really doing when she tapped away on her own keyboard.

She knew enough that she could use the computer he gave her to hack wherever she wanted—he'd never know any better—but it felt safer to keep her work separate from whatever it was he needed.

And wow, he needed a lot.

He'd asked her to look into a few airline flights coming in and out of Canada. He'd also asked for a few maps of wilderness routes from Alaska into Canada, Canada into Montana and Canada into Idaho.

Nobody would tell her where they actually were right now, but Uncle Richie kept calling it a dude ranch. He'd also made some weird excuse when he took her phone, saying how the owners thought cell phones made kids rude and he didn't want them to think less of her.

She'd nearly staged a full-on revolt at that but something in his eyes stopped her. Something she'd never seen before.

Fear.

He also told her he'd let her talk to her mom and he'd bring it to her then. In the meantime she was working on what she needed to get quickly off her phone when she did have it again.

The big house was nice, but she didn't like the people who owned it. John and Jane Smith. They acted friendly, but Olivia didn't like the overbright smile from the wife since it didn't match her mean blue eyes. And her husband seemed really clueless, since he didn't see how her uncle Richie kept touching Jane and making eyes at her each time John's back was turned.

Her mother had told her to humor Uncle Richie and help him with whatever he asked on their *little adventure out west*, but Olivia wasn't buying any of it.

Especially because those jerks were on their phones all the time.

Did they really think she was that naive?

She knew the only reason she was here was because her mom wanted to go off on another trip with her boyfriend, Lyle. An old man—Eloisa called him that when he wasn't around—but she went with him because he had a lot of money.

She'd met him through Uncle Richie, and Olivia didn't like it when Lyle was around. He had a calm voice, but he oozed something that made her uncomfortable. Like the way she felt when she looked at the snake her science teacher kept in the back of the room in their biology class.

It was supposed to be a big secret her uncle was involved in a lot of bad stuff, but Olivia wasn't sure why they thought they were all so secretive about it. Mom always called him her "innocent little baby brother," but Olivia knew it was a front for excusing Uncle Richie's behavior.

A fact she'd innately understood but which she got more wise about after overhearing Uncle Richie's ex-wife yell about him a few Christmases ago.

"You think of no one but yourself! You and that damn business and finding ways to screw people. You're a miserable man-child!" Aunt Siobhan had yelled before stomping out of the room.

Her father had been gone since she was small, so Olivia had never seen grown-ups fight like that. She figured she'd have missed that fight, too, if she hadn't been hiding on the staircase in her aunt and uncle's big house in New Jersey. She was staying there for a few days while her mom got wined and dined in New York by her boyfriend before Lyle.

Her aunt had also yelled some stuff about shipments and running supplies, and it had made Olivia curious. So that night she'd done some digging, hacking into her uncle's computer from her own laptop up in her bedroom. He'd been stupid enough to use a simple password— Siobhan—and she'd gotten into his home server really fast.

Once in, Olivia had read about the "shipments" her aunt had talked about.

A few files from Africa and Asia that had information about shipping routes. Then she'd stumbled on some other stuff. Things that talked about bombs and guns and ammunition, and Olivia recognized quickly that things didn't match.

The stuff from Africa and Asia looked like regular things businesses shipped, from fabrics to ceramics to plastics. But the other stuff?

Olivia had slammed the laptop closed and shoved her computer under her pillow that time, too, scared at what she'd discovered. Because whatever her mother had said for years about her "little brother," Olivia sort of thought those files made it clear Uncle Richie was anything *but* innocent.

Which was why she'd reached out to Nic earlier today through the agent's database. Olivia liked knowing she could access her that way and had kept that capability in her back pocket. The government got really pissy when you hacked into their networks, but she wasn't doing it to steal secrets.

She needed help.

She thought she could handle it all, but this morning her uncle asked her to look into the local police chief. Olivia had done it over breakfast, giving him the information he needed before heading back up to her room. They promised to take her out to explore the ranch today with some horseback riding, and she'd gone up to get ready.

Only when she'd gotten back to her room, she looked out her window to see the police chief out in the driveway with her uncle and John. The officer had looked mad as they all yelled at each other, and she got a funny feeling in her stomach.

Why did Uncle Richie ask her to look that man up and then go out and fight with him?

And who were the man and woman who owned the house? Her uncle kept talking about being college friends with John and Jane and how they went way back, but he didn't know small things like how long they'd lived in the house or if they had kids. Two questions she'd asked at dinner the night before.

Jane had laughed off her questions, but those mean eyes had stayed on her face a bit too long, and Olivia hadn't asked any more questions.

But it had all made her think about what was really happening. Something she'd wondered since Richie and Siobhan's fight at Christmas but which got bigger after Olivia met Nic.

Nic had found her at school and introduced herself one day.

"You can get in trouble for talking to me without my mom around," Olivia had sassed when the pretty woman started talking to her. What she hadn't expected was the quick agreement.

"You're right. I can. And I don't want to make you uncomfortable. But I am worried about you."

"Why would you worry about me? You don't know me."

"I was a kid who didn't have anyone to worry about me. So as an adult, I decided to make sure other kids didn't have to go through the same thing. Which is why I'd like to talk to your mom, too."

Nic had been really nice and had been adamant with her mom that she wanted to protect Olivia from something. But her mom hadn't believed her.

Only, Nic had nice eyes. And she hadn't lied. She'd given Olivia some information, all of which Olivia had corroborated when she did her own digging.

Which made her mad at herself now because she'd thought

about calling Nic when the trip came up but hadn't. And now there were weird questions about going back and forth to Canada.

And the police chief yelling in the driveway with her uncle and John.

And Jane Smith with the mean eyes, nearly walking in on her and discovering her talking to Nic.

Olivia ran her fingertip over the edge of her computer, stuffed beneath her the pillow.

And wondered if she'd ever see her own bedroom again.

THE TRUCK HAD been a bit of a joke, Trace could admit to himself now, but it had opened up something between them, too.

He knew damn well his equipment would see them through. He refused to surround himself with anything less, and the retrofitted truck was one small example of all he and Garner had invested into the ranch.

But the opportunity to tease Nic a bit had been... Well, it had broken the ice.

Maybe it had also given him a chance to prove to her, in a small way, that he was *in* on this. That he was still the competent agent she'd known. That he was still able to see a mission through.

And that he was still the person she could trust.

Of all that had come between them before he left DC, that was the part that had hurt the most. There at the end, when she'd questioned *them* because she questioned him.

That moment when his disdain for the organization they worked for spilled over to how she felt about him.

He'd put his life in service to the government behind him when he left and moved to Liar's Gulch. And up until that morning, he'd even believed it was all in the past. Which made it both surprise and challenge to realize how much of it was still far too close to the surface for comfort.

Was it the work and the potential for a new mission that had churned it up?

Or Nic?

Because you are in love with her, and I don't think you have it in you to watch her walk away twice...

He shook off Garner's words once more.

This wasn't about them. But if it ended up exorcising some of those lingering relationship demons, Trace would count himself lucky. Saving a child and giving himself some semblance of a future? Win-win.

Especially because those relationship demons were increasingly causing problems of late. Sure, he found companionship when he needed or wanted it. But it wasn't until recently that he'd realized just how infrequent that need actually was. Needs that came back awfully damn quick the moment he laid eyes once again on Nicola Miles.

"I do believe you mean that. Even without knowing her, I know you'll stand for her."

Nic's words drifted toward him on the cold breeze that had kicked up in the few minutes since he'd walked outside to find her.

"Why wouldn't I?"

"There were days I wondered if the work had taken that away from you."

He wanted to be suspicious of her sudden change in tone, but no matter how ruthlessly his gaze drifted over her face, he saw nothing but openness.

"Taken what?"

"That ability to stand for anything any longer."

It was a harsh statement and Trace wanted to be angry about it. The man he was two years ago would have been. Only now...

"Why would you think that of me?" he finally asked.

"Because I'm afraid it's done that to me."

It wasn't rational, and he knew damn well he didn't have a right to offer her comfort any longer, but before he could stop himself, he was moving forward and pulling Nic into his arms.

She went willingly—and wasn't that a surprise?—her arms coming around his waist like tight bands.

Trace didn't want to be affected.

He didn't want to *feel* like this.

But as her body pressed against his, he recognized he needed this as much as she did.

"It's not supposed to be like this." Her lips moved against his chest, the sound absorbing into his jacket.

"Like what?"

"You're supposed to be a part of my past."

"Yeah, well, ghosts have a way of coming back to haunt those they're not finished with yet."

She shifted at that, the vivid blue of her eyes meeting his as her head lifted. "You're not finished with me?"

It was a stark moment of truth. One he'd avoided diligently for more than two years. "I thought I was."

"And now?"

"I guess I was wrong."

A soft nod had her head moving, her hair brushing against his jacket. "I guess I was, too."

"What are we going to do about it?"

"The job. That's all we can do."

As if to punctuate the point, her arms dropped from his waist, and she took a few steps back. It didn't escape him that she just caught herself on that last step back, the slightest wobble visible in her stance.

Good. He wasn't feeling all that steady himself, Trace admitted, and it was a hell of a lot easier to brush it off when it was mutual. When it was something they both had to deny.

Which made that heat in his chest—the initial spark that

fired when he'd first laid eyes on her this morning and had built into a steady burn in the hours since—so fascinating.

Because she wasn't immune, either.

They could both talk about the job all they wanted—even use it to put a distance between them—but his memory of their time together was good.

Damn good.

And as he recalled, the two of them had done just fine multitasking between the work and their need for each other.

Chapter Six

Nic could still feel Trace's arms wrapped around her as she headed back into the house. Those moments in his arms had been her first easy breaths since Olivia disappeared, and she hadn't realized just how much she needed that sense of support. Of human contact.

Only now she'd gotten another taste of depending on him again, and it was dangerous to her well-being.

She needed to stay focused on finding a child and getting her to safety. *Not* on her own hormones.

Ghosts have a way of coming back to haunt those they're not finished with yet.

Where had that even come from?

That whole exchange between them had been like something out of a dream.

Nic had sworn to herself before coming to Wyoming that she would remain professional no matter how tense the moments with Trace might be, and yet here she was, barely a morning in his presence, and they were talking about ghosts and pasts and...and being *finished* with each other.

What was she supposed to do with all that?

Nothing, she thought as she stomped toward the kitchen table and snatched up her laptop. She wasn't going to do a damn thing about any of it.

Especially now that she had some distance and a chance to think away from the temptation of the circle of his arms.

That was the key to all this, she admitted to herself as she walked into the guest room Trace had said she should use and closed the door firmly behind her.

Keep moving.

Stay focused.

Don't forget the mission.

Finding Olivia Brigante and getting her back safely was all that mattered.

Although Nic had no hope of hacking her way backward to reach the child in the same way Olivia had found her earlier, those moments out in the driveway with Trace had given her an idea. It had been a whisper of a thought when he'd popped the hood on the work truck, but it had grown stronger in her mind with each foot of distance away from him.

Get under the hood.

Images of that truck engine, gleaming a shiny silver, flashed through her mind as she opened up her laptop and hunted through a few of her intake files.

"Where did they take you?" Nic barely realized she asked the question out loud as she searched through a series of files her team had put together.

The case they were building against Richie Brigante was complex and layered and had been going on for some time. There had been a tremendous amount of work before she ever came onto the case, and they'd acquired even more since she joined the team a little over nine months ago: shipping records; business filings; real estate holdings. All were legitimate, but they still painted a picture of a man with considerable wealth that didn't quite match his apparent earnings.

It had been that disparity that kept her hunting for where his real sources of income were coming from.

And it had also led her to the sister and her child.

She'd had to work for it, but she'd eventually gotten approval to put surveillance on Eloisa and Olivia. Eloisa had been a pretty easy sell to her manager, but she'd had to make a real case to monitor a minor.

But she had built it, step by careful step.

The child's intelligence. The amount of time she spent with the adults suspected of criminal behavior. And, most of all, the continued exposure to that world in much of her free time, especially when Eloisa dropped her child off for days at a stretch.

It had started as a surveillance exercise and had morphed quickly when the restless, unquenchable depths of Olivia's intelligence spilled over to Nic. Even now, Nic remembered those first moments meeting Olivia, the child's mix of intelligence and humor capturing something inside of her.

Reminding her of a time so long ago when she herself had watched the world with careful eyes and very big ideas.

I CAN SEE YOU.

Nic had blinked at the laptop nestled on her thighs where she was hunkered in the corner of the school cafeteria. A text window had popped up with those words, a cursor blinking at the end of them.

She'd started the job three days before, and while she was well aware kids noticed everything, most also had enough hormone-filled contempt to deliberately ignore her.

Which worked just fine for her.

Until then.

More words flashed on her screen.

YEAH, LADY. YOU. SITTING THERE IN THE CORNER.

Despite her training and preference to avoid getting made—even in a high school—Nic looked up, her gaze scanning the cafeteria. Only to find nothing out of the ordinary staring back at her.

Which made the pixie-size human who plopped down beside her, clad head to toe in black with a thick purple streak in her hair, more evidence that Nic was off her game.

"Who are you?" the pixie asked.

Nic stared at Olivia and considered how to play the moment. Her presence might be obvious, but she was more than confident she'd stayed off the radar in her surveillance efforts. This was hardly her first stakeout. "An adult."

"Yeah, there are lots of those around. Who are you specifically?"

"My name's Nic."

"I'm Olivia, but you already know that." Deep brown eyes twinkled with merriment. "You're watching me."

"I am not."

"Sure you are. I saw you outside of school yesterday and parked down the block the day before and in the bar of the restaurant my mom took me to last weekend in New York City. You were a blonde there in a black dress and really awesome heels."

"I—"

Olivia leaned closer. "Gotcha."

Nic hadn't felt this off her game since she was in her first year, on her first stakeout, and even then she had never felt quite so exposed.

Or, frankly, stupid.

"You're mistaken."

"Nah, I'm not. But you can play cloak-and-dagger if you want. I'll keep your secret."

Nic hadn't been a teenager in a very long time, but those years were still emblazoned in her mind as if etched in stone.

The frustration that no one gave you enough credit. For anything. And the deep desire to get out and get on with it.

It went against protocol and everything she'd been taught, but in that moment Nic went with instinct. Something Trace said once had drifted through her mind a split second before she did.

The rules are all fine and dandy until they're not. Quit using them when they don't work anymore.

"Why do you think I need you to keep a secret?" Nic asked.

"Because you've got questions about me. About my family. If I'm honest, there are days I have questions about them, too."

It couldn't be this easy, Nic had thought at the time.

And it hadn't been.

For all her bravado and smarts, Olivia didn't let on that she knew much of anything about her uncle's business. Nic figured a child as aware and as smart as Olivia likely knew *something*, but not a single bit of intel suggested the kid was involved.

She was at risk, living in the orbit of adults engaging in bad behavior, but she'd spent her life there and hadn't been involved.

Until recently.

The child she'd spoken to that day in the cafeteria—deeply precocious and terrifyingly brilliant—wasn't involved in Richie Brigante's crimes.

She was now. Nic would bet her life on that. And it was all likely beyond Olivia's understanding.

And against her will.

IT BOTHERED HIM that the kid got in.

Trace wanted to ignore that fact—scared, precocious kid and all—but it still bothered him.

Olivia Brigante had hacked a government database and communicated with a federal officer. And she'd done it on *his* Wi-Fi.

When he and Garner had made the decision to settle in Liar's Gulch, it was with the full knowledge they both knew too much. Way too much.

They'd agreed that while neither of them were interested in shutting the world out, they knew enough about it—and had made enough enemies between them—that they wanted to set up some security protocols from the start.

The work truck was one example.

State-of-the-art technology was another.

And a series of security cameras was yet another.

They'd made an investment in these tools as a way to ensure they had a future. To ranch how they chose. To step in and help others as they chose. Most of all, to live as they chose.

It wasn't off the grid, but it was managing the grid in a way that ensured their privacy, safety and, more than anything else, an opportunity to put the past behind them.

Olivia's hacking experiment meant they weren't nearly as safe and secure as they thought.

Trace pulled up the security application on his laptop and ran a series of protocols, trying to determine where it all came from. The kid was likely smart enough to bounce a signal off of several locations to avoid detection, but…

Trace tapped in a few commands, that *but* lingering in his mind. She was looking for help, not trying to evade detection. Would she be quite so concerned with hiding her digital footprint? He typed in a few more commands, looking for any sort of breach or even physical hack into his systems.

And fell back into the plush leather of his office chair a few minutes later when he came up with a big fat lot of nothing.

"I'll bet you we're looking for the same thing." A voice

emanated from his office doorway, and he looked up, surprised to realize that once again today, Nic had gotten the jump on him.

"Oh?"

"I've been tracing anything and everything I can find on Olivia and her family for the past hour."

"Find much?" Trace asked as he stood, gesturing Nic to one of the chairs opposite his desk.

"I don't think so, but I wanted to run something by you."

Since it wasn't a flat-out no, Trace sat down in his seat after Nic took one of the chairs. "What do you have?"

"I'm not wasting time thinking we can backtrack through her hack to find her. Instead, I'm going to focus on what I do know."

"You don't think you can find the breach?" That surprised him, especially knowing the phenomenal talent in the agency when it came to cybersecurity.

"I don't think I can find it with *my* skills." Nic's smile was more a soft tilt of the lips, but he caught her wry humor all the same. "And I'm not ready to call in anyone for backup. So I switched gears and focused on what I do know after watching the kid for a month, as well as keeping tabs on her family for the better part of a year."

As strategies went, it not only made sense, but it matched what Nic was very, very good at.

Trace had known her—or more, he'd known of her—for a few years before they got together. Her reputation was flawless when it came to understanding her targets. She saw someone's life in clear patterns—who they were, where they went, who they were related to—in ways he'd rarely seen in other agents.

Of course, people could be trained and those skills honed over time, but she had an innate sense of people and the details that made them tick.

"What do you know?"

"Although we have nothing but circumstantial evidence, Richie Brigante is running an illegal business. It's exceptionally well managed and maintained, but there are too many moving parts and slight inconsistencies for him to be clean."

Although he didn't doubt her, Trace was curious to know more. "Such as?"

"His shipping manifests don't match the inventory he carries. He's got contracts with ports that don't seem a direct match for his business and in locations that are even less specific to the goods he imports. And the business is just *bigger...*" she waved a hand for emphasis "...for lack of a better word, than it should be."

"And you think Olivia's involved?"

"I didn't at first. I thought she was in danger due to proximity and her skills, but I didn't think she had actual involvement. Until now."

"What changed?" Her cheeks took on a decided blush, and he was curious as to what caused the change. "Nic?"

"The kid made me."

"When?"

The pretty blush only deepened, and he couldn't deny how compelling she looked. It was a far cry from the kick-ass woman he knew her to be, but that touch of embarrassment flared something inside of him.

One more proof point that she wasn't unaffected by the world around her, no matter how cool and aloof she could play it.

"When I first started to follow her, after going through all the motions to get approval to track a minor. I was in character and in costume, fully disguised each time I followed her. And she made me, Trace."

What had been pure interest shifted inside of him, and he couldn't hold back the grin. "I'd have paid to see that."

"I bet you would. I even used my best dress and wig, and the kid knew it was me."

"The Morocco disguise?"

"Yep. It's one of my best because the wig hides portions of my face, and it was like she didn't miss a beat. Olivia saw right through it."

"Eidetic memory?" He smothered an urge to complain about the agency's psychologists. "Or whatever passes for the broader idea of it that doctors will actually believe."

"I think so. The kid's special. She's frighteningly observant. And she processes it all with a mix of computer-level accuracy and a funny sense of humor. She's—" Again, Nic searched for the right words. "She's unique and odd and wonderful in the best of ways."

In all the time they were together, Trace had never seen her quite so caught up in a case. Even more than that, she was caught up in the kid, that much was clear.

Yet even as he acknowledged it, Trace couldn't see how it was unhealthy. Focused, yes. But there was a sweetness to it and a very real level of concern he couldn't help but key into.

"For the obvious intelligence, and I'm assuming if tested she'd hit genius, there's a high emotional quotient there, too."

"Yes!" Nic leaned forward, excited. "That's absolutely it. She's not caged by her intelligence. But I am concerned that Richie or someone in his organization has figured out a way to use her."

"Why the change? You said you don't think she was involved when you first started tailing her."

"Despite her quick ability to make me, she was discreet about it."

Trace was starting to get a picture in his mind, and it was considerably more sophisticated than he'd first imagined when Nic briefed him on the assignment that morning. No matter how intelligent, the behavior Nic was describing had a layer of maturity to match that was maybe harder to believe than the depths of the child's intelligence.

"Discreet how? Most adults would tell someone about that sort of intrusion into their life. She kept it to herself?"

Nic nodded, that subtle swing of her hair brushing the edge of her jaw. "The whole time. Even when I finally went to her mother and told her of our concerns, Olivia kept it to herself."

"So she has to sense something is going on with the adults around her," Trace pressed, a deepening sense of unease at the child's proximity to all this. "Which possibly puts her in more danger. They've likely underestimated her up to now, but if she demonstrates any sense of understanding of what they're doing, the risk to her safety increases exponentially."

"Her risk is with the uncle. Eloisa keeps coming up clean."

"You really buy that?"

Nic stilled, something a lot like grief clouding her sky blue eyes. "It's a mother's job to protect her child."

"Yes, it is."

She sighed, the sound barely a whisper in the room. "Yet we both know not every mother is wired that way."

On that point, Trace admitted to himself, they'd always agreed. "Better than most."

BETTER THAN MOST.

Trace's words still lingered between them, weighted with a level of meaning neither of them had ever delved into too deeply.

All part of why your relationship was so easy at the start and so hard by the end.

That small voice, the one that hadn't shut the hell up since she'd started on this journey out west, reared its head once more.

Nic wanted to ignore it.

If she wasn't so head over heels at being in Trace's company again, she might have even been successful at doing just that. But something about being with him, in his home, near his brother and his friend and their collective new life, had all of it coming back. All the memories and feelings she'd spent the better part of two years placing in an emotional box that she kept firmly closed.

Much to her horror, but oddly not her surprise, was how quickly the lock that kept it in place snapped, breaking wide-open.

And just how easy it was to bring it all back.

They'd fooled themselves at the start, before the physical aspects of their relationship had ever begun. Before the fights and disagreements. And well before she'd realized her heart was in way too deep.

The conversations they'd both believed to be shallow—a simple way to pass the time on stakeout—had held depths neither of them had been willing to admit. And it was talk of their childhood, on the occasions the subject came up, that had been the deepest.

She'd shared her time in foster care and the changes in her life once she'd found her home with Jack and Lucy Baker. He shared—always in light anecdotes—how he and Garner had fended for themselves when his mother wasn't around. It was always the mother, Nic remembered, with no mention of his father.

Trace always laced the stories with humor and told them with a lopsided grin, but she'd sensed the pain underneath. Nic had been touched that she'd seen that small layer of vulnerability from a man who operated at the highest levels of a government organization. Like it was only for her to see. Because it wasn't something he showed anyone else.

Ever.

She'd seen him debrief some of the worst specimens

of human depravity without a single expression crossing his face.

Yet in those quiet moments together, she'd seen beneath the granite.

Saving Olivia Brigante and getting her to safety isn't about you and Trace.

Those internal admonitions reared up again, cutting through the morass of memory that threatened to pull her under.

She had to remember that. Had to keep it in the forefront of her thoughts. Old feelings and memories could not cloud this case or her judgment. The risks if she lost focus were simply too great.

"You think I need to look at the mother again?" she finally asked, surfacing from her thoughts.

Oblivious to her roiling emotions, Trace's response was as unyielding as his cold gray gaze. "Damn straight you do."

"Then on that we're agreed."

That gray heated slightly, and she took some small satisfaction that she'd tripped his expectations once again.

"That's what I've been doing for the last hour in my room. Digging into every single thing I know about the Brigante family and what we think."

"I thought you said Richie's business was the focus."

"It was. Until I asked the team to expand it and look at everyone in his orbit. His big sister and ex-wife were the top of the list since the Brigantes' parents are gone. There aren't any other close family members to consider."

"How deeply have you looked at the sister? The first time," he clarified.

"She was the first family member we evaluated after we put eyes on Richie. The ex-wife was duly reviewed, but early indications suggested she just wanted out of the marriage and that ultimately matched our discovery on her."

"Tell me what you know."

"Eloisa comes off like a caricature of a person. Part '40s movie star, part sly fox, part femme fatale. There's an affectation to her personality that's impossible to ignore. But—"

"But what?"

"I thinks she loves her family. And I do think she loves her child, but my assessment is she doesn't fully understand just how deep Olivia's intelligence goes."

"Surely Olivia's been tested through the years. Would a mother who cares about her child somehow miss that?"

It was a good question, and one Nic admittedly hadn't asked herself. Was she so determined to believe Olivia existed in a cocoon of protection that she'd misjudged Eloisa's intentions?

One more sign of how mixed up she was by this case.

"It's a fair point."

"Mothers know their children," Trace insisted.

Some don't.

The thought hung there, hovering between them, and she would have bet her very last penny Trace was thinking the same. But neither put voice to it, and before she could even think to find a way to manage that emotional minefield, he'd already moved on.

"So we go on the assumption Eloisa has a better handle on Olivia's skills than might appear." A thoughtful look carved Trace's features into deeply grooved lines. "And it would be the mother who had to let her go with the uncle if she's missing."

"He could have taken her."

"But nothing's pinged on the mother, right? No upset? No frantic calls."

"She's on a romantic trip with her new boyfriend."

"And isn't talking to the kid?"

They stared at each other, their next step immediately

obvious, but Trace got to it first. "We need to put a tap on the mother."

"I can't just do that, Trace. I have to follow procedure, and a warrant's at the top of the list."

His answer was swift.

Immediate.

And exactly what she wanted to do.

"I don't."

Chapter Seven

He had to tread carefully. It was the mental warning that had cautioned him since looking up to find Nic staring at him across the expanse of woods during his morning ride with Magnum. It had grown increasingly louder—like a drumbeat—as the day progressed.

It practically had his pulse thrumming out of his skin now.

But it was how he managed this current conversation that would really set the tone.

Trace eyed Nic, curious to see the quick expressions that flitted across her face—frustration to wry humor to what looked like acceptance. Nic seemed to experience them all as she considered his words.

"You with me on this?" he asked. "Or do you want me to go it alone?"

One last expression settled over her features at his question, a whip-quick flashover to anger. "I didn't come here to put this all on you."

"I'm not suggesting that. But you *are* still a federal employee. I've got a bit more latitude than you do."

"I came to you *because* you've got latitude," she said, winging his emphasis right back to him. "That doesn't change my responsibilities here."

"Okay then, we're agreed."

Nic looked about to argue, her mouth even opening before she snapped it shut as Trace continued.

"We put an illegal tap on the mother and see what we get."

"She's traveling with the boyfriend. She could be anywhere. Putting a tap on her home's not going to give us what we need."

"We'll go in through the phone. I can drop a piece of code via a text link, and we can get access to her calls and texts."

"You think she's just going to click it? From a strange text?"

"She will if we make it look good enough."

Trace was honest enough with himself that he could admit he was enjoying this more than a little bit. Nic might be determined to hold on to her bravado and do this the way he suggested, but she wasn't exactly comfortable, either.

It took him back to their earliest days together.

They'd disagreed about their work from the start. It had been fascinating at the beginning, getting her thoughts and opinions on the work and coming to understand how iron-clad her principles were.

Had he ever had those?

Oh, he had his own code of honor, to be sure. But rigid, inflexible principles when it came to the work? Not so much.

He'd had a lot of successful cases because of it, too. Tossing the rule book out when his instincts grew too loud and resonant to ignore had not only served him well but had proven itself a sound strategy many times over. Times that, Trace knew, he wouldn't have closed the work *without* breaking the rules.

But not Nic. She *was* the rule book.

Which made her willingness to go outside of it for this case all the evidence he needed to know that this mattered to her.

"How are you going to fool Eloisa?" Nic asked, obviously resigned to their next steps.

"We'll gin up a fake text based off of what she loves most. You said she's a fan of the fancy boyfriend. We can make a text from a high-end boutique or a high-end hotel for starters."

"She's not going to fall for it."

"It's my job to see that she does."

"Our job."

Although his memories of their time together had haunted him since Nic's arrival, something about the firm set of her jaw and the slightly mulish expression that thinned her mouth into a straight line pulled him up short. Like a rogue wave, the memory washed over him, so intense he wondered if his knees would have actually buckled had he been standing.

"What?" she asked, keying into his sudden mood change.

"Nothing."

"No, that look meant something."

"It's really nothing."

"Let me be the judge of that."

"I just—" He broke off, not sure why he suddenly felt so out of his depth when he'd distinctly felt the upper hand less than two minutes ago.

And yet…wasn't that the very definition of him and Nic?

"There was something about that expression on your face. It took me back for a moment."

She didn't speak and instead simply sat there with that intense gaze as she considered him. He was close to responding when she leaned forward a bit, her expression earnest.

"This whole day has been an experience in being taken back. Far more than I ever expected."

Whether it was the absolute honesty or just the fact that it was *her*—his Nic—back in his presence, Trace didn't know. "It's not how I expected my day to turn out, I'll give you that," he said. "But I am glad you're here. More than I'd have imagined I could be."

She extended her hand across the desk, laying it over his. "Even when I told myself it was a bad idea, I knew you were the answer, Trace."

He stared down at where their bodies joined, the heat of her palm searing the back of his hand.

They'd been the answer for one another for a long time, until one day, they weren't. It was that moment—the final one when he'd decided it was time to go away—that lingered now.

He hoped like hell he could be the man she needed this time.

MOMENTS—HEAVY ONES. LIGHT ONES. Soul-searing ones— had she really banked on all of this?

Nic asked herself that question as she slipped from Trace's office to go gather a few of her notes on Eloisa.

Her hand still tingled with heat where she'd laid it over his, and she fought off the urge to wiggle her fingers as if she could simply shake off the heat and need and sheer history that arced between them.

It was a quick trip to grab her file, but she used the time to try to regain her equilibrium.

Ignore the moments.

Keep your attention on the now.

Focus on what you came here to do.

It was a good idea until she was confronted by an impressive wall of men waiting for her in the kitchen.

"I pulled in reinforcements." Trace's comment was casual, but she sensed his intentions straight off.

Let them in, too.

It flew in the face of who she was—letting others in— but really, hadn't this entire case tested who she thought she was? More, who she *believed* she was.

"Sure. Great."

Garner and Jake—now fully clothed—both leaned back

against various points on the kitchen counter. Hogan settled down, his head between his paws, beside Jake.

"Trace gave us rather limited details on what's going on," Garner started. "Why don't you walk us through it?"

Nic hadn't expected to pull additional people into this project, but as she took in the other two men, she realized it wasn't an entirely bad idea to get some fresh eyes on the case. Yes, Trace was fresh as of a few hours ago, but he was also former CIA. He was trained to look at data the same way she was.

Would Garner and Jake see something different?

She further consoled herself with one other key point. Whatever new life Trace had created for himself, it unquestionably included his brother. Now it included Jake, too, even if she did get the sense Trace was still trying to get his footing with the man. Something she'd keep an eye on and ask about later.

With a nod, she gestured toward the kitchen table and launched into a quick debrief on the case, including the steps taken up to now and what had brought her to Wyoming.

"You think the child's been taken?" Jake was the first to speak.

Nic considered how to answer. While moving a child to a place where she could be used for nefarious purposes was absolutely kidnapping, up until recently Olivia likely hadn't seen it that way. But this morning…

Nic. It's me Olivia. I'm in trouble.

The breach of Nic's systems this morning now suggested otherwise.

"I think she's being maneuvered, her skills used as a point of manipulation. Her outreach to me this morning suggests she's aware of this, which now risks our working assumption that she won't be hurt by her uncle."

"So let's make a plan and get her out." Garner's eyes lit with a simmering excitement she could feel arcing around the table.

"I'd like to, but actually finding her is the challenge."

Garner seemed undeterred by her pushback. "One we can surely get around. If she's with the uncle, we'll do some digging into his whereabouts."

"We can't run the risk of tipping him off, and I have no idea if he's got someone in the agency watching out for him." It pained Nic to even think something like that about her colleagues, but nothing was off the table. Especially since her senses had been on high alert that something was off about this job from the start.

A child was in danger, which was obviously her first priority. But their inability to dig into Brigante's financials with any level of success felt like a blocker that shouldn't have been quite so insurmountable.

Garner barely held back a snort. "Multilayered, inefficient bureaucracy at its finest."

Trace elbowed his brother. "You want to cool it?"

"Because ignoring the reality of the situation is somehow better?"

Nic's initial impression of Garner was a mix of loyal hardass and lighthearted jokester, but looking at him across the table—even with Trace trying to quiet him—she saw something more.

A man who carried so much resentment it had become a simmering rage below the surface.

What had happened to him?

Trace had never said much to her in the time they were together, beyond the cursory explanation that he had a brother who was a navy SEAL.

But here? Now? She saw a man as damaged as she suspected Trace was. Would that make the two of them stronger? Or would it send them down a rogue path, only exacerbated by their new addition, Jake?

As if sensing a need to break the tension, their third musketeer jumped in. "So what do we do?"

"I'm going to put a trace on the kid's mother's phone. She may be out getting her rocks off with her rich boyfriend, but she's bound to talk to the kid from time to time." Trace shrugged. "Or at least text."

"You doing the full rock star?" Garner asked, and Nic could only puzzle at the question.

"Rock star plus pampered princess."

"Oooh." Garner nodded. "Good one."

"Care to clue us in?" Jake finally asked, his head swiveling between the brothers.

Trace tapped the back of his cell phone, face down on the table in front of him. "We're going to make her think she's got street cred equivalent to a mix of Taylor Swift and Princess Kate."

"How you going to do that?" Jake asked.

"We'll fake an invitation via text. I was looking at her social media, and she's got a fascination with a very specific high-end boutique in New York. I'll start there with an offer of a personal appointment and see if she bites."

"On a random text from someone she doesn't know?" Jake shook his head. "The temptation to bet you the next round of drinks in town is strong, but somehow I'm afraid you're gonna be right on this."

Subtle amusement at their byplay morphed into a full-on laugh at the three of them.

"Next round of drinks is on me if Trace can make this work."

Three pairs of eyes lit up at Nic's offer, but it was the subtle glee that filled Trace's that confirmed just how determined he was to win.

"You're on, Miles."

TRACE BUILT OUT the details of his phishing text for Eloisa Brigante, then shifted focus toward creating the small piece of malware he was going to use to monitor activity on her phone.

"You need help on that?" Nic asked.

She had flitted around the kitchen, pulling together something for a late lunch, as he worked on his laptop. Garner and Jake had headed out for the stables, Hogan following along in their wake.

Jake had mentioned something about getting the lay of the land, and while Trace didn't doubt it was true—the former cop was now going to be a horse trainer at least some of the time—he also figured it was an excuse to give him and Nic some privacy.

With the scent of soup now wafting from the stove—what did they have in the house to make soup?—she rejoined him at the table.

"I think I've got it. It's a pretty simple piece of code. I just need to mask the number to make it look legit if she calls it. We'll know pretty quickly if she bites or not."

Nic shook her head. "Don't people know better than to click on strange links?"

"They do until that link might lead them to something they want."

She shot him a questioning eye but didn't respond. They'd both been on enough jobs to know that people who should know better often didn't *actually* know better when something enticing tugged at them.

Since that thought sat a bit too uncomfortably close to how the two of them had gotten together, Trace didn't say anything further, just focused on finishing the job.

"Am I being unrealistic to think that this is going to get us to her?"

Nic's question hung between them as Trace considered how to play this. She wanted reassurance, and he wasn't in a position to give that to her any longer. He didn't have government resources behind him, nor did he have access to some of the tools he used to have to get the job done. Sure, he was confident in his own skills, but it was a hell of a lot easier with the government's slick and shiny toys backing you up.

Did he believe they'd find Olivia? Yes, absolutely.

Did he think it would be easy? Hell no.

But he didn't say any of those things. Instead, he looked at her over the edge of his laptop and purposely kept his expression blank. "It's a start."

"Right. Sure. Of course it is."

"I know it's hard when you're not accessing the snazzy tech we all got used to, but none of it replaces our training."

There had been a restlessness about her he'd observed since she arrived. It had ebbed and flowed, but since they'd made the decision to hack Eloisa's phone, it had ratcheted back up.

So it was a surprise to see her relatively still, that energy that had hummed around her leveling down.

"I keep falling back on the training, too. And then I second-guess myself that it won't be enough."

He understood that. Had discussed it at length with Garner when they made the decision to change their lives.

Yes, the move to Wyoming had a variety of facets, one of which was their desire to still help others. But they'd also realized that their training and skills were augmented with significant resources they could no longer access. So they'd agreed in advance they would take on the jobs they believed they had the skills to handle. Because while they both fully acknowledged their training was exceptional, neither of them were superhuman.

Extending the invite to Jake had included more of the same, ensuring his expectations were matched to what Trace and Garner had chosen to build in Liar's Gulch.

"It will be."

With the short malware program he'd written humming through its setup, Trace stood to get more coffee. He'd pretty well gotten rid of his hangover, but the lingering malaise from an evening full of far too many drinks—coupled with the intense emotions at seeing Nic again—needed some sort of battle armor.

Caffeine would have to do.

The more enticing options that refused to leave his mind, all of which involved both of them shedding their clothes, weren't on the table. That particularly tantalizing outcome sat firmly in the realm of never-ever-again. He knew that.

And he'd known it the moment he walked out of her apartment all those long, lonely months ago.

The fact she'd shown up here—hunted him down, really—seeking his help wasn't going to change it.

Trace was surprised to see the slight shake of his hand as he poured the coffee into his mug, willing away that small sign of weakness. They were well-trained professionals. Considered spies in some quarters, excellent government assets in others.

They weren't lovers.

Not any longer.

Wishing he could change that flew in the face of every bit of rigorous discipline with which he lived his life.

He took a sip of the coffee, the ping from his computer drawing his attention. Satisfied he had his armor firmly back in place, he took his seat once more and reviewed the malware program he'd compiled for this job.

Coding wasn't his favorite portion of the work, but he'd gotten proficient enough through the years to know he'd done the basic job needed to track Olivia's mother and her communications. More important, he did it outside of Nic's work, so the ownership remained his. Although, was it splitting hairs since she *was* involved? If they found out, the government would most certainly see it that way.

Since his skills extended to destroying the evidence when they were done, he'd gamble on that split anyway.

Satisfied they had a path forward, he turned his laptop around on the kitchen table. "I think we're ready. Take a look at the text I've pulled together and let me know."

Nic's curious gaze had remained on him throughout their limited exchange, but she leaned forward and scanned his screen, her gaze narrowed slightly as she took in the words. "This is good. Smart to lean into the offer of a private shopping hour at her convenience."

"It's low-risk. And if we get in and see she has any issues with the boutique, we can smooth it over with a separate call." He grinned at her, wiggling his eyebrows. "I can play an indulgent rich boyfriend, ensuring my lady gets whatever she wants."

"This is really good, Trace. It's quick, efficient and easy to manage on our side." There wasn't any hint of censure or dismissal in her tone, so it made no sense that her comment pissed him off.

No sense at all.

Even if it did feel like a small pat on the head that he was a good boy.

But there was no mistaking the tightening of his chest or the way his response came out harsher than he intended. "That's why I'm here."

"Well, yeah. I mean—" She stopped, seeming to catch herself. "Are you upset about something?"

"No."

"Trace—"

"I'm not upset. I'm being an ass, and it's all on me."

"Why?"

Once again, there wasn't a hint of censure in her voice. There was the obvious question in her eyes as to what his problem was, but how did he explain that even he couldn't explain it?

"Can I send the text?"

"Of course." Nic lightly pushed the laptop back to him before standing and crossing to the stove to check the soup.

He wanted to apologize—knew he needed to—but for what? Feeling grumpy that she was only here because he was some sort of professional tool that she needed?

It was tempting to marinate in that place, but he had a job to do and time was wasting. With a tap on the keyboard, he hit Send on the fake text.

"Done."

"Thank you." Nic turned after she laid down the spoon she'd used to stir the pot. "And now I think we need to talk."

"Haven't we been doing that?"

"A bit. But we've also been letting old animosities mess up a lot of the words in between snatches of conversation, and it has to stop. I trust you, Trace. Implicitly, or I wouldn't be here."

Of course she was right. And he could sit and marinate even further in resentment that she'd been mature enough to admit it first, or he could own his part in it all.

His vacillating emotions had no place in this.

"I don't want to fight with you," he said on a small sigh. "And I'm glad you're here. Even happier that you felt you could come to me with this."

"Why do I hear a but?"

She might have taken ownership of her emotions first, but

he wasn't that far behind. Whatever else they'd shared before it all imploded, they'd always been honest with each other.

Or he had been, save one small point. He loved her. To distraction.

And he'd never said a word.

That was his problem, and he'd spent the past two years working on putting it all behind him. Her coming to him for help couldn't change that. But it did mean there was history they needed to acknowledge. Maybe putting it out there would finally excise it from memory.

"Because we had a relationship. It doesn't matter how it ended, it doesn't erase that we had one. That's the 'but' between us, Nic. It's not going to go away."

"I know."

"So what do we do about it?"

"We put the mission first. Like always."

The words were straight up Nicola Miles. Sharp. Deliberate. To the point.

Even if the small hitch when she said *always* was as audible as a gunshot.

"Of course we do." He nodded as he stood from his seat and slowly crossed the kitchen toward her.

He knew she was right. He even agreed with her. But something had settled deep inside of him at that subtle hitch in her voice. That small, ever-so-slight clue that she wasn't as unaffected as she claimed, no matter what.

Like catching a tiger by the tail, he had no idea what he'd do once he proved his point, but he seemed determined to try anyway.

So he moved forward, narrowing the distance between them.

And leaped to cover her, dragging her to the kitchen floor, when the distinct sound of gunfire erupted just beyond the window.

Chapter Eight

"Let me up!" Nic struggled under Trace's heavy weight—
how did such a lanky man have such muscle mass?—
desperate to get outside. Who was shooting at them? And
what horror had she brought to his home? "Trace! Let. Me.
Up."

He rolled to the side, still holding tight to her forearm when
she lifted out of a crouch to look out the window.

"You don't know what's out there," he hissed.

"Which is why." She gritted her answer through her teeth
as she tamped down on the immediate instinct to break his
hold—and possibly his arm. "I'm a federal agent trained to
go handle it."

Something shifted in his demeanor, and she sensed she'd
finally gotten through to him when his grip loosened, but he
still held her down by his side. "We can stay below the window line if we go behind the table."

"Let's go then."

She didn't wait for a response and instead dropped to her
belly, army crawling past the exterior wall. Who had found
her? It was the only question racing through her mind as she
crawled through the kitchen.

The distinct ring of a cell phone pealed, and she heard

Trace answer gruffly before he shouted to her. "Wait, Nic! It's Garner."

With the wall still at her back, Nic leaned against it, her gaze on Trace's face as he switched to speaker.

"What have you got?"

"Jake and I are in the stables. Bastard's roaming around outside and thought he could get a shot off at us."

"That's a pretty bad way to announce your presence," Nic murmured.

"Exactly!" Garner's words came winging through the speaker. "It's a message, and I'm not quite sure what he's hoping to convey. Especially since we can't find a second, either, and we've both been on the cameras in the office."

Nic didn't recall seeing a video array in the stables but didn't doubt they had one.

"You have eyes on him?" Trace asked.

"I did until he moved out of sight toward the house. That dead space you and I keep meaning to fix. Jake and I will cover you from out here. Keep me on the line so I can watch your back and watch yourselves."

"We've got it. I'm leaving the line open and putting my earbuds in."

"You on dual use?" Garner asked.

"Of course." Trace tucked the phone back in his pocket, Garner's voice evaporating with the switch to his earbuds.

Nic extended a hand. "Give me one."

He nodded, pulling out an earbud and handing it to her before pointing toward the sliding back door. "Let's bypass the living room and head for the laundry room."

"Or we can split up and have a better chance of finding him."

"It's a risk. You're not armed."

She grinned before tapping her calf. "Oh, sweet summer child, guess again."

Where the old Trace might have taken offense at the sarcasm, this version simply grinned and nodded. "Of course."

"But you're not."

"Shall I make you eat your words?" Trace reached behind his back and pulled out a handgun. "I snagged a bit of backup after the kid hacked into your system."

"Then we avoid the living room. You take the utility room, and I'll take the front door. Let's figure out what we're dealing with." Nic didn't wait for his agreement but headed for the front door, bypassing the living room and the wide sliding door that overlooked the back of the house.

Garner's assessment rang in her head as she moved rapidly through the space. *It's a message, and I'm not quite sure what he's hoping to convey.*

Who knew she was here? And so soon? She'd been careful, damn it. Was it someone from the agency, trying to thwart her attempts to find Olivia? If it was, she had a much bigger problem than she could have imagined.

Or did Richie Brigante actually act this quickly? If he did, that meant he and his goons were a lot closer than she initially estimated.

Nic sighed as she approached the oversize steel front door. First they had to catch the intruder, and then she could figure out where he'd come from.

She opened the door, careful to move it inch by inch so that she wasn't an immediate target. When the crack was wide enough, she took a chance to look outside, only to see the air continue to bluster in thick swirls, kicking up leaves and grass in its wake.

The direct line in her earbud carried a steady stream of instructions from Garner. She could even hear Jake giving updates on what he saw on the cameras. All of which confirmed the intruder had wisped away like smoke.

Slipping outside, she held still, trying to listen for

some clue as to where their attacker had gone. Although Garner's comments were direct and issued only when necessary, it was still distracting to have the noise, and she listened with focused attention, trying to catch something—a snapped branch or a scuffed foot on the driveway or *anything*—on the air.

Only to still come up with nothing.

She'd nearly begun moving again when she caught the faintest glimmer of something. An instinct, really, that had her whirling toward the far side of the driveway.

Only to feel the distinct press of a gun at her temple, the air blustering around her in thick gusts.

TRACE HATED THE WAITING.

He'd always hated the waiting part of his job but had managed to forget just how much of it he used to do.

Waiting for orders.

Waiting for the time to take action.

Waiting for the object of his mission to make a move.

It had always held an endless quality that never fully faded, even after the adrenaline rush when things finally shifted into all-out action and fierce battle.

He wasn't sure what that said about him, but he knew himself well enough to know it was his own personal truth.

It wasn't a lack of patience, either. He had plenty of it—and had proven it to himself over and over in his work with the horses.

But he had zero tolerance anymore for the endless waiting that came on an op.

Which made the small, calm voice that echoed in his ear both a shock and an instant cattle prod into motion.

"Trace. Do you remember Reykjavík?" The tone in her voice was as fragile as glass.

Already on the move, he cycled through the ops they'd

shared during their time working together, before landing on the memory she wanted him to recall.

Iceland.

New Year's Eve.

And a shooter waiting just outside the door, somehow managing to get the two of them apart.

"Garner." He whipped out orders with deadly calm as he moved. "Get Jake and get out of the barn. He's got her at the front door. Approach right flank. I've got the left."

An expletive exploded in his ear, a match for the one cycling through his head.

How had they missed this?

But Garner's mention of their dead spaces was spot-on. They had one at the side of the house, too. A problem he'd been meaning to fix, but he'd tabled it knowing they had enough other cameras around the house that they'd know of an intruder long before one got to the front door.

How's that working out for ya, Withrow?

Vowing to go over it endlessly later, he stilled just shy of the front of the house. His head was already upside down because Nic was here. Barreling in without taking a moment was akin to putting a bullet in her head.

"I'm almost there." Garner's voice was a whisper in his ear, and Trace took some solace that Nic would have heard it too.

"I'm closer."

"Jake stayed in the office. He's got eyes on them, and guy's got her just outside the front door. I've got comms in my other ear. On my mark, Trace."

"Noted," Trace whispered, well aware Nic's captor might hear him but not caring any longer.

"Now!"

Trace moved in time with his brother's shout as the world went eerily still, even as his body was in full motion, operating on sheer instinct and adrenaline. He ran straight for Nic, Garner coming from the other direction.

As Trace rounded the corner, the vision of her held in the grip of the intruder nearly felled him, but he kept moving, focused on neutralizing the situation.

He couldn't think about the fact that it was *her*.

He had to focus on the threat.

Focus, damn it.

His head swirled at the risks to her, but he kept moving. Kept straight for the man who held her in his grip, who now had the immediate threat of Garner heading for him as well.

But it was Nic's war cry that erupted into the air, her arm lifting and slamming into the guy's arm and chin, disrupting his equilibrium with the mix of motion and noise.

The three of them worked as a unit, Nic making the immediate hits to the intruder's body to disable him while Trace approached from the back and Garner ran point, removing the man's weapons from the front.

"Who are you?" Trace pulled hard on the man's arms, now behind his back.

"Amateurs." The man spat the word, followed by an actual well of spit in Nic's direction.

Trace tightened his hold, but it was his brother who moved right into the potential line of unsanitary fire.

Garner's gaze was hard, but his smile was pure menace and mischief all rolled into one as he leaned in close to the man's face. "Since we're the ones standing here and you're trussed up like a turkey ready for dinner, I'd guess again."

"Spare me. You didn't know I was here until I wanted you to know."

Although it was true, Trace held still, not wanting any response to seem like weakness or worse, agreement.

"Again, I repeat my point," Garner said. "You're the one standing here trussed up between the three of us."

Even though he couldn't see the intruder's face, Trace easily pictured the sneer that settled there. "You have no idea what she's dragged to your door."

"Then enlighten us." Nic's voice was steady and deadly calm.

"You think this is about a kid."

Nic's stare was unrelenting as she gazed at the man Trace held still. "I think there's a child being used as a pawn, but I don't think any of this is about a kid."

"They're never going to let you have her."

The flash in that crystal-blue gaze was brief, but Trace saw it all the same.

They.

It was small, but it was a slip.

"She's not a bargaining chip," Nic insisted.

"Then I guess you're out of aces," the man said.

Their quarry had remained eerily still through the exchange, not displaying any signs of struggle as he remained inside of Trace's hold. All that vanished when he moved suddenly, obviously determined to do some sort of damage.

Trace held tight and nearly had him in place, Garner moving up to add his additional weight, when the guy got free of both of them. Where the man thought he'd go with three people immediately on his tail, Trace didn't know, but he keenly understood the need for escape.

Trace, Nic and Garner took off in pursuit, racing down the front path of the house following the intruder.

Only to come to a slamming halt as the man's body shook violently, felled in the face of an unstoppable force.

NIC FELT THE rush of air before she even registered the bullet. She ran past the intruder, as did Trace and Garner, until they all realized what happened and doubled back.

"Sniper!" Trace called it first as they all quickly dropped to the ground. "Get to the tree line!"

Employing the same belly crawl she'd used in the ranch kitchen, Nic moved away from the body, seeking cover in the foliage that surrounded the property.

Foliage that had hidden a sniper and who-knew-what level of backup for the guy who'd made a run at them.

"Who is he?" Trace asked as he assessed their surroundings.

"No idea." Nic shook her head. "He's not familiar nor have I seen him in the Brigante files."

"Highly paid mercenary, most likely," Garner added before shifting back to work with Jake on their linked comms.

"Who's tracking you, and how the hell did they find you here?" Trace glanced at the body, his features taut from the stress of the moment. "And if you keep holding out on me, you can get off my property now."

"I'm not holding out on you. I've told you everything."

"Including whatever BS you've been facing in the home office?" Anger filled his lean features, driving deep, craggy lines into his forehead and around his eyes.

She knew that look—had seen it more than once—but never had she seen the absolute exhaustion behind it. Nor had she seen the very thin threads he was hanging on to as he worked to keep it together.

"I have told you what I know. Everything I know. But you have to know I came to you because I wasn't comfortable in the home office." She kept her gaze on his, willing him to understand.

"You haven't told me who. Who do you suspect, Nic?"

"I would never have taken this option if I thought there was any other way back in DC."

"Not what I asked you." He shook his head. "I asked you who."

"I can't tell you that."

"You come to my home. You hold a gun on me. You drag me into this. And I don't have a right to know?"

"I can't tell you that because I don't know."

"Well, hell."

Well, hell was right. But Nic didn't know how to fix it or how to give him a different answer. She did think the problems were buried somewhere deep inside the agency, even if she couldn't prove it.

But it was that belief that had spurred her on to find Trace.

She'd never have come to him if she'd had a choice. But she couldn't work inside the office, either. And she couldn't do this alone. Whatever else she'd figured out these past months, it was that.

So she'd gone to the one person she believed would handle this as faithfully as she would.

And the broken heart of the woman who'd loved him once upon a time would simply have to bear it.

"We need to go deal with the body."

She was already on her feet and moving to do just that when Trace spoke. "We don't know the scene is clear."

"I'll take my chances."

It was risky, but her gut told her if a sniper was waiting to shoot them they'd have not only done it sooner, but they wouldn't have wasted time with the goon they sent in as advance reconnaissance.

Which only added to the mystery of it all.

Was the goon a mercenary sent in by the Brigante organization? Or was it someone back in DC trying to send her a message?

I asked you who.

Trace's words still echoed between them, a lingering admonishment that she wasn't doing anything to build trust with the one person she couldn't afford to piss off. But since she'd obviously passed that milestone more than a few times since arriving, she'd have to push it aside.

Kneeling down beside the body, she felt around his thick coat looking for any form of ID she already knew she wouldn't find.

She searched anyway because action was better than inertia. Trying to find answers was better than accepting that someone was trying to hide them.

And immersing herself in work was the only possible protection she had to get through this, find Olivia and get out of Wyoming.

"ARE YOU SURE you trust her?" Garner asked as he dragged a tarp, laden with the body, between him and Trace.

"I do."

"Is this ancient history talking?"

Trace considered his brother's question—well aware *ancient history* increasingly felt like the present—as he came to a halt at the stable doors.

"I actually do, in spite of our ancient—" He broke off, done with the euphemism. "In spite of our past relationship."

"So you're staying in this?" Garner pressed.

"I am." Trace pulled open the heavy stable doors. "That doesn't mean you and Jake have to."

"Ride or die, brother." Garner sighed as he bent to grab handfuls of tarp again. "I'm yours."

"I know." Trace stilled and stared at his brother. "And I also know what that support means."

"Don't get mushy."

Despite the intense day—and the dead body between them—Garner's grin was broad and full of humor, and Trace couldn't help but smile back.

"You're an ass."

"Of the first water."

Trace shook his head before adding his muscle to move the body. They ultimately settled the dead man in an empty stall. He'd call local law enforcement and explain the situation. The fact that they had cameras on the property would work in their favor, the videos showing clear proof they were attacked and defending themselves.

The issue was how quickly should he call them in.

The bad weather that had been reported all week looked imminent, the skies growing darker since morning. He wasn't interested in putting local law enforcement in danger if there were others lurking around the property.

Garner stepped around the body and headed for the long pathway that ran down the length of the barn. "Let's go see if Jake's found anything else."

"I was coming to find you." Jake met them halfway down the stable aisle, several horses poking their heads over their stall doors at the man's obvious excitement.

"Someone else out there?" Trace was already on the move, heading for the office and the high-tech security setup they housed there.

"I haven't found anyone else. I've rewound the tapes by twenty-four hours but will keep looking. But I did find our dude lurking around this morning, just after ten, on what looks to be the very edge of the property."

Trace did the quick math and realized he'd already run into Nic in the woods and brought her back to the house by then. Had it really only been that morning? "Can you cue it up for me?"

"Already there." In the office, Jake tapped a few keys, obviously well-versed in visual technology tools the way he seamlessly shifted between screens and various commands to view the footage.

Trace focused on the top screen where the video was cued up, Garner leaning in with him. They took in the intruder's familiar figure, lurking around the edge of the property. The guy moved with purpose, but he didn't communicate via any device, nor did he refer to any digital technology.

"It's a match." Trace knocked his knuckles on the narrow table that ran the length of the viewing console. "He's not using any tech, and we didn't find anything on him."

"You'd give up your tech?" Garner glanced toward Trace.

Jake let out a low whistle and added a quiet "hell no."

"Not if given an option." Trace considered some of the more difficult missions he'd run. Tech was dangerous because if it got into the wrong hands, the ramifications on discovery were huge. But to be without anything?

"So who took away his option?" Garner reached over and tapped a few keys, rewinding the video before pausing it on a specific frame. "There. See how he's looking backward?"

Trace had seen the same and intended to look once more when they ran through it again. "How much you want to bet the sniper is who he was looking at? Maybe he was still communicating with him in some way."

"I don't take sucker bets," Garner said. "And that would be the very definition of one. He's working with someone, and once he wasn't useful anymore, that someone shot him."

They watched the recording a few more times before shifting to the other items Jake had cued up.

"You've got a few dead spots, but I was able to piece his movements together, going out of frame on one camera and back in on another."

"That was a deliberate decision. We can't reasonably cover the entire property, so we picked key spots."

"Except around the house," Trace corrected his brother. "We need to fix that."

"Yeah, we do."

Garner's agreement was obvious, but it still stuck an incredibly hard landing in Trace's gut that Nic had been attacked the way she had. If the mercenary—and Trace was working off the assumption the guy *was* hired muscle—hadn't gone after Garner and Jake first, who knew what could have happened?

"We need to find the sniper. We've got general direction, and there may be something up there we can use."

"You really think so?"

Trace turned at Nic's voice, eyeing her where she stood in the doorway to the office.

"I think that's the next step. The guy didn't get on the property by accident, and he sure as hell wasn't murdered because he stumbled into the wrong place."

"I'll get the body dealt with," Nic said, "and then I'm going to get backup. They'll either send a field team to me, or we'll work the project from DC. Either way, you don't need me bringing this sort of violence to your door."

"You think we're afraid of a few bullets?" Jake asked.

It was unexpected to hear their newcomer pipe up so quickly, and all heads turned toward the former Vegas cop with a past full of baggage. Or at least that was what Trace assumed, and Jake hadn't given him any reason to think otherwise.

"I think we should all be afraid," Nic said. "What just happened out there was a major escalation."

Obviously undeterred, Jake persisted, "It was also a really bad tip of the hand." When no one said anything, he laid out his argument. "If it's Brigante's people, they tipped their hand. And if it's your old office mates…" Jake tilted his head toward Trace "…it's extra bad form."

Although he couldn't fault the logic, Trace was fascinated by how quickly Jake pulled the pieces together without the benefit of time or experience with the federal government. "Some of the boys and girls at the agency were never taught to play nice." He couldn't resist adding, "I know because I was one of them."

"You played by the rules."

Nic's ready defense captured him, and he couldn't resist poking that old topic just a bit. "We both know only when it suited me. It was the biggest reason we broke up."

"No it wasn't."

Trace suddenly recognized his tactical error as his brother and his new roommate both became very interested in whatever was coming next.

He'd put their personal life on display and based on the light of battle filling her vivid blue gaze, Nic wasn't going to wait to argue with him outside the surveillance of two deeply interested parties.

"We broke up because you didn't trust me to have your back."

"I always trusted you."

"No, Trace, you didn't. Not when it mattered most."

Chapter Nine

Nic cursed herself a million ways to Sunday that she'd let something that personal slip out. In front of others, no less. One more sign the feelings she carried for him—the ones she never actually dealt with, just buried deep—carried the very real risk of overshadowing what she was here to do.

And she could not let that happen.

Olivia was the focus.

All the rest—catching Brigante, dealing with possible rot back in DC, even those overwhelming feelings—they all had to come second.

A child's life was at stake.

She had to keep that focus, or else…

The thought faded away, replaced with the truth.

For all her armor and all her belief that she could have a physical affair with Trace Withrow and move on, it had been the biggest lie she'd ever told herself. The relationship had been the most impactful one of her life, and she hadn't survived the end of it quite the way she'd believed she could when it all began.

But that was her secret.

Her burden.

She'd remained strong for two years, moving on in life if not in spirit. And she had to keep doing it.

Because right now, Olivia's life was all that mattered.

"Much as I'd like to stand here and continue this little coffee klatch slash jaunt down memory lane, we need to find where the sniper set up. I doubt we'll find any clues, but we have to try." She turned on a heel and headed for the exit to the stables, not surprised when she heard footsteps behind her, stopping her before she hit the door.

"Nic. Wait."

"We don't have time to wait."

"Nic!"

She felt the light tug on her hand, and she turned to face Trace, pulling her hand free of his grip. "Can we at least talk on the move?"

"Fine. We keep extra tools here in the stables. Let's suit up in Kevlar and take the truck. I have an idea of where the sniper set up to get that sort of view on the front of the house."

Since going out unarmed with a sharpshooter on the loose was the height of stupidity, she nodded and followed him to a long wall of closets. She'd assumed they all held tack and other items for the horses when she passed them earlier, but when Trace opened the last cabinet in the row, she saw what he'd promised.

State-of-the-art physical protection.

"How much did you and Garner put into this place?"

"Enough," he muttered as he pulled out a jacket for her, followed by one for himself.

The thick body armor was tight when she zipped it up—well fitted as it should be—and she felt an odd calming inside at the additional layer of protection.

It was a counterpoint to just how vulnerable she'd felt outside with the guy who'd attacked them. While the body armor wouldn't protect her from a head shot, it went a long way toward making her feel better if they got into a skirmish.

"Let's go," Trace said and she didn't miss the light of battle that filled his gray eyes.

She headed for the work truck parked outside the stables and climbed into the passenger seat. Trace climbed into the driver seat and in moments had them turned around and heading down the long driveway that led to the ranch house.

"What are you going to do with the body?"

"We have a good relationship with local law enforcement. Working with them isn't the problem." Trace glanced over at her as he took a right onto a dirt road that would take them into the heart of the ranch. "The question is when. I don't want them tipping off anyone at the agency that you're here."

"You don't have to hold off on my account."

"I think I do. And I think you're fooling yourself if you think otherwise."

Trace's words were calm and level, a counterpoint to the muscle that ticked in his jaw and the hard set of his face.

He was pissed off.

She recognized the surly attitude. Faced it before, as a matter of fact. Trace was a world champion blusterer when properly ruffled. It was actually a trait she'd admired. There was no hiding his emotions. No faking a smile when he was pissed off or giving someone hell for making mistakes on an op.

Or, as most often was the case, giving that hell to himself because he hadn't met his own exceptionally high standards.

So yes, she'd seen this side of him. But then they were colleagues. Mission buddies. And later lovers. There was an intimacy to all that had come before that they no longer shared.

Memories of intimacy weren't the same as actual intimacy, and that suddenly seemed very important.

In the past, she'd known the right words or even a joke to ease the situation. Now she had nothing to defuse the tension. Which only left her to her silence and him to simmer beside her, a bubbling cauldron building steam.

They continued on the trail for a short while before he turned off, the land beneath the truck growing increasingly bumpy and rough. They didn't go much more than half a mile when he came to a halt, pulling the truck to the side.

"We'll walk the rest of the way."

Nic followed Trace through the thick brush, this portion of the land rugged and harsh and likely why the ranch house was set where it was. Although she hadn't seen the full property, the thick ridge that made up this portion likely made it difficult to manage with livestock or to use for farmland.

"Is this ridge the reason the house and stables are set where they are?"

"Yep. Workable areas were left open while this area below the ridge made it ideal to hold people and animals."

"It's clever," Nic observed as they walked, taking in the land and the rising height.

"It was one of the things that sold me on the place. That thoughtfulness about the layout and the use of the land. People on a ranch have to live somewhere, so put them in the place that's least useful to the business endeavors of the property."

"Hearty people conquered this land." She glanced sideways, curious to see the fresh air and walk hadn't done anything to change his mood or the dark look that rode his features. "Hearty people continue to make it home."

"Yes."

"Look, Trace." She stopped, trying to get him to slow down for a minute and snap out of this mood that he seemed determined to marinate in. "I get this is not ideal, and I've shown up in your life and created chaos with seeming ease. But talk to me. What has you so upset?"

"You mean besides the gun aimed at me to start my day, the very real knowledge a child is in danger, and then an assassin on my property who was determined to kill you and whomever else got in his way?"

"We're handling it."

"By slapping on Kevlar and hunting down a sniper? That's handling it?"

"Trace, I—"

The words died as he stopped and stared at her. Right there, in the midst of the dying afternoon light and the cold air that swirled around them and the very real knowledge that they had no idea who hunted them. "You what? You going to apologize again?"

"No, I think the time for that's past. I just…"

The words faded out again, an embarrassing state that she couldn't seem to shake. She didn't forget her words. Nor did she back down from the face of a fight.

But this? The sheer anger that rode his features?

"What has you so riled up? I get this is all an inconvenience, and I've dropped your old life smack in the middle of your new one. But we've got a plan. We'll get Olivia, and I'll be gone."

A harsh laugh escaped his lips, and she felt that tugging sensation that pulled her from way down deep inside. "Same old Nic. Blind devotion to the job and blithe ignorance to your own personal danger."

"What does that mean?" Just because she was willing to acknowledge his anger didn't mean she refused to allow her own to rise. Whatever had him in knots didn't mean she had to bear the brunt.

"Did you give any thought to the danger you've taken on, doing this by yourself? Outside the auspices of the agency?"

"I came to you."

"Now! But how long have you been in the thick of this? Alone!"

Whatever worry they'd both carried about being spotted

by the sniper had faded. Lunacy? Yes, probably. But if they were really targets, they'd likely have been shot at already. "I came to you, Trace. You have to know what that cost me!"

"Yes, I know. I know exactly what it cost you because I'm paying the same damn price, with interest."

"What's that supposed to mean?"

"I watched him hold you. Press a gun to your forehead. That's the danger that's been stalking you. You, Nic!"

With startling clarity, the reason for his ire and frustration became clear. This wasn't about a shooter or a case or even her holding a gun on him this morning.

It was about *her*.

Before the knowledge had even fully sunk in, she felt herself being dragged forward. The thick Kevlar made a hard barrier between them when he pulled her close, but she didn't have time to worry about it as his mouth came over hers.

Crushing.

Devouring.

Feasting.

As she wrapped her arms around his waist, just below the thick band of protection, she matched his ardor.

And gave up the ridiculous notion that there was any possible way she could ever keep her heart out of this.

TRACE KEPT A firm hold on her, the sheer wonder at having her in his arms again juxtaposed by the thick protective material between them and the reality that they were standing in the woods mere yards from where a sniper had hid less than an hour before.

Had he lost every bit of training and ability he'd honed over decades?

Even as something in the back of his mind recognized they were still in danger, something more present—and far more fierce—beat in his blood.

He needed this. Desperately.

Because one wrong move, and she'd have died today.

The man who attacked Nic had been determined to cause problems, and it was only by sheer luck Trace had gotten to her first. It was only the man's extreme bad fortune to get himself involved with some ruthless machine who only ever intended to use him as a pawn.

Trace knew he should pay attention to all of that. That he should dig down deep and let his exhaustive training and years of reading the worst of humanity's actions be his guide.

But all he wanted was Nic. And these quiet, nearly desperate moments to hold her close and make them both remember what had burned so bright and clear between them.

God, he'd missed her.

More, he'd missed *them*. What it felt like to be with her and how he felt when he was with her. Free in a way he'd never experienced before or since.

With all that swirling in his mind, Trace pushed every one of those emotions into the kiss. It was hot and carnal and oddly sweet at the same time. Because whatever he'd remembered of her, nothing could compare to having her in his arms once more.

Danger be damned.

"Trace." His name was half moan, half sigh against his lips. "We can't do this here."

His response was wholly inappropriate, but he found he couldn't stop the smile as he pulled back slightly to look down at her. "We've already made easy targets of ourselves, and no bullets yet. I think we're safe."

Her eyebrows rose over those gorgeous blue eyes, and he saw skepticism rapidly chasing away desire. "That's a way to look at it."

"I'm not apologizing for taking a moment."

"I'm—" She took a deep breath. "I'm not apologizing, either. But we need to focus on the sniper."

"I'll bet you another kiss we're not going to find anything."

"Not taking that bet, and we're not kissing again."

Trace nearly laughed out loud at the prim response and decided to save any smart-ass remarks for later. Because after what they just shared, he was quite sure that wasn't their last kiss.

But he'd leave her to her illusions.

"Fine then, let's look."

He continued tramping up the dirt path that led to the upper portion of the ridge. While he wasn't convinced they'd find anything left behind, like shell casings or a lost glove, he was interested in what they could potentially track.

Footprints. The imprint of heavy equipment like a tripod to balance a rifle. Or even a body print if the sniper lay prone on the ground to take the shot.

Their recent weather was a positive in the tracking work— the late winter snows and the corresponding snowmelt after a few unexpectedly sunny days had made the ground soft. And no sniper, no matter how good, could erase the pull of gravity.

The path they walked was clear, so Trace shifted his attention to the scrub grass alongside the trail. His patience was rewarded when he got the distinct imprints for two pairs of shoes.

"Here." He waved Nic over. "Look here."

"So they were together."

"Yep. And that's cold. They come up here like partners in crime, but one knows the other's unlikely to leave."

Nic knelt down to inspect the footprints before looking back up at him. "You think he was expendable from the first?"

"If he'd succeeded, maybe not. Likely not, as the sniper would have needed to come play backup to deal with the rest of us." Trace looked around, curious now that he considered that angle. "Jake would have been a surprise since he just got here. Maybe they figured they could take us three to two. It's not a secret my brother lives here."

"And your ranch hands. They would have been targets, too. It seems risky to think anyone could have come onto this property and thought they could simply slaughter everyone." Nic stood, shaking her head. "And even that. I just got here this morning. How could anyone plan it so fast? Even if Brigante is that connected, Olivia just hacked into my computer a few hours ago. None of this makes sense."

Trace had to agree with her assessment. Nothing about the attacker and the shooter up on the ridge fit any logical pattern. "You thought someone back in the home office could be involved. They'd have time to get here and set this up."

"Trace, I know you don't fully believe me on that front, but I've been careful at the office. And that's with not even being quite sure anyone at the office is even the problem."

"But you've considered it?" he pressed.

"Of course. I won't rule it out until everyone can be fully ruled out. It's why I haven't shared my theories with anyone and covered my tracks on my trip out here."

"How'd you get here?"

"I scheduled a few personal days. I flew to Florida first and spent the weekend there. Then I went on to Denver. Then I rented a car to drive up here."

"You could have been tracked."

"Could have been, sure. But I was careful, I was on my guard every step of the way and never saw a tail, and I truly played up being out. I briefed everyone on my plans and had an action plan for covering my work while I was gone. Other than my computer log-ins, which I said I'd do to be available while remote, I've been careful."

Every point was fair and logical, and Trace wanted to believe she was right. But he also had a dead man on his property and a case suspicious enough that Nic was keeping it close to the vest *and* coming to him for help.

He wasn't ready to rule out his old employer as the root of the problem.

But, Trace admitted to himself on a sigh, he couldn't let his old resentments lead the witness, either. "Let's keep going."

They followed the dual footprints until they came to the top of the ridge. Trace turned and could see the front door of the house clearly from where they stood. The ground was trampled in a circle around what was clearly three divots from a tripod. "Sniper was here."

He moved to stand in the line of sight again, but Nic beat him there, positioning herself as if she stood behind the sniper's rifle, looking through the sight down toward the house.

"Right here." Nic pulled out her phone and started snapping photos.

Trace busied himself with the footprints. They were large—he placed his own size twelves next to both sets and could see a fairly close match. "Looks like both snipers were male based on the prints. Since they didn't go back down the ridge side by side, I'm going to check the descent and see if anything's there."

He moved toward the other side of the trail, curious to see that there was one set of prints. He would investigate further but assumed he and Nic would be able to follow them back down. Likely this was the attacker leaving the vantage point to head down earlier and make trouble at the house.

But where were the other ones?

Retracing his steps, he moved back up to the vantage point and looked around, finally spotting the second set of prints down the back side of the ridge.

The escape.

It still bothered him that either man had gotten on the

property undetected, but the exit was interesting. Since it was different from where the pair ascended the ridge, Trace questioned if there was some sort of getaway car waiting on the other side.

"Nic, play something out with me." He waved her over, memories of their time in the field together filling his mind unexpectedly.

How seamlessly they worked together.

The way he'd bounce things off of her, spinning theories and watching as she was able to poke holes where needed or where she helped make the thread even stronger.

She came up beside him, oblivious to his wandering thoughts, her gaze on him telegraphing that she was firmly in huntress mode. "What are you thinking?"

"Two pairs of prints up the ridge. One down the back here. They didn't come in from this direction." Trace pointed to the back side and the lone set of footprints.

"You think there was a getaway car?"

"Yep. One our dead guy had no idea about."

"A driver and a third person involved?"

"A third doesn't make a lot of tactical sense. Why only send one down to deal with us if you had backup? You only need onc sniper."

"True." She nodded, warming to the topic. "But that means if they came in together, they were in a different vehicle than the getaway car."

In unison, their gazes clashed, a triumphant note echoing from their words at the same time. "Let's find the car."

It was a good plan.

An excellent one, Trace knew.

They could come back later, but it was time to head out and find the car.

His focus was on the end game, so he'd chalk it up to his

training that at the last minute he stopped and took one last look at the ridge, his gaze drifting over the ground.

That was when he saw it.

A glint of light, reflecting from where something metallic was buried in the grass.

He moved closer, curious, even as a wave of anticipation flew through him. Shell casing or maybe something that fell off a sniper's equipment?

That was his expectation when he bent down.

But as his fingers grazed the edge of a round disc, something dark and dangerous flashed in his mind as he picked up the small coin.

He knew what this was.

"Nic. Come here."

"What?" She moved closer immediately, obviously drawn by the urgency in his tone.

"Tell me you know what this is." He extended his hand, the coin lying flat in his palm.

"It's a challenge coin."

"It most certainly is. And last time I checked, these were most definitely a law enforcement thing. Not the work of shipping magnates."

NIC STARED AT the challenge coin displayed on Trace's palm and tried to catch her breath. She knew that coin.

Had one of her own, in fact.

"Those were given out when Roger Bane retired."

"Yeah, they were." Trace nodded, his gaze dark yet surprisingly unreadable. Even with the strangely damning evidence, it was the fact that she couldn't read him that ratcheted up her anxiety.

Roger had been their collective lead when they worked together. Incredibly well respected, he'd run his unit at the agency with a mix of humor, grace and integrity.

"Roger's been gone a little over two years."

"I know. His retirement was the reason I finally put in my resignation. I wasn't interested in staying in that place if Bane wasn't there, and Rannell wasn't sad to see me go. After all those years, he accepted my resignation and said it was probably 'for the best.'"

Unbidden, one of their last conversations before their relationship exploded ran through her mind.

There's an undercurrent here, Nic. Can't you feel it? Don't you sense it?

We work for a highly respected government agency.

With huge pockets of work subject to no external oversight. We're keeping state secrets. What do you expect?

She'd argued those points at that time. They had latitude because of what they did. And the reality that in order to keep the world safe, elements of that safety hinged on secrecy and the ability to get the job done.

Even with that conviction, Trace's words had haunted her in her quiet moments since.

Undercurrents.

Although she'd fought him mightily at the time, she'd felt them, too. And had continued to feel them more and more as time passed.

"The place hasn't been the same since Roger retired." *Or since you left.*

She wanted to say that part, too, but their kiss was still too fresh on her lips. And the raw emotions that came from admitting to herself just how badly she wanted him kept her from saying anything more.

"Who else was there at the time?" Trace turned the coin over before holding it up. "Who else has one of these?"

"They had a few hundred made for his retirement. Anyone on his team at the time could have one, but he could have shared some with family or friends outside the agency, too."

It was the reality of challenge coins. What started in military organizations now extended well past that to police, fire, EMS. Even universities and sports teams had gotten into the idea of customizing human belonging within a group of people.

In their case, Roger's retirement had generated a coin specific to him and his team, honoring his many decades of service.

She'd accepted hers with pride and knew Trace felt similarly about the one he'd received.

But there was something about this one, left right here for them to find, that sent a message.

"You know as well as I do this wasn't left here by Roger's family or his friends."

She stared up at him, the lips that had so recently kissed her, taking her back to a place that still ached in her heart, suppressed into a flat line. Rigid.

And telegraphing an anger she could feel sparking off him.

"No, Trace, this isn't by accident. Someone's sending us a message."

"Which means this isn't just about Brigante. And following you here, finding you here? With me? That wasn't an accident, either."

Deep down, Nic had known that from the start. Was that why she was so invested in this? She'd told herself it was about a child, and that fact remained absolute in her mind, but there was something more.

Something dark and rotten from the inside.

"I was careful. I kept my search for you out of work computers and off the grid."

"Then someone already knew where I was and figured I was the first one outside the agency you'd come looking for."

"Why would anyone think that?" she pressed, an oddly

sinking feeling settling in her stomach. "We were discreet. No one knew about us."

That dark, haunted look on his face faded, replaced with a layer of humor she knew wasn't actually about anything funny.

"What's that look for?"

"People knew."

The roiling in her stomach dropped clear down to her feet, a gaping pit. "Like hell they did."

"Nic." Trace shook his head before moving closer. He settled one hand on her shoulder while the other moved up to cup her cheek. "For someone so street-smart, you really do miss the forest *and* the trees sometimes."

"What's that supposed to mean?"

"Roger warned me off of you before anything even started."

"He never said anything to me."

"He didn't have to. You weren't the one looking at you. I was."

Even as those words arrowed straight to her heart, a big part of her struggled to believe it was possible. Did everyone really know about them?

It struck hard, the idea that people had watched them. Had known about their intimacies.

And yet…it dropped a few more pieces into place.

"Was that why you were so reluctant to start anything with me?"

His thumb brushed the edge of her jaw. "Well, yeah. You're the golden girl, and I was just the ass who had the hots for you."

"You were a top-notch agent and well respected by everyone who knows you. What you do as an adult in your private moments is no one's business."

That grim smile shifted—morphed, really—into a broad

one to rival the sun desperately struggling to cut through the clouds. "People have a funny way of making their own observations all the same. And if it's considered remotely scandalous or interesting that goes double."

"People need to mind their own business," Nic snapped. Hearing the harshness, she could be honest enough with herself to know it was out of embarrassment more than anything else.

"Since they don't, we have to figure out a way forward."

She laid a hand over his, still pressed against her cheek, and saw the reality of what she'd brought here to his corner of paradise. "I'm sorry."

His gray eyes, always so expressive, narrowed at the apology. "For what?"

"For bringing this here. For drawing you back in. For all of it."

"I told you I was in this, Nic."

"When it was about a child, yes. But this is more." Her gaze drifted to where he'd found the challenge coin glinting on the ground before coming back to him. "That coin says this is so much more."

"Then we face it together."

"I'm still sorry. For all of it."

"I'm not. If this is about me or my time at the agency, it's been out there, waiting to strike."

"And I brought it here."

That smile—the heartbreaking one that she still saw in her private moments—flashed strong and true. "There's no one I'd rather face it with than you."

Chapter Ten

Garner turned the challenge coin over in his hands before passing it off to Jake.

They all sat around the kitchen table, the lights dim against the darkness now settled outside the window, steaming mugs of coffee in front of all of them. Hogan lay on the small area rug they kept in front of the fridge, where he'd been all day. Making himself at home and claiming his spot.

Trace was oddly glad of it, even if it was going to take a bit of getting used to having such a large presence in the house.

But Hogan had been a sentinel for Jake throughout the intruder's attack. And even now, head on his paws, the German shepherd's eyes kept opening each time Jake spoke.

A unit, Trace thought. A man and his dog. Had they only just arrived the day before?

It's been a hell of a day.

Trace nearly said the words aloud but stopped, instead taking in the dynamics at the table. He watched his brother and his friend work through the implications of the coin, sharing a few theories between them, before allowing his gaze to drift to Nic.

She was one of the strongest people he'd ever met, male or female, so he wasn't worried that she'd wilt under the reality of all this. But he did worry about her.

Most of all, he was concerned she somehow felt this was all happening because of her.

In reality, it was happening because of him. He'd bet his life on it.

Leaving the agency and DC behind hadn't just been about getting away from her. Nor had it been about simply leaving a place that no longer filled him with pride and purpose.

He'd known something was wrong. He'd sensed it in Roger long before the man retired with honors. A sense that his respected boss was doing everything he could to keep his fingers in the dam.

But there were cracks.

The unrelenting pressure to expand their remit and take on more shady responsibilities in reaction to the bad actors in the world. Points Trace understood, yet couldn't fully reconcile with the Mom, baseball and apple-pie reasons that got layered over it.

Murder was murder, and you couldn't change that with a slice of pie.

There had also been a change in the tone of their missions. While espionage had carried shades of gray since time immemorial, their reasons for the missions had become more nuanced.

A *suspected* arms dealer acting badly in the Horn of Africa.

A *presumed* scientist in the Middle East selling state secrets.

An *inferred* connection in South America with a group of local militants and an upcoming political election.

He'd been in the game long enough to recognize that all of the suspicion had a place, but the speed with which they acted on it had become difficult to explain away to himself. A truth that had grown even more challenging when he'd seen their secret actions directly benefiting businesses who operated in those places, from shipping to technology to pharmaceuticals.

Was he jaded? Sure.

Was he still right? Hell yes.

"This was from the man you both worked under?" Jake asked as he laid the coin on the table. "Was he a good guy?"

"The best," Nic quickly asserted before her gaze drifted to meet Trace's. "I'm not backing down off of that point, Trace. Roger was a good man. Is a good man."

"I agree. He's the reason I stayed so long." *Him and you*, he thought as he looked at Nic.

But she didn't need to know that. Even as he suspected his brother was well aware of what he'd held off saying.

"So there's no chance he's behind this?" Jake persisted. "Some inability to actually retire and leave the game?"

"It's a consideration, and running down all angles has to include it," Trace added. Jake's police training and years of detective work would ensure he looked under every rock, and Trace appreciated the perspective.

He also knew Roger Bane.

"But I think it's a consideration to drop way further down the list. We'd be better off thinking through who was on his team during the time he retired and who has an interest in extracurricular activities, using agency influence."

"Anyone come to mind, Nic?" Garner had remained quiet up to now, and his directed question held more censure than Trace was comfortable with.

He trusted his brother and knew that was returned tenfold.

So why was he swiping at Nic?

Yet true to his belief in her, she held her own, her chin held high and her voice firm and direct. "No one's off-limits, but there's no one who pops for me, either."

"But you came here," Garner pushed. "You sensed *something* if you went outside your own resources."

"That's the problem. It's a sense, but it's broadly distributed."

That was new. What did she mean *distributed*? Before Trace could ask, Jake stepped in, his tone calm. "Walk me through it."

Nic glanced at Trace, as if willing him to keep quiet, before launching in. "I've given you the overview of the Brigante case. The shipping and manifests that don't quite match. The size of the business overall and the suspicion Richie Brigante has friends in low places."

"Right," Garner said as Jake nodded with a "yep" of his own.

"So we've been following it. The moment he moved into international waters and began his work with other countries, it moved into our jurisdiction, even as I argued it belonged with coast guard or even FBI to manage, with us assisting."

It was an interesting angle and one Trace hadn't considered, but Garner was already probing further. "You can make that decision?"

"We can recommend. If the base problem was Brigante putting dangerous cargo on his ships and leaving US waters, coast guard should have a role."

"But they didn't on this?"

"They were the ones who brought it to us," Nic said, her gaze going slightly unfocused as she recounted the work. "I was pulled into a briefing meeting and figured that would be the extent of it for a while. We would agree to share some data resources and any intel we had on Brigante. Next thing I know, the work's being taken over, and I'm on the team working the case."

"How'd the coasties take it?"

Nic flashed a smile at Jake. "They don't call them Bears for nothing. Not well."

Trace took it all in and had to admit he'd let his feelings for Nic cloud quite a bit. The overwhelming emotions of being around her again had ruled the day, and it was only now, with the realities of all they'd faced in less than twenty-four hours, that he had to admit the situation went far deeper than he first suspected.

But it was the interagency battle that said the most.

Sure, there were turf wars from time to time. But people also knew their responsibilities and their roles. A decision this overt suggested someone trying to hide their involvement in the core problem.

"Who made the decision, Nic?"

"That's the problem. I can't find who ordered it. I've dug, and I've discreetly asked, and I've even bitched and moaned about the assignment in hopes of getting some detail. But no one seems to know. Or the ones who do are mum."

"So let me play it back," Garner said, his expression flat.

Trace had always thought of it as his brother's SEAL face. The one that said *don't mess with me*. It hid a lot, Trace knew. Emotions that ran far deeper than Garner allowed anyone to see. And a rapier-sharp intelligence few truly understood until it was too late.

"You have murky leadership now that Roger's departed. Interagency battles that no one seems bothered by. And now, based on this coin…" Garner tapped the table "…the assumption that we've got a rogue agent."

"It looks just like that."

"Well now," Garner drawled, shooting Trace a large, wolfish smile. "Looks like things just got good."

"THAT'S ONE WAY to put it," Nic said in as dry a tone as she could manage. Did he think this was funny?

Even as the thought flitted through her mind, she knew better.

Garner had questioned her from the start—and since she'd held a gun on his brother, she couldn't quite say she was blameless—but it still rankled a bit. They weren't playing a game.

And yet…someone in DC obviously was. Maybe she'd be better off looking at the situation through that lens, identifying her next move like a chess piece on a board.

Which made Garner's next retort sting a little bit less. "I think it's the only way to put it. You've got an ogre situation going on here."

"I'm sorry?"

"Ogres. Onions," Jake said.

"Layers," Trace added. "Lots and lots of layers."

Awareness finally registered at the pop culture reference. "This is hardly a children's movie."

"Hardly," Garner said. "But it's still true."

Nic gave herself a moment to gather her thoughts, looking at each man in turn. It was a skill she'd figured out early on, when she was new to the work and trying to make a name for herself in a male-dominated world.

Nic Miles held her own.

Always.

"I want to go out and take a look at the surrounding roads," Trace said finally. "We'll see if anything looks out of order or where there might have been an entrance onto the property. I have a few ideas where they might have come in."

His words seemed to have a quieting effect on his brother because Garner only nodded. "Why don't I take care of calling out law enforcement? I can introduce Jake to the locals in the process."

Jake rubbed his hands with a half smile. "My first day and already meeting local law enforcement."

"Start as you mean to go on, I always say," Garner said as he stood up from the table.

Jake followed suit, catching Hogan's attention from where the dog had settled in front of the refrigerator. He obediently followed, as silent as a wraith other than his nails clicking on the kitchen tiles.

Nic considered all they'd learned up at the sniper's perch and the risks of running around in the dark. The ranch was in the middle of nowhere. They'd gotten lucky earlier, but was it really wise to go out at night without any knowledge of what lurked nearby? "It's dark. Do you really think you'll see much?"

"Doubtful." Trace picked up his mug and took a sip of coffee. "But you never know. We could find something. Or we find nothing and keep on driving to pick up some dinner at the diner. No one will argue with takeout tonight."

"I—" She broke off, unwilling to continue the thought. What was she going to do? Apologize again? Or worse.

Ask him to kiss her again?

When her face grew decidedly warm at the image, Nic recognized it was best to make a hasty retreat. "We can take my car if you'd like."

"The rental?" Trace shook his head. "I hope you don't mind, but I'd rather we looked a bit more incognito in my truck."

"Sure. Of course. Right."

She pushed back from her chair, suddenly needing to get away and regroup for a few minutes. All of it had grown heavy. Almost too much to bear, really.

She'd nearly made her escape when she felt a tug on her hand. Trace had reached for her, stopping her movement. "I just need a minute, and then I'll be ready."

"Take all the time you need."

As the mortifying reality that she was staring at a place just over his head took hold, Nic shifted her vision, her gaze clashing with his.

What she saw there nearly took her breath.

"I'm glad you're here. I'm glad I'm the one you came to."

"I don't know why," she murmured.

"Because you need me, and you came to me." His hand tightened around hers. A soft squeeze of welcome and connection, and so achingly familiar it was a wonder she didn't dissolve into a puddle right there. "I'm glad you did."

She'd never considered herself a woman of vast emotions. Appetites, yes. There'd been a time she was insatiable for him. At moments, even now, she could feel that need echo through her body in harsh, clanging waves.

But emotions? They'd always been her downfall.

She didn't like them. Had never wanted them. In fact, she'd figured out the only way to survive her childhood had been to ruthlessly root them out and live in a way that didn't allow her emotions to exist.

How humbling to realize Trace had pushed through all that.

Effortlessly.

For reasons that made no sense, a night several years ago filled her mind's eye. It was before they'd become intimate, one of several jobs together that had preceded the fall into their ill-fated relationship.

"Do you remember that night?" she asked. "The stakeout in Budapest?"

"I do."

"Do you remember what we talked about?"

"You told me about the kid whose mom came to school and talked about her work as a chef."

Those emotions she wanted to pretend didn't exist speared through her, piercing internal organs as they zipped around her insides like pinballs.

"Why do you remember that?"

"Because you told me." His gaze searched hers. "And because I got the sense as you were telling me the story that long, boring night on stakeout that you were leaving out a very large part of it."

She had left something out, but she was shocked to realize that *he* knew it. "I told you everything. The way she talked about her job and how she told us funny stories about patrons who wanted weird things or how someone brought a dog to her restaurant in their purse and it got loose, wreaking havoc in the kitchen."

His hand hadn't let go, and his gaze hadn't left hers, and Nic recognized somewhere way down deep that she was well and truly lost.

Because there was no way she could deny what was uniquely and innately *them*. No way she could deny how he saw her and heard her and touched her and...just how she felt when she was with him.

"What were you holding back?"

"How much I wanted that to be my mom. This was before the Bakers when I really didn't have anything beyond three squares and a rotating group of foster parents." She closed her eyes against the memory, not even sure anymore why she'd brought it up. "I wanted that to be my mom so badly. To have someone who told funny stories and who came for me at school and who hugged me when it was all over."

"Why didn't you tell me that part?" Trace asked, his voice husky. "Seems like it was the most important."

"That's the point I'm trying to make. I deliberately left it out because I have no interest in feeling that way. Emotions are poison. I don't want them. I can't do them. In fact, I sort of suck at them."

She tried to tug her hand back but he held firm.

"I don't think you suck at them."

"That's because you want in my pants."

"Perpetually and eternally. But news flash. I've been in your pants. I still don't think you suck at emotions." He stared up at her. "I can, after all, keep two distinct thoughts in my head."

The intimacy—one that had nothing to do with sex or nakedness—embarrassed her even more than the frank talk. "I don't do this. So can you just accept that it took a lot for me to come to you?"

His hand dropped away from hers and something shuttered, shadowing those deep gray eyes. "I know it took a lot." He stood then, towering over her but not touching her again.

Nic felt her pulse trip at his nearness. At the way that deep gray seemed to see everywhere at once. The way that gaze seemed to simply envelop her.

"Just so you know, that goes both ways."

"You expect me to believe you've spent the past two years pining for me?"

"Believe what you want, Nic. I know what I know."

And then he was gone, slipping from the kitchen and leaving her standing there staring into space.

The pressure of the case.

The long, exhausting days of searching for a child.

And now this.

Her living nightmare, having to confront all the feelings inside she'd long believed buried.

Or worse.

Admitting she was full to the brim with emotions she'd believed herself incapable of having.

WHAT IN THE ever-loving hell was wrong with him?

Trace left that question to marinate as he prepared himself for the trip out to the edges of the property, well aware he needed his full focus to go hunting for a killer.

You expect me to believe you've spent the past two years pining for me?

The fact that he almost said yes was proof his head was not where it needed to be.

In the game and totally focused on catching a killer. That's where he needed to be. Especially after their discovery of that little clue up on the ridge.

The challenge coin haunted him, and he knew Garner and Jake had similar responses. A challenge coin meant something, most specifically belonging to a team.

A unit.

Hell, Trace and Garner had discussed creating a few of their own once they made the decision to move to Liar's Gulch and set up the training facility. Old habits died hard and all that. But both of them innately understood what it meant to belong to something bigger than them.

Which was why that discarded coin packed the exact punch its owner intended.

Trace knew how a challenge worked. A person carried the coin on them so they could hold it up when someone called for it in a social setting, initiating a coin check of the members present. It was both a game and a very real test of emotional commitment.

He still had every challenge coin he'd been given. Most professionals he knew were the same.

So the purposeful discard of one had several messages layered through it.

The person shooting at him and Nic *knew* them.

And they no longer cared to be a part of the team.

Trace finished pulling weapons, ammo and a few other supplies out of the cabinets in the stables and walked into the office for one last check on the cameras. Jake had flagged several points when he was watching the recordings earlier and had encouraged Trace to watch them before heading out. The man might be new, but he was quickly making himself invaluable. Trace appreciated the immediate willingness to help.

He also appreciated the keen eye the seasoned detective brought to the work. An eye that had encouraged him and Nic to get out of the house before Garner called the local cops to help with the body.

Settling himself at the keyboard, Trace ignored the distinct unpleasantness that filled him, knowing there was a dead body not that far away. Distractedly, he wondered if it was bad for the horses. None had seemed worse for wear when he came in and greeted them down the line, but was he risking equine harmony in his stables with this?

Since there wasn't anywhere else to put the guy, they were going to have to risk it, but Trace was anxiously counting the minutes until they had the body off the property.

The videos were queued as promised, and Trace played the first three, each showing the same span of time from different angles. It was only when he got to the fourth—showing the same time stamp and a view on the farthest edge of the property capturing the road into town—that he saw Jake's intention.

Because right there, about forty-five minutes before the incident out front, was a large black SUV barreling down the road. The windows were tinted, but Trace was able to make out two distinct forms in the front seat through the windshield.

It wasn't much, but it was something.

He rewound the tape, the angle of the camera only capturing the license plate for the briefest moment. Even with that quick slip of time, Trace could see the plate had been covered over with mud.

One more indication they had the vehicle of the intruders, if not the identities.

It wasn't ideal, but at least they'd have an image to show

police. One more element in their favor when they also pro-
duced a body, one who just happened to get himself shot
dead on their property.

Trace left the recordings queued where they were for when
Garner and Jake walked the local sheriff through the details
and picked up his stuff to leave. He had a renewed sense of
purpose, even as he knew it was highly unlikely they were
going to find anything.

The ridge had been clean before, and Trace had no doubt
that was by design. The only clue they were meant to find
was the challenge coin.

It was just their sniper's bad luck that he and Garner had
been paranoid enough to set up far-perimeter cameras at
the very edges of the ranch. Their video strategy left way
too much acreage uncovered—it would be impossible to do
otherwise—but in moments like this he was grateful they'd
thought that far ahead. At least they had a set of eyes on anyone's approach.

He was briefly tempted to rewind the tapes even further
and see what Nic's approach had been that morning, but he
didn't have the time. Besides, based on where she'd found him
in the woods, he likely wasn't going to find it; her hike into
the back of the property was inaccessible by the local roads.

Trace was already wearing his Kevlar as he bent to pick
up the rest of the items he'd collected and headed for the stables. The material was thick against his body, and he realized it had been some time since he'd had to suit up like this.

A stray shot of adrenaline zipped through his system at
being on an op again, a map of the property filling his mind's
eye as he shut off the office lights.

The horses whickered a loud greeting, the notes slightly
discordant as they filled with restless overtones.

It should have been his first clue.

It might have been if he hadn't had the simultaneous

thought that the sniper would have had the same training as Nic. So why did the intruder drive past the ranch instead of come in through the woods the way she did?

A flash flared at the edge of his vision as a blend of instinct and training had him dropping to a crouch, but it was too late.

Something hard slammed against his head, and the pain consumed him as the world went black.

Chapter Eleven

Nic finished pulling her things together. Her gun. Her two clutch pieces—another pistol and a wicked knife that fit against her ankle. And last, another suit-up in the Kevlar.

She'd given herself five minutes while Trace gathered what he needed in the stables, but she still felt like she was moving underwater.

Slow and ungainly.

And shaken.

It was the *shaken* that pissed her off, but instead of focusing her movements into quick bursts of speed, she couldn't seem to keep her thoughts in any one place.

Why had she brought up that stupid story from school?

To this day, she'd never understood why she told it in the first place. If she were honest, she wasn't even quite sure if she could remember the zigzagging discussion that had gotten them to that point in the conversation.

But stakeouts were often endlessly long and boring to boot. If you were lucky enough to have a partner you liked talking to, the conversation could go anywhere.

Theirs certainly had. From Budapest to Moscow to Cape Town, they'd worked well together and fallen into an easy rhythm. One that had been surprisingly easy to tap into today.

Souls know each other.

Her foster mother, Lucy, had said that frequently. She'd thought it a sweet statement, but Nic had never quite believed it until she met Trace. But once she had? Lucy's sage wisdom had made a tremendous amount of sense.

"You're not soulmates. Or twin souls. Or any other fanciful notion that dances through your mind in weak moments," she whispered fiercely to herself, ignoring the twinge that hit just below her breastbone.

Even if Lucy Baker was one of the wisest—and best—women Nic had ever met.

Instead, she gathered up her things and headed for the living room. A quick glance at her watch showed that despite the treading water feeling, she'd gotten all her stuff together in just shy of five minutes, after all.

It was only when she hit the hallway to the living room that all hell broke loose.

Hogan started barking like a madman, racing toward the door in leaps, his frantic howls and snarls focused on one thing: getting outside.

Jake ran to let the dog out, but Nic raced past him, already reaching for her weapon. Since Hogan was already creating a ruckus, she didn't bother to go easy, screaming as she followed the dog. "Trace!"

Heavy footsteps pounded behind her, Jake and Garner already following, but Nic was beyond caring. She had to get to Trace.

The dog headed straight for the stables, his frantic barking meeting nothing but resistance at the closed door. Up on his hind legs, Hogan pawed to get in, but the large sliding door wouldn't budge, even once Nic got there throwing her weight against it and dragging on the slider.

"Why is it locked?" Garner shouted as he got there, slamming a fist against the door.

"Is there another way in?"

"Back, but—"

Whatever else he had to say faded in the air as Nic headed around the far side of the barn. She trusted the protection around her midsection but slowed as she neared the back side of the barn.

Was there only one other person?

Two?

Had the sniper come back with a partner?

Gun in hand, she moved along the side of the stables, her back to the structure. She paused, doing a quick sweep of the area, before continuing on.

With deliberate steps—and the hope that the barking dog would drown out any noise she might make—she moved around the corner, only to see someone racing off in the distance, a body over one shoulder in a fireman's carry.

Trace!

Or was it the body?

Uncaring, she took off again, positive she could take him down based on the increased load he carried. That had to work in her favor.

It was a good plan. A sound plan, one she was armed to take on and trained to handle.

Only her plan was no match for the trip wire that she ran straight into, falling to the ground as a cacophony of explosions lit up the night sky.

THE MAN BREATHED hard as he ran with the body over his shoulder. The mercenary had been expendable, but he was still a liability, even dead, so he'd circled back to pick up the body.

Besides, it was fun to match his wits against his old friends from the agency.

Even more fun to show them how outmanned they were.

He kept up the grueling pace, a testament to his training and his own personal fortitude. But even with the hundred and ninety pounds of deadweight, he wasn't going to get caught.

He'd made sure of it.

The little trip wire had been fun to rig, and the small batch of explosives tied to it would keep them busy—and moving more carefully—to give him ample time to get away.

What was more fun was letting them know their small corner of Nowheresville, Wyoming, wasn't safe from him. Hell, he'd spent three days here, and he'd gone undetected. But that was the price you paid for choosing a damn ranch to live on in the middle of nowhere instead of keeping your ass in a city.

Because there was no place, no matter how remote, he couldn't find. And if you were separated from civilization, it made his work that much easier to manage.

His nickname hadn't been Bloodhound for nothing. He had the natural skills of a hunter and the tenacity to hunt down his quarry no matter how long it took.

And Trace Withrow had been enemy number one for a long time.

He'd bided his time on getting his revenge, but Nic Miles had been the key to putting his plan in motion. After she'd interfered in his work with Brigante, he'd known it was time to make his move.

And she'd made it all so easy.

The car he'd driven into town was parked just where he'd left it, hidden in brush on the back side of the property. With efficiency born of working in the shadows, he tossed the dead mercenary in the trunk and slammed the lid.

In moments he was heading for the lonely stretch of highway that led out of this wilderness. He'd stop just shy of Jackson Hole where he'd already stowed another car and all he needed to get out of here and hang for a few days.

He had to hand it to Richie, the guy had delivered on the tools to do the work. It was one more aspect of their partnership that had proven rather fruitful. He erased the man's deeds from the agency databases and got a very nice cut in exchange for the work.

What he hadn't banked on was the sister. The woman was a piece of work, and he was already spending far too much time thinking about her. She was a distraction, but now that he'd put his plan in place, he could lie low and turn his attention toward her. Get her to shake off the old dude she was hanging with and spend some time with someone who could satisfy her baser urges.

Yep, he thought as he hit the highway, he had it all planned out.

Just as soon as he doused the car with gas and the body inside of it, he was taking a few days for himself. Working off a bit of energy was just the thing to get him limber and loose and ready to finish up his plan.

Because Trace Withrow was going down.

That little hit on the head was just a preview of how well he worked in the shadows. When he came at Withrow again, he was going to make damn sure of two things.

Withrow would know who was after him.

And he wasn't going to wake up next time.

SPIKES HAMMERED INTO his skull as Trace struggled to open his eyes.

The first thing he heard was the frantic neighing of the horses, followed by the equally frantic barks of a dog.

They had a dog?

The hammering continued, even as he knew he needed to get up—to move—so he struggled to open them as he rolled over. Something fell off his chest and brushed his fingers, but he had no idea what it was, nor could he fully open his eyes to find out.

And then he didn't care as a wave of nausea rolled through him so hard he nearly blacked out. It was close, but he caught himself before falling straight back against the hard floor of the stables, just rolling to the side before he hit.

"What the—" His words faded off before a harsh expletive spilled from his lips as memory returned. On a deep breath, he opened his eyes and willed himself to sit up, nausea be damned.

It was a close one, Trace had to admit, as he struggled to sit up and worked desperately to keep the contents of his stomach. With a hard inhale to steady himself, he suddenly became aware of the heavy drafts of air coming in through the wide-open back door of the stables.

He hadn't come in that way…

The large spotlights on the back of the barn lit up the land beyond it, and despite the blurred vision he couldn't quite blink clear, he could make out a figure running in the distance. Staggering to his feet, he headed for the door.

Was it the person who'd hit him?

The urge to sit back down and close his eyes nearly won until something in him dimly registered the running form.

Nic.

What was she doing? Why was she running outside? Why was…

Nic!

Clarity returned with all the finesse of a freight train slamming into his skull, but he ignored the pain as he realized it was Nic racing through the property out beyond the barn.

Had she found the intruder?

He took off, determined to keep moving, even as his legs trembled with the lack of equilibrium and the pounding in his skull.

"Trace!"

Garner's large form suddenly filled the space in front of him, his brother's arms going around him to hold him steady.

"Whoa, buddy. Stop."

"Nic. She's—"

"I know. Stay here, and I'll follow her."

Trace pushed against his brother's arms, not quite sure why he couldn't break Garner's grip, but that tight hold moved him toward one of the stalls.

"Hold on here and don't move. I'm following her and will bring her back."

Garner's form wavered before his eyes, but Trace nodded. "Go."

He should follow. He needed to follow. But the best he could do was hold on to the stall door and give his brother room to move.

It was only as Garner cleared the wide-open door that the sky beyond lit up like the Fourth of July.

Vision be damned, Trace took off at a run.

He had to get to Nic.

NIC SPIT OUT a mouthful of dirt and struggled to get to her feet. She'd missed the trip wire and had gone down hard. Her puffy oversize coat and the Kevlar broke her fall, thankfully preventing too much damage with all the padding.

It was the fireworks display that was even more jarring than the trip wire.

She recognized it for showmanship—the smoke still lingering in the air—but the bright lights had already faded without leaving any fire in its wake.

Showmanship and diversion, she amended to herself as she got to her feet. Especially because the figure she'd followed—the one weighted down by a body—was nowhere to be seen.

"Nicola!" Garner ran up to her, his gaze skipping past her and all around them. "Are you hurt?"

"No. Where's Trace?"

"In the stables. Dude took him down with a nasty hit to the head."

She didn't wait to hear any more, just took off and circled back the way she'd just come. Even from a distance, she could see Trace come stumbling out the back of the stables, his movements exaggerated before he lost his footing.

The sight of him tumbling to the ground spurred her on, and she dragged off her coat as she ran, dropping to his side. "Trace. Are you all right?"

The spotlights mounted on the back of the stables filled the area with bright light. She used her coat as a makeshift pillow and was careful to lift his head. Only after she had him settled could she see how disoriented and foggy he was by the blown pupils and unfocused gaze.

"I'm fi…" The word slurred off into a hiss as he squinted against the bright overhead light.

Opting not to argue, she bent over him to shield him from the glare. "Is that a bit better?"

"What happened to you?"

His words came out like *wazzz hazzen yew* and didn't do much to make her feel better, but she kept her voice calm and measured, not wanting to confuse him. "A trip wire and some fireworks. I'm fine. I wish I could say the same for you."

"I'm fi…"

Once again his words faded off, and she fought the rising concern that there was something really wrong with him.

"Can you sit up for me? Slowly," she added when he jerked impulsively to sit up. Keeping a firm hold, she pressed one hand to his shoulder while the other went behind his neck to gently help him up.

Trace shot her a dark glare, which she took odd solace

from. If he could process enough to be irritated at the question, it meant he was making more connections in his head than his condition might suggest.

He struggled to sit up, but she only had to help him a little as he got into a sitting position.

Before she could ask him how he was, Trace was asking questions of his own. "Are you sure you're okay?"

The question was a bit fuzzy, the words slightly slurred, but he completed the sentence and was slowly refocusing his eyes on her.

And then Jake was beside her, Hogan at his side. "Let me help you."

"Keep the dog here. I hit a trip wire, and I don't want him to do the same."

Jake looked at her for a moment, an immediate kinship springing up at her concern for the dog, before he gave Hogan a few commands. The dog's training was impeccable, and he remained close, following behind them as she and Jake managed to help Trace to his feet, each of them taking one of his arms around their neck.

"We can get him to one of the chairs in the office. It'll give him a chance to resettle a bit before we try to get him to the house."

"I am walking. I can make it to the damn house." The words came out in a snarl, but once again, Nic took heart that each was distinct and layered with irritation.

"Let's try the stables first anyway," Jake said. "We've got work still to do in there."

Realization dawned, and Nic let out a heavy exhale as they crossed the threshold of the stables. "He got the body."

"Yeah, he did." Jake nodded, his mouth set in grim lines as they headed toward the office. "Left a little present this go-round, too."

"Another challenge coin?"

"Yep. I left it on the ground for you to see before touching it."

That sense of being toyed with ratcheted higher—hadn't that been the very definition of all that had happened today?—but she held back the ire and the frustration. There'd be plenty of time for that later.

Right now she needed to focus on Trace.

They settled him into a chair at the extensive console. It had a high back and a place for him to rest his head while she looked at him.

"I cleared the barn," Jake said. "No one else is here."

"While I think we'd all love a shot at him, I'm not surprised," Nic said. "This was one more attempt to stage things according to his own plan."

"You see that, too?" Jake looked at her over the top of Trace's head.

"I'm afraid I do." Nic kept splitting her focus between Jake and Trace, working through what was in her head even as she worried over Trace's injury. "Which now makes me certain Olivia's in even more danger than I first thought."

"How so?"

"The one point that's eased my mind up to now is that she's with family."

"Presumably she's still with family," Jake pointed out.

"Her uncle's a pawn," Trace piped up, his voice clear even as his eyes remained firmly closed. "Whoever is doing this is using Brigante to his own ends. Once he outlives his usefulness, the uncle's in as much danger as the kid."

Nic leaned down and laid a hand on Trace's cheek, the move so like his gentle touch earlier. "Look who's joined the land of the living."

"It was a close one." He smiled as he opened his eyes.

"Too close."

His large hand came over hers, holding her in place. "Bastard's playing games. We're going to use that to trip him up."

She heard the conviction, even through the groggy tone. Oh how she wanted to believe him. But they'd been played every step of the way so far.

And since she wasn't even sure who they were playing against, it was impossible to know what their next move should be.

HOWEVER MANY WAYS Trace had imagined Nic in his bedroom—and he'd imagined plenty—sitting beside him on the bed and holding an ice pack to his head hadn't made the cut.

"How are you feeling?"

She'd asked him the same question at least every five minutes for the past hour, but the aspirin had finally kicked in, and he could at least give her a slightly more honest answer than *fine*.

"The ice pick has dulled down to a ball-peen hammer."

"That doesn't sound entirely promising, but it's improvement, so I'll take it."

"I really am fine. And I'd like to be out in the kitchen with Garner and Jake as they talk to the sheriff."

"They have this covered. You're staying here."

"Bossy much?"

"Grumpy much?"

Even though it hurt, he couldn't hold back the smile. "I can hold the ice pack myself."

"Fine."

Despite the irritation in her voice, she placed his hand gently on the pack before letting go of it and standing up to move around the room. She'd already dimmed the lights, using only a small lamp in the corner that he rarely, if ever, turned on, and it left the room bathed in a golden glow.

"We'll get him, Nic. I promise."

"He planned this. Down to an escape plan out behind the stables."

"He did."

"He's been on your property for who knows how long. Moving around and creating chaos. Hell, if Hogan wasn't here, I don't know how long you'd have been lying there in the stables."

"You would have come looking for me."

Even with the softer light, he'd kept his eyes at half slits, but opened them fully as he watched her storm around the room.

"I shouldn't have had to come looking for you. None of us should have. Whoever the hell this is shouldn't even be here. He wouldn't be here if it weren't for me!"

Although Trace had expected this—and her unnecessary guilt—the explosion still caught him a bit by surprise. Not for its intensity but for the obvious upset she still carried.

"Come over here."

When she only stared at him, he patted the place beside him that was still warm from where she'd sat ministering to him. "Please."

Her cheeks were flushed, and he could see her chest rising and falling from the frustration, but she did as he asked, moving over toward the bed. She even sat without any further coaxing.

Without giving her time to pull away, he took her hand and linked his fingers with hers. "You didn't bring this here."

"I did."

"No, Nic, you really didn't. This situation with Olivia might have brought it here and now, but this storm was coming. Those challenge coins are proof of that."

She'd picked up the second one in the stables—the one the bastard intruder had left on Trace's chest—before they headed in the house. Trace had looked at it before setting it down on his end table.

It was another retirement coin, this time from a colleague who'd started in the agency with Roger, Stewart Gaines. He wasn't as respected as Bane, nor was he as adept at playing politics, but he'd been sent off into retirement with a proper goodbye and gratitude for his years of service.

And now his challenge coin had been left behind.

The message was clear. This was a vendetta.

"You can keep arguing with me, but if I hadn't come for your help, this wouldn't be happening."

It hurt to shake his head, but he did anyway, determined to make his point. *Willing* her to understand.

"Don't you get it? Other than my brother, there's no one else on this planet I'd want having my back besides you. And if it wasn't this time and place, with you here, it would be another, without you here. Can you stop blaming yourself for a minute and understand that?"

Although he didn't miss the clear skepticism that had her shoulders set in hard, tense lines, he saw a few shots of understanding light up her gaze.

"I need you, Nic. Olivia is our focus. She has to be. But finding her also means cleaning up whatever is haunting me from the past. Whoever wants to see me go down has obviously wanted that for some time. You and I are going to work together to make sure that doesn't happen."

He wasn't sure if he'd fully gotten through to her, but in that soft light he sensed that something had changed.

One more shift in the give-and-take between them that had been happening all day.

From the way they'd started just this morning—and God, was it only this morning?—to this very moment, it had been a slow yet determined weakening of the walls between them.

And defenses be damned, he wasn't willing to fight it anymore.

With that only thought driving him, Trace reached up and laid a hand at her neck, pulling her gently forward for a kiss. He sensed the briefest moment of hesitation just before their mouths met, but it quickly vanished as their lips came together.

Warm and needy and wanting.

Oh how he wanted her. How he'd never stopped wanting her. And in this stolen moment, he was determined to show her just how much he'd missed her.

With soft, aching slowness, his tongue lined the seam of her mouth, teasing her, tasting her. On a soft sigh, she opened for him, her tongue meeting his in blending so carnal he physically ached.

He'd dreamed of her, and he'd longed for her. Both far more often than he was comfortable with. But he'd never believed he'd see her again. Never imagined, no matter how wild the fantasy, that she'd be in his arms again.

So in this moment, with the reality far better than he'd ever imagined, Trace took the precious gift that had been given to him once more.

And vowed to himself that he wouldn't discard quite so easily what had willingly come back to him.

Chapter Twelve

She was falling.

Deeper and deeper, and she didn't care.

Further and further down the path where memory met reality and would leave her with a whole new set of decisions to make.

No matter how much she'd denied it or believed herself strong enough to resist him, there was no force on earth that compared to what she felt for Trace.

So she'd fall.

And hope like hell she would find her feet again someday.

All while fervently hoping that day was far, far away.

Trace's hand settled at the back of her neck, his thumb lightly stroking the skin beneath her ear. It was erotic and gentle all at once, and she shifted, bringing their bodies in closer contact as she leaned into him.

On a hard groan, his free hand came around her waist, and he pulled her fully against him where he sat half-propped up in bed.

It was in that place, in a half sprawl neither of them were in any rush to move from, that she heard the hard knock on the door, followed by Garner's deep voice.

"Trace, we just got word that—"

Nic scrambled to sit up at being caught, even as Trace's arms still wrapped around her in a tight band.

"Trace!" she hissed, pulling against his hold until she finally wiggled out in an ungainly move that nearly had her falling off the side of the bed.

"Nic." Garner nodded his head. "I'm glad you're here, too. I need to talk to you both."

If he thought anything about finding them in such a position, Garner didn't say, but she didn't miss the twinkle that filled his eyes and had his mouth tilting in a lopsided grin. "I'm sorry it can't wait."

"No, of course not," she said as she smoothed down her hair, taking a few discreet steps away from the bed. "What's going on?"

"Jake and I've been briefing the sheriff. While we were talking, a report came in about a car torched about fifteen miles outside Jackson Hole. With a body inside the trunk."

Trace sat further up on the bed, his expression sharp and holding steady as he moved. Nic moved closer, holding his arm to help him up.

"Maybe we should go talk to the sheriff then," Trace said, looking at her. Despite the tightness of his features indicating he still had some pain, there was a clearness to his gaze that had her breathing a bit easier.

Was kissing restorative? Were raging hormones a strong counterpoint to a likely concussion?

Tamping down on *that* line of thinking, she just nodded. "Maybe we should."

"How do you want to play this?" Garner asked. "I gave him the base information but haven't expanded on Nic's involvement or the possibility that we have a rogue federal agent running around the wilds of Wyoming."

Nic had braced for this possibility from the start. While she'd come here with the expectation that she could handle the mission, local law enforcement being none the wiser, she'd also run the scenarios if the opposite happened.

It looked like the thirty-four percent probability she'd calculated was more likely than she'd given it credit for.

"May I take the lead?" she asked.

Garner tilted his head, something that looked like acceptance and appreciation in his eyes. "The show's yours."

Since it was, Nic made her excuses to slip from the room and headed for the one she'd been using. Might as well pull her credentials from the start and make every effort to play nice with the locals.

Technically she had the advantage as a federal agent, and she knew it—and the sheriff would, too—but she wanted this to go smoothly. For this case and for whatever Trace, Garner and Jake needed in the future. Add on that she was here on her own devices and technically without supervisor approval, and that only made the whole thing murkier.

Best to go in with a smile and an air of collaboration.

Less than twenty-four hours in Trace's company, and you're already working outside the lines.

The thought would have been funny, she realized as she pulled her badge out of her bag, if the stakes weren't so high.

Nic headed down to the kitchen, which had proven to be the heartbeat of the house, and found a man who looked as lean and mean as Jake only with Garner's height.

"Hello." She extended a hand. "I'm Nicola Miles."

"Sheriff Dawson Kane." He maintained eye contact, but she didn't get the immediate sizing-up feeling. Oh, she had no doubt he was taking his own impressions, but he was damn good at concealing the fact that he was.

"Sheriff. Good to meet you."

"Life has certainly gotten interesting since the Withrow boys moved to Cage County."

"You flatter us," Garner joked as he came into the kitchen,

his hand on his brother's elbow. Although Trace was doing a decent job of holding his own, Garner kept close watch and did help him into a seat at the table.

"Trace." Dawson nodded.

Trace's greeting was equally simple. "Dawson."

Goodness, they'll be grunting next, Nic marveled to herself before taking the empty seat beside Trace. "I'm afraid what I'm going to share is going to ratchet up the interesting scale."

Dawson remained impassive, but his hazel eyes were sharp and laser-focused on her. "Please go on, Ms. Miles."

"Nic will be fine."

"Nic, then."

"I realize I'm putting you in a difficult position, but I'm going to start with asking you if you could consider keeping this to yourself for a few days. I understand if you can't, but I believe once you hear the full story, you may consider my request."

Although Dawson had remained fairly unflappable since they'd sat down, she saw her words made a dent.

"I'll tell you how I came to be here and the reasons why we think trouble has followed me."

"What sort of trouble?"

"Kidnapping and murder, Sheriff Kane."

NIC HAD BROUGHT a hell of a lot more than kidnapping and murder to Cage County, but Trace held his own counsel on that as she launched into her story for Dawson. From her initial suspicions in DC to her search for Trace to the contact with Olivia, she shared it all.

Garner and Jake added in context about the intruder and subsequent movement of the body and offered to take Dawson out to the front porch as well as the stables so he could get a few photographs.

Nic wrapped up the story with what they assumed was the

sniper returning to retrieve the body and the attack on Trace, as well as the trip wire on the run to the woods.

"That takes some time to set up. And it suggests he's been on the property," Dawson hypothesized.

Trace hated the reality that they'd been unaware of an intruder, but he couldn't argue with the facts. "It does."

"I'm happy to send a few deputies out to help you cover ground. I don't lie to my men and women, but for now I'd be comfortable saying you had an intruder, and we're looking to understand where they might have hid out."

"We appreciate that."

Dawson nodded, and it was as good as done.

Trace respected the sheriff and knew the man was good for Cage County. Dawson had dealt more than fairly with him and Garner since they moved to Liar's Gulch and had supported what they were looking to do.

Yes, they had military and covert skills, their decades of training too valuable to fully waste, and they wanted to put them to use selectively helping those in need. But they were also committed to their horse-training-and-rescue business. Jake had come to the ranch committed to the same after leaving the Las Vegas PD.

It was "what came next." That change in life stage that began to haunt him a few years before he officially left the CIA. Garner had experienced it in the SEALs as well, though his was a bit more tied to the physical rigors of his job and the reality that no matter how well he was trained, his work had a shelf life.

The horses—a path Trace had never anticipated for his life—had brought passion and a purpose that meant something. He no longer depended on higher-ups or missions or the ambitions of others to rule his days. Instead, he worked with animals whose only purpose was to live day by day.

The work had centered him. Given him a new focus for his life. And hell, he just plain enjoyed it.

Which made the fact that he'd sunk back into his former life so easily something of a surprise. And, if he were honest with himself, a bit of a concern.

He wasn't that man any longer. Even if today had made it clear that life seemed to have other ideas.

"This is quite a case, Nic. You think Brigante's operating here in Wyoming?" Dawson asked.

Trace keyed back into the conversation, the extra set of eyes something they couldn't underestimate.

"I think he's farther north, lying low in one of the border states. My money's on Montana, but it could just as easily be South Dakota or Idaho."

"You don't know?"

Nic had been open and honest with Dawson, and she didn't veer off that course. "He's been to all three states in the past three months."

"Staking out territory?" Dawson probed.

"That's what we don't know. Brigante runs a legitimate shipping business. There's every reason he could be in any of these states, setting up contracts for warehouse space or legitimate contracts to move goods across the border."

"But he operates in New York. Why come this far west?"

Nic grinned, the look triumphant, and Trace didn't miss how Dawson sat a little straighter at her bright smile. "That's part of what has us concerned. He could just as easily move goods through upstate New York or Pennsylvania or Ohio. It's suspicious, especially since he doesn't have any business outposts in the Pacific Northwest."

Dawson paused, considering all Nic had relayed. It was one of the qualities Trace respected about the man. He was thoughtful and he listened, two traits that made him good at his job.

"Tell you what. I'm willing to give you seventy-two hours before I file my notes. You could keep me from doing anything if you had a mind to, but you've dealt fairly with me, and you've kept me informed. I can give you that in return and hopefully keep you off the radar of anyone with prying eyes in DC."

"I appreciate that, Sheriff."

Dawson's attention shifted to Trace. "You took a pretty hard hit today. How are you feeling, Withrow?"

"I've downgraded from ice picks to the skull to hammers."

"Improvement, but not enough to go running around. You want to think about calling in a doctor?"

"I'll take it easy and up the aspirin dose."

"Why'd I get the feeling you were going to say that?"

While Trace appreciated the sentiment, his vision had cleared fully and he was no longer seeing double. And the hammers had dulled to a steady throb, even easing up as the medicine took hold. He was fine.

"And why do I get the feeling no one's taking it easy?" Dawson continued.

"We need to see this through," Trace said. "I was committed before someone came onto my property, tried to hurt all of us and got the jump on me from behind. It's personal, Dawson."

"That's what I'm afraid of."

Nic chose that moment to stand up, effectively ending the conversation. "You've given us seventy-two hours. I intend to use every minute of it. Thank you."

She exited the same way she came in, gliding out and presumably heading for the guest room. Each man watched her go, but it was Garner who spoke first.

"I'm shooting straight with you, Dawson. I was the first one to give her a hard time, but this mess is way beyond her. And she needs all the support she can get."

"And you, Trace?" Dawson said. "You think she's on the up-and-up?"

"Yeah, I do. We worked together a long time. And whatever's really going on here, I think they've made Nic a pawn to get to me."

"Who'd you piss off?" Although Dawson said it with a smile, there wasn't a trace of humor in his voice.

"Hell if I know, Sheriff." Trace shook his head, using the pain to fuel him. "Hell if I know."

OLIVIA SPENT A sleepless night, worried about the hacking computer call she'd made to Nic. It didn't seem like anyone had figured out she'd done it, especially since her uncle and his friends, Jane and John, had basically ignored her all day.

But it was their absolute lack of interest that had her wondering if she'd done something stupid by reaching out.

She trusted Nic, even if she didn't like that she hid stuff. Well, Nic didn't hide things the way her mom did. It was more that Nic hid some bigger reason why she wanted to keep Olivia safe but didn't want to tell her what was so dangerous.

Olivia didn't actually think her mom or her uncle would hurt her. They were stupid adults, but they were her family. But she really didn't like their friends.

Even with all that, had she overreacted?

She'd been on her best behavior, only coming down to the kitchen for lunch and a soda in the afternoon. Her uncle was on his phone like always, and when she asked about John and Jane, he told her they were running errands.

What was dangerous about that?

Since no one would tell her where they actually were, she had gotten busy after lunch hacking the Wi-Fi. You couldn't get an exact address off a router, but it had given her some basic details. She did get the provider, and it was a local service available in the northwest, mostly in Montana, based on a quick search of their coverage map.

The whole dude ranch thing didn't really seem real, but a walk outside hadn't shown much but an empty stable and an old chow house with a dated kitchen and long rows of tables. It seemed odd that the ranch part was so run-down and the main house was so big and beautiful, but it was one more thing no one wanted to explain and she innately knew she shouldn't ask about.

Jane finally came back late in the day, but John wasn't with her. Jane did bring a few frozen pizzas back with her and made them for dinner, but it was so quiet as they ate that Olivia decided to tell them about her explorations for the day, telling Jane how cool it would be if she and John fixed up the dude ranch and held weddings here.

Jane didn't seem that impressed with the idea, but Olivia really played it up, making up a big story about how her mom could be their first bride. That at least got a laugh out of Jane, but it was sort of a mean laugh, like it was a joke instead of something that could happen.

Olivia just pretended she didn't hear the mean part and said that she was going to her room to work on a business plan and mock up a website.

It gave her something to do—not that it was real—but she was bored, and it also meant no one would pay a lot of attention if they found her on her computer.

But she kept worrying about the fact that she'd called Nic. Would she come try to find her? And if she did, what would happen?

It really did seem like they were on a dude ranch, visiting friends of her uncle's. The main house was big and elaborate, and the rest of the property was run-down, but it wasn't like anything else was happening.

Olivia loved her computer and knew how to occupy herself, but she was sick of being cooped up and couldn't even get excited about playing around on the computer for another day. Maybe she'd ask Uncle Richie if they could go somewhere or head into whatever town they were in or just... It didn't matter. She was bored, and she wanted to do something.

Wrapped up in her thoughts, she nearly walked into the kitchen when the sound of voices stopped her. Uncle Richie and Jane were yelling, and there was a third voice, but it was too deep and low for her to hear.

She briefly thought about ignoring it—adults yelled all the time—when she heard her uncle shout, "You killed John!"

"Shut up, Richie!" Jane shouted. "We talked about this. About what had to happen."

"You never said you were going to kill him."

Olivia didn't stay to hear the rest. Whatever feelings had her messaging Nic the day before came flooding back, making her stomach hurt and her mouth water in fear.

Something bad was happening here.

When she heard heavy footsteps inside the kitchen, someone pacing around, she stepped backward, keeping her own footsteps light.

Quiet.

Even once she was out of earshot, she walked softly, not wanting anyone to hear her.

It was only when she got back to her room that she grabbed her computer where she'd stowed it under her pillow and pulled up the VoIP calling program she used. She'd never called Nic before, but she had already saved her number in the program in case of an emergency.

If someone was dead, this qualified.

Nic was part of something big. Olivia had always known that and had always feared being traced or tracked because of it.

But now?

She needed help.

And somehow knew that Nic was the only one who she could turn to.

TRACE WAS STILL pondering the question of who he'd pissed off the next morning as he tried to ignore the light flooding his room. It was muted and gray—the impending snowstorm looking more and more like a done deal—but it was still daylight.

And the headache he'd managed to get under control the night before protested.

Mightily.

He hadn't expected to fall asleep, assailed as he was by tortured images of what he and Nic had been doing in his bed before Garner's interruption. But the hit on the head as well as the exhaustion of the day caught up to him and he'd fallen asleep almost immediately.

After a quick shower and another handful of aspirin, he managed to feel semi-human. A cup of coffee and some breakfast might go all the way toward getting him back to the land of the living instead of feeling like an invalid sent to his room.

Trace figured he'd eat and then quickly run through morning chores feeding and exercising the horses before diving back into the Brigante case. He needed to check if Olivia's mother had taken the bait on the text messages, and then they needed to map out a plan for finding Olivia. Hopefully spying on Eloisa's texts would give them an idea of where to find the child.

And if there was an ex-colleague lurking behind it all? They'd deal with that when they got to it.

The scents of coffee and breakfast meats hit him as he

walked into the kitchen and found Nic at the stove, spooning something out of a large casserole dish.

"Good morning."

She turned with a bright smile, and he was taken aback, the domesticity of the moment hitting far harder than he'd have expected. "Good morning. Hungry?"

She'd always been an early riser and claimed that breakfast was her favorite meal. Something he'd seen firsthand when he would sleep over and wake up to the scent of her cooking something.

Nic Miles wasn't a bowl-of-cereal or a cup-of-yogurt eater, either. Eggs were nearly always a part of what she made, and she actually cooked things to go along with it. Bacon. Sausage. Sauces if she was feeling extra creative.

"I made a breakfast casserole. Garner and Jake are out feeding the horses and will be back in soon."

Trace tried to shake off the memories and get his head back in *today*, but he couldn't quite regain his equilibrium. And it had nothing to do with getting hit over the head.

Garner and Jake had taken the final feeding last night, too, after walking Dawson through the crime scene. Garner's expletive-filled don't-mess-with-me response when Trace had protested that he could help had been enough to keep him inside, but now here he was stuck again— eating eggs fraught with memories, and Nic flitting around his kitchen like some goddess of the morning, bright-eyed and ready to take on the day.

Was he the only one who'd been affected by last night's kissing in bed? Or *on* a bed, he amended. He dumped sugar into his coffee, sloshing the hot liquid over his hand as he dragged the mug off the counter.

"Damn it!"

"What's wrong?" Nic was by his side in an instant, but

that only seemed to fuel whatever irritation gripped him like a too-tight pair of shoes.

"I've got it. Just clumsy." He marched over to the counter with his coffee, running his hand under cold water before wiping the mug dry. Couldn't even get his damn coffee in order.

"Are you having headaches this morning?"

"Hell yes, I'm having a headache."

"Sit down and let me look at your pupils."

Although neither of them were trained physicians, they had received basic medical training before being sent out in the field. Enough to make basic diagnoses or understand things to watch out for on routine injuries.

"I'm fine, Nic."

"Sit. Down."

She took his mug off the counter before he could grab it and walked it to the table, him following along like she was the damned pied piper. Dancing to her tune.

Wasn't that his lot in life?

It was only when he was in a chair, her leaning over him, that he realized his tactical error.

He wasn't concussed.

He was in love.

Had never really been out of it. He mentally regrouped as the reality of it all came crashing in with far more force than last night's blow to the head.

"Look at me. How many of me are standing here?"

"One."

She bent closer, an exercise in torture as his body tightened uncomfortably with her nearness. "Your pupils look good."

"Pupil dilation isn't a reliable sign of concussion."

"It's not wildly off base, either," she muttered as she held his face in her hands, her gaze searching his. "And you fumbled the coffee mug, which concerns me."

"I'm fine, Nic."

He heard the warning notes in his own voice, but for some reason she didn't seem to, her gaze still searching. "Do you have any eye pain or any sensitivity to light?"

"No."

"Did you sleep last night?"

Would have slept better if you were with me. Only he didn't say that, opting instead for, "Like a baby."

"What about stiffness?"

"Damn it!" He pushed her hands away, standing up. Was she messing with him?

"Trace! What is wrong with you?"

"You can't be that oblivious." He stalked back over to the counter, putting distance between them because he had no other idea what to do. He wasn't going to beg for her attentions, and he certainly wasn't going to get into her personal space if she didn't want him.

"What the hell is that supposed to mean? Oblivious to what?"

"Us, Nic! You and me. Together. We were interrupted last night, and then I was sent to my room to sleep like a child. But us is what I'm talking about."

She stared at him from across the room, the initial shock that rode her features changing—morphing, really—until her face crumpled into hysterical laughter. "I actually asked you if you were stiff!"

Before he could register what was happening, she'd doubled over, dropping into the chair he'd just leaped out of. "And...and..." Another fit of convulsive giggles took her over.

"It's not funny." He might not want to be considered a truculent child, but even he heard the whiny notes in his tone. Damn it to hell, what did this woman do to him? Why was he reduced so quickly by the simplest things?

He might have even asked that question if her phone hadn't vibrated on the table.

Nic's eyes went wide as every bit of laughter died in her throat. "It think it's Olivia."

"Answer it."

Even from across the room, he saw her hands tremble as she picked up the phone.

"Hello?"

He watched Nic's face, the humor nearly all gone.

"Where are you, Olivia?"

Whatever the child was saying wasn't audible to him, but he could see Nic getting more and more tense as she scribbled notes on a pad left on the table from earlier.

He moved closer, eyeing what she wrote down even as he itched to hear the conversation.

THINKS MONTANA WITH A COUPLE SHE'S NEVER MET BEFORE.
NEW ARRIVAL AT THE HOUSE.
ANGRY UNCLE.

Trace considered the notes, curious when Nic underlined *angry*. What was Richie angry about? Had he figured out Olivia was communicating with Nic? Or had something else upset him?

"I'm coming for you. I—"

Nic pulled the phone away from her ear, staring down at the face, the home screen still lit up. "She's gone."

"What did she say?"

"She's gone, Trace. I don't know where she went, but she was talking to me, and then her words just stopped."

Trace saw the swing of emotion and the way fear rapidly took over her thoughts. "Call her back."

"The connection was bad. I don't think it was a standard cell phone."

"May I?" He extended a hand, and she gave him her phone, the calling app still open. He redialed the number, putting it on speaker and getting nothing but a ring. Over and over it pealed through the kitchen, no one answering. After ten rings, he tapped it off and focused on her notes.

"She's in Montana?"

"She thinks so. She hacked the Wi-Fi, and the router owner is a regional provider."

He filed that away, aware it would be hard to use a utility as a resource, but it was information. "What else?"

"They won't tell her where they are. She's been smart enough not to keep asking, but all they keep saying is how great it is that they're at a dude ranch. There's a couple there with her and her uncle."

"Names?" He kept firing questions, trying to pull out whatever information she'd gleaned from the call.

"Has to be fake. John and Jane Smith. She said she found out the husband is dead, and there's a new man there at the house."

Trace avoided a sarcastic remark on the originality of the names and kept firing the questions. "Did she see him?"

"I don't know."

"A new guy and a dead guy." When she only stared at him across the table, Trace pushed. "We had a sniper and a dead man here yesterday. If she is in Montana, he's had all night to get there."

"What are they doing in Montana?"

"Border access. There's a crossing about seven hours north of here into Alberta."

"Why would they use a major crossing?"

"They may not be hiding anything yet. But they're setting themselves up for it. Setting up patterns of coming and going."

All things they would need to set up a proper smuggling business.

What didn't play was Olivia. Why involve a child, no matter how precocious?

But it was Trace's conviction that gave her the boost she needed.

"Let's go find her and get her back safely. Then we take them down."

Chapter Thirteen

The border-crossing angle made sense. As did the sniper and the dead man. What didn't make sense was Olivia.

Nic went over it and over it as she loaded up her gear. Trace had already gone to update his partners, and they'd agreed they would start on the road, running whatever they could on their computers while Jake and Garner worked the same from home base.

She'd overheard some stern words as Trace fought with his brother about Garner's loudly stated view that he and Jake should come along. It seemed like Trace won the day—especially when he pressed the fact that the ranch was breached the day before, and someone needed to guard it—but Nic figured it was a close call that there weren't four of them heading out of Liar's Gulch fifteen minutes later.

"I can drive."

Nic glanced over at Trace, not at all surprised by his mulish expression. "You're operating on a likely concussion. I'll drive for a while, and you take over in a bit. It's probably not great for you to stare at a phone, either."

"I loaded up on aspirin. I'm fine."

"We'll agree to disagree." Before he could argue, she pressed her point. "We have no idea what is waiting for us on the other end of this drive. You were injured yesterday, and it makes sense to conserve as much energy as possible. I need you to have my back."

She'd like to believe it was her reasonable tone that had him agreeing but suspected it was the risks of the sobering reality they faced.

"I get it."

Since he did, she couldn't resist teasing him a bit. "And I know you hate it when I drive, so put one in the win column for me."

"I don't hate it when you drive."

"You do, but I never really knew why. You're not normally a sexist pig, so what is it with the driving?"

"I'm not—" He broke off, and there was something in what he didn't say that hit her with all the force of a lightning strike. "It's stupid."

She had no idea why she was pushing it, but there was something in his tone, and they had a long drive, and well… it was Trace. "I'm sure it's not."

Trace didn't say anything for quite a while, and she gave him his space. He might be a hard and often unyielding man, but he'd never dismissed her because she was a woman. Nor was that unique to her because they had a relationship. She'd always seen him equally forthright and collaborative with all their female colleagues.

"The last time I saw my mother, she drove Garner and me to our grandparents' house."

Whatever she expected him to say, something about his mother was nowhere on the list. She'd always suspected he'd had a difficult childhood by virtue of the fact that he avoided the topic. Since hers had carried more than a few challenges, she'd always given him that measure of privacy. But now she had to wonder if it was one of the reasons they'd bonded the way they had…if there was something they each recognized in the other.

"So it's not about you or your driving," he finally said after a long stretch of road had passed.

"How old were you?"

"Eleven. Garner was nine."

"I'm sorry she did that."

"It was a long time ago."

"It doesn't make me any less sad for those two boys in the car."

She didn't have to look at him to see the wry smile on his face. "Yeah, well, those two boys channeled it all into being big, strong men. Who knows what we would have been if she hadn't dumped us."

"Was life with her bad?"

"She wasn't particularly stable in her child-rearing. My dad took off when I was three, but I was too young to remember him. I don't know a whole lot about him, but I do know he was found dead a few years later, so no looking for a reunion with dear old dad when we got older."

Nic let him talk, the joke about her driving somehow releasing a dam of memories.

"I don't know that they had a great relationship, but it was enough to give her a measure of stability. And raising kids is hard in the best of circumstances with a partner who's there with you through it all. I think there was one day where she just broke."

"And your grandparents?"

This time, she heard the real smile under his words. "Gigi and Pops are great. Were great. We lost them a few years ago, within six months of each other. But they were the best. Real. Solid. Pops is who taught Garner and me to fish and ride horses and love the outdoors."

"And Gigi?"

"She's probably the biggest reason I respect women with as much awe as I do." He turned to face her, and she risked pulling her gaze from the open stretch of road to look at him. "She didn't take any crap from either of us, but she showed us love every day. She did her damnedest every day to show us that we mattered. And she was a seriously kick-ass lady. She hunted and fished. Dressed her kills, too."

"Impressive."

"It was. And it wasn't just the nature stuff. She had a wide group of friends and was part of the community. She wasn't a great cook, but she was an awesome baker, so there were always cookies in the house. She was—" He broke off as if trying to find the right words. "She wasn't just a great woman, she was a great person. And it took me a long time to realize just how important it was that Garner and I saw that. And lived it with her."

It did make Nic wonder if his mother had done him and his brother a service in the end. As if parental abandonment could ever be a service to anyone. Yet even as she considered it, she had to admit that she felt the same about herself.

She'd hated foster care but ended up okay. The Bakers had made sure of it. But even without their steadying influence, she'd developed her own moral compass and had always felt she would have found her way. She was forever grateful she didn't have to know if that were true but felt it all the same.

And if she'd stayed with her parents? Whoever they were? She might not have ever gotten any of that. The Bakers. Or the future. Or her own sense of self.

It wasn't anything you could have proof of, but she'd come to a place over the past few years where she'd found a level of acceptance she could live with.

Trace spoke again, and her heart cracked a little bit more at the blend of strength and vulnerability threaded through his words.

"I always sensed Gigi was disappointed her own daughter hadn't stood up for us. That she'd found it easier to walk away than to fight. But she never said it. Never left Garner or me with any words that would burn into our memories and ruin our mom."

Nic reached for his hand, laying hers over the back of his where it rested against his thigh. He didn't brush her off, which she took as a good sign.

Along with the fact that he'd decided to say anything at all.

It was a hell of a lot more than she knew about her own parents, but it was interesting that both of them had found their way into adult roles as operatives.

They were both the "type," as it were—individuals who had less to ground them to a family and were therefore potentially more open to risk-taking and the demands of a covert lifestyle.

And yet based on Trace's story about his grandparents and her own experience with the Bakers, Nic couldn't quite take on that idea and believe it applied to either of them. They did have something to lose. They also recognized how precious life was.

It hadn't made her reckless, it had made her determined.

A trait she saw in Trace as well.

"Your grandparents sound like incredible people."

"They were."

"They raised two incredible men, too."

He turned his hand over beneath hers, linking their fingers. "I'm not sure I'd go that far."

With the road ahead flat and empty, she turned to look at him, shockingly full of emotion. "Without question or hesitation, Trace Withrow, I most certainly would."

TRACE FINISHED FILLING up two coffees at the gas station convenience store about halfway through their drive. Black with too much sugar for him and just milk in hers, no sugar.

He still knew how she liked her coffee.

And what she tasted like.

And those soft moans that filled her throat when they kissed.

He *knew* her.

And he'd spilled his guts like some lost little boy who still missed his mommy.

Only...

He slammed the last lid in place and headed for the register to pay for the drinks and their gas.

Only it hadn't felt like spilling his guts. It felt like being honest. It felt like opening a door he'd kept firmly locked to everyone including himself. It felt like healing.

He wasn't quite sure what to do with it. Because she wasn't staying. No matter how quickly they'd fallen back into intimacy over the past thirty-six hours, they'd left each other for a reason.

He couldn't lose sight of that.

The truck was done filling up when he got back outside. Nic had opened the driver side door to wait for him, her head down as she focused on her laptop.

"What are you working on?"

"Garner texted while you were inside. Said he had something for us to consider."

Trace handed her one of the cups before leaning closer as she tilted the laptop toward him.

"The Sweetgrass-Coutts crossing." She already had a web page pulled up that showed the various United States and Canada border crossing stations. "It makes sense if they're in this part of the country."

"That would work. If they're looking for border access, that's the most likely one."

"Agreed. But here's what's got me really going." Nic smiled. "Take a look at what the guys did with the dude ranch angle. Garner's sending me a list of three properties that have changed hands in the past eighteen months. One of them is eight miles from the crossing."

"Looks like my brother and Jake have more mad skills than I gave them credit for."

"I told him to send me the properties, and I'd dig into the actual ownership on my side. You drive while I do that."

Confessions aside, he'd wanted that from the start—to drive and not feel helpless and injured. Take back a bit of control by being behind the wheel.

So why was he still grumpy as hell?

Garner and Jake had helped. Nic had her computer in hand. He had the drive.

"Why are you all squinty and irritated?"

He glanced over at Nic as he came to a stop before turning onto the highway. "I'm neither of those things."

"Sure you are. You want to run this op, and you're irritated we're all taking pieces."

"I'm pissed you're all taking *all* the pieces."

"You're on point for any texts from Olivia's mother."

"Which I checked an hour ago and still nothing."

They'd been using their mobile phones as hot spots, and he'd logged in to the small program he'd written convinced he'd see Eloisa's engagement with the fake text messages.

Only to see she hadn't even opened the text.

Great game he had.

"Pull over," Nic ordered.

"We need to get going."

"Please pull over."

Although the highway gas station was busy, it was a slow enough time he was able to make a U-turn away from the entrance and turn back into the parking lot. Finding a space out of the way from incoming traffic, he pulled back into the lot and put the car in Park.

"What, Nic?"

"What has you upset?"

"I'm not—"

Without warning, Nic leaned over the large center console that separated them in the truck and pressed her lips to his.

The light flavor of coffee met him as her mouth moved over his, and despite his frustration and irritation and all around general pissiness, he caught on quickly to what she was doing.

A spiral of need opened up in his chest, the kiss rapidly spinning out of control as their mouths met, then met again. That soft sigh he loved so much echoed between them in the cocoon of the truck cab. In this moment that was both carnal and comforting, Trace recognized just how well this woman knew him. What made him tick and what drove him wild.

And what smoothed out the rough places inside he avoided with everything he was.

Pressing one last light kiss to his lips, she shifted back into her seat and smiled brightly. "You in there?"

"Yeah, I'm here." He glanced out over the parking lot, his gaze taking in the big wide-open sky beyond. "Yes, I'm upset. About feeling helpless and out of the action."

"You've done so much."

"That remains to be seen."

And it did, but he'd also done work like this long enough that he recognized the value of teamwork and partnership. He was also honest enough with himself to know that wasn't the real problem.

She deserved to know it, too.

With his own gaze steady on that crystal blue that *saw* him, he admitted the truth. "I'm not sure why I told you that story about my mom earlier."

He saw a series of expressions flash across her face, surprised to realize the pity he expected wasn't one of them.

"I'm glad you told me about her. She's a part of you, and

that experience is a part of you, and I have to confess, I'm rather greedy."

"About what?"

"I want to know you, Trace. I've always wanted to know you. And that story is you."

"It was a long time ago."

Something shifted on her face, her expression set in the fierce lines of an argument. Which was at odds with the gentleness in her voice. "And you spoke of it like it was yesterday."

"Don't make it more, Nic."

And then fierce shifted whip-quick into matter-of-fact. "Don't make it less. Whatever you want to say about it now or even if you regret what you told me, don't make less of your feelings or your experiences. Most especially not the ones that made you the man you are today."

It shouldn't have bothered him. He'd shared the most intense moments of his life with this woman, and barring his brother, no one knew him better. And still it all burned, somewhere dark and shameful inside of him.

Those memories of abandonment.

He laid his head back against the seat rest, his gaze continuing to follow that wide arc of sky. "She never came back."

"I know, baby."

"I don't want it to matter. By now it shouldn't matter."

"But it does."

"It never goes away." He turned to look at her, keeping his head against the rest to center himself. And what he saw in her eyes nearly broke him.

"It never leaves you. Whether you can rationally appreciate why those feelings are there or whether you try to dismiss them because of time and distance and life." A few tears spilled over her cheeks as she continued. "It never leaves you, Trace. And maybe on some level, it shouldn't."

"Even if life moves on."

"Because life moves on. But that child doesn't. You will be forever eleven inside, and that's okay. It's what made you an incredible agent. What makes you a man who has the patience and the fortitude to work with horses and give them a new life. It's what's made you the man you are today."

Throat tight, he wanted to keep dismissing it all. Just keep pushing it away with both hands and a shovel if he had to. Yet despite everything inside of him wanting to deny that truth she spoke so eloquently, he knew she was right.

"I'm still not sure why I said anything. I don't think about this every day. That child may live somewhere inside of me, but the man knows how to get up and get to work every day."

She reached for him, once again linking their hands over the console between them before those depths of blue captured him once more. "Maybe you told me because it was time."

TIME.

It did its work, Nic reflected as the miles passed by them outside the truck windows. For good and for bad, time did its work.

Her conversation with Trace in the gas station parking lot kept echoing through her head, those moments of raw vulnerability leaving an echo of quiet softness between them on the drive.

Neither of them had said much these past few hours. A few comments about the drive. A quick parry-and-thrust of theories as to who Brigante was working with. A discussion about who they could remember at Roger Bane's retirement party who might have received one of his challenge coins.

Despite those shots of conversation, the two of them had

remained quiet, lost in their own thoughts and the weight of what they'd shared.

"What's the end game here?" Trace asked, breaking the silence.

Nic turned to look at him, captivated as always by the solid lines of his profile. There was a strength there, and a resolve that spoke to her on a visceral level. And he was just so damned attractive.

Sheer need filled her, heat flushing her skin.

Since there was nothing to be done for the rash of hormones in the middle of a long stretch of highway, she did her best to mentally swat it away. She could pine later.

More to the point, she mentally admonished herself, she knew she would.

"I know what you're asking but don't get the context. End game for Brigante?"

"Him, sure, but if he's running as many nefarious practices as you believe, his world is already a lot of 'live by the sword, die by the sword.' It's the idea of a rogue agent that I keep circling around."

"Why is he doing it?" Nic clarified.

"Not that I'm excusing it, but the temptation to get a side gig can be explained. But why risk discovery with this showboating? Because if this is about running a side gig with access to Brigante's influence and business, taunting a former colleague is a hell of a way to go about it."

What else *could* it mean? People made bad choices all the time. His mother leaving him and his brother. The criminals the world over they used to thwart together. The scale might be different, but the capacity to do damage was sadly the same.

"Every move so far has been a tactical assault in the vein of a game," Nic mused. "I'm not sure that speaks to long-term thinking and stability."

Trace tilted his head, considering. "Maybe not, but then what was the trigger? You and I have cycled through everyone we know together as well as individually and can't come up with a candidate for those challenge coins. No one even pops a bit as a loner or disgruntled."

"What about triggers? Were those retirements a part of it? Overlooked for a promotion? Passed up for a desired field assignment?"

They could be triggers, but it still suggested a level of instability she didn't understand. Everyone knew the risks in the job. Even those who romanticized the work knew what they risked, especially once trained for the field. Would someone really take that training and use it as a form of vengeance if they didn't agree with something in the organization?

Their earlier conversation drifted through her mind. The difficult childhoods that had made both her and Trace into good agents could be a consideration for who they'd become as adults. Even as she turned that over, she couldn't deny that both of them also found their way to adults who cared for them.

Was that the difference?

Or was there a third piece that couldn't be underestimated, either?

Her college psychology classes had called it nurture versus nature, which she had understood in the end just to be the realities of life and the choices they made every day. "What if it's in their profile?"

Trace glanced her way. "What profile?"

"You know, the idea that organizations seek operatives who have difficult childhoods. Loner personalities. Genius aptitudes. Even those who might have underlying adjustment issues."

"That's been glamorized a bit for entertainment, don't you think?"

"Even if it is, those traits could lead someone to the job. So whether by deliberate design or by personal choice, the work draws people who choose to operate outside the norm."

He was quiet for a minute, and she was surprised to see the emotions that played over his face. As a man who normally held back those reactions, it was humbling to see his willingness to be vulnerable. "Like you and me?"

"This isn't about our conversation earlier, Trace."

"Maybe it should be. Maybe if we acknowledge the vulnerability, we can also wield it."

It was a fascinating idea, Nic realized, catching on to where he was going. Even if she needed to stress the bigger point. "It's still choice, Trace. You and I chose differently, even with less-than-ideal childhoods. People the world over, in all walks of life, do the same."

"You've been in the agency for a while now, and our training is similar, so you'll know what I mean when I say this. Didn't you ever get the vibe off someone that they got more out of being an agent than actually doing the work?"

She could come up with a dozen people who fit that bill. "It's a component of the work."

He grinned. "Probably something you don't hear a lot of from dentists."

"Oh, I don't know about that. Bicuspids can be awfully alluring."

"I'll give you that, but you know what I mean. There's a distinctly different set of motivations here that go beyond greed. *You* came into the job with the conviction to do the work. Whoever is doing this wants the power. That's the dynamic we can't disregard here."

"Which further reinforces that Brigante's a pawn. Useful only until he isn't."

"Which may be soon." Trace eyed the mirror before drifting to the side of the highway and pulling over. Once stopped, he shoved the truck into Park and turned toward her, excitement lining his features. "That's what we have to find. The escalation has to be tied to the culmination of some big play with Richie Brigante. Our former colleague, whoever he is, thinks he's getting out with a big score, and he's going to take me down along the way."

"Which means Olivia's really not safe."

"No, she isn't." Grim determination carved deep lines around his mouth and eyes. "Getting her out is the first and only goal. Only after we've done that can we push for the rest."

"I think we start with the property Garner and Jake found. The one closest to the border crossing."

"We need to do it in stages. Reconnaissance first." His gaze was deep. "We can't let Olivia know we're there right away. You know that?"

"We can try."

"She's the priority, Nic. You know she is. But we need to know what we're up against. If there's more danger to grabbing her than laying out a plan, we may need to leave her there a bit longer."

She knew he was right. No matter how desperately she wanted that child out of all of this, safely away from the adults in her life, she knew how to run an op. How to take part in one.

And sometimes, heedlessly racing through the door was the absolute worst way to meet the end goal.

"I understand."

And she did. Olivia's life was the first priority.

But she also understood herself. This case had become personal. Both because she increasingly believed that she was some sort of pawn in the home office to get to Trace, and because in order to do that a child had been put in the gravest danger.

This was no longer *just* a rescue op. It was a mission to get data to take down a rogue agent and bad actor in an organization that way down deep she still believed in.

Despite it all, Olivia came first.

If it mean sacrificing her own life, Nic would keep the child safe.

Chapter Fourteen

Trace scanned the various images Garner had sent to him and Nic when they stopped for a quick bite to eat. They didn't dare look at any of this in public, so they'd picked up sandwiches and chips and settled back into the cab of the truck.

The air outside had grown whiplash cold, and the skies had progressively darkened as they drove north. The winter storm that had been promised for nearly a week increasingly looked inevitable, and Trace wasn't sure if that worked for them or against them.

It would offer some additional protection, potentially, as the occupants of the dude ranch weren't as likely to be outside and catch them moving around the vast acreage. But it was a distinct disadvantage if they were traipsing around and got caught. Add on the fact that escape was a hell of a lot easier when the roads weren't blocked by blizzard conditions, and Trace was worried the storm was a factor they couldn't fully prepare for.

With that thought, he weighed the benefits of waiting it out, knowing Nic well enough to understand that waiting was highly unlikely. So they'd plan as best they could and take their chances.

Focusing on what he could control, Trace looked over more of what Garner and Jake had been up to while he and Nic drove north. In addition to the maps and intel, his brother had already gotten them a room at a small hotel about fifteen miles away from the property they'd prioritized—the one eight miles from the border—and Garner had done some additional digging into the deed transfer.

"The property changed hands ten months ago."

Nic swallowed a bite of her sandwich, something thoughtful settling in her eyes. "I was put on the Brigante case about nine months ago. Coincidence?"

"Never was a big believer in them myself."

She smiled before taking a sip of her soda. "Me, either."

They continued to bat ideas back and forth. He still wasn't convinced Nic wasn't going to prioritize Olivia above all else, and he got it—he didn't like the idea of leaving the girl in that nest of vipers, either—but they'd deal with it when they got there.

On some level, a part of him wanted her out of it. If Nic rushed Olivia away, he could get down to brass tacks with whomever their rogue agent was knowing both of them were safe.

He took a bite of his own sandwich, well aware of his own personal irony. Since she'd arrived on his property, worried over this child, Trace was concerned Nic had let the op become personal. And now here he was, considering facing whatever this was all by himself if it meant Nic was safe.

"It looks like there's the main house and several outbuildings we can use for cover." Nic stilled.

He knew what she was thinking. "What if they have dogs?" Trace was transported to the same memory. "Moscow?"

"Yes. I still have nightmares about those guard dogs." She shivered. "But the point stands. Dogs or not, there's no way they're in the middle of nowhere, planning whatever this is and leaving themselves open without some sort of security."

"We'll plan for any eventuality. Luckily we're in beef country, so we can pack a deterrent to bring with us."

"Adding it to the grocery list."

It was amazing how easily they fell back into it. The exchange of ideas. Each of them taking on various responsibilities so that they maximized the time they had to plan.

It was easy.

And just like those memories of their close call in Moscow, it was something they shared. Those common experiences that bonded them in ways he hadn't fully realized until she came back.

"I'm glad you found me."

Nic paused typing up the grocery list on her phone. It took a heartbeat or three before she looked up and met his gaze. "I'm glad I found you, too."

"I know we left things in a bad way, but I need you to know I never wanted it to end that way." He took a deep breath. "Even though I take full responsibility for my part in how it ended."

"I wasn't my best self there at the end, either."

"I insulted what you believed in and what you stand for. I was in the wrong."

And he was. However much anger he'd left DC with, the time since had given him much-needed perspective. The reality of it all was that he'd equated his relationship with Nic to his job, and when he blew up one, he hadn't known how to preserve the other.

It was his biggest regret.

But now that she was back, he couldn't help but feel like he had a second chance to make things right. "I know I hurt you, and I'm sorry."

She nodded, swallowing hard around what looked suspiciously like tears. But it was her quiet acceptance that nearly did him in. "I'm sorry, too. Sorry I couldn't see my way to where you were at or why you were so done with it all."

"How could you know if I refused to tell you?"

He knew he didn't have a right to touch her, but oh how he desperately wanted to change that. Not just be worthy of her again but to find some way forward.

Some way past all that came before.

It made no sense, and the two thousand miles that stretched between their lives only reinforced that.

But a man could dream.

And he could burn from the wanting.

With all that clamoring inside him, he pressed a hand to her neck, gently pulling her toward him to press a kiss to her lips.

It was chaste and gentle, but he felt its impact clear through his entire body.

Because if he was lucky, it was the pathway to washing his soul clean.

Nic saw the change in him as much as felt it. A strange sort of acceptance flowed between them, connected by their lips but, as she well knew, connected by so much more.

For better or worse, Trace Withrow was the catalyst of her life.

There was who she was before him and who she became after, and nothing could change that. Not even the way they ended things had managed to change her steadfast belief in him.

The question was if they could get past all that had come before.

It was only when he pulled back, his gaze soft and full of a yearning that would likely have weakened her knees had she been standing, that she pressed for more. "Tell me about it. Tell me what happened to drive one of the best field operatives out of the organization."

Renegade Reunion

He took a long sip of water, but it seemed more in preparation for the discussion than stalling.

"I saw what they were doing. The guise that it was all in the name of being the good guys, yet it was hard to see where we ended and the bad guys began."

The ops world had an endless number of shades to it, and she accepted it when she went into the field. But…if she were honest, she could also acknowledge what he was saying.

When the work had purpose and clear lines that were being crossed by an enemy, it made sense. When it seemed a bit more opportunistic, she'd chafed a bit. And whether it was because more of the work was becoming opportunistic or because she'd been at it long enough to understand, she hadn't yet figured out.

"It's a difficult line to figure out because the edges are so soft."

"Are they?" The question came out as an edgy laugh, but she sensed what he meant.

"At times, I do think that's true. But at others?" She couldn't deny his point. "I agree with you."

"Well, I had one with edges so soft they were squishy. Right before you and I met. We had to get intel for one of the SEAL teams to take out a wannabe dictator in a small African nation."

"Someone who could have done damage," Nic said. Yet even as she pointed it out, she recognized the reasons for his underlying anger and disillusionment. "But let me guess. The dictator angle wasn't great, but his ascension to power would put a key shipping channel in danger."

"Called it. It's one thing to take someone out for human atrocities and genocide, but someone who potentially wanted to control waterways that his country had genuine rights to?"

Nic did understand. And while she'd been sheltered from

something quite as questionable as Trace's experience, she understood why it had disillusioned him.

"That was the third op in a row where I spent more time questioning what I was doing than simply acting. I knew my job, Nic. I understood my role and also understood in many ways I was a tool to get a job done."

"You're more than that. We all are."

When he only stared at her, his gray gaze so cold and bleak, she remembered part of that last fight between them.

You think this is about any of us? That they really see any of us as truly valuable?

Of course they do. Why else would we be trained as elite operatives, able to get in and out of any situation?

We're expensive tools, nothing more. Don't fool yourself, Nic. There is nothing keeping us safe except for each other.

Nic had shuddered at his attitude at the time, but she'd be lying if she didn't admit how often those words crossed her mind in the two years since. How that assessment—as stark as it might have been—had felt more and more real as she went through her assignments.

Expensive tools.

And now they were going up against someone who likely matched the same description.

"But you used that term...before," she finally said. "Tools. A means to getting a job done."

"And I was okay with it for a long time. I figured if I understood it, I could handle what came my way. For quite a while, that attitude worked just fine."

"Until it didn't."

"Until I woke up and realized that I wasn't a tool, I was a weapon."

NIC BUSIED HERSELF in the refrigerated meat section of the grocery store Trace had found about five miles from their hotel. Although she wanted nothing more than to go straight to the property Garner had shared with them and nose around, she recognized the benefit of regrouping and taking stock of their assets.

And picking up plenty of attack-dog deterrent.

She'd already hit the pharmacy area and picked up an economy-size bottle of extra-strength sleep aids. It was crude, but it would hopefully do the trick, especially when stuffed deep inside balls of ground beef.

If, you know, there were dogs.

Meanwhile Trace worked through the rest of their list. Food supplies for the next few days, several large packs of bottled water and some easy-to-carry trail food, depending on how long they needed to stake out the property.

What each of them seemed to tacitly understand yet didn't voice was the need to double whatever they were purchasing because of the unpredictability of the storm.

The conversations they'd had that day continued to roll through her mind as she picked up a few more food items. From a basket of fruit—portable energy—to a trip down the snack aisle for the canned potato chips she and Trace both had a weakness for, those conversations ebbed and flowed through her mind.

The story about his mother had hit a deep chord, but it wasn't unexpected. Sad to be sure, but a reinforcement of the story she'd pieced together in her mind. Trace's deliberate shift of conversation each and every time they talked about his parents had always left her with the assumption that something unfortunate had happened there. Now that she had the specifics, those long-ago conversations made sense.

What hadn't been quite as clear were the demons he carried over the work.

Until I woke up and realized that I wasn't a tool, I was a weapon.

Was that really the work? She'd believed they were doing what was right. What was noble, even.

Was that belief all a lie?

Because while she understood his point of view—and didn't excuse the missions that had left him feeling that way—she couldn't look back over more than a decade of her own work and feel it was meaningless or in service only to underhanded or shady objectives.

Nor did she think, for a minute, that she hadn't made a difference.

And it wasn't just looking back and trying to make herself feel better. From an international human trafficking ring that she'd help dismantle to a cybersecurity protocol that had protected banks and utilities and schools to other missions that had made the world a safer place.

It mattered.

But his experiences mattered, too. And it was that perspective that…

She nearly bobbled the can of chips she held as the implication of it all hit her.

"Nic?"

She looked up from picking up the chips to find Trace, his concerned expression at odds with the triumphant feeling coursing through her.

"I think I might know what's going on. Or have a theory at least."

Although the aisle was empty, he looked around before stepping in to push the cart. "Did you get everything? Let's get out of here and talk about it."

"Yeah, I'm good."

He looked at the chips in her hand and shook his head before reaching behind her and snagging two more cans. "Now we're good."

Fifteen minutes later, they'd paid for it all and were heading toward the hotel. Snowflakes had started swirling as they loaded the truck and fell steadily as they drove, one of the chip cans open between them in the cupholder.

"What has you so excited?"

"You. The conversation we had earlier."

"We had a few."

"I'm sorry about your mother. About what her leaving did. But that's for us." When he risked a look her way, she added, "Just us."

"All right."

"I'm talking about the work. The experiences you had. Oddly, even taking it back to the fights we had. You and I were on the same team and didn't see eye to eye about the work. Or our purpose."

"We had a shared purpose."

"But different perspectives." Again, Nic realized this was her chance. If not to make things right, at least to make the two of them whole again. "Not wrong perspectives. I don't think that or feel that anymore. I'm sorry that I ever did."

His phone dinged just as the GPS indicated their next turn, and she half thought he might answer. But he only took the turn and waited for her to continue.

"What if the person we're looking for had one of those perspectives? Was somehow at odds with their management or was on an op that broke them somehow?"

"And that excuses it?"

"Not at all. But it does give us a place to start looking. A person with bad intentions and whole lot of rage can do a lot of damage."

"We've been through the list of people who'd have those challenge coins. No one fits."

No one did fit, and that was the other problem. Add on sniper-level marksmanship skills and a sizable enough build to fireman-carry a dead body, and they were looking for someone who was *noticed*. Someone with a physical presence and a set of skills his fellow operatives would understand to be valuable.

"There's no one I can come up with, either. And I saw him. The back of him as he ran from the stables last night, but I did see him."

"What do you remember?" Trace turned into the parking lot of the hotel Garner had booked. The property had hotel suites and would give them an opportunity to spread out.

"He was a physically large male. Which is important because he not only lifted the dead guy, but he ran with him, too." She let out a harsh expletive that earned a grin from Trace. "I would've caught him, too, if not for that damn trip wire."

"He was prepared."

"Bastard."

Trace pulled up under the portico and put the truck in Park. "Let me run in and get the keys. It'll be less noticeable if I go in, and then we can finish this discussion in our room." His grin widened before he leaned forward and pressed a hard kiss to her lips. "I love it when you talk dirty."

"That wasn't talking dirty. It was just a few swear words."

"I'll take what I can get."

Before she could say anything else, he was out of the truck and heading inside to complete their check-in. She watched him go, the simple act of being with him and talking things through making her feel less alone.

Hadn't that been one of the worst things about him being gone? There had been many, but it had dawned on her a few months after he left just how much she missed having Trace in her life.

Yes, the sex and the intimacy absolutely. They were incendiary together and had been from the start. But it was so much more than the physical.

She missed *him*.

The way he knew her and listened to her. The way they bounced ideas off of one another and never really got irritated with each other. The way they could just sit and be with each other, not needing to fill the spaces with conversation.

One of her favorite memories was of a day they'd spent walking the monuments in DC. They'd started early, cups of coffee from a street cart near her apartment in hand, and just roamed. The Lincoln Memorial to the World War II Memorial and all the other amazing stops along the Reflecting Pool. They'd held hands as they stared at the soldiers that made up the Korean War Veterans Memorial, and she'd felt…connection.

Looking at those statues, just larger than life-size, still and yet suggesting movement all the same, she'd had an overwhelming sense of belonging that she'd never felt in her life.

Those statues and the culmination of the monument captured the reality that freedom was not free. Her work epitomized the same. And she had a partner who understood that. Who understood her.

That had been one of the hardest things to understand about their fights over the work, because they really didn't fight about anything else. They were oddly compatible and in tune with each other. Other than a minor irritation or terse comment from time to time, they got along and worked well together.

But in the end, it was the work that brought them together and the work that tore them apart.

A police SUV drove through the hotel's portico, pulling her attention from those memories that had been so close to the surface these past few months. The driver had a large brimmed hat on, low over his head, but she got the distinct sense he was keeping watch all the same.

It was…

It was a small-town patrol, she reminded herself and sat back in her seat. She briefly considered flagging him down and sharing her credentials, but just like speaking with Sheriff Kane the night before, bringing in law enforcement put her on the radar. Here and back home, because there was no way any cop worth their weight wasn't going to run her and then get curious and call back into DC.

She didn't need that.

Even if it would be nice to know she and Trace had some backup.

The cop kept driving, his arc through the portico slow but steady, and she dismissed the thought of asking for his help. If they needed resources, they'd find a way to ask for it, but now wasn't the time.

But it didn't escape her notice that the cop stopped once he cleared the portico, his gaze on Trace as he came back to the truck with the keys.

Nor did she miss the way he kept his gaze on them when Trace followed that same arcing path to the parking lot to find a spot.

That thought about reaching out for local assistance flared again, and she considered getting out and flashing her badge to set the right tone. But before she could make her move, the cop moved on and headed for the exit.

"HE WAS WATCHING YOU?" Trace asked as he unpacked the cold groceries and put them in the hotel suite's refrigerator.

"You going to keep being paranoid about this?" Nic asked from where she was logging in on her computer across the room.

"A local cop stares you down, and it doesn't bother you? It's not paranoia."

"Okay, fine. When he looked the first time, I didn't think

about it. The second, when he watched from the parking lot, I did reconsider."

"Reconsider doing what?"

"Going over and flashing my badge. Introducing myself and telling him we might need help."

Trace restrained himself from slamming the fridge door, but it was a close thing. "Why would you do that?"

"Why'd you call in the local sheriff at home? We're two people, and we have to get a kid out of a situation we have no intel on. Trained backup isn't a terrible idea."

Trace trusted himself, and he trusted his instincts, and her description of the cop made him itchy. Why the hell was the man looking at them? A cursory glance, protecting his town and all that crap, fine.

But to look again? To focus on them? It didn't settle well, and he knew better than anyone it hadn't settled well with Nic, either. So why was she trying to brush it off?

"I had to wage war with my brother to get him to stay behind and keep watch on the property and any other problems that might come to the house. He'd have gladly come along. Jake, too."

"I already brought one civilian into this. I don't need to drag in two more."

"We're not civilians."

"Yeah, Trace, you are. I know that chafes a bit, but you don't have a badge or a federally supplied gun or access to top-secret information any longer. Neither does your brother or a former Vegas cop, no matter how well-intentioned."

"So you'd rather go it alone than admit you need their help?"

"I'm trying to keep them safe and avoid any of this blowing back on any of you. You and Garner have built a nice life up here. You have your equine program and your side jobs when you choose to take them on. You've built something good and continue to build on that every day. I don't want my choices to take that away from you."

"We chose to help you. I chose first, but Garner and Jake are all in, too."

Battle lights filled her eyes, but she kept her voice deadly calm and even. "And I'm choosing what I'm willing to accept."

"Damn it, Nic! You don't get to do that." Trace stalked across the living area of the suite. "Why come to me at all if you're going to be like this?"

Before he could say anything else, she was on her feet, facing him down. "I can't take this away from you. What you've built in Wyoming. The life you're living. I appreciate your support and your help and all you've done, but I need to figure out how to keep this on the up-and-up and ensure you don't lose your new life because of me."

"Too late. You don't get to make that choice any longer."

"I'm not going to see you go down again. You left DC in disillusionment. I won't see you lose your business now, too."

"This is about me! Damn it." He shook his head, frustrated that he couldn't seem to get through to her. "Why won't you see that? You've been used in this. They're after *me*. It's revenge against *me*. And I can't sit here and worry you're going to take off on some half-formed idea that I need protecting."

"Are you trying to insult me?"

"I'm trying to make you see what's going on here. And maybe—just maybe—accept the reason you've lost control of this is because it wasn't about you from the start."

Trace hated that the work could drag them back to this place so quickly. Hated even more that they still couldn't seem to find level and common ground for very long when it came to the work.

"I appreciate this display of chivalry, but what I really can't understand is how you've managed, in twenty-four hours, to make a case I've been working on for nearly a year all about you. You, who raced away to live in the far reaches of the Western wilderness, a lifetime away from DC and office politics and the agency, are somehow important enough to generate all this."

"Because it is about me. It's about someone gunning for me." God, how did he make her see this?

It was like every bit of progress they'd made before they started out for Montana had vanished, replaced by the by-the-book woman he believed had faded in favor of the realities of the op. Had he been that wrong?

Or had something changed her mind?

"The murder on my property yesterday wasn't about you. Neither are the challenge coins, including one left on my chest, or the mercenary bastard who tried to do damage to all of us. I need you to stop looking at this like a field op and start seeing it for what it is. A twisted game."

"And you're the prize?"

"Yeah, Nic. I'm the one some out-of-control mind has decided has to pay some price. And I'm afraid if you don't get in line and understand this, you've been played harder than I thought."

"Damn you, Trace!" She threw up her arms before turning and facing the window. "We're back where we were two years ago. All about you. What you think. What you claim to 'know'..." she added air quotes "...and the lines you think only you can draw. What about me? What about my life and my career and my efforts? Why won't you give me the proper credit on this?"

And there it was.

The raw vulnerability that suggested she did know—on some level—what he was saying. But she was bound and determined to fight that truth in favor of all the places where she felt overlooked or overruled.

Or where she had to admit her precious agency could do wrong. Or even worse, could house a traitor in its midst and never even know.

It was that truth that straightened her spine as she turned away from the window to face him.

"The whys of it don't matter, Trace. Don't you see that? I brought the monster to your door. Me. No matter how it happened or if I was manipulated or if it was just a hoped-for outcome on the part of an enterprising disgruntled employee, who knows? But I brought this to you. Can you understand how that weighs on me?"

He took a few steps closer, the ravages of the storm between them fading a bit. "That's why we're stronger together."

"You shouldn't be in it at all."

"But I am in it. I—" He broke off as something caught his attention outside the window. Despite the bright white of the snow that had increased even since they'd been inside, he could see a dark shape moving around in the parking lot.

It shouldn't have registered or mattered, until he realized…

"Hell! What's going on with my truck!"

Nic turned toward the window, her training kicking in apace with his.

Before either of them could head out to confront whoever was messing around with the truck, a wall of sound filled the air. The building couldn't fully withstand the pressure, shaking around them as a ball of fire filled the parking lot.

Chapter Fifteen

Trace raced out of their room, headed for the exit. Nic would have followed but realized he hadn't grabbed anything in the way of firepower, so she diverted to where they'd set up their small arsenal of weaponry in the bedroom. As she picked up two pistols, she sent up a silent thank-you that they'd gotten everything out of the truck.

Even if they were now stranded with no means to find Olivia.

She remembered to snag her cell phone off the desk and shove it into her pocket, along with one of the hotel key cards.

"One problem at a time," she muttered to herself as she followed Trace's path. They'd focus on Olivia after they got this handled.

After...

The parking lot had filled with people, several trying to get closer to the now-smoldering truck to see what was going on. Every last person had a cell phone in their hands, recording the damage.

And Trace stood closest to the burning vehicle, staring at the wreckage.

The sound of sirens was heard in the distance, and Nic had another flash of that police officer's attention on her and Trace when he'd driven through the parking lot.

Was he responsible?

It hardly seemed likely, but who else knew they were here? They'd used minimal communications, and she hadn't yet logged in to her work VPN. She was about to once they got settled in the hotel room, but she hadn't since they'd left Liar's Gulch.

So who found them?

And why was it only that too-attentive cop that kept coursing through her mind?

Although people were interested, the snow was whipping around all of them in increasing spirals, and it was enough to send quite a few back to their rooms. A few of the phone-wielding diehards stayed, but as soon as the cops and fire trucks pulled in and obscured their view, they headed off as well.

Which left her outside in the driving snow wondering how to play this and just how wide-open she was to discovery.

Even still, a growing voice inside roared with excitement that they'd finally broken something open. This wasn't an accident. She wasn't even convinced it was a message. But she was damn sure it was a deterrent, designed to keep them from getting to Olivia and whatever her uncle was hiding this close to the country's border.

Trace caught her eye as a cop and her partner got out of their vehicle to come closer. She read his intention immediately and came to stand with him, taking a spot under his arm and putting on her most worried face.

"Oh gosh, Officers, we're so glad you're here. Who would do something like this?" She added a soft little moaning wail at the end, pleased to see a shot of sympathy in the partner's eyes.

"It's okay, ma'am. We're going to figure out what's happened here."

"And in the snow that's just getting worse. How will we ever get home!"

Trace tightened his hold, and she recognized the direction to ease up on the histrionics but couldn't resist one last hiccuping sob. When she got another gentle smile from the second officer, she took it as a good sign.

The lead officer asked a series of questions and moved them a small distance away so that the fire department could see to putting out the blaze. Trace answered each question, his answers slow and deliberate and ever-so-slightly misleading.

In the course of the officer's questions, Trace managed to pepper in that they wanted to spend one last visit seeing this part of the country before they moved away for a new logging position he got in Washington. That he'd just proposed on this trip and how awful it was that they were starting their life together with a car fire. And his last salvo was how upset his dad was going to be that he went and ruined his truck.

By the end of it all, the cop asking the questions looked uncomfortable enough to want to wrap it up and the partner had already gathered a few sweatshirts for them from the trunk of the police vehicle to keep them warm. Nic thanked him profusely and the cops shared cards and promised to file a report for insurance.

All in all, the increasing snow conditions did them a favor. There would no doubt be a host of new questions once the truck was towed and an incendiary device discovered somewhere in the chassis, but for now the aw-shucks answers and the increasing snowfall bought them a few days.

Nic stood with Trace's arm around her shoulders, matching shell-shocked expressions painting their features, as first the fire trucks drove away, then the police vehicle.

"Dad'll be right mad, no doubt about it."

The deep voice held distinct notes of laughter as Nic

whirled around to find Garner behind them, with Jake and Hogan beside him. Jake and the dog moved on toward the truck, Hogan making a circle around it before stopping midway down the passenger side of the truck bed.

"That's a good boy." Jake fed him a few treats and pointed toward the frame. "You'll find the device under there."

Garner nodded. "We'll remove it in the morning after it cools."

Nic glanced around, pleased to see the parking lot was empty. The driving snow continued to support their desire to remain hidden. "What are you both doing here?"

"You don't think we'd let you two have all the fun, do you?" Garner shook his head as Jake added a "no way in hell" to punctuate the comment.

"Let me guess, there are two rooms booked?" Trace said, his voice dry.

"Three actually," Jake interjected. "I'm not sharing a room with him. Hogan and me need our space."

It was a bit silly, and an odd counterpoint to the fight she and Trace were having moments before the explosion, but Nic couldn't deny she was happy to see them. A new vehicle was essential if they were going to get Olivia out safely.

And she hadn't quite shaken off Trace's words or his determination to make her see reason. His comments had hurt, but now that they'd just seen the truck explode into a raging fireball, she had to admit there was likely a strong thread of truth to his position.

I'm the one some out-of-control mind has decided has to pay some price. And I'm afraid if you don't get in line and understand this, you've been played harder than I thought.

The backup was welcome.

The additional firepower was welcome.

But the two more able bodies—well equipped to keep Trace safe—were the most welcome of all.

CALL NIC.

The small voice that had whispered to her all morning drifted through Olivia's mind once again as she sat stretched out on the couch in the media room watching a movie.

She'd have to be careful about when she made the call, but she could probably do it. Especially if she waited for when she knew Uncle Richie and Jane were hushed off somewhere.

They kept doing that, like no one could figure out they disappeared to make out.

And then there was Jane's husband. Her uncle's *old friend* from college who was dead but no one seemed to care.

Olivia stayed out of their way, and no one seemed to care that she kept to herself, either. But she felt safer that way, and that worried her.

Just like Jane worried her.

The new guy who came yesterday didn't seem to even notice her or see that she was there. He hadn't actually said a word to her. It was Jane who kept looking at her with those watchful eyes.

Suddenly, it all felt like too much.

Why had her mom sent her here? And why wasn't Uncle Richie making a point to spend any time with her? Her father didn't care, only showing up every so often.

Why did everyone *not* care about her?

The tears came hard and fast, and she let them roll. Not like anyone was here in this stupid place to even care.

Not like anyone cared.

Except Nic.

She'd cared from the beginning. Wasn't that the weird part? Someone Olivia didn't know had more feelings for her than her own family did. And Nic meant it, too. Olivia got the sense that something about her own situation was important to Nic, even if she didn't understand why.

But Nic had been the only one to believe that nothing in Olivia's life was normal or even felt very real most of the time.

Call her.

Do it.

Call Nic.

The thought had been steady, and it kept getting louder the longer she sat there.

The only problem was if Olivia did call her, she still didn't have anything to tell her. She had no freaking idea where she was, and even if she could figure it out, she didn't get the sense Jane and the new guy would take very kindly to someone coming to pick her up. Uncle Richie might just let her go, but the other two wouldn't.

That she knew with absolute certainty.

Which meant she had to figure out how to get out and get to a place where Nic could find her.

The media room didn't have much in the way of helping her figure out where she was, especially since there weren't even windows in here. And the view from her bedroom only showed a lot of land and a ton of trees at the edge of it.

She could try to figure out how to get to the trees. Of course, she needed her stuff. But if she only kept to the essentials of her computer and her phone they still had stashed somewhere and that small piece of her baby blanket that she kept stuffed in the bottom of her backpack so no one could see it anyway, she would be okay.

Only problem was she didn't know where her coat was.

Which hadn't seemed like a big deal until she realized that she hadn't worn it since she arrived, and she had no idea where it was.

It was cold outside. Her breath had frosted up the glass in her room when she was looking this morning.

Could she really do anything without a coat or her phone?

Because even if she got a hold of Nic and even if she got to the woods, she'd still have to keep going outside.

Coat aside, it was time she figured this out. Olivia needed to get to Nic—that was all that mattered—and she needed information in order to do that.

Since her bedroom was the only thing besides the media room that she was allowed into on this floor—and wasn't it interesting that all the other rooms were locked?—she headed toward the staircase. She couldn't hear anyone, which probably meant—and ewww gross—that Uncle Richie and Jane were making out somewhere. Still, if they were otherwise occupied, it would give her a chance to nose around a bit.

She just needed one item that would tell her where she was. Maybe a piece of mail on the counter or a take-out bag with an address on it or a credit card slip from somewhere local. If she got a location, even the city she was in, she *knew* Nic would find her.

The house was so silent it felt eerie and creepy around her, but she kept on. If anyone found her, all she'd have to say was that she was hungry and looking for food. It wasn't like she lived here. If they caught her in a drawer or cabinet, she'd make up an excuse.

Or she'd pull the same routine she saw some of the girls in her class do and just complain that she was bored. Everyone hated a whiny teenager, but they also expected it, so she'd use that to her advantage.

The kitchen was quiet and way too neat—did people actually live here?—so she started with the drawers first. The wall of cabinets was huge so she just went down the row, pulling drawer after drawer. Several were empty, but then she got closer to the sink and the dishwasher and found utensils and one full of spatulas.

Not a bill or restaurant menu in sight.

She'd just hit a drawer that had some junk in it, her hand

closing over a magnet for a local pizza place, when the lights flipped on.

"What are you doing in here?"

Olivia's heart slammed her chest and her stomach clenched hard, but she scrambled to hide the magnet in her palm as she came face-to-face with Jane.

Act bored. Act bored. Act bored.

Images of Madison Townley and her group of picture-perfect friends filled her mind's eye, and Olivia did her best Madison impression, hoping beyond hope her voice wouldn't crack. "This place sucks. I'm so bored."

"You have a full media room and a full pantry. Why are you in the drawers?"

"I told you, I'm bored. There's nothing to watch."

"There are about five hundred DVDs in that room."

"Nothing good." Olivia added a pout. "And I've seen all of it anyway. Why don't you have anything streaming?"

Jane's eyes narrowed, and Olivia thought she might have overplayed her hand. She'd already asked about the streaming and got told the media room equipment wasn't compatible with a Wi-Fi signal. Was this 2010?

"Why are you a whiny child?"

"Where is your husband?" Olivia shot back.

The moment the words were out, Olivia wanted to pull them back. A feeling that was only made worse by the narrowing of the woman's eyes.

"I'd suggest you keep your mouth shut and your thoughts to yourself."

It surprised Olivia that Jane didn't just look mean, she actually looked a bit unhinged. There was something not right behind her cold eyes. Eyes that matched the dark smile on her face when she pulled Olivia's phone out of her pocket and held it up in a taunting motion.

It dawned on her a split second before it happened that Jane's intention was to ruin her phone.

Olivia tried to snatch it back, but the hateful woman moved back out of her reach. "My house, my rules."

A low-level panic settled in that was rapidly morphing out of control. If she didn't have her phone, she didn't have her hot spot out of range of the Wi-Fi.

Which meant she couldn't call Nic on her VoIP when she got to safety.

"That's my phone."

"You can have it back tomorrow."

"I want it now."

"Too bad."

Before Olivia could do anything, Jane stared down at the phone in her hand and threw it on the ground, stomping it with the heel of her cowboy boot. Without another glance, she turned on that same heel and left the kitchen.

Raw panic ate at her all the way out of the kitchen and back up to her room, hot tears threatening the whole way.

It was only when she slammed the door that she realized she still held the restaurant magnet in her grip.

Opening her fist, she read the name of the restaurant: Ted's Pizzeria.

And underneath it in tiny letters were the words that could make all the difference.

SUNBURST, MONTANA.

She knew where she was.

Now she just had to figure out how to get that information to Nic.

TRACE STARED DOWN at all Garner had managed to procure in the past twelve hours and marveled at his baby brother's skills. He knew the man was a badass—nearly two decades as a SEAL had ensured it—but he was tactical as hell.

And his ability to piece together disparate information that actually fit together was nearly otherworldly.

It reminded Trace that, of the two of them, he'd always been the big-picture guy. He made the connections between implications and outcomes. He could calculate possible and probable end results, spinning out scenario after scenario in his mind. That skill had done him well, preparing him for any eventuality and giving him the needed mental bandwidth to pivot if the inputs changed.

Garner's skills were more grounded and focused, his array of maps and satellite imagery—all publicly available—an absolute marvel.

Add on Jake's tactical abilities and Nic's exceptional knowledge of the case and the agency itself, and the four of them made a formidable team.

"I want to run something by all of you," Trace said at last.

When everyone settled, fortified by the food he and Nic had bought earlier, Trace laid it out.

"First, Olivia is the priority. However she was initially identified as the pawn in this, our latest intel suggests the danger around her has likely ratcheted up."

"Walk me through that," Jake probed, reaching for his water. "Hasn't she always been in danger?"

Trace spun out one of those probabilities for them. "With her family, she likely wasn't in physical danger. Yes, being near the misdeeds of the uncle and the vapid lifestyle of the mother is a problem, but we can assume they care for her and love her and aren't looking to harm her."

Garner snorted at that. "The association with them is enough to do that."

It was Nic who stepped in. "Trace is right, though. Her family cares for her. Has her in the best schools. They even tolerate her precocious technical skills. She's loved, albeit ignored or underestimated much of the time. But she wasn't in physical danger in New Jersey."

"So what's changed in your scenario?" Garner asked.

"The uncle's business associates. If someone in the agency is after me…" Trace's gaze drifted to Nic, but he no longer saw resistance to the idea "…we have to figure this case was the one he identified as the pathway to lure me in."

"How many people knew you two were a hot item?" Jake asked, reaching for a handful of chips.

The question was fair, and Trace had to admit, one he should have considered a lot sooner.

"Management knew."

Nic's eyes widened, their discussion on the day she arrived that their team likely knew about their relationship obviously rushing back to her, but she just nodded slightly. "They know everything else. It's safe to assume they knew that, too."

"They don't know everything, but they do know how to use operatives who work well together. Add in a bit of romance, and we become catnip to them in a partner scenario."

"How do you figure that one?" She took a sip of the coffee she preferred over water. "We're a liability."

"Not while we're together. Together we're even more incentivized to keep the other safe."

"Or romantically go down with the ship," Garner added.

Nic's quick "what?" and puzzled face must have matched Trace's as they both swung toward his brother.

"What does that mean?" Trace asked.

"You're operatives. To your point, you're incentivized to keep each other safe. You're also going to be more keen to protect one another. No squealing secrets if the other is captured for fear of putting them in danger."

"That's good." Nic nodded. "It's very good. And it explains some of the grunt duty I got after Trace left."

"Grunt duty?"

"Oh yeah. I wasn't totally persona non grata, and I pushed for new assignments pretty quick once I realized what was going on, but I got a bit of scut. A few protection details in Europe that were ridiculous in the extreme. A wild-goose chase in the Middle East that had me looking for old security files that had long since been destroyed. And an investigation of a new communications satellite in India that was so on the up-and-up clergy could have written the code."

Jake held up a hand. "How long did this happen?"

"About five or six months."

"For five months after Trace left," Jake pushed, "how often did they keep you out of the office?"

"Every week. I finished one job and moved right into the next. In that stretch I think I slept in my own bed three nights."

"That wasn't scut." Jake shook his head. "That was housecleaning. They got you out so they could reassess what you knew and how dangerous you were from Trace's influence."

"Oh, come on…" Nic broke off, and Trace would bet anything that forgotten conversations had begun spinning in her head. Her voice was quiet when she finally spoke. "I was played."

"Not the right answer," Jake shot back. He wasn't unkind, but there was something unyielding in his tone that snapped Nic to attention.

"What else could it be? There I was, buried in my own head and missing Trace, and I just went along with it."

"They used that all against you. If you weren't a possible threat to them, they'd never have tried any of it," Jake persisted, his attention laser-focused on her. "You're good, and you're passionate about what you do. They had to be sure you weren't going to follow Trace's rogue attitude and employ it in your work going forward."

"But they used me. They're still using me." She looked up, her gaze meeting Trace's, and he saw a world of understanding layered with raw pain. "You're right. About everything. It was you they wanted all along."

NIC STARED AT the computer screen and filtered through her notes files from the past two years. She knew her own style—matter-of-fact layered over observation—and read and reread her own impressions, memories of each of the jobs coming back to her.

Every word was written with serious dedication to the work and the belief she had in what she was doing. Even those boring jobs—protecting a low-level government flunky in Milan and searching for any anomalies in the satellite plans—had been handled with thorough professionalism.

She'd accept nothing less from herself.

Trace had settled in the bedroom to watch TV, giving her a bit of space. Updates on the Sonics dominating play kept echoing back through the open door.

He hadn't said much to her after Jake's masterful ability to drag her down memory lane and come out with a completely different understanding of what she'd experienced. Instead, all three men seemed to sense that she needed a bit of room to process her thoughts and had agreed to regroup in the morning to finalize plans to get Olivia.

They'd all agreed the child was the focus, and everything else could come after. Taking down Richie Brigante and whatever rogue agent was masterminding the situation took a distant second to Olivia's safety.

"You okay?"

It was only as Trace's words found her that she realized the TV was no longer blaring sports updates. She turned to find him in the entryway of the bedroom.

"I'll take the hide-a-bed out here, and you can have the bed. It's probably a good idea to turn in."

She glanced at the time stamp on her computer and realized just how much time she'd spent lost in her own head. "Sure. Of course." Nic closed her laptop and vowed to put it away for the night. They were meeting early, and she needed the sleep, too.

"How's your head?" She'd watched him throughout the day. He hadn't exhibited the aftereffects of a concussion, so she'd taken that as a lucky outcome. There could have been a far different ending if his attacker had gotten a slightly different angle from behind.

His grin was a bit lopsided. "Fortunately quite hard and stubborn. I've managed to get it down to two aspirin, and I even went six hours since my last dose." That smile fell, replaced with a more serious demeanor. "I'm trying to figure out how we fell right back into old habits earlier. I'm sorry for it, but I've also spent the last few hours trying to figure out the why of it. I don't want to be in that place with you, Nic. For whatever time I have left with you, I'd like it to be positive. I don't want to fight with you."

While it shouldn't have been a surprise, it was an unintended gut punch to hear him mention their time left.

But of course.

It wasn't like she was staying here. Nor were they back together. A few kisses weren't rekindling a relationship, and nothing changed the fact that she had a home and a job to go back to once they found Olivia and got to the bottom of what was going on.

End of story.

So why did it make her so sad to think about leaving?

"No, I don't want to be in that place, either. I want—" The words died in her throat as the reality of what she *did* want simply took over.

She wanted Trace.

Not because their time was limited, though she could admit that was a factor.

And not because they were risking a lot to save Olivia, though that was a factor, too.

But this was so much more.

She wanted him because she'd never stopped wanting him. Not one single second of a single day since they'd been apart.

"What do you want, Nic?"

Trace hadn't moved from his position in the doorway, but he'd gone very still, his neck corded with lines as if he was straining every muscle in his body in order to remain that unmoving.

Time seemed to pause in the space between them as the unspoken promise of what they could have arced between them.

And then she didn't want to wait any longer. Didn't want to argue herself out of it or tempt herself into it. What she wanted didn't sit on either side of that equation.

Oh no, it was so much more.

She wanted the absolute belonging she felt when she was in his arms.

She wanted the heat. The physical union. The endless pleasure. All of it wrapped up in that glorious intimacy she'd never felt with anyone else.

Nic crossed the room, her steps deliberate, until she reached him. Without hesitation or question, she moved into him, wrapping her arms around his neck and gently pulling his head down for a kiss.

Trace hesitated for the briefest of moments. A fraction of a second, really, yet she felt it.

"Is this okay?"

"Oh yeah." He nodded, and she could feel his smile against her lips as he murmured the words. "It's okay in every way."

And then she gave in to all of it.

TRACE WRAPPED HIS arms tight around her and savored the feel of having Nic pressed against him. Oh how he'd missed her.

It wasn't just the physical—it could never be just the physical—but that had been a part of it all. The sheer want and desire he held for her, every day since they'd met, was a living thing inside of him.

Even when they'd been together, he'd never found a point where they'd had enough of one another. Or had fully sated the most elemental desire between them.

But wow, had they tried.

In the time since, he'd dreamed of her, spent sleepless nights because of her and woken up wanting her. And as he walked them backward into the bedroom, he was determined to make up for the misery of every one of those very long years.

He had the heavy sweatshirt she wore up and over her head, the thin T-shirt she had on under it quickly following. His own clothes came off just as quickly, her hands as impatient as his. Their jeans came next, and she had the advantage over him when she simply reached inside and took him in hand, not even waiting until they were fully naked.

Desire had claws, quickly filling him and taking over. No matter how he'd imagined this—and how slow he'd sworn he would take things—the need between them burned far too hot to wait.

Trace matched her movements, slipping his fingers beneath the elastic of her panties, and was rewarded with a sharp cry of pleasure as her inner muscles clenched around his fingers. She was wet with her pleasure, and he used it ruthlessly to take her up, over, setting a pace that she more than kept up with.

They pushed each other on, a delicious battle of touch and taste, of want and long-denied hunger. Somewhere along the way, they lost the rest of their clothing, falling onto the bed pressed to each other.

And long, endless kisses later, as he rose up over her and slid into that welcoming warmth, Trace was forced to admit the truth. Home had always been the most elusive of places for him.

But Nicola Miles was his home.

He'd known it on a soul-deep level from the first.

And he knew with everything he was that she would be forever.

Chapter Sixteen

Nic lay wrapped up in Trace and gave herself a moment to simply enjoy. To ignore the endlessly circling thoughts that always filled her mind. And to just be in the moment. Present and perfectly sated as the heavy weight of his body kept her warm.

The wind howled outside the windows, the promised storm doing its work.

"What time is it?" Trace's voice was heavy with sleep as he turned his head to look at the bedside clock. "Three thirty. That wind is something else out there."

Despite her best efforts to be in the moment and enjoy what she'd wanted for so long, reality crashed back in. "We're going to have to find her in what's left behind after that storm's blown itself out."

His hold tightened around her. "We will find her, Nic. I promise you that."

"It's what else we're going to find that worries me. People know we're here, Trace. The truck is proof of that. How they know, I have no idea, but they know, and we're going to have to plan for that now. Our ability to sneak onto the property has likely vanished."

They'd tossed around a few theories with Jake and Garner earlier, but the fact that they were detected in town so quickly was a concern. It suggested that someone expected they would be found here and on some level had shared their identities in advance.

But who'd seen them?

She supposed the employees of the hotel could be in on it, but Trace had checked them in while she stayed in the truck, and they'd kept a low profile overall.

"Jake had a few theories on that. Because he's the newest one of the group, he was going to spend some time in the lobby bar. See if he could get anyone talking or if he overheard any of the staff talking."

"I get the sense he can be rather persuasive."

Nic took definite solace knowing Jake was looking into things. And it also reinforced Trace's point yesterday. He and his partners were all in on this. It was incredibly reassuring to know she and Trace weren't facing this alone.

If she were even more honest, it was the first time since Trace left the agency that she felt like someone truly had her back. Which should have been an even bigger sign she'd stayed in DC too long.

But what was the alternative?

Wyoming.

With Trace.

Supporting the private work he and Garner and now Jake are doing.

"I know what we're facing, Nic." Trace settled a finger beneath her chin, gently lifting her head so their gazes met. "I know the danger, and I'm prepared for it. But I don't want to give any more of these moments up. I have you until daylight, and I can't see my way to being sorry for that."

"I know." She lifted her lips to his, pushing all that was to come outside of the bed.

They were committed to seeing this job through and getting Olivia back safely. That couldn't happen tonight, nor could it happen in the middle of a snowstorm. So they'd take the time until daylight. Especially with the knowledge it might be all they would get.

NIC WAS ALREADY up and out of bed when he woke up again. They'd made love twice more before dawn, and he let the sheer joy of that move through him as he showered and got ready for the day.

It was a gap in time—a few hours for just them—and now it was over. He needed to bury the emotions that came from being with her again and get his head firmly in place.

In less than forty-eight hours, his home had been breached, and he'd been targeted within an hour of arriving in a small Montana border town.

He was the target.

And unlike every op he'd run before, he had no intel to support the work they were doing. It was all theories and scenarios, with nothing concrete or certain.

Except the location. Every instinct he had told him the property they'd narrowed in on was the right one.

"Trace!"

He nearly collided with Nic as he headed into the suite's living room, excitement riding high on her face. "The texting program. On Eloisa's phone. Did she bite?"

With all that had happened the day before, he'd forgotten about checking the program last night. "She hadn't all day yesterday, but I forgot to look last night." He pulled his phone out of his pocket, vaguely remembering a notification ding that he hadn't answered.

"Hot damn."

The words escaped him on a hard exhale as he reviewed the program he'd set up. Not only had Eloisa taken the bait, but he had full access to everything she'd done on her phone since five o'clock the day before.

"I'm in."

Nic hovered near his elbow, and Trace kept the phone turned her way as he scrolled. His program didn't capture the names of her contacts, but they could reverse look up the numbers. In the meantime, he could gather context from several. "Looks like text messages with her brother. What looks like her lover on this one."

"There's her text back to the boutique." Nic leaned closer, her voice growing puzzled. "And another string of texts on a different number. Purring about her lover's anatomy, among other things. Those are some graphic compliments," she added.

"Puffery at its finest."

She glanced up at him. "What do you mean? It looks like she's keeping two fish on the hook."

"She's keeping the rich fish on the hook." Trace reread the last few messages. "But read them. The sex talk to the fish is over the top. Especially when you look at the other one. It's sexier and way more subtle."

He handed Nic his phone so that he could get his computer and look at the texting program there. In a matter of minutes, he had the two text strings pulled up side by side onscreen. He set his laptop on the kitchen counter so they could both look at the variance in the messages.

"See there," he said. "Look at the cadence and the tone. It drips with fake praise."

"I see your point. Especially knowing his age and life stage."

"She's his prize, and she's going to make sure she stays that way."

"There's something else there. Look." Nic pointed at one of the last messages to the man who seemed to be her actual paramour. "She's mentioning how she can't wait to see him.

She's supposed to be in New York with the old beau. But here she's looking to get with the other guy."

"It's a sign. And—" He stopped, registering the number of the boyfriend she probably actually wanted. "That's a 571 area code."

"I have a 571 area code."

"So do I."

"What's Eloisa doing sending seductive messages to a Northern Virginia area code?"

"I could give you two guesses," Trace said, "but you're probably only going to need one."

GARNER AND JAKE arrived shortly after they made the discoveries on Eloisa's phone, and Nic got them up to speed while Trace looked through whatever other data he could get off of Eloisa's phone.

The text messages were the most informative, until he hit the mother lode with her last mobile credit card transactions.

"She's in Montana."

"Olivia's mother?" Nic looked up from where she was studying maps with Garner.

"She flew in yesterday morning and made mobile payments at LaGuardia and Chicago O'Hare before flying into Bozeman. She had one more transaction there, which was food."

"Layover to a smaller plane?" Garner asked.

"Maybe, maybe not," Trace said. "It's a four-hour drive so someone could have picked her up. But she made a purchase, so we've verified location."

"Any texts with Olivia?" Nic asked. "When I scanned the details before, I didn't see anything but wanted to check. She's got a 973 area code."

Now that Nic flagged it, there *were* a lack of texts with

her own child. It was only as he moved down through the list that he saw the sad reality of Eloisa's parenting.

Her last text to Olivia was three days ago.

"I found it. She sent a note three days ago telling Olivia to be good for Uncle Richie and a smiley face blowing a kiss."

"Three days?" Nic asked. "She's had plenty of time for sexy texts but can't be bothered to check in on her child?"

"Mother of the year," Trace muttered, well aware of the judgment that dripped from his tone. With his own mother's actions so recently churned up in his thoughts, he understood how easy it would be to equate the two women.

Only those feelings of abandonment and inadequacy didn't come.

And with that realization—that he could be angry for Olivia and not channel it into his own pain—Trace recognized the victory.

Instead, all he felt was sheer anger for a child who deserved so much better. From all the adults around her, yes, but from her mother most of all.

"So we need to plan for the mother, too." Garner turned to Nic. "We'll play this how you want, but if we snatch the kid out of her family's hands with no clear evidence she's been harmed, we're risking kidnapping charges."

"Child endangerment," Trace snapped, unwilling to get into the gray areas of what they were going to do. "We have every reason to believe the child's life is at risk, either directly or indirectly via the people her uncle has aligned himself with."

"Your sheriff's support would go a long way toward reinforcing that as well," Nic said, obviously undeterred on their course of action.

"I'm not saying we don't do it," Garner added. "I don't want Olivia sent back to those people."

Trace didn't want that, either. Those nonexistent text messages checking in on her only reinforced it.

Jake had been fairly quiet up to now, adding in a few tactical thoughts but giving them room to plot and plan.

But his assessments from the start had been spot-on, and Trace admired the man's ability to listen and work toward a solution.

"That doesn't change the fact that the mother is another layer in this we have to plan for. And since it is her child," Jake added, "we can assume she'll either be a loose cannon or will use the situation to act like one."

DESPITE REPEATED ADMONITIONS to trust her instincts, Nic found little to feel good about as she prepared to head out with the men. Jake and Hogan had already gone out and inspected Garner's SUV, finding nothing of concern. The two feet of snow they'd gotten overnight had likely helped as a deterrent, but it created new problems this morning.

Namely, how were they going to navigate a major op in the biting cold and wintry landscape? And also, how were they going to avoid detection wearing full gear as they traipsed through fields of blinding white?

Garner was packing up the additional firepower he and Jake had brought along. After that, he planned to go out and join man and dog to dig out the SUV, and then they'd reassess from there.

Nic and Trace had been left to finalize their entry point into the property and then determine how they were going to navigate the snow-covered terrain.

"It's a blinding white nightmare," she muttered as she once again considered their options. They'd narrowed it down to what looked like a work road in the back of the property or an entrance on the west side of the acreage that sloped downhill and wasn't easily visible from someone standing on higher ground.

Either option still put them at least a half mile from the house, tromping through a landscape that would slow them down.

Should they wait?

Each time she asked herself the question, she quickly dismissed it. Olivia might not have the time, and that made it an unacceptable option.

But getting her out in these conditions was damn near impossible.

"I heard you muttering all the way out in the living room," Trace said.

"Did you get the pack made?"

Trace nodded in the direction of the living area. "Food and water as well as blankets and a few more layers of clothing. If we need to snatch Olivia, we can't assume she'll be in winter attire."

They couldn't, and it had been his advance thinking that had ensured there was a pack at all. One more sign Nic was swirling in various scenarios that refused to settle in her mind.

"At this point we should just walk up to the damn front door." She tossed her phone on top of the small pile she'd built on the bed, the frustration mounting.

"We could."

"We most certainly cannot."

Trace quickly warmed to the idea. "Yeah, actually, we can."

"They're expecting us. Showing up at the front door isn't exactly a surprise attack."

"Right, *us*. But Garner and Jake showing up at the front door, us hidden in the back of the SUV, is not what they're expecting."

It wasn't just his excitement, Nic admitted to herself. His point had merit. Brigante and whoever he was working with would be on high alert for any intruders, but they were expecting her and Trace.

"With what excuse?"

"Jake's got the dog. We say they're tracking a missing elderly man who is presumed lost in the storm. Could they come onto the property to look?"

"A house full of criminals isn't going to see through that?"

"That's the beauty of it. It's so obvious, why would they question it? And all we need is to get close enough to go find Olivia. You and I slip out the back while they're creating the distraction at the door."

The idea skated that strange borderline of nearly brilliant coupled with practically insane.

Which made it so enticing.

"All we need is Olivia, Nic. The rest of this can wait. The only goal is to get her out of there."

That had been her only goal, but as they'd learned more over the past forty-eight hours, it had shifted. Expanded. Because now it was about keeping Trace safe, too.

"One thing at a time, Nic." He reached out and pulled her close, and she went willingly into his arms.

They hadn't spoken today about what happened last night. A part of her wondered if she should feel strange about that, but the bigger part of her had simply gone about her day, secure in the knowledge she'd made the right choice.

The only choice.

There was a future that yawned in front of them, one that had always looked like it would be spent apart. A night making love wasn't going to change that.

But at least she got the night.

And more than that, she'd gotten a chance to address and maybe repair what had torn them apart. It didn't mean they were getting a happily-ever-after—was that a real thing?—but it had given her an opportunity to perhaps erase some of the destruction that had been left in their wake two years ago.

It was a gift, she realized as she lifted her head from his chest and looked up at him. Their old lives and old relationship were gone, but they no longer needed to be painful memories.

In a dreamy sort of slow motion that belied the urgency of what was happening around them, their lips met, sweet and trusting and full of that banked passion she'd always associated with him.

There was no *easy* with Trace Withrow. No smooth, frictionless ride. No part of his personality that didn't demand everything from his partner.

It was no less than he demanded from himself.

The night before had been amazing. A chance to steal back some of what the past two years had taken from both of them. But this? Now? It was the quiet acknowledgment that they could still comfort each other, even after all this time.

Her fingertips explored the broad planes of his back, drifting over the firm, lean muscle there. His hands spanned the length of her spine, holding her close and pressing their bodies together, keeping them connected.

So much waited outside the door, and they would face all of it.

But for these last few lingering moments, Nic wanted to take the time for herself.

For them.

And for all they'd never have again.

THE SNOWFALL WAS as bad as expected, Trace acknowledged as Garner drove slowly out of the hotel parking lot. He'd brought chains for the tires, and they'd put them on as the last step before leaving the hotel. The measure would offer significantly more protection for the drive, but it was going to sorely limit their speed. One more thing they'd discussed and turned over, going through the tactical considerations for and against.

It was Nic who'd suggested they could use the chains as an element in their story, talking about how bad the roads were, yet how desperate they were to find their fictitious missing elderly man.

Garner and Jake were game for the ruse and had already worked out their cover and the patter they'd employ between them.

It was a good plan.

He and Nic had made a hiding spot in the far back of the SUV and had agreed to at least ride there, even if they hadn't covered themselves in the reams of items. They figured they could risk comms devices based on the ruse of the search, and he could hear Garner and Jake as they worked through a few tactical points.

Nic had Trace's laptop open and was reading through Eloisa's texts again as well as what had come in overnight. More over-the-top sexy texts with the boyfriend back in New York. And nothing with the other one.

"Anything new?"

"Beyond the nauseating sex talk?" Nic gave a mock shiver. "I will never be able to scrub that out of my brain."

"But still nothing with the other one?"

"Not a thing. They're together," Nic said, excited. "Can you track GPS on the phone?"

"I can triangulate off the last text."

Nic handed over the computer. "Beware your eyes don't burn."

He grinned at her. "I never took you for a prude." Since he knew for a fact that she most certainly wasn't, it was fun to tease her.

"Those are pornographic."

"Way to tease a guy," Jake said through their comms. "You can't read me a few?"

It was enough to break the tension that had risen with each slow mile, a reminder of what it was like to work in a team. Sure, it was gallows humor, but how many missions had Trace been on through the years that carried that light-hearted teasing as a bonding method? Wasn't that part of why he and Garner worked so well?

The intimacy of the work—the familiarity and rapport that was one person knowing another, trusting another—was fundamentally essential to the outcome.

It played through his mind as Trace went to work capturing the GPS coordinates.

Eloisa was the wild card in the mix they hadn't been able to plan for. They could only assume she was somehow a part of things and present at the ranch. But if she was the side piece, hanging out somewhere else, it split the focus of their quarry, potentially in their favor.

The snow was slowing their movements, but it would slow everyone else's, too.

And if Eloisa wasn't there, that meant someone in Brigante's orbit wasn't, either.

"The mother's the connector."

"To what?" Nic asked.

"All of it. Think about it. She knows the brother's business. She knows how smart the kid is. All the vapid behavior and running with the boyfriends? It gets her out of the way and makes her look innocent."

"But she isn't." Nic shook her head. "She's been the out-lier from the start. And there hasn't been a damn thing we can pin on her."

"Queen bee who won't get her hands dirty." Garner's

voice boomed through the comms. "But she's running the whole thing."

"How could we have missed it?" Nic pressed, spiky frustration in her voice. "If she's this close and running the whole damn thing, why is nothing implicating her? At all?"

"Because her number one drone is in your organization. She's got him doing her dirty work for her. Which likely means missing or doctored files and a whole lot of 'look over here' distraction."

As he tried on Garner's assessment, Trace had to admit it fit. Even if he gave his old workplace the benefit of the doubt, the volume of work was overwhelming. A well-respected operative could work with that, doing his dirty work in small batches over a long period of time so as not to get caught.

Patient, just waiting to strike.

Wasn't that the message in the challenge coins?

I've been here all along.

"You got those coordinates?" Jake asked.

Trace tapped a few last keys, and the coordinates popped up. He read them off, knowing Jake was mapping to the coordinates of the ranch.

"Damn it." Jake added a few more inventive curses full of excitement. "The latitude and longitude's a match for the ranch."

"She's pinging off the same cell tower," Nic said. "But that doesn't mean she's in the house. The property's large, and there hasn't been a single text between Eloisa and her brother or to her daughter that she's arrived in Montana."

Again, Trace thought, there was that proof point that stuck a hard landing: no communication with her child. It didn't necessarily mean everything, but it meant something. He'd stake his life on it. What bothered him was the fact that he was staking everyone else's on it, too.

Everyone, he realized as he heard the chatter in his ear as Nic, Garner and Jake talked through it all, that mattered.

Chapter Seventeen

With coats, blankets and several backpacks layered over top of them, Nic lay nestled beside Trace in the back of the SUV. In any other circumstance, it might have bordered on cozy—minus the sharp metal handle of who-knew-what that poked her back.

But that sharp tool was just the discomfort she needed to keep her head in the game. They had more intel now that Trace had access to Eloisa's phone, but they were still flying blind on so much.

Who was the operative from the agency involved in all this?

What were they running here in the far north?

And who was the mercenary who'd gotten killed in the midst of it all?

"Push it aside," Trace whispered in her ear.

She turned to him, his features shadowed under the thick cover. "We don't know what we're facing."

"We're getting Olivia. That's the only goal here. The rest can and will come later."

"It might not be that easy."

"Maybe not, but we'll deal with that if it comes. We've got the element of surprise on our side. We've got firepower. And we've got a really mean-looking dog."

"I heard that," Jake said in their ears.

"Hogan's beautiful," Nic rushed to add. "But he's got a serious intimidation factor."

"That's why I love my boy," Jake cooed, obviously sweet-talking to Hogan, who'd patiently waited in one of the passenger bucket seats behind Garner.

Nic left him to the pre-op pep talk. Which, like the blanket overlay in the back, would have been cute and funny if the stakes weren't so high.

"Pulling into the driveway," Garner said, detailing everything he saw as he drove slowly. Nic pictured each place he described, matching it to the aerial photos they'd reviewed of the property.

"Outbuilding is just where we think it is," Jake added. The old decrepit stables they'd read about on the property's real estate listing were the closest to the house. "Should be condemned," he added, "but it's got a roof, so it'll work in our favor."

They'd aligned on specific hiding places if Nic and Trace felt they needed one with Olivia, and the stables had topped the list. The short distance from the house would work in their favor as they spirited her away, and the likely hiding places inside from stalls to tack room to a hayloft added to the building's potential.

Trace's hand closed over Nic's as the SUV came to a stop. "We're getting her out of there."

She squeezed back and closed her eyes. They'd prepared, and all four of them, as well as the dog, were trained with the highest degree of skill.

They had to be flawless on this, and she knew they would be.

Because anything else could get a child killed.

TRACE KEPT CHECKING his watch. Garner and Jake had been out of the SUV for more than four minutes, and so far no one had come to the door. They'd kept up congenial conversation, talking about the search for anyone who might be listening, playing their roles as search-and-rescue to perfection.

"No one's answering," Garner drawled. "Maybe you and Hogan start the search, and I'll see if I can find anyone and let 'em know why we're here."

"Man's been missing for a few hours. I'm not hopeful on this one."

"Talk like that's not gonna help." Garner pushed some heat into his words. "He's depending on us."

"Yes, sir."

Trace pictured the slightly cheeky expression that likely matched the words before he heard Jake give Hogan a few commands, the sound of them walking echoing through his earpiece.

"Hello! Anyone home!" Garner pounded on the door once more, hollering as he did. "Hell—"

His words ended abruptly as a new voice floated through the comms. "What do you want?"

The female voice was low and smoky, and Trace turned to face Nic. "Eloisa?"

"Not her," Nic whispered. "Voice is too low and not accented."

Garner kept up his congenial tone, one he knew his brother could project in spades. He was a big man who knew how to disarm people with big personality charm, and that was pumping full-bore through their earpieces. "I'm sorry to bother you. I'm local search-and-rescue. We've got an elderly man missing. He's got dementia, and his family's panicked he got lost."

The woman didn't sound convinced. "Out here? I'm sure he couldn't be on our property. We're rather remote."

"They broke down about a mile up the road. While the

husband and wife were working on getting the truck back up and running, the old man took off."

"That's hardly my problem."

"My partner and I will stay out of your way. Just wanted you to know we're here."

The comment was easygoing but punctuated with the underlying point that she didn't really have a choice in the matter.

"Well, I'll need to see if my husband is okay with this."

"Sure. We'll get started. Have him come on out." As if an afterthought, he added, "Name's Garner, ma'am. Garner Pinnip."

"Cheeky bastard," Trace muttered, his brother's joke not lost on him. When Nic just looked at him askance, he smiled. "Garner's long-standing joke. The scientific name of seals are pinnipeds."

"It's an oldie but goodie," Garner said under his breath. "She's flustered but didn't kick me out. Let's figure the husband'll come out and make a fuss, and then you two can get to work."

Time moved like a drip-feed, but Trace and Nic waited it out. Nothing suggested there was anyone else around beyond the purported husband, and Jake kept a steady relay of information from his side as he and Hogan moved over the property.

Garner did the same routine with the man who came to the door. Although Nic added color commentary identifying the man as Richie Brigante based on his voice, all Jake and Garner got from him was the fake name John Smith.

"So they're keeping that routine up," Trace said.

"Olivia said the other man was John," Nic hissed.

"More to suggest that he's the one who was killed at my front door."

"Our front door," Garner corrected as he'd obviously

moved out of the front door's line of sight. "You're clear. I'm coming around the back to get my gear. Duck out when I do."

Garner made a big show of hollering instructions to Jake, who was some distance away, not even looking in the back seat. Nic scrambled out first, and Trace followed, staying low behind the body of the SUV.

Garner slammed the back door closed while Trace and Nic remained low and out of sight. Jake kept watch at a distance, giving instructions as he kept an eye on the house.

"Couple's still in the windows, looking out at us. Stay behind the SUV until I give the signal."

Trace and Nic remained low, but he knew she was as desperate to move as he was.

"Stay the course," Garner's voice echoed in their earpieces. "Wife left the windows. Brigante can't be far behind. He might not stay gone, but it'll give you a chance to get up against the house."

"What if Olivia's not even in there?" Despite her whisper, Nic's question was as powerful as a gunshot.

"Then we find a new plan," Trace asserted.

"Jake and Garner are out in the open. We're at risk of discovery. I've put you all at risk."

He heard the increasing notes of panic and turned to face her. "We will find her. Here or wherever these people have taken her. We've done the work and made our plans. Now's the time to see them through."

"They're gone." Garner's voice filled both their ears. "Make a run for it."

Trace took another few beats, his gaze holding hers. "We're getting her out of here. Believe me when I say that."

Nic nodded. "I believe you."

"Then let's go."

NIC FOLLOWED TRACE, moving for the spot on the outer wall of the house they'd identified as their goal. It got them out of view from the main windows and a chance to regroup.

There wasn't any sign of Olivia, but it wasn't like they were going to advertise the presence of the kid, either. And even if she was perfectly fine, it wasn't a stretch to think she wasn't going to be outside the morning after a blizzard.

Although heavy, the snow had a powdery consistency that was easier to navigate than a thicker wet dumping, and they crossed the space between the SUV and the house quickly.

Trace looked at the distance they'd run and shook his head. "I don't like the tracks in the snow."

"Hogan and I will come back that way," Jake offered, already circling back toward the driveway. "We'll make it look good if they're watching and get something else out of the back seat. I'll have Hogan mess up the footprints a bit."

Satisfied they'd done as much as they could to avoid detection, Nic kept on, Trace behind her.

She stared up at the house, assessing where Olivia might be. The living room was at the front of the house, and some instinct had her moving opposite of that. Would they have wanted her near them or would they put her in a room farther out of range of whatever they might be discussing and planning?

"I think we should start at the back," Nic suggested. "They'd either want to deliberately keep her out of earshot, or she'd pull a teenager move and take the back of the house anyway. Either way, I think we start there."

"Let's do it."

The house was large, two stories tall and far more modern than the rest of the property. Nic mentally pulled up the real estate images and remembered the large bedroom at the back of the second floor. Picking up the pace, she stilled at the corner before slowly edging her head around the back of the house.

The yard was empty, the ground still pristine and untouched from the snowfall.

"We need something to throw at the windows." Nic reached down and tried to pack some snow in her gloves, but the light, fluffy consistency floated through her fingers.

"We can use some of the nuts from the trail mix we packed." Trace dug a single serving out of his backpack and ripped it open, dumping some nuts into her palm. "Give it a try."

She tossed a handful up toward the windows, lightly grazing the glass but doubtful she'd made enough noise to attract attention. "You try it."

Trace already had his gloves off and tossed a few more nuts at the window, a light ping echoing down.

"Olivia." Nic used a heavy whisper as she tossed another handful up. "Olivia!"

The window flew up suddenly, before a head peeked out. "Nic!"

"Shhh." Nic lifted a finger to her lips, relief flooding through her at the confirmation Olivia was safe. Now they needed to get her out. "Can you get out of the house? I just need you to get to a door."

"I don't have a coat or my phone."

"We've got a coat for you. Shoes, too."

"Can I toss down my computer?"

It was Trace who spoke up beside Nic. "Send down whatever you need to, honey. We'll keep it safe."

Olivia ducked back in the room, and Nic turned to face him. "That's sweet, but we need to go."

"She needs to feel some measure of control. And she needs that laptop. And you can't afford to miss out on whatever's on it."

Before Nic could press him, Trace held up a hand. "I deliberately kept that as a distant third because it *is* a distant third. But you don't want these people getting their hands on it, either. Two birds, Nic."

Olivia's head reappeared along with a pillowcase in her hand. She leaned over as far as she could, the pillowcase still ten feet above them.

"Drop it," Trace ordered. He easily caught the machine before dragging his pack off and stuffing it inside.

"I'll meet you out front," Olivia promised before ducking back in the house.

"Let's get out of here." Trace extended a hand and Nic took it. "We're getting her home."

"I wouldn't be so sure about that."

The voice was eerily familiar, but it wasn't until Nic and Trace turned that she had the confirmation.

Because the man about ten yards away? The one with the gun at the end of his arms pointed directly at them? He was her boss.

Dirk Rannell.

"What are you doing here?" Nic blurted.

The gun never wavered as Dirk looked first at her, then at Trace and then back to her again. "What I've been aiming to do for the last three years. Getting rid of both of you."

DIRK RANNELL WAS the operative who wanted to take him down?

Trace kept going over and over that truth and couldn't reconcile the deeds of the past few days with the man he knew. Or had known.

Dirk Rannell had been on every list of teammates he and Nic had gone through over the challenge coins, and they'd each dismissed him without thinking, never once considering him capable of not only going rogue but creating such a nefarious mess.

"Dirk," Trace said at last. "What is this possibly about?"

"Haven't you figured it out, Withrow? It's all been about getting to you. I knew she'd run straight to you the moment things got tough. And it was easy to see just how attached she was getting to the kid. It practically dripped from every report she wrote."

"Why would I ever figure this?" Trace edged in front of Nic, putting her out of immediate firing range. He sensed her frustration but refused to let her take any more risks on his behalf. "You're one of the most respected operatives in our office. You and I came up together. We worked together. I trusted you!"

The anger rose along with the litany of their working relationship, and Trace was shocked to realize just how badly it hurt. A knife not just plunged in deep but twisted round and round to cause maximum pain.

"You know the work, Withrow. The job's changed since you and I went in. The good guys have decided to make rules that only favor them. Doesn't matter what the rule of law is. Or international rules of war. Or even the most basic rules of diplomacy. It's all about who's got the best intel and the balls to wield it. Which is why I decided to get my fair share."

Although Trace couldn't find it in him to deny Dirk's points, it was that last comment—the flip over into acceptance and self-dealing—that he refused to accept.

The work had always been the work. Those in charge were going to keep managing the tools in their arsenal to advance their own gains.

That was why Trace got out.

And it was why he believed in the future he was creating here in the northern wilderness with Garner and Jake. He took the jobs. He helped the ones who had no one to stand for them.

Most of all, Trace had channeled that very same anger Dirk

carried into something that worked for the benefit of others, not destruction. And then he got to go home and work with his horses and live a life that, while not exactly simple, wasn't about navigating other people's shades of gray.

"Why'd you kill that guy on my property?"

"John was a tool."

"And kidnapping a kid?"

"It's hardly kidnapping for her to spend time with her beloved family. But I have to say, she's an even more useful tool."

"How so?"

Three more people stepped from the side of the house. The man he recognized from photos as Richie Brigante. A woman who stood beside him and hadn't been a part of Nic's intel. And a man wearing a police chief's uniform.

"Her skills have given us all the support and contacts we need here in our little corner of the world."

But it was the fourth person who stepped out that made Trace realize just how badly they'd all been played.

Eloisa Brigante stood head-to-toe in winter gear.

And held her daughter tight in her arms, a gun pressed to the child's head.

"No!" THE SCREAM welled in Nic's throat, primal and raw, as she fought to get around Trace.

What was this? And how had she missed so clearly that Dirk Rannell was a lying scumbag piece of crap and Eloisa Brigante was the devil?

She held a gun to her child's head. Her own child. It was the epitome of every bad cop movie Nic had ever seen.

And it hurt. Deep down where she'd buried all the aching grief over her childhood and those years in foster care when she'd have given anything to know why her mother abandoned her.

But now? Based on the gaping maw of pain watching Olivia deal with the same, Nic realized that wound had never truly closed.

She'd simply covered over it with work and training and field ops.

"Give me Olivia," Nic begged. "She's not a part of this."

"Oh but she really is." Eloisa held her daughter more tightly against her. "Her skills and abilities are like a secret weapon. One no one can even see coming."

"I'm sorry, Nic." Tears spilled down Olivia's cheeks, making them raw and red in the cold air. "I'm so sorry you're here. Because of me."

"I'm here to help you." Nic edged her way out from behind Trace's back. "You will never, ever owe me an apology for that."

"Please let them go." Olivia's sobs grew harder, her shoulders shaking in her mother's grip.

"Olivia." Eloisa shook her. "Stop it! Right now!"

The yelling only made the child cry harder, and Nic moved a few steps closer.

Eloisa's hand shook from holding the gun. "Don't move!"

And then it all broke wide-open.

From behind Eloisa and Olivia, Hogan leaped over a snowbank, snarling and feral as he knocked Eloisa down.

Trace moved the moment the commotion began, as dark and feral as the dog as he leaped straight for Rannell.

Jake and Garner followed up with additional rear attacks on Richie and the woman.

Nic trusted they'd all do their work and used the commotion to race to Olivia, dragging the girl to her feet and spiriting her out of the mess.

"I'm so sorry." Olivia continued to sob, but Nic only pulled her closer, half holding her, half supporting her as they ran toward the SUV.

"Stay with me, sweetie. It's okay."

Nic got to the SUV and opened the door, shoving the child inside. "I need you to stay here until I—" She broke off as a wall of field agents came racing toward them.

She recognized a few as fellow operatives from the office. They moved in unison and carried enough firepower for a large army.

And they'd come to help.

It was the last agent, bringing up the rear, who stopped her. Dirk's boss, Abraham Squires.

"Good work, Miles."

"Thank you, sir."

An all clear was hollered from the direction of the house, angry shouts and dog barks echoing along with it.

But it was the gentle smile that lit up Abraham's face that had her taking her first easy breath. "You don't think we'd let you face this one alone, now, did you?"

"Honestly, sir, I thought—"

He nodded, his face instantly going sober. "You did think you were alone on this."

"Well, yes, I did."

"I'm sorry I couldn't tell you. And I'm sorry it took us so long to get here today." He glanced around. "Damn snow."

"It worried us, too."

"Us?" His eyebrows rose. "Withrow's here, too?"

"Yes, sir. Around back."

"I figured as much."

"I know I broke protocol, and I fully own my actions. Please don't hold Trace or Garner Withrow or their friend Jake Stilton accountable for my actions."

"While I appreciate the self-sacrifice, it won't be necessary. Nor am I holding any civilians accountable for ensuring a rogue agent on my team is no longer able to continue his dark deeds." Abraham glanced over to the SUV where

Olivia was huddled in one of the back bucket seats. "Now, I think there's someone who needs far more of your time than I do." He patted Nic on the shoulder. "She's far more important than the trash out back. I'll go clean that up for you."

The man walked off, leaving her to Olivia.

Nic closed the SUV door before walking around the back and climbing in the other side, taking the seat next to her. "How are you?"

"Fine."

"How are you really?"

"I'll be fine."

Nic picked up one of the blankets they'd packed for the express purpose of staying warm in the event they got stranded, and covered the child.

For all her bravado since that first time they met, Olivia looked very small as Nic spread the blanket over her.

"You don't have to be fine, you know. Not right now. Or next week. Or even next month. But one of these days, I promise you, you will be."

"My mom—" Olivia broke off on a sob. "My mom tried to hurt me."

"I know she did." Nic shifted out of the seat and wedged herself on the floor of the SUV, kneeling beside Olivia. "She won't hurt you again. She's not going to get the chance."

"She's supposed to love me."

"Yes, she is."

"And she doesn't."

In reality, Nic knew the answer wasn't that simple, but now wasn't the time to try to explain it to Olivia. It would be a journey she'd face for the rest of her life.

But in that moment, as she reached out and took the young girl into her arms in a tight hug, Nic vowed she would be there to help her find the answers.

Always.

Chapter Eighteen

Trace navigated the stream on the south end of the property with Magnum, giving the horse a late-afternoon treat as a reward for the riding they'd done all day across the ranch. Spring was doing its steady march toward summer and now here in early June they were dealing with a scorcher.

Three months.

It had been almost three months since Nic arrived and they'd had their adventure taking down Dirk Rannell and saving Olivia.

Trace had learned a lot since then.

The ways they'd used the child's intelligence to map out an illegal trade route up into Canada.

The hot love affair Dirk had been carrying on with Olivia's mother.

Even the local police chief who'd been bribed into supporting them and who had ultimately made him and Nic at the hotel when they arrived in Montana. It was that same police chief who'd firebombed the truck and damn it if that still didn't chafe.

But he and Garner had already begun work under the hood of a new one, and it was coming along. Jake was settling into ranch life, his patience and skills with the equine program something special.

Jake and Garner had held the fort down when Trace flew to DC for a week to testify in front of an oversight committee. He saw a lot of old colleagues and kissed the asses of several politicians who had questions about the events that went down in Montana. He got those garlic-and-butter mussels he loved at his favorite restaurant in Georgetown. He even spent an aimless afternoon roaming a few of the Smithsonian buildings.

But he hadn't seen Nic.

Nor had she reached out.

He'd heard rumblings that she was up for Rannell's job, and he hoped like hell she got it. He'd like nothing more than to see her get a promotion out of all the crap that had gone down.

So he'd come home to Liar's Gulch and dedicated himself to putting it all in the past.

He knelt down at the stream and cupped his hands, drinking the crisp, fresh water. The snowmelt had been running for weeks on end, and the water had finally lowered enough to actually look like a creek bed again.

All of which would have been just fine for a late spring day that felt like summer if the hairs on the back of his neck hadn't stood up.

Whirling, he was on his feet, his hand reaching for the gun at his back when he came face-to-face with Nic.

She stood about ten feet away, her gun in hand.

"You like pulling a loaded weapon on innocent men drinking from streams?" The words came out as he'd hoped they would—lazy and insolent—even as his heart slammed in his chest at seeing her again.

"Maybe I do."

"What are you doing here?"

"I was looking for someone."

"Find him?"

She smiled at that, even though she never lowered the gun. "Well, I'm trying to decide if Annie Oakley had words of wisdom or if she missed the mark."

"I thought she never missed the mark."

Ignoring the bad pun, she kept on with her thought. "She's the one who claimed, if Hollywood show tunes are to be believed…" Nic moved a few steps closer "…that you can't get a man with a gun. Do you think that's true?"

"I don't particularly love being on the receiving end of one."

She opened the gun to show it was empty before dropping it to her side. "I don't love aiming one, so I guess that makes us even."

"What are you doing here?"

"I came to share my news."

"You got the promotion?" Even with his pounding heartbeat and desperate need to touch her, he couldn't deny how happy he was for her.

"I did."

"That's great. You deserve it."

That crystal gaze never moved off his face. "I turned it down."

"You did?"

"It didn't seem like a good choice. Now that I'm the legal guardian to a teenager."

"You're fostering Olivia?"

"Yep. She's been with me since Montana, but the courts made it official last week."

"That's great, Nic."

And it was. He'd known from the start there was something special about her bond with the child. Olivia had a long road ahead as she worked to accept the failings of her family, and Trace knew Nic would be the ideal person to help her through it.

"It is pretty great. She's an amazing young woman, and I'm just grateful she's willing to follow me."

"To DC?"

Nic took a few steps closer, the empty gun hanging at her side. "We're looking to go a bit farther afield."

"Virginia's got some great places. Great schools, too."

She stepped a few paces closer, dropping the gun at her feet. "Not my style."

"Maryland's good."

And then she closed the gap completely and was so close he could feel the heat of her body. "Olivia and I both agree Wyoming feels more like our style."

That wild ride of adrenaline kept pumping through his body in a rushing stream. "And do what?"

"Well, it seems as if I'm in the market for a job. I hear there might be room on a team-for-hire for someone who's not always willing to play by the rules."

Trace stared at her, hardly able to believe she was here, let alone what she was asking. "You want to live here?"

"Live here. Work here. Play here." She lifted her arms and wrapped them around his neck. "Love here."

"What changed your mind?"

"Nothing changed my mind. Not when I got it set on coming here. Well, really on staying here, since I was already thinking I could make this place home about an hour into my last visit."

"Could have told me."

It was the first hitch he'd seen since laying eyes on her again. A sadness that turned down her lips in a subtle frown. "I should have told you. But my mind was also set on that amazing kid. She needs me, Trace. And I think I need her, too. And I had to make sure this was right for her."

"You're going to be a great mother figure to her."

"She needs a father figure, too."

The unspoken question slammed into him with the force of a bullet, and he staggered back a few paces. "Me?"

"I think we'd make a pretty great family. If you're up for it?"

Not even an hour before, he was imagining the endless days of his life stretching out before him, without Nic.

And now she was offering him not just herself but a family of their own?

It was…

Well, it was everything.

"I have one condition." He shook his head. "No, that's not right. I have three."

"Tell me."

"No more separate decisions. It's killed me being apart these past months. Not seeing you. Not talking to you. Even if Olivia hadn't wanted to come here or the courts didn't agree, I'd have supported you. We'd have found a way."

"Okay," she said, her voice quiet. "What's the second condition?"

"You'd better not think we're stopping at one."

"One what?"

"Kid. I'm thinking we need at least three more. Maybe four."

"You gonna do something about that, Trace Withrow?"

He saw the deliciously wicked gleam in her vivid blue eyes and couldn't hold back any longer. Stepping forward, he laid his hands on her hips and pulled her against his body before he pressed his lips to hers. He gave her his answer as their lips met. "You better believe I am."

"And three?"

"Marry me, Nic. Make a life with me."

"That doesn't sound like a condition."

"What does it sound like?"

She smiled up at him, and he realized all the reasons he loved her were right there in her eyes. "An offer."

"Then I guess it is. Because I love you."

And right there, beside a cold mountain stream two thousand miles from where they first met, Trace heard the words he'd longed for his whole life.

"I love you, too, Trace. I will love you forever."

* * * * *

COMING SOON!

We really hope you enjoyed reading this book.
If you're looking for more romance
be sure to head to the shops when
new books are available on

Thursday 24th April

To see which titles are coming soon, please visit

millsandboon.co.uk/nextmonth

MILLS & BOON

afterglow BOOKS

Afterglow Books is a trend-led, trope-filled list of books with diverse, authentic and relatable characters, a wide array of voices and representations, plus real world trials and tribulations. Featuring all the tropes you could possibly want (think small-town settings, fake relationships, grumpy vs sunshine, enemies to lovers) and all with a generous dose of spice in every story.

♪ @millsandboonuk
⊙ @millsandboonuk
afterglowbooks.co.uk
#AfterglowBooks

For all the latest book news, exclusive content and giveaways scan the QR code below to sign up to the Afterglow newsletter:

SCAN ME

afterglow BOOKS

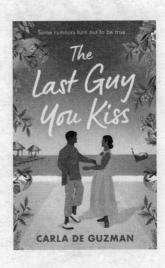

(((♥))) Forced proximity

💻 Workplace romance

🛏 One night

✈ International

⌛ Slow burn

🌶 Spicy

OUT NOW

Two stories published every month. Discover more at:
Afterglowbooks.co.uk

LET'S TALK
Romance

For exclusive extracts, competitions and special offers, find us online:

- **f** MillsandBoon
- **X** @MillsandBoon
- **◯** @MillsandBoonUK
- **♪** @MillsandBoonUK

Get in touch on 01413 063 232